A Shred of Evidence

'She had been in school uniform the first and last time Judy had seen her alive, and she had wondered what it would be like to be her mother. Now, she thanked God she wasn't.'

Detective Inspector Judy Hill had seen the girl that evening, talking and laughing with friends on the bus home. Now she lay dead in the glaring arc-light of a scene-of-crime investigation; beaten, strangled, and possibly raped.

Oakland School in Stansfield comes under a no less glaring spotlight as Judy and Detective Chief Inspector Lloyd begin their investigation into the murder of Natalia Ouspensky, aged fifteen, on a piece of open parkland in the centre of town.

It is an enquiry which will uncover the secrets of staff and pupil alike, not least Natalia herself; an enquiry which will produce suspects and motives but no witnesses; an enquiry which will deeply affect the lives of the innocent, but might well fail to convict the guilty.

An enquiry, it seems, which is not going to yield a single shred of evidence . . .

By the same author:

RECORD OF SIN
AN EVIL HOUR
THE STALKING HORSE
MURDER MOVIE

The Lloyd and Hill Mysteries

A PERFECT MATCH
REDEMPTION
DEATH OF A DANCER
THE MURDERS OF MRS AUSTIN & MRS BEALE
THE OTHER WOMAN
MURDER ... NOW AND THEN

A Shred of Evidence

Jill McGown

MACMILLAN

First published 1995 by Macmillan London Limited

an imprint of Macmillan General Books
Cavaye Place London SW10 9PG
and Basingstoke

Associated companies throughout the world

ISBN 0 333 60535 7

A CIP catalogue record for this book is available from
the British Library

Phototypeset by Intype, London
Printed by Mackays of Chatham PLC, Chatham, Kent

Chapter One

The buzz of excitement and anticipation in the classroom turned to hushed expectancy as the new teacher walked in. Teachers, however new and interesting, didn't always merit instant attention on the first day of term, but today there was a particular reason for this unusual reaction.

Someone, for some reason, had written on the board every rude word they could think of, in or out of the dictionary. Whoever it was, if he or she was in Mr Murray's class, was keeping very quiet about it, and Kim Walters was waiting, like everyone else, to see how the new teacher would handle this pre-planned challenge to his authority.

He was quite young; late twenties, at a guess, Kim thought. Nice looking, in a way. The same pleasing build and colouring as Colin Cochrane, but not as handsome, of course. He had a friendly face, though; Kim liked the look of him. Short, dark, wavy hair, beginning to recede at the temples already, but it suited him, somehow.

She could see, even from the back of the classroom, the little beads of perspiration on these exposed temples, and she wondered if he was nervous. She supposed he would be; he was starting a new job, after all. Kim worked in a supermarket at weekends, and she knew how she had felt on her first day. It was hot, though – too hot for the school uniform they were obliged to wear now that the school had opted out of local authority control, and had given itself a new image. A grey skirt or slacks – after much discussion, they had decided that girls could wear slacks as well as boys – navy blue sweatshirt, and grey blazer. Those wearing skirts, the guide-lines had said – presumably that included any boys who felt so inclined – should wear knee-length navy blue socks if they were in first, second or third year, and flesh-toned tights in fourth, fifth and sixth year.

Kim, now a fifth-year student, had opted for the skirt and tights, and her legs felt slippery already. Mr Murray's equally formal grey suit wouldn't be helping him to keep cool either; he hadn't, unlike his pupils, removed his jacket. Perhaps it was that rather than apprehension that was making him sweat, but Kim wished whoever it was hadn't done that, all the same. It didn't seem fair, not on his first day.

1

He smiled, told them that his name was Patrick Murray, and that he would be their form teacher. 'That means,' he said, 'amongst other things, that if you have any problems with the school, or fellow pupils, or even at home, you're welcome to come to me and I'll see what I can do to help. But I'm sure you all organize your lives a lot better than I do,' he added. 'So if I've got any problems, can I come to you?'

He had an Irish accent; it was nice. He was nice – funny. Kim almost wished that she had some problems to take to him.

'And I see from this – ' Mr Murray held up his timetable, pulling a face. 'If I'm reading it right, that is, that I also have the honour of taking this class for English.' Latecomers were straggling in as he spoke. 'Find a seat,' he said. 'I haven't taken the register yet – I always give people time to get here and sit down and get the Maltesers out before I raise the curtain. Speaking of which,' he said, turning back to the class, 'there isn't a theatre in Stansfield, is there?'

A couple of negatives were murmured in reply.

'Well, maybe I can wangle a trip to Stratford or something,' he said, to groans. He laughed, and began to call out their names, asking each of them to stand. 'Not every time, you understand,' he said. 'Just for today, so that I can pretend to fix your faces in my mind. It takes me all term to sort out who's who really, but I like to show willing.'

The usual people were absent, and he had the predicted and laughed-at trouble over the Polish and Ukrainian and Russian names which were commonplace in Stansfield. He stumbled over Natalie's.

Kim smiled at his attempt, and glanced at Natalie, who sat across from her at the next table, but she wasn't laughing, and hadn't even stood up, as he'd asked. Kim frowned a little. Natalie wasn't usually touchy about her name, and poor Mr Murray was really embarrassed about it.

Kim had known Natalie since primary school. Her first name was Natalia really, but she called herself Natalie; Natalia was nicer, Kim thought. But if that was too difficult for most people, then they didn't stand a chance with her surname, which was Ouspensky. She was looking a bit pale, almost hiding behind the curtain of long blonde hair which Kim had always envied. By her eighth birthday, Kim had reluctantly come to the conclusion that she was not going to turn into a blonde until she was old enough to choose to be one, but she had thought that she could grow her hair long like Natalie's. She had tried, but as soon as it started getting in her eyes or having to be untangled, she would get her mum to cut it again.

Kim's mum was a hairdresser, and she wished that Kim had Natalie's hair too. Natalie's hair always looked wonderful; Kim's would never have looked like that even if she had managed to grow it. But in this warm weather Kim was glad of her urchin cut, as her mother called it.

Mr Murray carried on with the register, closing it with a smile. 'Now then,' he said. 'What's all this groaning at the mention of Stratford-upon-Avon?'

He spoke a bit about how much better it was to see Shakespeare on the stage than to read him, but the class wasn't listening to a word as they whispered to one another and willed him to turn round to the board. At last came the moment of truth, when he finally stood up and turned to the board, and the room went silent.

He turned back to the class. 'I expect you're all taking bets about who wrote this stuff,' he said. 'And I'll bet that all bets are off. Because I wrote it.'

He must have been very satisfied with the gasp of surprise, but he didn't show it.

'Why?' someone asked.

'I'll tell you,' he said. 'Two reasons. One is – if you really feel obliged to write all or any of these words on walls, that is how they are spelled. If I'm going to be responsible for your command of English when you leave here, then at least do me the favour of proving you can spell when you deface public property.'

They laughed.

'And the other reason,' he said, 'is to indicate to you that I know all these words. I've used them all, in my time. There isn't an Irishman born that hasn't, I shouldn't think – well, give or take the odd priest, but I wouldn't be too sure about that, either. So I'm not going to be all that impressed if you use them. Now, I don't know why some words are taboo – I think if we sent explorers to another planet and found a tribe of people with a language some of whose words they weren't allowed to use, we would think that very quaint. But we are that tribe, so here's the deal. I won't use any of these words in class if you don't. That way we can all keep out of trouble.'

'Would you get into trouble if we told the head that you'd written them on the board?' someone asked.

'Of course I would,' he said, wiping them off the board as he spoke. 'But you're not going to tell, are you? If you do, I'll deny everything – and I'm a powerful liar.'

Kim laughed. She liked Mr Murray.

Acting Detective Chief Inspector Judy Hill ran a hand through dark, short hair dampened with perspiration, wound the window down, and breathed in petrol and paint fumes with a modicum of the fresh air she had hoped to admit.

They were parked on one of the new industrial estates in a cul-de-sac of mini units out of which worked small concerns, mostly in the motor trade. A body shop, a paint shop, a car repair place, and a motor-cycle spares and repairs made up the court they were in. They were watching Humphry Davy Close, the one across the road, where two men also sat in a parked car. These two were not police; they were would-be receivers of stolen goods.

And they were all, good guys and bad guys, sitting in hot cars waiting for a lorry full of electrical goods which had been due at nine forty-five. Lorries came and went all the time; none of them had been the lorry they were waiting for.

'Do you think it's going to come?' asked Detective Sergeant Finch.

'No,' Judy said, with uncharacteristic shortness. Knowing the kind of day she was having, there was no chance, she thought.

It had started all right. The sun had awakened her as it always did in this sort of glorious weather. She enjoyed the extra time, the quietness. Sometimes she just lay awake, watching the room come into sharp focus, her mind wandering where it would. Sometimes she got up and allowed herself to wallow in the bath rather than have a quick shower. Always, she left enough time for breakfast, the best – and quite often the only – meal of the day. Bacon, egg, tomato, toast and tea.

The clamour from the body-repair shop brought her back to her current surroundings, but she kept the window down. Even with the noise and the fumes, it still had the edge over being baked alive, she decided. 'It always did seem a funny time to deliver a lorry-load of stolen goods,' she muttered.

The repair firm began work on an ancient black cab, which operation involved racing the deafening engine with the bonnet up, forcing black clouds of exhaust smoke out the other end.

'That's the idea, guv,' Sergeant Finch said, raising his voice above the noise as the smell of spent diesel mingled with all the others in a sort of essence of automobile. 'They think no one will pay any attention to a lorry delivering mid morning in an industrial estate. Give it another fifteen minutes?'

This morning, her early-morning meditation had been spent looking forward to Detective Chief Inspector Lloyd's return from the course that he had been on for weeks. The silence that she so enjoyed palled a little when it had no counterpoint; Lloyd's occasional but sometimes turbulent presence in the mornings made the solitude all the sweeter.

'It's almost eleven,' she said. 'I think your informant's let you down.'

There was a moment before Tom Finch answered. 'He never has yet,' he said.

4

'Between nine-thirty and ten, you said.'

'The villains haven't called it a day yet, guv. Just another fifteen minutes?'

Guv. Villains. She smiled. Suspected stolen goods were iffy, known stolen goods were hookey, according to Tom. His immediate superiors were guv, the public were punters. It had begun in an effort, Judy felt, to counteract his fair-haired, well-scrubbed schoolboy look, but then Tom had discovered that it drove Lloyd mad, and now sounded like a veteran of a dozen police series.

He had once told Lloyd that he had spotted a couple of well-known brasses in a boozer – it was some time before Lloyd understood that Tom was not a keen connoisseur of the heavy horse regalia often used to decorate public houses. Or so Lloyd would have people believe, at any rate.

'All right, Sergeant,' she said. 'Fifteen minutes, then we pack this in before we all melt or die of boredom.'

She had committed two cars and four people to this, Tom's information having been that there would be two people in the lorry, and two in the car, all of whom would, in his words, try to leg it. The uniformed officers had had to be begged; they were parked at the rear, where they couldn't be seen from the road.

If it was a success, then fifteen thousand pounds' worth of stolen goods would be recovered; if the information was wrong, then her name would be mud. She was acting DCI in Lloyd's absence, which she was rather enjoying, but it did mean that you carried the can, and it looked like that was what she would be doing.

It was thanks to Lloyd, whom she had known almost all her adult life, that she had ever been anything other than a uniformed constable, but at times she wasn't sure that thanks were in order. Her relaxed morning hadn't prepared her for the day ahead; she had set out into the warmth of yet another beautiful day, pleased that Lloyd would soon be back, pleased with her handling of the job in his absence, pleased with her lot, and in an undeniably good mood, until she had tried to start her car. When it had finally consented to go, she had spent the next half hour queuing up behind the lorries at the lights before she ever got on to the dual carriageway, which she had had to share with the same lorries, all suddenly strict upholders of the speed limit, as though they had had an astral tip-off about what she did for a living.

In other words, despite her early start, she had arrived late for work, and almost, unforgivably, late for the stake-out. Her mood had been shattered, and nothing short of an entirely successful operation would restore it.

Only two things in her life could get to her like that. One was the internal combustion engine; the other was on a seven-week course at the Police Staff College, and would be home soon.

Detective Chief Inspector Lloyd knew that the others all had him marked down as the short bald bloke who lived in the past. He was short – shorter, at any rate, than all of them. And he was, he now had to admit, bald. There had been a long time during which he had thought of himself as thinning, then receding, then even, though it had taken severe soul-searching to admit it, balding. But now there really was no *ing* about it. He was bald.

What hair he had grew back from the middle of his forehead and down from about an inch above his ears; he had cut the latter crop very short at Judy's suggestion, and was glad of that decision on the dreadful day when he had realized that it was turning grey into the bargain, because hardly anyone had noticed yet.

He did not, however, live in the past, though that was the impression he was quite deliberately giving. That was his platform, that was the character he was playing. Judy said he was always acting, which wasn't entirely true, but he certainly was this time. And he was glad that it was this short bald bloke who was doing this course instead of him, because he would have loathed it, worthy though it undoubtedly was.

Lloyd had always had trouble with the unreality of education; however complex and difficult a situation on a course was, it could never match reality. The final week had provided a very realistic set-up, but Lloyd's solution to it, though it had worked, had had the same hint of theatricality as the problem.

Judy had done this course shortly after her promotion to inspector; Lloyd wondered with which practical problem she had been faced. One to which she had found, no doubt, a practical solution.

As a method of assessment it had stood the police in reasonably good stead, he supposed. And now he was even attending a computer studies class, of all things, because he had admitted shortcomings in that area. He was once again head of Stansfield CID, and had been getting to grips with all the state-of-the-art egg-sucking technology now available to him; he had been paying close, if reluctant, attention to the advances of modern science, and didn't think he was showing himself up too much.

Computers were almost miracle tools, as far as Lloyd was concerned. They had revolutionized life itself, never mind policing. He just didn't know how to work them, that was all, and he felt that he never would, but he was doing his level best to learn. The short bald bloke, however, thought they were the invention of the devil, and if the police were going to rely on cameras and computers, then the detective was going to lose his most important asset – his nose. Talking to people, asking questions, wondering.

Wondering why a known car thief had suddenly apparently gone straight, or why the little woman who had had a flower stall on the market for years had suddenly not been there one day.

Each of these things had netted him a career-enhancing arrest in his time, he said to the assembled company, and neither was something that a computer would have had any time for.

Neither of these things had ever happened, or if they had, they had certainly not happened to Lloyd. They might have happened to the short bald bloke, though.

'Thief takers,' one of his fellow DCIs said in response, 'are a thing of the past.'

You are not joking, mate, the short bald bloke thought. You would not chuckle. And Lloyd had to agree with him.

Colin Cochrane waited until the last of his charges had gone noisily off before having a quick shower himself, and pulling on his tracksuit. He had had only one gym session so far, its being the first day of the new school year, but he wanted to grab a quick cup of coffee, and teachers of more intellectual subjects had a morbid fear of the smell of good honest sweat.

He ran a comb through his thick, dark, longish, permanently damp hair, and liked what he saw in the mirror, giving it a smile.

The sun, which had perversely arrived just as the school holidays were ending, was warm on his back as he walked from the gym, across what was left of the once-extensive playing fields, to the main school building. Oakland School had started life as a grammar school, with all the facilities that any educational élite could possibly need or want. Now, you couldn't have a decent game of cricket without threatening the windows of half a dozen supposedly temporary buildings through which a second generation of pupils was passing.

Colin's wife Erica was the school secretary; she had been married and divorced before coming to work at the school, and meeting Colin. He had known, from the moment he had caught a glimpse of her, that she was the one for him.

He had played the field; it had been time to settle down, and Erica, early thirties, slim, elegant, tumbling dark hair, had come made-to-measure. They had been together for three years and had finally married in March.

'It's over there,' she said, as he went into the office.

'It' was his fan-mail. Erica had been impressed by the steady flow

7

of letters in the beginning; she would open them for him and sort them out into bundles.

Kids wanting advice about running, and advice about all manner of other sporting endeavours about which Colin knew little. He would pass the hurdlers and the pole-vaulters and the hammer-throwers on to the appropriate people, and answer the ones about middle-distance running himself.

Kids simply wanting his autograph – he had had photographs taken with a band at the bottom so that he could write a message, which was usually *Yours in sport, Colin Cochrane*.

Kids telling him their problems. If they seemed serious, Erica would find out which organizations they could contact, and write sympathetic letters for Colin to sign.

And love letters, which used to make Erica laugh, until the one that hadn't. Not all from kids, the last category, but they had made her laugh all the same, even the raunchy ones. Not any more. But it was hardly his fault that females of all ages fell for him.

The mail was always like this after the long summer break. People saw him on television during the summer and wrote to him at the school. Much too much mail for the pigeon-hole in the staff room, which was where it usually went. For the first few days after the long holiday, his pigeon-hole could only accommodate internal mail. Erica had dealt with that too, once upon a time.

Colin was famous. Not for what he had done, particularly; he hadn't been all that spectacular at what he had done, which was one reason why he had never given up the day job. But he was telegenic. The TV people had liked interviewing him, having him in the studio to discuss the merits or otherwise of competitors at the odd meeting when he was nursing an injury and couldn't compete.

He had been to three Olympics and had been knocked out in the first round of the fifteen hundred each time, but had reached the semi-final of the eight hundred once, failing to qualify for the final as a fast loser by two hundredths of a second.

Now, he was in his mid thirties, and he wanted to move up to five and ten thousand, perhaps even the occasional half-marathon, where stamina was more important than sudden bursts of speed. He didn't really like long distances, and stamina wasn't his strong point, but he was working on that. Mostly these days he appeared on television, and got very well paid for it.

'Will you be training tonight?' Erica asked.

'Yes. Well . . .' Colin thought that perhaps he ought to be more aware of Erica's needs than he was tending to be at the moment. 'Not if you'd rather I stayed in,' he said.

'No, you do what you want,' she said, her voice cool. 'There's a film on that I want to see anyway.'

'Good,' said Colin. 'I won't stay out too long.'

'It doesn't finish until ten,' said Erica.

'And you don't want me coming in in the middle of it and spoiling it?'

She managed a smile, for the first time that day.

Colin smiled back. 'I'll be home at ten, then,' he said. 'I'll make it a long run tonight.' He picked up his unopened mail as he spoke. 'I'll put this lot in the car,' he said. 'Get it out of your way.'

The frost was fairly thick in the office, and he went out into the warmth of the late summer day with a sigh of relief. Those who liked to mind other people's business had suggested that it was a mistake, her keeping on her job at the school after they had got married, but it had been during the summer holidays that things had got sticky, so that seemed to have had very little to do with it. Not that she had to work, but she wanted to, she said, and it made very little difference to Colin one way or the other.

He dumped his mail on the back shelf of the car, locked it up again, and went up to the staff room, taking the stairs two at a time as the others came down.

'Stop showing off, Colin,' said Trudy Kane, the pleasantly plump divorcee, who, if Colin was any judge, fancied him more than a little. He certainly wouldn't kick her out of bed either, but their relationship had never progressed beyond banter and never would.

He poured himself a coffee in the deserted staff room, opening the dusty venetian blinds to persuade some of the smoke out of the window. They objected to the smell of sweat, but he was supposed to put up with breathing in their stale smoke. Maybe he should campaign to make the staff room a non-smoking area.

He smiled, and closed the blinds again, absent-mindedly trying to straighten the bent slat that had been like that for as long as he'd been there. He didn't care if they smoked, really, and anyway it was only a couple of them who did, these days.

He studied the timetable, clearly designed to have as many staff and pupils running round in circles looking for where they were supposed to be as it possibly could. He had a free period, then another gym session before lunch. He was looking forward to the afternoon, and the chance to get the older boys out into the sunshine for a double period.

His pigeon-hole had the usual stuff; memos from the head, notes about staff meetings, union business . . . He saw the envelope and closed his eyes briefly. He had thought – he had hoped – that the letters would have stopped, but they hadn't. He opened it, read it,

9

stuffed it into the pocket of his tracksuit top, and threw the envelope into the waste basket.

He would dispose of the letter somewhere safer than here.

Erica sat in the office, watching through the window as Colin walked back towards the gym, and the clock showed that it was one minute to the final period before lunch. Colin was never late, never early. He had said he would be back this evening at ten, and that was when he would be back – not a moment earlier, not a moment later. In a way she wished he was unreliable, like Patrick.

She had met Patrick in March, when he had come for an interview at the school, and Colin had been away, as usual, at some indoor athletics meeting.

Despite the fact that she was still practically on her honeymoon, Patrick had made a play for her. She hadn't let anything happen, of course, but it had been nice, having someone pay attention to her. Colin's attention had lapsed even then, before he had begun training practically every night and had lost interest in her completely.

Patrick had moved to Stansfield at Easter, though his appointment wasn't until September. Erica imagined that his decision to leave his previous school had been forced upon him, having got to know him quite well since then. His wife had only just joined him – obviously, she had been doing some serious thinking about whether she was going to come at all.

Erica had been the only person in Stansfield he had known then, or so he had said, when he had come calling, and she had resisted his little-boy-lost act. Then she had found that letter, and Colin had tried to talk his way out of it ... It would have been very easy to succumb to Patrick's overtures after that. But she hadn't.

Patrick had become a frequent visitor, whether Colin was there or not, and he had never really given up; she had seen more of Patrick than she had of Colin during the summer. But Colin liked him too; they had become friends. Patrick had, of course, found consolation elsewhere, but that wouldn't prevent him starting something with her if she would let him. He was engagingly open about it, though she doubted if his wife found it all that attractive a trait.

The season proper had started then, and Colin had been away most of the time. She had still resisted Patrick's advances, which were by then made purely because it was expected of him. She liked the mild flirtation, but she had not been tempted, not then, because she had thought that perhaps she had misjudged Colin, that there really was nothing to the letter she had found. She had thought that once the season was over, once he'd finished with all the athletics meetings, he'd find time for her again, but that wasn't how it had worked out.

She wouldn't have believed it was possible to feel so lonely, but Colin was out practically every night again, doing whatever it was he did, and she was at a permanent loose end.

He had said the letter was just some silly little girl indulging some fantasy. Perhaps it was; perhaps if all those silly little girls who wrote to him knew what it was like to live with their heart-throb, they wouldn't be so keen. Erica hardly saw him; when he did come home, it was to flop into bed and go to sleep.

She still felt lonely. She still felt unwanted. And she still didn't really know what Colin did when he was out at night.

Hannah saw Colin Cochrane too, and watched him until he went out of sight, her thin, pointed face lit with the intensity of her feelings for him. She wore her long dark hair down; it would be a little more comfortable up in this hot weather, but he had once said that it suited her down, and now she wore it no other way.

The others had gone; she would be late for her next lesson, but she didn't care. Every glimpse of Colin was precious. He lived on Ash Road, in one of the houses set back below the level of the road, behind a bank of trees. A whole gang of girls from school used to go there last term and climb the trees to try to catch a glimpse of him and his new wife and their dog – a weird creature with more skin than it needed when it was a puppy – until he asked them not to because his wife didn't like it.

Hannah hated Erica Cochrane. Hated her for marrying Colin in the first place, hated her for stopping them going to the house. They hadn't been doing any harm – they weren't Erica Cochrane's own personal trees. So she had carried on going there, until it had struck her that that was just kids' stuff. From that moment, she had worked hard to put her relationship with Colin on a much more personal footing, one that might break up the marriage, with any luck.

Colin only took the boys for sports, so she didn't get the chance to talk to him at all during school hours. At least he was still in the drama group, and they were meeting tonight. They would just be discussing possible productions, though, so she wouldn't be able to wander up and start a would-be-casual conversation; they would be sitting down, talking, like a formal meeting.

But that didn't matter, because she would see him later on, and there wouldn't be anyone else around then.

Patrick Murray was spending some of his lunch hour trying to get himself acquainted with the school, which had been built in the fifties to house four hundred pupils and had been extended and added on to and partitioned until it now accommodated eight hundred and fifty. There were several annexes – one was a mile away, across the Green.

11

The Green was a piece of common land down on Ash Road, too small to be called a common, too unstructured to be called a park, that linked the east side of the town, the older, more established part, to the centre of the new town created in the fifties.

Even that older part only dated back to the thirties, when Mitchell Engineering arrived to set up its once-enormous operation. What had been there before was a tiny, one-horse village. It was still there, that piece of the sixteenth century; a little oasis of history in this relentlessly modern desert.

Patrick's knowledge of the town was much more extensive than his knowledge of the school, which he just found bewildering, even after Colin had shown him round.

Colin was the first friend Patrick had made in Stansfield, or to be more accurate, and more honest, Colin's wife was the first friend he had made. Colin had left her on her own for hours on end, and Victoria, Patrick's wife, had been in two minds about joining him in Stansfield. Erica was a very attractive girl, and Patrick would be Patrick. He hadn't cracked that particular nut yet, but it was fun trying. Sure, what was life for, if it wasn't to be enjoyed?

And what made Patrick's life enjoyable was the opposite sex. And snooker, and jazz, and teaching, of course. And tinkering with cars, and reading books, and seeing plays ... but all these things went down even better with a girl by your side, if you asked Patrick.

It had got him into trouble before, and he was going to have to execute some very fancy footwork if it wasn't to get him into trouble now. But Patrick preferred not to think too hard about things that might disrupt his enjoyable life.

He had almost forgotten why he'd had to leave his last place – an eminent public school with an impeccable record which Patrick had done nothing as regards his teaching to besmirch – but his close acquaintance with a female member of staff had caused Victoria to create a bit of a scene in front of a group of parents who were looking round the school.

There was no real harm done. They had had their sons' names down from birth; there was no way they were backing out, even if they had found Victoria's outburst a bit on the embarrassing side. But the school had very politely asked him if he might not be happier elsewhere, like by Easter. That, Patrick had to admit, had not been the first time they had had occasion to talk to him about his enjoyment of life. It was just the first time Victoria had made a public fuss.

They would be prepared to tell any prospective employer that they were letting him leave before the end of the academic year to pursue private studies, he had been told, but he had to go.

12

Patrick wandered round, eavesdropping on conversations as the kids took their lunch break, and he thought that it was entirely possible that he would indeed be happier here. There was no class system in operation, either in the school or the town, and that was refreshing, to say the least, in England's green and pleasant, especially after his last place.

Yes, he could be very happy here. Providing he boxed clever, of course.

Natalie Ouspensky sat on the low wall which ran along the front of the school, eating her packed lunch with a group of other girls, but not taking part in the endless conversations about boys that the others were having. It bored her now, all the boasting and baiting.

'Barry's dead worried because he thinks I'm pregnant,' Julie said.

Natalie doubted that Julie had ever been with a boy in her life, but to hear her talk you would swear she was on the game. Natalie had been with boys, but they bored her too, with their frantic fumblings and their crude goals, because she had a man. A grown man, who knew what it was all about. She wasn't interested in what Barry or anyone else had or – more probably – had not done with Julie.

But there were problems with the relationship. There always had been, but they had been on the horizon, and she had shut them out of her mind. She couldn't do that any more, not now. She was determined not to lose him, and she had to think about what she was going to do.

'There's Mr Murray,' said Claire, in a stage whisper.

They all cast covert glances as he passed.

'He's nice, isn't he?' sighed Claire.

'Is that him?' asked Hannah. 'The new teacher?'

'Yes,' said Claire. 'He wrote rude words on the board this morning,' she added, with a blush. 'Really rude. We didn't know who'd done it, but it turned out he'd done it himself.'

'He never,' said Julie.

'He did, didn't he, Natalie?'

'What?' Natalie looked up.

'Mr Murray wrote all those words on the board.'

'Yes.'

'See! I told you!'

'What words?' asked Hannah.

'You tell her,' said Claire to Natalie.

'Tell her yourself.'

'No! They were rude.'

13

'Oh, grow up!' snapped Natalie.

Claire went into a huff; Kim eventually told them what he had written.

Natalie sighed, as the others giggled. All except Hannah, who was merely looking puzzled.

'Why did he?' she asked, but those who knew were giggling too much to tell her, and Natalie was too preoccupied.

They were all so childish.

Detective Sergeant Tom Finch was in the DI's office, being chewed out. No arrests, no recovered property, nothing except the blame for a useless exercise and a lecture to double-check his informant's integrity.

'Someone tipped them off, Tom,' she said. 'And it obviously wasn't the purchasers, or they wouldn't have been there.'

'I don't think he set us up, guv,' he said. 'Something went wrong.'

'Maybe they're still trying to get through the one-way system in Malworth,' she said, smiling at last.

'You could live somewhere closer at hand,' said Tom, grinning. Everyone knew that DCI Lloyd and his acting Chief Inspector were more than just good friends, though they liked to pretend it was a secret.

Her eyes widened slightly at the remark, and Tom felt uncomfortable. It was a very subtle piece of rank-pulling as a result of his unsubtle teasing, and he was being put in his place.

'Well, now that we've wasted an entire morning, let's get on,' she said. 'I may as well sign your expenses now.'

Tom smiled.

She smiled back, a professional smile. 'Do you have those receipts?' she asked.

Tom's jaw fell. 'I told you I'd lost them,' he said.

'I assumed you would look for them.'

'I did! I know what must have happened – I must have thrown them out by mistake with that other lot ... I've told you all this,' he said.

'But you haven't produced them,' she said.

'Oh, come on!' said Tom. 'Those expenses were legit – I shelled out the money! I'm entitled to get it back.'

'I've no doubt they are,' she said. 'But I have to justify them. I can't just take your word for it. I need receipts, Tom.'

'But you know I had to go to Liverpool! You told me to go! So you can sign it without the receipts!'

'Why would I want to do that?' she said. 'You could take advantage of me if I started doing that.'

14

Tom ran a hand over his face. It might not seem like a lot of money to her, but she didn't have kids growing out of clothes and shoes and a mortgage she could barely afford.

'I'm owed that money,' he said. 'I need it.' He did. He was taking Liz out for an anniversary dinner on Friday that was going to cost a bomb.

'You should have taken better care of the receipts, in that case.'

Tom looked at the implacable brown eyes that still held his, and swallowed. He had worked with her for almost a year, and had got, he had believed, to know her pretty well. He had warned other people not to be taken in by the big brown eyes; he had told new recruits to the department that she was easy-going and friendly, didn't even like being called ma'am, but that there was a line, and you overstepped it at your peril.

But he had said that she was fair, and he'd been wrong, obviously, because this wasn't fair. Liz would kill him.

The inspector grinned suddenly. 'The claim's on your desk,' she said. 'Authorized. It has been since half past three yesterday afternoon – if you ever did any paperwork, you'd have found it.'

Tom blew out his cheeks and looked at her for some time before he spoke. 'Sorry,' he said. 'I was out of order.'

'If and when I want advice concerning my domestic arrangements,' she said seriously, 'I really will ask for it.'

He had been well and truly kippered. She had done him for his manners, his carelessness, and his reluctance to do anything approaching paperwork all in one neat movement. And conned him rotten into the bargain.

'And, Tom – the paperwork on that aggravated burglary has got to be done today.' She smiled sweetly at him. 'Your desk's the one nearest the window,' she reminded him.

'Yes, ma'am,' he said. And grinned back.

It was nice to know that he wasn't that bad a judge of character after all.

Chapter Two

By the time he had worked up another two good honest sweats in the gym and got rid of another two lots of kids, by the time he had had yet another shower, and slicked down his hair in the mirror, by the time he had sat beside Trudy in the dining hall and was eating to the unholy noise of adolescent table talk, Colin had forgotten all about the letter.

He sat with Trudy because Erica almost always brought sandwiches to eat in the office, or if, as today, the weather was kind, out in the sunshine, with a book for company. Colin read books in bed; Trudy's was the sort of company he preferred at lunch time. He made no bones about enjoying admiration, which was one of the reasons that he had such a large following; he had no time for those in the public eye who professed to shun publicity.

Colin was that elusive animal, the television personality. He liked being recognized in the street, and he liked knowing that he could be famous full time if he wanted to; he was increasingly in demand for chat shows, game shows, studio panels – you name it, Colin had done a guest appearance on it. Advertisements were the most lucrative form of exposure, and now they wanted him for a whole series of ads for men's toiletries. But he wasn't quite ready yet to throw himself completely into the spotlight, to depend entirely for his living on the fickle public, who might very well have a different favourite this time next year.

But as long as he was running, the school would give him a steady income and time off when he needed it, so his present situation suited him admirably. And as long as he did nothing to incur the displeasure of his adoring public, he could have the best of both worlds.

The letter did cross his mind again then, as his thoughts took that turn, but no more than that.

Kim Walters liked Mr Murray a lot, she had discovered by the end of registration. She liked English, too, though she wasn't much of a speller, and she was sure it was going to be fun now that it was Mr Murray.

She sat beside Natalie as usual, but Natalie was still in a funny mood and didn't even look up when Kim spoke to her, never mind answer. Kim wondered if she wasn't well.

'Show of hands,' said Mr Murray. 'How many of you believe that this is going to be your last year in full time education?'

About half the class put their hands up.

'Keep them up,' he said. 'Now, of those of you with your hands up how many think that this year is a waste of time? If you do think that, keep your hands up.'

Some hands went down; not many.

'And how many of the ones with their hands up have a job to walk into when they leave school?'

All the hands went down.

'None of you?' said Mr Murray, looking startled. 'I thought you must all have, if you think this year's going to be a waste of time.'

'What else is Shakespeare and stuff like that?' Dave Britten asked.

'Well, what do you think you might do for a living?'

'Plumber,' said Dave. 'Like my dad.'

'And you don't think a basic understanding of Shakespeare's use of irony will help in this endeavour?'

Dave's eyes widened as he tried to work out the question. 'I don't see that I need to learn about Shakespeare,' he said defensively. 'You might, if you want to be a brain surgeon or something.'

'Brain surgeons need a good education, you mean?'

'Yeah.' Dave nodded, relieved to have got his point across. 'But plumbers don't need to know all that stuff.'

'Why not?'

'Well . . . it's not as important.'

'Plumbers aren't as important as brain surgeons?'

'Well, they're not, are they?'

'I don't know,' said Mr Murray. 'I'm willing to bet that there are thousands of plumbers who have gone from cradle to grave without once requiring the services of a brain surgeon. But I doubt if even one brain surgeon has gone through life without . . .'

The class laughed, supplying for themselves the end of his sentence, and Kim was gratified to see that even Dave looked thoughtful, for possibly the first time in his life.

She really liked Mr Murray.

Tom Finch walked across the little car park to where his acting chief inspector's car sat, screwing up his fair lashes as the late afternoon sun slanted through the trees that hid the police station from the houses opposite.

The car was making disconsolate and distinctly dodgy noises as

17

Judy tried to start it. Even Tom's rudimentary knowledge of the internal combustion engine was enough to tell him that this car was not going to start, whatever she did, unless something mysterious was accomplished under the bonnet.

He watched, amused, as her face grew pink with frustration. She sat back, pushing her hair away from her face, and saw him.

'Having trouble?' he asked.

'No, I enjoy doing this,' she said, then took a deep breath, and tried again. She hit the steering wheel in frustration, and gave up, getting out. 'It took me about fifteen minutes to start it this morning,' she said. 'I knew this would happen.'

'Do you want me to get one of the lads from the garage to have a look?' asked Tom.

'No,' she said. 'It isn't worth having to put up with all the remarks about women drivers.'

Tom smiled. 'I don't know anything about what goes on under the bonnet either,' he said.

'You're allowed not to.' She sighed, then smiled, turning her puppy-brown eyes his way, and giving him the benefit of her very best smile. 'I don't suppose you could give me a lift—'

'Sorry,' said Tom. 'I'm waiting to interview a witness who is on her way here as we speak.'

'Would you believe the next bus to Malworth isn't until quarter to seven?' she said.

'You've already checked on the buses, then,' he said, with a grin.

'I knew it wouldn't start. Quarter to seven! And it takes over forty minutes.'

'It's probably something and nothing. One of the lads could have it fixed in a jiffy.'

'No,' she said firmly, heading back into the building.

Tom caught her up.

'Tell me something,' he said. 'Why do you give a monkey's what some oily rag has to say about women drivers? You could have him crying for his mum inside a minute.'

He held the door open for her, then wondered if it was a bad time to be chivalrous. But she was his senior officer, so it was probably all right. Life did get very complicated at times.

She went in, anyway, without comment.

'Why?' he persisted.

'Oh, I suppose it's because I'm being seen as some sort of representative of all female police officers,' she said, as they walked along the back corridor.

'So? You're a bloody good representative.'

'Maybe. But I still feel I'm letting the side down.'

18

'Because you can't strip down a car engine?' asked Tom incredulously, stopping at the inner door to punch in the security numbers.

'In a way.' She pushed open the door that led down yet another corridor, past the collator's office, past the duty inspector's office, to the CID suite, so called, in the new extension. All that that meant was that two reasonably large offices had been made into three that were too small for their occupants.

'They unnerve me,' she said.

The woman who had achieved what a gunman and two desperadoes with knives had failed to do, and had made him break out in a cold sweat of sheer panic, would sooner leave her car sitting out there on the car park than admit that she didn't know how to mend it?

Tom risked overstepping the mark again. 'I know if you want my advice, you'll ask for it,' he said. 'And it might seem odd coming from someone you reduced to a jelly this morning, but if you ask me, it's advice on believing in yourself that you could do with.'

'Oh, I get more than enough of that,' she said, as they went into the empty CID room.

'Maybe you should listen to it,' Tom said, sitting down at his desk for the first time that day, and picking up the precious expenses claim. 'Ma'am,' he added, mischievously.

'Maybe I should,' she said, going into her office, and snapping on the light. 'Sergeant.'

Tom smiled as she went in and closed the door. She was all right, Judy Hill. Even if she did have a wicked line in wind-ups. He'd had much worse governors than her.

'You're not forgetting the stuff for the CPS on that aggravated burglary, are you?' she asked, popping her head round the door again. 'I want it on my desk first thing tomorrow. And I mean it, Tom. No excuses. I don't care how many witnesses you've got to see.'

'Right after I've seen this one,' said Finch, and looked at the pile of work that awaited him, his shoulders drooping. He reached for the phone to call Liz.

Worse governors, anyway. Maybe not that much.

Patrick was preparing his lessons for tomorrow; he always preferred to do all his school work at school, so that he could forget about it once he got home. Or wherever. But tonight he was going home. He enjoyed his home, his married life. He really didn't want to give his wife a hard time. He had, of course, more than once. And he would again, if she found him out again. But not tonight.

The staff room was hot and dusty, and had the smell of coffee and Pledge and a hint of cigarette smoke. They all did, really. Patrick

19

liked staff rooms. He liked schools. He liked teaching. He pulled his
shirt away from his back, and stretched. When he was little, all he
had wanted to do was work in a garage, like his dad. Mending cars.
And as he grew up he often did help his dad out, once he'd started
his own business. He had had every intention of being a motor
mechanic, despite the kind of marks he was getting at school, which
suggested an academic career.

His father hadn't tried to influence him one way or the other; all
that had happened was that one day he had looked up from the
book he was reading and realized that what he wanted to do more
than anything else was tell other people about the joys of learning.
Learning anything. Everything. How to mend cars, how to read
Shakespeare. How to play the saxophone. He wanted everyone to
realize that learning was fun.

'How was your first day, then?' asked the head, suddenly appearing
beside him.

It ruined the stretch. 'Oh, not bad at all, thanks,' said Patrick. 'Is
it all right to leave my jacket off tomorrow, though?'

'You weren't wearing that thing all day, were you?' said the head,
horrified. 'You must have been abominably hot.'

Patrick smiled. 'I was,' he said. 'Only at my last place you had to
wait until you got the word that jackets could be removed.'

'Did you?' The head's brow cleared. 'Oh yes – of course, you
taught at . . .' He moved his hand backwards and forwards in what
Patrick was already able to recognize as his substitute for any name
he couldn't remember, which was most names. 'Yes. But we're not
that formal here. No, no. Actually – I was thinking. The uniform . . .
I mean, the children must have been too hot.'

'They were,' agreed Patrick. 'But I don't think you're supposed to
call them children any more.'

'Oh, no. Pupils. Students. It's so difficult trying not to offend . . .'
He waved his hand. 'Anyone,' he finished. 'I keep forgetting that I'm
not a headmaster any more. Head teacher, head teacher, I have to
say to myself.'

Patrick smiled.

'I was going to say that they should wear summer uniform while
the weather continues like this,' the head went on. 'But most of them
won't have the summer uniform. This is the first year we've had a
uniform at all. Well, since the sixties, that is.'

'Yes.' Patrick wasn't sure what he was supposed to be saying.

'I like them, myself,' said the head. 'I think it gives the . . .
students . . . a touch of pride in their school. It makes them look
smart. And you can't tell the well-off ones from the ones whose dads
are on the dole.'

'No,' said Patrick.

'But they must be far too hot,' said the head. 'Do you think I should say that the uniform needn't be worn until further notice?'

'Well, it's not up to me, but it would be easier teaching people that weren't wilting before your eyes.'

'Yes. Yes – I'll get...' He waved his hand in the direction of the office.

'Erica?' suggested Patrick. The lovely Erica, who had repulsed him yet again, only this evening.

'Erica. Yes. I'll... yes.' He peered at Patrick. 'I'll get her to do a letter to the parents,' he said, absently.

'She's gone,' said Patrick.

She had left at five, walking home so that Colin would have the car when he came out of the drama group that he belonged to. Colin needed the car because he always had a lot of stuff to lug backwards and forwards, she had told Patrick. He didn't dare leave good equipment and kit at the school.

Patrick hadn't demanded an explanation; he had just been given one. In his experience that meant Erica was justifying what seemed to her to be unreasonable, and that meant she might no longer be off-limits, if 'Cocky' Cochrane, as the papers were wont to call him, was beginning to get on her nerves again.

Patrick had offered her a lift but she had said that it wasn't far. She had thought, though, just for a moment, before she had refused. If he had pressed her, she would have accepted, and he might not have been doing his lesson preparation, or going straight home, after all. But he mustn't make things even more complicated than they had already become.

'Is everything all right?' the head demanded. 'You look worried.'

'No,' said Patrick. 'Hot, that's all. Just hot.'

'You'd tell me if anything was bothering you about the school, or anything like that?'

Not on your life, thought Patrick. 'Yes,' he said cheerfully, turning back to his work.

'The caretaker locks up at eight,' said the head.

'I'll be out from under his feet before then, sir,' said Patrick.

'Yes, er...' The head waved his hand about, as Patrick's name escaped him. 'And it's Max... We don't stand on ceremony here.'

At least he could remember his own name, Patrick thought. It was a start.

'Cheer up,' said Lloyd's table companion. 'You're supposed to be enjoying yourself.'

Lloyd looked up from his meal. 'How?' he asked, uncomprehendingly.

The surroundings were very pleasant, particularly during this surprising weather, and the house had been built by the sort of Elizabethan yuppie that he always found intriguing, but he wasn't here to soak up the atmosphere. He had applied himself with considerable determination to the course, but he was not, and never had been, a career policeman, and enjoying himself was not what he was doing.

Why other police officers apparently broke their necks to get on courses was a mystery to him, or, at any rate, to the short bald bloke, who had no apparent interest in boozing or betting or women, all of which pursuits were made easier when you temporarily had no wife to whom you had to account for your doings.

But that lure would never have been Lloyd's, either, fond though he was of a dram and the occasional flutter and the pleasures of the flesh; he had no wife, and what he did have wasn't something from which he needed escape.

'You're off the hook, man! It's all over bar the shouting. So now you get to unwind a bit, let your hair down while you're out of the missus's clutches.'

'I haven't got a missus,' Lloyd said. 'Not any more.'

Lloyd wasn't at all sure that the short bald bloke should be divorced, but even he drew the line at inventing a wife.

'I've had two. Still got the second. Shows you what a glutton for punishment I am, doesn't it?' A dig from his elbow accompanied this remark, causing Lloyd's fork to ship its cargo on its way to his mouth.

'Look round. They're not half bad. See her?' He pointed to a young woman at a far table. 'She's a DI from up north – a right little goer, by all accounts.' He laughed. 'I'm all for women getting into the higher ranks if they're lookers,' he said.

'I don't think that wins points for political correctness,' said Lloyd, in some danger of stepping out of character. The short bald bloke might not mind having his evening meal thus interrupted, but he did, and he wanted this moron to go away. He would probably be Chief Constable somewhere in about five minutes, he thought sourly.

'Eh?'

Lloyd smiled. 'Nothing,' he said. What was the point in getting into an argument at this stage, he asked himself.

'Aren't there any that take your fancy?'

Some of them were, as his friend had so poetically put it, not half bad, and this had not gone unnoticed by Lloyd. But he could survive without dragging one of them off to his room, even supposing that any of them found him not half bad. That was what intrigued him about his companion; the certainty with which he was looking forward to the gratification of his carnal desires.

22

'They're off the leash, too,' said his fellow diner, proving Lloyd's point about the policeman's nose being as important as the wine expert's was to him. Knowing what your interviewee was thinking went a long way towards getting a result. 'Get a few gins down them, and you're away.'

Lloyd's one and only attempt to seduce a female police officer had finally borne fruit over ten years and two broken marriages later, but that was another story, and not one that he was about to discuss with this Romeo or anyone else.

He asked himself, all the same, what would have happened if he had met Judy at one of these things rather than at work. It had been the idea of getting into a relationship with a married man that had scared Judy off, that had made her marry Michael, and all the rest. She might well have entertained the idea of a one-night stand.

He wondered, a little uncomfortably, if she ever had. He knew there had only been two serious relationships – Michael and him – but he didn't really know about anything else.

And if they had met at one of these things, would they have ended up together? If you called living in two flats being together, that was. Perhaps the sort of instant gratification apparently on offer to his companion would have been enough, and they would have gone their separate ways.

But he doubted it. He and Judy had something special, and even she, unromantic and down to earth as she was, knew it. And now he came to think of it . . . He took out his glasses and checked the date on the newspaper that he had rather been hoping to read. Damn. It was tomorrow. Not that Judy would know that, of course, but he would much rather be celebrating with her than bedding any of his fellow students, that was for certain. No point in sending a card or anything. She wouldn't know what it was all about.

'No,' he said, pushing away the remains of his meal and getting up. 'There's no one takes my fancy. They're all yours.'

'What's he still doing here?' asked Julie.

They were standing in the late-evening sun, a group of them, at the bus stop just beyond the gates, having been to the drama group. The school was just on the edge of the town centre; until five o'clock there was a little shuttle bus service that came along every ten minutes, but after that the buses slowed down, and, for reasons best known to the now privately owned bus company, acquired another deck, though they had fewer passengers.

Natalie turned to look in the direction of Julie's gaze.

'Mr Murray?' said Kim. 'He said he marks books and things at school before he goes home. I think he always stays late.'

23

'He taught at some posh boys' school before, didn't he?' asked Julie.

'Yeah. He's nice, though, isn't he?' said Claire, dreamily. 'I'm going to ask him if he'd like to join the drama group.'

'Didn't work with Colin Cochrane, did it, Hannah?' teased Julie.

'What's that supposed to mean?' asked Hannah, instantly on the defensive.

'You only joined the drama club because Colin Cochrane was in it! She was hoping she'd get a love scene,' Julie went on, addressing Kim, who smiled. 'But no such luck.'

Everyone laughed, except Natalie. She was tired of Hannah and her one-sided romance with Colin Cochrane.

'There he is,' said Kim, as Colin Cochrane emerged from the gym.

Natalie turned her head and watched as his tracksuited figure strode round to the car park.

'Why does he have to wear a tracksuit all the time?' demanded Julie. 'In case no one recognizes him?'

'He's training most nights,' said Hannah, protective, as she always was about him. And she always called him Colin when she spoke about him; that irritated Natalie, but it made the others laugh.

'Is that what he calls it?' said Julie, her voice acid.

'What do you mean?' asked Hannah.

'The woman who works with my mum knows his wife,' said Julie.

'So do we,' Natalie pointed out.

'No, I mean really knows her. She's a friend of hers. And she says that Erica Cochrane reckons he's seeing someone else. Someone from school.'

'Some friend she is,' said Kim. 'Telling people Mrs Cochrane's business.'

'Who's he seeing? Mrs Kane?' asked someone.

'No. A pupil, she says.' Julie grinned. 'So you've missed your chance, Hannah,' she said. 'Sorry.'

Hannah bridled. 'How do you know it isn't me?' she demanded.

'Because even he's not that daft,' said Julie.

Everyone laughed; Hannah didn't like that, but the remark hadn't been personal, as Julie was quick to point out once she saw Hannah's face.

'I just meant that it'll be one of the sixth-formers,' she said. 'He's not going to go with someone our age, is he?' she said. 'He could go to prison if he got caught.'

Kim drew in her breath sharply and looked at Natalie, then went pink and stared at the ground.

Natalie could only hope that she kept her mouth shut and that the others hadn't noticed. She had had to confide in someone just after it had started, and Kim was her best friend. Hannah had noticed, perhaps, but no one else had.

Julie obligingly changed the subject to her evidently numerous boyfriends, and one sticky moment had passed, but there would be plenty more, Natalie was sure.

The bus came then, a double-decker with about a dozen people on it, drawing to a noisy stop, its engine rattling, its brakes sighing; they all got on except Hannah.

'Aren't you coming?' asked Kim, half on, half off the step.

'No,' said Hannah, looking at Natalie, not Kim. 'I'll walk.'

'You get on if you're coming, girl,' said the driver testily to Kim, revving the engine as the bus shuddered. 'Or you'll be walking too.'

Judy Hill sat upstairs in the bus, from force of habit. She hardly ever smoked anyway, and the buses had all been smoke-free zones for years, but her feet, on the odd occasion that she found herself on a rare double-decker, still took her upstairs, and along the length of the aisle to the very back.

So, that was where she now sat, unobserved by the girls who had come on at the bus stop outside the sprawling Oaklands School.

'Did you see her face?' one of them said as they came upstairs. 'When I said he wouldn't be daft enough to go with her? I thought she was going to hit me!'

The others laughed, obviously at someone else's expense. You would probably have deserved to have been hit, Judy thought.

There were only four girls, though they somehow contrived to seem like double that number as they spread themselves around the upper deck, lazily insolent, carefully unconcerned by the faintly disapproving looks being cast in their direction by the handful of other passengers. They took up four double seats in the empty bus so that they could stretch out long legs, almost lying back in a literal evocation of their would-be state of mind.

One sat up in order to inscribe graffiti on the back of the seat in front with black felt pen; *BABY OTTER AND PINK CHAMPAIGNE WAS HERE*, she wrote.

'I spell *champagne* wrong,' she said.

Judy wondered how Lloyd would deal with that one. Someone who knew she couldn't spell a word, but spelt it that way anyway. As an officer of the law, she supposed she ought to be worrying less about their spelling and more about their behaviour, but she didn't advise them against writing on the seats.

They fascinated her, these languid, self-confident creatures as they talked and laughed and wrote on the seats; she didn't want to inhibit them.

25

The girl behind leant over the seat and took the pen to cross out the intrusive I. She, presumably, was Pink Champagne; at any rate, she could spell it. She sat back again, flicking her long blonde hair over her shoulder.

Baby Otter, cute, short, sandy hair, added (*KIM AND NAT*) to the inscription.

'He really thinks I'm pregnant,' said one of the others, to laughter. 'Aren't you going to put him out of his misery?'

'I've told him I'm not, but he doesn't believe me.'

Judy shook her head slightly, recalling her own school-days, and the desperate crushes she had developed on the older boys. Men, it seemed to her, from her twelve-year-old perspective. One such had dropped a coin as he was putting change in his pocket; she had dived to retrieve it for him, and he had told her to keep it. She probably still had it, somewhere. It had meant everything to her for at least six weeks.

But these girls were older than that, and, Judy knew only too well, a great deal better versed in such matters than she had been at their age. Quite possibly than she was now, come that. She watched and listened as these nearly-adults did their best to shock the other passengers.

She could be the mother of one of these fascinating creatures, she realized, with a jolt. She didn't think she'd mind; she could believe having given birth to one of them, even if they did exhibit slightly anti-social tendencies and an alarming readiness both to indulge in and subsequently discuss matters sexual. She had never given any thought to motherhood, never wanted the responsibility; now, sitting upstairs on a bus, she felt faint stirrings of regret.

It wasn't too late yet, she told herself, partly in fun. Mostly in fun. It was impossible: she was too old to be a first-time mother, it would disrupt her career, change her life for ever ... Of course it was in fun. Lloyd would be all for it, naturally, if she were ever to suggest such a thing. But she wasn't serious. It would pass. Besides which, it was babies that were supposed to make women in their late thirties broody, not tall, leggy teenagers who would probably all be pregnant before they were twenty.

Linda wasn't that much older than these girls – two, three years, perhaps. The thought of her sticky relationship with Lloyd's daughter checked Judy's brief moment of regret.

One by one the girls alighted from the achingly slow bus as it did a tour of Stansfield. Those left after each departure became visibly more conventional, less noticeable, taking up less room than before. And then there was just one. Blonde, slim, sexy Pink Champagne –

Nat, presumably. Self-assured, still, but now she was sitting up, her feet on the floor, quiet and well-behaved, indistinguishable from the other passengers.

The girl rose as the bus approached the last stop in Stansfield before it took to the dual carriageway, and pressed the bell. She made her way to the stair, then turned and said cheerio to the young man at the very front whose presence she had not once acknowledged. A sudden, broad, and quite unexpected smile transformed her expression from sophisticated *ennui* to friendly openness, as she ran down, no longer the languorous sophisticate of the upper deck, but the girl who went home to her mum and dad, the girl they worried about, and expected to come home.

And she did come home, thought Judy, as the girl set off in a half-run. She did.

Perhaps she was missing something after all.

'Erica? Colin. Look – the car won't start, so I won't be home.'

Erica frowned a little at the phone. There had been nothing wrong with the car this morning, and besides it was only a ten-minute walk home from school.

'I'll get something to eat in the town,' he said. 'And I'll be back at ten as arranged. All right?'

'All right,' she said.

All right. She only saw him for about an hour on Tuesdays between the drama club and his training, and now he was avoiding even that. He wasn't even training *for* anything, as far as she could see. Nothing specific, anyway; he had practically retired from athletics.

Erica made a meal for one, as she so often did, eating it on a tray in front of the television.

Colin would be back as Big Ben struck for the ten o'clock news; it was an obsessive trait that would make deception childishly simple, and the fact that he was obsessive was one of the reasons that she was contemplating deception at all. Marrying Colin may have been a dreadful mistake.

Patrick had offered her a lift home; anyone overhearing the conversation would have thought nothing of it, but she had known what was on his mind. And there had been an instant, the merest fraction of a second, when she had almost accepted. Colin safely out of the way for two hours at the drama group . . . It would have been easy to say yes.

The dog shifted his position at her feet, with a little throaty growl of contentment, and Erica felt a pang of envy. Patrick might have made her feel like that, if she had said yes. But she hadn't.

27

The film started at eight, but it failed to catch her attention and she switched it off just as the door bell rang.

Hannah cursed the dark blue sweatshirt as she had cursed it all day. It was far too thick to wear in this weather.

She had gone to the burger bar, and stayed there reading until just before nine; now she waited on the darkening Green for Colin to arrive. She hoped the temperature would drop a little when it got dark, which it was just beginning to do. It had been so hot all day, and even the breeze that was getting up, whispering in the wood that bounded two sides of the long, wide rectangle of grass, was warm, like the ones you got abroad.

Across from the adventure playground, where she sat waiting, across the areas marked out for rugby and football, was Beech Street, with scarcely any traffic in the evening, its commercial buildings all dark. To her left was the much busier Ash Road, along which she could hear but not see the traffic as it rumbled past. A hedge of trees separated the Green from the road, and from the service road which branched off it, down to the council depot, which was hidden in a dip, on a level with the houses that lined Ash Road.

It gave the illusion of countryside, of loneliness. But she wouldn't be lonely when Colin came. They had laughed at her, laughed at the very idea of her and Colin. She'd show them.

She got up to wander through the columns of tyres and wooden climbing frames. She didn't know when Colin would appear; she just knew that he would, because he always came home this way, and on Tuesday nights, hidden by the structures of the adventure playground, she always waited for him.

But tonight was going to be different; she had made that clear to him in her letter.

Chapter Three

Ten past nine. Lloyd sipped an indifferent whisky, and looked round the bar, where huddles of people sat actually discussing the stuff they had been listening to all day. They used jargon as though it were holy scripture, and spoke about modems and windows as though they were the deity.

Judy had, not unnaturally, asked why he had been so keen to go on the Leadership Development Programme. His answer had been that he had a few years to go before he would have put in his thirty years, and early retirement on a reduced pension did not appeal.

That, he had told her, was the likely outcome of the changes about to be forced on the police, unless he got a rank that kept him clear of it, and to do that he had to be up to date with current command thinking.

In truth, there was a possibility of his being kept on at his current salary with the rank of inspector, and a desire to continue to outrank Judy might have quite a lot to do with his late-flowering ambition, but he tried not to think about that. His male chauvinist tendencies bothered him a little.

Neither of those reasons, needless to say, were the ones he had given Them. He had been scheduled to attend a Junior Command Course, to which this was the successor, after his promotion to Chief Inspector, but had been prevented from doing so by, of all things, appendicitis. He had never reapplied, and now, some years later, it should have been too late. But They had understood his belated desire to reach, if not for the sky, then at least for a hand-hold on the rooftiles.

So many senior police officers had been on accelerated promotion that, in Lloyd's official opinion, the opinion of the short bald bloke, there was a danger of a lack of empathy with the officers under their command, most of whom had achieved whatever rank they had by putting in years of service.

And if, he had said earnestly, in his man-of-the-people Welsh accent, as opposed to his expensively educated Welsh accent, his sinister Welsh accent, or his literary Welsh accent – the one that got

Judy going – if a them and us situation was to be avoided, it seemed to him essential that a balance of old and new be maintained at the top.

Every round of interviews had seen him expand on his theme, which he found even more boring than they did; they had let him go on the course simply to shut him up, he was sure.

He had mistakenly thought that no one else had discovered this pub, its being a considerable distance away from Bramshill and not exactly the most welcoming place on earth, but it hadn't remained undiscovered. The serious mob had found it. The ones who didn't want to let their hair down, who had probably never let their hair down in their lives, had found it.

He would find a phone box and phone Judy. He hadn't spoken to her for over a week, as the course work had got more and more demanding, and he had simply not had the time or energy to do anything other than work and sleep.

He wanted to hear her voice.

Daylight faded beyond the windows, and Patrick really hadn't meant this to happen. But the bare, suntanned leg that pressed against his was . . . well, irresistible.

He had meant just to talk to her, that was all; there had been no ulterior motive. He had honestly not meant this to happen. He hadn't expected her to come on to him the way she had, for one thing, but he had never been one to refuse what was on offer. He ought to, he knew that, but he had acquiesced thus far, and now his hand was on her knee, and . . . well, they weren't going to talk, were they?

He knew he ought to put a stop to it now, while they were still both respectable, still hadn't removed any clothing, were still able to stop, but her parted lips were on his, her tongue slipping into his mouth, and, well . . . he didn't have the willpower.

He never had had. He slid his hand up her thigh and muttered something about Colin, but she said what harm were they doing Colin?

None, really, he conceded. He didn't suppose, he added, with what might have been a twinge of conscience, except that she was wriggling out of her pants, kicking them off, smiling at him.

What Colin didn't know couldn't hurt him, she said, and she was . . . Well, what was a man supposed to do?

He didn't feel right about it, not really, all the same, and, anyway, Colin was hardly the only issue, he said, when he could speak. There were numerous other bars to what they were inevitably about to do, to what they were in fact, to all intents and purposes, already doing. There was his wife, for one thing.

30

She said he hadn't been too bothered about her in the past, so what had changed?

Nothing, he supposed. Nothing. God knew, he hadn't changed. And he never would.

She had changed; she was making all the moves, and his far from robust conscience couldn't possibly withstand what she was doing to him now.

The minimal resistance that he had put up melted away; the immorality of it all, the danger in which he was placing friendships, career, marriage, well . . .

There was only so much a man could resist.

'So how's it going?'

'Drearily,' said Lloyd. 'If there is anything more boring on this earth than a computer buff, I hope I never meet it.'

Judy laughed. 'You're bored because you're not joining in,' she said. 'It's end of term. You're supposed to be getting smashed out of your skull and pushing naked women into fountains by now.'

'No, that's in a couple of hours or so. About eleven, that starts. Why do drunks always shout? They're about two feet away from one another and yelling as if they're all stone deaf.'

Judy tutted. 'I can see that you are not entering into the spirit of things,' she said. 'The idea is to compromise as many female police officers as you can, in order that it might be used against them should there be any possibility of their actually being promoted to superintendent.'

There was a little silence at the other end.

'Hello?' said Judy. 'Are you still there?'

'You know when you . . . when you were doing this course,' Lloyd began, haltingly.

Judy had known him much too long to be taken in by the shy, tongue-tied mode. 'Yes,' she said warily.

'Did you get . . . What's that dreadful expression Finch uses?'

'You know perfectly well, whatever it is,' she said crisply.

'Hit on?' he said.

'Lloyd – the only qualification for being hit on at one of these things is to be female. Of course I did.'

'What did you do?'

'Mind your own business,' she said.

Another silence. This time she didn't break it.

'I wish you were here or I was there,' Lloyd said.

'It's nothing like as bad as you're making out,' Judy said. 'None of it. My translation is that the course is really quite interesting, but you won't admit it.'

'Have you missed me?'

She had seen him twice in seven weeks. The first time she had been working all weekend, and the second she had been called in to work before he'd been there an hour and had got back just as he was leaving, because he'd only come for the day. It had been worse than not seeing him at all.

'I managed,' she said.

'Good,' he said. 'Are you going to resent my coming and taking charge at work again?'

'No,' she said, truthfully.

'Good.'

'So – what have you got on for the rest of the week?' she asked.

'Oh, this and that. I think I get released some time on Friday.'

'Maybe I can wangle Friday off,' said Judy. 'We can have a nice long weekend.'

'That sounds very good,' said Lloyd.

'I'll see what I can do.'

'And what sort of day have you had?'

'My new car won't go.'

'It is not your new car,' Lloyd said. 'You bought it nearly a year ago. It was never your new car. It was someone's new car once, but that was about twelve years ago.'

'Well, it won't go.'

'Get rid of it. Get a proper new one. With a warranty, and AA membership, and . . .'

Judy settled down comfortably, lying on the sofa, as Lloyd got into his stride, moving smoothly from how she should buy a new car to how she should run her entire life. She wasn't listening to the words, just to his voice. Even over a phone line, Lloyd's voice, with its carefully nurtured just-Welsh accent was top of the list that she kept in her head of Good Things about Lloyd.

What he was saying was patronizing and infuriating, and top of the list of Bad Things about Lloyd, which was why she didn't listen. But eventually he got off the lecture, and just talked about the people he was meeting, about the course.

He made her laugh. He had always been able to make her laugh, and she could forgive him almost anything for that. But there was more, much more than that.

She wondered if she should tell him one day how much she loved him, but she thought he might just become unbearable if he knew.

Sherlock whimpered as soon as Erica closed the door; he had thought that he was going to be taken out, obviously. She had forgotten all about him – Colin always took him out when he came home from school, but of course he hadn't come home from school.

She heard the car drive off, and looked at the dog. Colin would be back soon – he would take him. But . . . well, perhaps she could do with some fresh air.

'Come on, then,' she said. 'Let's go walkies.'

The bloodhound, which looked ancient but was in fact just a year old, lumbered along the hallway, into the kitchen, picked up his lead, and lumbered back.

She strolled down the busy road, Sherry on the lead, trotting obediently at her heel as cars zipped past at head height with the occasional burst of music from their open windows on this soft summer night. There was open land across the road, through the underpass, but she walked on down towards the Green. She would get there at about five to ten; Colin would be there on the last leg of his run, or she would meet him on the pathway.

If he really was out running, that was.

'It's Natalie's mum,' said Kim's little brother, who had dived for the phone as being yet another thing that would delay the dread moment when he had to go to bed. He was far too late as it was.

Kim took the phone. 'Go to bed,' she said.

He stuck his tongue out at her. God, she hated baby-sitting. 'Hello, Mrs Ouspensky,' she said.

'Kim – is Natalie with you?'

'No,' said Kim. 'Did she say she was coming here?' she asked, her tone guarded. Natalie's love-life was a bit too complicated, and she might have said she was with Kim. Well, if she had, she should have warned her.

'No. She went over to see her gran, but she should have been back an hour ago. Her gran said she went for the ten to nine bus. She should have been home by ten past. I saw the bus go by.'

Oh dear. Natalie had obviously not counted on Gran reporting her movements. 'I haven't seen her,' she said.

'It's not like her,' said Natalie's mother.

Well. It was like her, really. Natalie's mother had a bit of a blind spot about Natalie. Not that she would go out of her way to worry her mother, but you couldn't pick and choose when to see someone if he was married. And she was only an hour late, after all.

Kim hated having secrets. She didn't like her own secrets, and she certainly didn't like having custody of someone else's. 'I'm sure she'll be all right,' she said. 'I expect she just missed the bus – I think there's only one an hour out to your place.'

'Not from her gran's,' said Mrs Ouspensky. 'They're every twenty minutes until twenty to ten. It's the little buses up there, and the

33

garage is down our way, so they come right until ten. But the last bus has been.'

'Well – maybe she . . . went to see someone else.'

'Who?' Mrs O. jumped on the statement practically before Kim had stopped speaking.

'I didn't mean anyone in particular . . .'

'Look – Kim – is Natalia seeing some boy?'

'No,' said Kim, with absolute truth. Not a boy.

'Oh, I'm sorry,' she said. 'You're right, I'm probably worrying for no reason at all. I'm sorry to have bothered you.'

'No bother,' said Kim, lying in her teeth. 'And I'm sure she's all right, Mrs Ouspensky.'

Hannah left the adventure playground, and walked along the service road, towards the footpath up to Ash Road. She could get a bus home from there, and that seemed the best idea, really.

The figure that almost bumped into her at the alley tried, for a moment, to turn away, but then turned back, and looked at her.

Hannah saw who it was, and froze to the spot.

Ten past ten. In the almost-deserted Stansfield police station, Tom Finch rubbed his eyes and moved on, with considerable lack of enthusiasm, to the second witness statement on the aggravated burglary. He had little stomach for the task of presenting a case to the Crown Prosecution Service; sometimes it seemed to him that whatever you did, they would throw it out for lack of evidence.

Right now, he'd welcome anything that would rescue him; the job wasn't getting done while he was stuck here, pen-pushing; the villains were out there, and they didn't need to shuffle bits of paper around before they could get a result.

Still, at least he wasn't at Bramshill, like the DCI. He'd be back any day now, and acting Chief Inspector Hill would be back to taking orders. Tom wondered how she would take it. Professionally, of course – but she had enjoyed being in charge, all the same.

Women sometimes found it just too difficult, and even she had problems, it seemed, with the rampant sexism. Tom didn't think he was too guilty of it – he had been a bit leery of having a woman boss, but she was all right. He was supposed to moan about her, so he did, but that was just the way it was. There was that time they had been at the scene of a stabbing, and the blood on the floor had made her queasy . . . that was pounced on, of course, and he'd had a laugh at her expense with the rest of them. He felt just a touch disloyal about that; she was his governor, and he should have stood up for her. Lloyd would have.

He was beginning to get used to calling him Lloyd; at first he'd felt a bit as though he were addressing the butler. But Lloyd's first name was of such awfulness that no one except Judy knew it, and she had had to work it out from inadvertent clues.

Work, he told himself sternly, as the clock moved on to quarter past ten. Work, or you'll be here until midnight. But maybe something would happen out there in the real world, something that he could hardly ignore in favour of paperwork. A murder would be favourite. That would be a good enough excuse even for DI Hill.

Colin finally found the key, and got into the car, starting the engine. His whole body shook, and he wasn't sure he could drive, not like this. But he was late already, and he couldn't stay here for ever.

Still breathing heavily, he put the car in gear. His hands were still shaking, but he seemed to have got control of his legs at last.

He had to get home. He had said ten o'clock, and it was after that now. Erica would be worried, even if he was only a few minutes late. Colin's punctuality was obsessive, he knew that. Everything about him was obsessive, and always had been.

Time-keeping, showering; it wasn't the other members of staff who were scared of sweat, it was him. He showered constantly, in case he smelled, whether he'd been exerting himself or not. He reached into the glove compartment, unzipped his tracksuit top and sprayed himself with more deodorant as he sat there.

He was like that about everything he did. All the time. He wanted to stop, but he couldn't – it was always like that. Erica just laughed at him about the showers, but she didn't really know what he was like, what he had been going through. She knew their marriage had been suffering, though. She just didn't know why.

His new obsession. Erica didn't believe he had been running; she had got into conversation with a coach at an athletics meeting and he had told her what sort of training was needed if you wanted to run long-distance races. It didn't, of course, make any sense when she compared it to what he was doing.

Now he was going to have to go home in this state and she would want explanations. He drove slowly out of his parking space and along the school drive to the rear gate, his heart still hammering painfully, his temples throbbing.

Chapter Four

Patrick drove home, trying to work out how much damage limitation was going to be possible.

That girl had seen him; there had been no point in trying to go back. A second later and he would have been in the darkness of the depot; as it was, he had been in the well-lit alley. She had seen him, and he had seen her.

A girl, a pupil of Oakland School, her eyes wide with apprehension. Half the bloody school must have been on Ash Road Green tonight, he thought sourly.

He had had to do something, and yet he hadn't been able to do anything useful, not with her there. In the end, he had walked across to the depot, trying to look as though he had some business there, and had gone to the doorway, pretending to try an obviously locked door to an obviously dark building. But he was Irish; she would have put that down to Mickness, he hoped.

He had put the shoes down and turned, then walked quickly back up the footpath to the road. He hadn't stopped until he had got to the car; he had looked back, then, and she had been at the top of the path, watching him curiously. Then she had walked quickly away along Ash Road, towards the bus stop.

He had got into the car and driven away in the opposite direction, rehearsing the lies he was going to have to tell Victoria.

He didn't know the girl, but the chances were that she had recognized him. He just had to keep his head, that was all. He just had to keep his head, and hope that the girl wasn't too good at putting two and two together. Trouble was, Oakland didn't go in much for pupils who couldn't do simple arithmetic, not now that they had an image to maintain.

Victoria was watching television when he got in; she didn't acknowledge his presence.

'Sorry, love,' he said. 'I got tied up.'

'By whom?' she asked drily, as he got between her and the TV.

Patrick smiled. 'Ah, nothing like that,' he said. 'I offered to fix Colin Cochrane's car, that's all.'

36

Victoria looked pointedly at the clock, got up, and went into the kitchen, where she proceeded to fill the kettle as noisily as she could.

Patrick went in after her. 'Swear to God,' he said. 'You can ask Colin, if you like.'

'And fixing his car took until ten o'clock, did it?'

Patrick nodded, shrugged. 'Yeah,' he said. 'About that. It was harder than I thought.' He put his arms round her as she stood waiting for the kettle to boil, his chin on her shoulder. 'Ask him,' he said. 'I was mending his car.'

She turned. 'And then what, Patrick?' she asked. 'Did you take it home for him? Pop in to see Mrs Cochrane?'

Patrick's eyebrows rose. 'What's Mrs Cochrane got to do with anything?' he asked.

'I've heard all about you and Erica Cochrane,' said Victoria.

Patrick laughed. 'Sure, what's there to hear about me and Erica Cochrane?' he asked.

'You were never away from there during the summer, or so I was told today.' She looked away from him. 'I nearly didn't come here,' she said. 'You persuaded me. You were never going to be unfaithful again – you had learned your lesson, you were a changed man. And all the time you were sleeping with Erica Cochrane, weren't you?'

'What?' said Patrick. He put his hand to her chin, and turned her face to his. 'Who's been telling you that?' he asked, in truly injured innocence. He had done nothing with Erica Cochrane during the summer, though it hadn't been for the want of trying.

'A friend of hers that I met today,' she said. 'Dropping hints about what a great friend of the Cochranes you were, and how you were company for Erica while Colin was away.'

'I am a friend of the Cochranes,' said Patrick. 'But there was nothing going on between me and her. And I think I know the friend you mean – she's started more rumours than any ministry of propaganda ever did.'

'But you were there when he was away at athletics meetings and things,' said Victoria. 'Weren't you?'

'Sometimes,' said Patrick. 'But he was there as often as not. Erica would make a meal for me now and then, that's all. There was nothing going on, Victoria. I swear to God.' It had been so long since he'd told the truth that he had almost forgotten how; he embellished it now. 'The man's a friend of mine, for God's sake,' he added, as though that made the slightest difference.

'Then where were you tonight?' she said.

'I've told you. Mending Colin's car.'

She didn't look convinced.

Patrick gave her a cuddle. 'If I'd been with some woman, I'd hardly come up with a lame excuse like that, would I?' he said.

Victoria smiled. 'No,' she said. 'You're usually more inventive.'

He'd usually had some time to think up a story; tonight hadn't been planned. He kissed her. 'I'm not daft,' he said. 'I know if I start all that again you'll leave me.'

'Yes,' she said. 'I will.'

'I'm not going to risk that, am I?'

They kissed again, she made a nice cup of tea, and Patrick convinced her, not for the first time, that he was a reformed character who would never again have a bit on the side.

He had told his class this morning that he was a consummate liar, and it was no more than the truth; he believed the lies as he spoke them. And when he was reassuring Victoria, he really did believe what he was saying; he believed that he had done nothing at all that night to worry her or anyone else.

But he had, of course, and there would be a reckoning, one way or the other.

The call had been the answer to Tom's prayer. A body on Ash Road Green took precedence over paperwork, even in his inspector's book.

He was there now, feeling just a touch guilty about his wish coming true; something superstitious at the back of his mind made him feel that he had somehow caused it to happen.

The duty inspector had cordoned off the children's playground. Tom had asked him to seal off the depot area too. There were tyre marks, rubber on the paved surface down by the depot that seemed out of place where all you should have was the odd van picking up equipment and more or less obeying the five-miles-an-hour limit on the service road. It looked as though someone had shot out of there at speed. And up on the main road there were skid marks in the nearside lane, where the service road met it.

Joyriders? The depot courtyard was a good area for showing off your handbrake turns, Tom supposed. If so, did one of them get over-excited, and work off his excess energy on the victim?

The lady whose dog had found her was still too upset to be of much use. She had stumbled away from the body, and run up the overgrown embankment to the phone. She was a mess; all that anyone had got so far was that her name was Cochrane, and that the dog's name, of all things, was Sherlock. Then she had started to cry almost helplessly when Tom had tried to talk to her. A WPC was with her now, trying to calm her down.

Not a nice thing for your dog to turn up, Tom thought. Not a nice thing at all. A young woman, beaten, strangled, probably raped; her blouse was unbuttoned, her skirt pulled up to her waist, and she had nothing on underneath.

Tom squatted down and shone his torch into the concrete pipe where the top half of the body lay, and sniffed. He could still smell it. Something not right, something that didn't belong. He shook his head, and stood up. He knew that smell, but he couldn't place it. A perfume of some sort, but it didn't seem right.

On one level, he was as shocked as the next man, as shocked as Mrs Cochrane, even, at the brutality, the horror of it all. On another, he was a little like the dog, who sat beside his dishevelled mistress, tail wagging, tongue out, pleased that his discovery had produced all this activity. Finding people was a bloodhound's job, he was saying joyously, and that's what he had just done.

Finding their killers was a policeman's job, and Tom's tail was wagging too. The duty inspector had got two teams doing house-to-house along Ash Road before it got too late; they had arranged for scene-of-crime officers to come, set the wheels in motion. Now, they needed something to go on.

'What's the score, Tom?'

He turned to see acting Chief Inspector Hill coming towards him along the lines of ribbon.

'Lights will be here any minute,' said Tom. 'If it means anything, I think a car came out of the service road going very fast,' he said. 'I think someone might have had to skid to avoid him.'

'We can appeal for the drivers to come forward,' said Judy, making a note. 'At least eliminate them if nothing else.'

'And the doctor's on his way to confirm death. She's in there.' He nodded towards the big section of concrete pipe that sat half embedded in the grass, part of the adventure playground. Only the girl's legs were visible in the dim light from the street-lamps.

Judy went over and bent down. 'Can't see a thing,' she said, and took his torch, shining it into the pipe. She straightened up, swallowing a little, looking, it had to be said, even less happy than she usually did about dead bodies. 'Do we know her name?' she asked.

'Not yet,' said Tom, and frowned. This body was having a hell of an effect on everyone; it was bad, but he'd seen worse, and so had she. Maybe he was missing something. 'Are you all right?' he asked.

'I think she was on my bus tonight,' said Judy. 'She's younger than she looks, Tom. She's a schoolgirl. The others called her Nat.'

That would be a bit hard to take, thought Tom. It was difficult to know what to say, really. You could hardly offer your condolences, but he knew how she must feel. 'Are you sure?' he said. After all, she had just glimpsed someone on a bus. Teenage girls were much of a muchness, really.

'Yes, I'm sure. Sure enough to get the head teacher here, if possible.' She got brisk and efficient again. 'Have we found her underwear?' she asked. 'Or her shoes?'

39

'Not yet,' said Tom. 'She's got her tights round her neck, though,' he added, with a sudden surge of outrage, now that the body had a name, an identity, however vague, and now that he knew she was little more than a child. 'We've not found anything else.' He glanced over to where Mrs Cochrane sat. 'That's the lady who found her,' he said. 'Beside the smug bloodhound. I haven't been able to get any sense out of her so far – she was too shocked.'

'Right – let's go and talk to her now,' Judy said, as the police surgeon arrived and disappeared into the concrete pipe.

Mrs Cochrane was calm now; she apologized for breaking down, after Tom had introduced Judy.

'Nothing to apologize for,' said Tom. 'It must have been a very nasty shock. Do you want the doctor to have a look at your leg?'

'Oh, no – it's just a scratch.' She examined the graze through her torn and laddered tights. 'I didn't know if she was dead,' she told Judy. 'Sherry found her, and I couldn't see into the pipe. I was going to ring for an ambulance. I fell when I went up there. I should have used the road, but all I could think of was getting to the phone box as fast as I could.'

'If you're sure you're all right,' said Judy. 'I'm afraid we have to ask you some questions.'

'Yes, of course,' she said.

'Did you see a car, Mrs Cochrane?' Tom asked. 'Or hear one, maybe?'

'A car?' She shook her head. 'No,' she said firmly.

Pity. But it added up. Joyriders, kids watching the fun and games, getting themselves all hyped up. Car goes, crowd goes. Just the girl and some youth left, out of his mind on drugs or booze or both.

'But the thing is . . .' she said, 'I saw a girl just before.' She looked at Tom, her face drawn. 'It can't be her,' she said. 'It can't be. I saw her not twenty minutes before Sherlock—' She broke off.

'Can you describe the girl you saw?'

'I know her, sort of. She goes to Oakland School. I can't remember her name – it's Russian, I think. She has long blonde hair, and she was wearing—'

She broke off again as Tom glanced at Judy.

'It is her, isn't it?' she said, dully. 'I thought . . . the skirt. It looked the same. I don't believe it. I don't believe it.'

'Where did you see her, Mrs Cochrane?' Her voice was gentle, despite the importance of the question, because Mrs Cochrane was on the verge of becoming incoherent again.

'Down by the depot. I had come down the footpath from Ash Road. She was just standing there, by the depot,' she said.

'Did you speak to her?' Judy asked, in the same even tones, not getting excited. Keeping things calm.

'I asked her what she was doing there. She just told me to mind my own business and walked up towards the adventure playground.'

'And you saw no one else hanging round the adventure playground?'

'No. But I didn't go that way – I took the dog on to the grass down by the depot. He ran around for a bit, and then he went into the wood, and I had to go in after him . . .' Her eyes brimmed with tears. 'I don't understand,' she said. 'I don't understand. How could that have happened to her in such a short time? How could I not have heard anything, seen anything? Why didn't I make sure she was—' She wiped the tears, and held herself under control.

'Why did you ask her what she was doing there?' asked Judy.

There was just a moment's hesitation before Mrs Cochrane answered. 'She's very young to be here at this time of night,' she said.

'Was she distressed? Frightened?'

'No. She was just – rude, I suppose,' said Mrs Cochrane.

'How do you know her?' asked Tom.

'I work at the school. I've seen her there.'

'Do you teach there?' Judy asked.

'No – I work in the office.'

Tom realized who she was. 'Are you Colin Cochrane's wife?' he asked.

She nodded.

'He teaches sport at the school, doesn't he?'

'Part time,' she said.

'Is he at home now?' asked Judy. 'He might be able to tell us her name.'

'He will be,' said Mrs Cochrane. 'He was due back at ten. He might know her . . .' She didn't finish the sentence, still fighting tears. 'I . . . I just took the . . . the dog on to the grass,' she said again. 'I let him go, and he ran into the wood. I went in after him – how could she have died in that short time? How?'

'How long were you in there?' asked Tom.

'Just—' Tears threatened again.

'Take your time, Mrs Cochrane,' said Judy. 'There's no hurry.'

She took a moment to compose herself. 'He played about in there for . . . I don't know, five, ten minutes. Then we came out and I threw things for him to chase for a little while. Another ten minutes or so. Then I put his lead back on, and we walked back past the playground. He was straining to go and look at something, so I just followed him, and he went into that awful pipe, and—'

'Do you know what time it was when you saw the girl alive?' asked Judy.

'About five to ten.'

'Would you mind showing us where you saw her?'

They walked down the service road to the cordoned-off depot, with the dog, tail wagging, walking beside them, his nose to the ground. Tom kept an eye on him; his own keen sense of smell had detected a scent he couldn't place, and which he hadn't discussed with anyone; a bloodhound's sense of smell might actually lead them to something, and Sherlock was following some scent of his own.

They arrived at the police line which had been slung across the road where it widened out into the courtyard.

'Just there,' said Mrs Cochrane, pointing towards the wall opposite the depot, steep, brick-lined banking up to the road above. The depot building was faintly lit by the road, but the wall was in deep shadow.

The dog confirmed Tom's belief in him, straining at the leash to go beyond the barrier.

'Do you mind?' asked Tom, taking the dog's lead. 'I think he's on to something.'

He ducked under the ribbon, and followed the dog towards the door of the depot, both of them sniffing. Tom's smell wasn't there, but Sherlock's obviously was. He shone his torch down into the darkness. 'Over here, guv!' he shouted.

The shoes sat neatly in the doorway, rather as though they had been put out for cleaning. Tom thanked God he had had the foresight to cordon off the depot, and got a glance of gratitude from Judy when she came running over in answer to his shout.

'Get one of the scene-of-crime people down here,' said Judy quietly. 'Tell them we'll need lights down here as well, and then I think you should take Mrs Cochrane home. See if her husband can help with identification.'

Tom took Mrs Cochrane home. He still hadn't entirely abandoned the idea of joyriders, even if she had seen the girl alive. Mrs Cochrane had been told to mind her own business; that suggested that the girl had had some business she wanted to keep private, and whoever she had been with could have been waiting up at the adventure playground. He tried again as they walked up her path.

'What time did you leave the house, Mrs Cochrane?' he asked.

'Quarter to ten,' she said.

'Did you hear anything odd as you were walking down to the Green?' he asked. 'A car – noisy braking, that sort of thing? Kids making a bit of a racket?'

'No,' she said, fumbling with her door key. 'Nothing.'

Colin Cochrane, looking just like he did in the ad he had made

42

for deodorant, came to the top of the stairs clad only in a bathrobe.

'Erica?' he said, startled. 'I thought you were in bed.'

Tom looked up at the handsome Mr Cochrane, his dark hair wet from the shower. He had been due home at ten, Mrs Cochrane had said. He could have seen something, if he had driven along Ash Road recently. But he'd have to explain to the man what he was doing there before he started asking him questions.

'DS Finch, Stansfield CID,' he said.

Cochrane's eyes widened when he really looked at his wife, the trickle of blood on her leg, her torn tights, her grass-stained clothes. 'What is it?' he said. 'What the hell's happened?'

Mrs Cochrane didn't enlighten him; she just walked into the sitting room with the dog.

'Your wife's had a rather unpleasant experience, Mr Cochrane,' Tom said.

'What?' He came downstairs. 'Is she hurt? Has some bastard—?'

That was it. The smell. The smell he had noticed when he had bent over the body. It was deodorant, the stuff Cochrane advertised. The stuff he was wearing now. That was it. That was why it had been wrong. It was a man's deodorant, and that girl had smelt of it.

'No, no, nothing like that,' said Tom. 'But I'm afraid your dog found a body, sir.'

Cochrane stared at him, then went into the sitting room. 'Erica? Are you all right?' he said.

Tom followed him in, watching with interest as Cochrane tried to put his arm round his wife, who moved away in a neat, obviously much practised, manoeuvre.

'Where were you, anyway?' Cochrane was asking her.

'Just on the Green,' she said.

'But . . . but why?'

'I had forgotten to take Sherry out,' she said.

'But the Green! At this time of night?'

'It was an hour ago! It was only ten o'clock.'

'But it's very dark down there – why did you go there, for God's sake? Why not across the road in the light?'

'Because I thought you'd be there!'

Tom had thought that there was more to this than Mrs Cochrane had been letting on. Something about that tiny pause before she had replied to Judy's question.

Erica Cochrane's face turned pink as she waited for the inevitable question.

'You were expecting to meet your husband at the Green, were you, Mrs Cochrane?' he asked.

'Well . . . he's usually there,' she said.

'And were you there, Mr Cochrane?' asked Finch.

'Obviously not,' he said testily.

'Why did Mrs Cochrane think you would be?' Tom persisted. He had smelt that deodorant, and now things were getting interesting.

'I do a training run. I usually finish by crossing the Green.'

'From the Byford Road area?'

'Yes. I come back along Byford Road, then down into Woodthorpe Close and across the Green from there.'

Tom nodded. 'And did you do that tonight?' he asked.

'No. Tonight I went along Byford Road until I got to Beech Street, and went down that way.'

'Why?'

'I had to pick up my car from school,' Cochrane said.

'Sorry – I still don't see why you didn't cross the Green,' said Tom stolidly. 'I mean, Beech Street takes you further away from the school, doesn't it?'

'Does it?' said Cochrane testily.

'I think you know it does, sir,' said Tom. 'The school's got an annexe on Byford Road, hasn't it?'

'Yes.'

'And the kids come across the Green when they have to get from there to the main school, or vice versa, because it's the quickest route – Larch Avenue is practically across from the Green. So why didn't you? Especially if that's your usual route?'

'I just changed my mind! Is that against the law?'

'No,' said Tom. 'It was a schoolgirl, by the way,' he added, watching Cochrane closely as he spoke, 'who was killed.'

He needn't have bothered; close scrutiny was hardly necessary, as Cochrane went pale and sat down with a bump on the arm of his wife's chair. 'Oh, no,' he said. 'No.'

Tom stepped closer to him. 'Does that mean something to you, Mr Cochrane?' he asked.

Cochrane looked up, his eyes barely focused. 'For God's sake!' he said. 'Doesn't it mean anything to you? A *schoolgirl*? I thought Sherry had found a wino, or . . . I don't know! Not a schoolgirl, for God's sake! What had happened to her?'

'She had been murdered, Mr Cochrane.'

Cochrane closed his eyes.

'Your wife knows her by sight, but not her name. We thought you might be able to identify her.'

Cochrane shook his head. 'I doubt it,' he said. 'I only teach the boys.'

Tom nodded. Erica Cochrane had hardly said a word since she had got in. Tom had had to tell Cochrane what she had found,

44

what had happened to her. Erica and Colin were not exactly the best of friends, Tom thought. Not right now, at any rate.

'You could do with a drink,' Cochrane said, finally attending to his wife.

She shook her head.

'Tea, then. A cup of tea. Will you have one, Sergeant Finch?'

'Thanks,' said Tom.

'Maybe you wouldn't mind giving me a hand,' Cochrane said.

'Sure.' Tom followed him down the corridor into the kitchen, interested to know what couldn't be discussed in Mrs Cochrane's presence.

'You said this girl had been murdered?' said Cochrane, as he filled the kettle and switched it on.

'Yes.'

'Are you sure?'

'There's not much doubt,' said Tom.

'Do you know when it happened?'

'From what your wife says, it has to have been between five to ten and ten-fifteen or so,' Tom answered. 'You see, she saw her alive about twenty minutes before your dog found her body on the adventure playground.'

'The adventure . . .?' Cochrane's voice trailed away, as he turned haunted eyes to Tom's, and shook his head slowly, disbelievingly. But if he had been going to say anything else, he'd changed his mind.

'Mr Cochrane,' said Tom, as Cochrane looked away again, 'do you know something about this?'

'No,' said Cochrane, his voice barely audible.

'Do you know who this girl might be?'

'No.'

The washing machine was going, Tom realized. He looked at it as the spin cycle slowed down, and could make out something blue and yellow, and . . . something else. A trainer. Two, presumably.

He pointed to the machine. 'Is that what you were wearing when you were out running?' he asked.

Cochrane turned and looked at the machine, as though it might suddenly have something different going round in it. 'Yes,' he said. 'A tracksuit and trainers.'

Tom smiled. 'You do your own laundry?' he said.

'Sometimes,' said Cochrane, striving to sound normal but failing. 'You don't want to leave sweaty running things and shoes lying around, do you?'

Tom never had sweaty running things and shoes, he was glad to say. If he did have, he expected that he would leave them lying around, like he did most things, much to Liz's annoyance.

But he was looking at a man who had not only done his washing himself, he had done it the moment he came in. And then he'd gone and showered. A man who always crossed the Green, according to his wife, except for tonight, according to him. A man whose relations with his wife were not at their sweetest. A man who taught at the school that the dead girl went to, a man with a TV commentator's contract, an advertising contract, a squeaky clean image and a great deal to lose.

A man whose deodorant Tom had smelt on that girl.

Freddie was finishing off his *in situ* examination, his tall frame bent over inside the pipe, the light from outside casting a huge, disturbing shadow inside. He was dictating his findings on to a tape, and his voice echoed in the pipe, the words indistinct, the sound eerie in the quiet night.

He had arrived dressed in dinner jacket and bow-tie, plucked away from the dessert. It was lucky they had got him before he'd got to the brandy, he had said cheerfully to Judy. A forensic pathologist's lot was not a happy one, he had added. His demeanour had belied this sentiment; Freddie always seemed to be at his happiest when poking about in dead bodies.

Judy looked round the area. Houses ran right up to the edge of the Green, and no one had heard these joyriders of Tom's, no one had heard the girl call for help, no one had seen anything remotely out of the ordinary, according to the door-to-door enquiries. No joyriders, then, thought Judy. The noise of a car being put through its paces would have reached the houses.

Someone was trying to get hold of the head of Oakland School, so far without success. The girl was called Nat by her classmates, and she possibly lived on the Malworth Road; that was all they had to go on even if they found the head, so identification would still be far from certain, unless he knew the girl. Freddie had found her knickers in the pocket of her skirt, so at least they were accounted for, too, now. There was a purse in the other pocket; the money was still in it. These items, along with the shoes, had gone to the lab.

Freddie emerged, and nodded to the body. 'She can go to the morgue now,' he said.

Judy looked at the girl in the glaring arc-light, half in, half out of the pipe, her legs sprawling. A soft, full skirt bunched up at her waist, and a matching shirt, open to expose small breasts. She wore make-up and jewellery; it made her look older.

She had been in school uniform the first and last time Judy had seen her alive, and she had wondered what it would be like to be her mother; now, she thanked God she wasn't.

She raised her eyes to Freddie's. 'Well?' she said.

Freddie sucked in his breath. 'First impressions?' he said. 'She's been dead under two hours, I'd say. There are considerable head injuries, but, from the temperature readings the police surgeon took, I'd say that she died by asphyxiation due to the air passages being constricted by nylon material wound round her throat.'

'Her own tights, in other words,' said Judy angrily, moving out of the way as the body bag was brought in.

Freddie smiled. 'I didn't do it, acting Chief Inspector,' he said. 'I was at a rather good dinner party at the time.'

'Sorry,' she said. 'Was she raped?'

'There's no obvious bruising or injury other than the head injuries – the shirt is unbuttoned, rather than torn open. I've taken swabs, of course, and I'll know better after I've examined her properly.'

'Are we looking at someone who might do it again?'

Freddie shook his head. 'You need a forensic psychologist for that,' he said. 'And he'd need to talk to the perpetrator, and cross his fingers for luck when he answered you.'

'What do you think?' Judy persisted.

'What do you?'

She had to assume that he would. A murder room was being set up, because no one thought that this would be cleared up by morning. But Tom had noticed the tyre marks, which was good work. Cars were very visible, and if this one left in a hurry, someone on the busy Ash Road might have seen it, even if it hadn't caused the skid. But it quite possibly had; an angry driver always noticed what sort of car had cut him up, and that was a good start.

And good old Sherlock had found the shoes down there; there was a chance of fingerprints, and the depot area might yield other clues, since it had been cordoned off immediately and not used as a makeshift car park by the investigating officers.

He was good at his job, was Tom. He looked like a choirboy; people often underestimated him, which gave him a considerable edge. Judy hoped he would take the inspector's exam again; he just needed to think a bit more than he did at times.

She looked at the section of pipe, now busy with scene-of-crime officers who took scrapings, made sketches, took photographs. A car had driven away at speed. Dumping the body? 'Was she actually killed in there?' she asked. 'Or could someone have been trying to conceal the body?'

'She was murdered in there. The head injury bled for a time before she was strangled. It looks as though it all took place here – there's blood on the rim at the entrance, see?' Freddie grinned at her reluctance to look. 'Here, at the top, and lower down. Her head came into forcible contact with the edge of the concrete. Then it looks as though she slid to a sitting position, where the action was repeated.'

Judy thought about that, and looked at those houses, where eminently respectable people had heard nothing, though all this was going on just up the road.

'How strong would her assailant have had to be?' she asked. 'Tom thinks that there might have been joyriders here.'

'You want to know if a young boy could have done it?'

Judy nodded. 'I think it was someone she knew. No one heard anything, Freddie. Mrs Cochrane was only in the woods – she would have heard someone shouting for help. I think it's possible that the girl didn't realize she was in danger until it was too late. That suggests a boyfriend.'

'That makes sense,' said Freddie. 'There are no signs of a struggle, as far as I can see from a first examination. We may find something under her fingernails, but I doubt it. There are no bruises on her arms, or her hands, like you would find if she had tried to fight off her attacker.'

Judy frowned. 'No struggle at all?' she asked.

'Not that I can see,' said Freddie. 'It's almost as though she was just standing talking to someone who suddenly bashed her head against the concrete without any warning, then overpowered and strangled her.'

'Overpowered her? Does that mean you think it was a man?'

'Not necessarily. She had probably lost consciousness, from the way she seems to have slid to the ground. All you'd need to do what's been done here is the element of surprise, not strength.' He smiled. 'Child's play,' he said. 'Not inappropriate, given the location.'

Freddie's graveyard humour was hard to take at times. Judy looked back at the scene. The pipe had a diameter of five feet two inches. The girl was five feet eight, according to Freddie. The edge of the concrete would have been level with the base of her skull. One vicious push would have been enough to render her semi-conscious. But it hadn't stopped at one push.

'How many blows?' she asked.

'I'll try to answer that tomorrow,' he said. 'Ten o'clock sharp – don't be late, acting Chief Inspector.' He smiled. 'You'll be catching Lloyd up any day now,' he said.

'Do me a favour, Freddie,' she said. 'Just don't say that to him.'

He grinned. 'Is that why he's knocking himself out on this course?' he asked.

Judy shook her head. No. Of course it wasn't. She hoped. 'He just wants to be clear of any rationalization that might be going to take place,' she said.

'Mm. Think he'll make it?'

'I think he already has,' said Judy. 'The course is finished, really. He'll be back on Friday.'

'Not the course. Do you really think he'll get promotion?'

'He's overdue for it,' Judy said.

'Quite,' said Freddie.

Judy walked away. She liked Freddie, in a way. He could be good fun. But his matter-of-factness overrode everything; a fifteen-year-old had been savagely murdered, but Freddie just saw a corpse, the way a businessman would see a memo, as something to be dealt with, something that could be joked about. Lloyd's future was less than certain, so Freddie saw little point in pretending that it wasn't.

She could have done with a little less frankness. She could have been more positive herself, come to that, and not given Freddie the opening.

'Have I offended you?' he asked, coming over to her.

She turned. 'No,' she said. 'You've probably saved me a great deal of grief. I'll remember not to say that to Lloyd.'

'But he is overdue,' he said.

Judy shrugged. 'He's never been that bothered about promotion,' she said. 'He's no respecter of rank – that doesn't help. And they think he lets his subordinates become too familiar with him.'

'Some more than others,' said Freddie. 'I don't imagine you call him sir between the sheets.'

Judy checked the sweep of anger, and took a breath before she spoke. 'They don't pass you over for promotion on the grounds that you have a private life,' she said.

Freddie gave a short laugh. 'I knew someone who had one of them,' he said. 'But he didn't have to get up before the pudding to go to work on a corpse in a surplus piece of storm drainage pipe embedded in a field. Just as well you and Lloyd did get it together, Judy – you'd have a hell of a job hanging on to anyone normal.'

Judy's anger subsided a little as she began to realize what this was all about. 'Are you having wife problems?' she asked.

'Well . . . let's say that I'm under some pressure to give up the Home Office work, and will be going home to more of it.'

Judy nodded. 'Would you mind giving it up?' she asked.

Freddie thought before he answered, the way he did when she was asking for an opinion about a death. 'Yes,' he said. 'So – if ever you get tired of being Lloyd's private life, I may well have a vacancy.'

'I'm sorry,' said Judy, honestly, ignoring the rest of what Freddie had said.

'I don't know if I am or not,' said Freddie, and strode away to where his sports car was parked, raising his hand above his head as a farewell.

The probationer was on his way towards her, his face eager to

49

impart information that Judy knew she didn't want to hear.

'Ma'am, a young girl's just been reported missing. Her mother says she hasn't come home,' he said, arriving beside her. 'She answers the description, including the clothes.'

Judy sighed. Nat, we've found your mum, she thought.

'Her name's Natalia Ouspensky. I've got the address here, ma'am.'

Nat. Natalia, but people couldn't be bothered with four syllables. They couldn't be bothered with two; she got called Jude as often as she was called Judy. And Natalia had become Nat.

Judy looked at the constable. 'Have you ever had to do this?' she asked, taking the piece of paper with the address on it, glancing at it. Malworth Road, as she had supposed from where the girl had got off the bus.

'No, ma'am.'

'Well, come with me. Everyone has to do it some time.'

But it never got any better.

Kim's mother came in, talking excitedly about what was going on down at the Green.

'There's loads of police, and they've roped it all off,' she said. 'We kept hearing the police cars – we wondered what was going on. When we came out, they were everywhere.'

Ash Road ran along the bottom of Oak Street, where the bingo club was; the police had been outside, asking the customers what time they had arrived, and if they had seen anyone on the Green. Kim's mum had got there early, so they weren't interested in her, but her friend hadn't come until about nine, and they had asked her a lot of questions.

'They asked her if she'd seen a young woman with long blonde hair,' she said. 'But she hadn't.'

Kim stared at her. 'What?' she said.

'What's the matter?'

Kim took a deep breath. 'Mrs Ouspensky rang and asked if I'd seen Natalie,' she said.

Her mother's hand went to her mouth, and she stood up. 'I'd better ring her,' she said.

'No, Mum! You can't do that! You'll worry her sick!'

'I'm not going to tell her all that!' said her mother. 'I just want to be sure that Natalie's got home all right.'

Kim shook her head. 'She can't have, Mum,' she said. 'Mrs Ouspensky would have rung me back. I know she would.'

Her mother sat down again. 'Oh, Kim,' she said. 'What are we going to do? Should we tell the police?'

'I think she might already have told them,' said Kim. 'She was really worried then, and that was over an hour ago.'

'I think I have to do something,' said her mother. 'I have to call the police, or Natalie's mum, or something.'

Oh, no. No. Supposing Nat was just with her boyfriend, and they got caught because of her? Kim couldn't bear to think of it.

'Kim, love . . . That description could fit lots of girls.' She stood up. 'I'm going to ring her mother,' she said.

Kim waited miserably while her mother dialled, and the phone rang out. She asked to speak to Mrs Ouspensky, then asked who was speaking, said, 'I see,' and 'Thank you,' and hung up. 'It was a policeman who answered the phone,' her mother said quietly.

It didn't mean that anything had happened to Nat. It just meant that her mother had reported her missing, and they . . . Her mother's arms were round her.

'I have to phone Hannah,' Kim said.

'It's late, love,' said her mother.

'I know. But I have to.'

She had to talk to someone, share her secret with someone. Not her mother. She would have the police round here before Kim could think. And she had to think, she had to remember what Natalie had said. She needed to talk to Hannah, tell her, see what she thought.

Hannah's mother said that she had gone to bed, but Hannah came to the phone anyway. Kim had taken the cordless extension into her room, and now she unburdened herself to Hannah.

'Colin wouldn't do anything like that,' was Hannah's first, instant response.

'I know,' said Kim. 'That's why I . . . but . . . we don't know that he wouldn't, not really. I mean, you hear about it all the time.'

'*I* know,' Hannah said firmly.

But she would say that; she thought the sun rose and set on Colin Cochrane.

'But she said she was going with a teacher, and Julie said that Colin Cochrane was—'

'Julie's a gossip. You don't want to take any notice.'

But she had to.

'Kim – don't say anything, not yet. What harm can it do to wait? The police might find who did it, and you won't need to say anything then.'

'What if they don't?' implored Kim.

'We'll talk about it,' said Hannah. 'Properly. Just don't say anything yet. Please, Kim.'

'All right,' said Kim.

'Promise,' said Hannah. 'Promise, Kim. You know that Colin

51

wouldn't do a thing like that. If you tell the police, he'll be in terrible trouble. Promise you won't say, not yet.'

'Promise.'

Kim didn't feel much better after her phone call, but at least someone else knew what she knew.

Finch was still here, still asking questions. They were still in the kitchen. Erica, Colin and Sergeant Finch were having a cup of tea together, of all things.

'Why all the questions?' Colin asked.

'It's my job,' said Finch.

'It's your job to catch this girl's killer,' said Colin. 'I don't see how sitting here asking me about my training run is going to do that.'

'There are lots of people working on this besides me,' said Finch. 'Right now, I'd like to know what exactly you were doing tonight, sir.'

Colin looked at Erica, but she was just staring into her tea. She hadn't opened her mouth since Finch had started asking questions.

'I was running! This is ridiculous! My wife's dog finds a body, and you seem to suspect me.'

Finch sipped his tea. 'How long were you out for?' he asked.

'I did a three-hour run.'

The sergeant pulled a face. 'How often do you do that?' he asked.

'Most nights,' said Colin.

'Blimey,' said Finch. 'You can't see much of him,' he said to Erica.

Erica lifted her eyes to the sergeant, then looked back down into her mug.

'That's really none of your business,' said Colin.

'No, of course it isn't. But that means you left the house at ... what? Seven?'

'That's when I began the run, yes, but I didn't leave from the house. I went from the school. I told you I had left my car there.'

Finch smiled. 'So you did,' he said. 'So ... what were you doing at the school until seven?'

'I belong to the drama group. It meets on Wednesday nights – starts at half four, finishes about half six.'

Finch finished his tea. 'Drama group, you said?'

'Yes.'

'How long have you done that?'

'About three years or so.'

'What ... just teachers?'

'No,' said Colin. 'Teachers, pupils, anyone who's interested.'

'Aren't any girls interested, then?'

Colin frowned. 'Of course they are,' he said. 'It's mostly girls.'

'Thought it might be,' said Finch. 'Only when I asked if you might

52

be able to identify our body, you said you only knew the boys.'

Oh, God.

'But it seems there are some girls you know quite well.'

Erica got up then, her chair scraping loudly on the floor, and left the room.

Colin half rose to go after her, then thought better of it. 'I . . . I just wasn't thinking,' he said.

'Think now, Mr Cochrane. Who are the girls in the drama group?'

'It's very informal – we're all on first-name terms. I can't give you surnames.'

'First names'll do.'

Colin sighed. 'There's Julie,' he said. 'And Ann, and Carol. There's Kim and Claire and Natalie—'

'Natalie?' said the sergeant. 'Can you describe her?'

'Tall,' said Colin wearily. 'Slim. Long blonde hair.'

Finch stood up. 'Can you remember her surname?'

'Are you saying that that's who—?'

'Can you?'

Colin shook his head. 'It's Russian,' he said. 'I know that. It begins with an O.'

'Can I use your phone?' Without waiting for consent, Finch went out into the hallway.

Colin sat at the kitchen table, his head in his hands, trying not to think about his part in this dreadful business.

Finch came back in. 'Ouspensky,' he said. 'Her name is Ouspensky, Mr Cochrane, and her mother is already on her way to identify the body.'

Colin groaned.

'Mr Cochrane?' Finch asked quietly. 'Would you have any objection to my taking those items away for forensic examination?'

'What?' Colin lifted his head and saw Finch pointing at the washing machine. 'Why?'

'Because you knew the dead girl, Mr Cochrane. You had been with her this very evening, and yet you led me to believe you would be unable to identify any girl from the school.'

'And that makes me guilty of murder?'

'No, sir,' said Finch, writing out a receipt for the clothes in his notebook. 'But your wife went to the Green expecting to meet you on your way back from your run. You tell me that you changed your route, but you haven't given me any explanation.'

'I don't see why I should!' said Colin.

'And you washed the clothes you had been wearing as soon as you came in, and showered immediately, without even checking up where your wife was. I think I would be neglecting my duty if I didn't make an attempt to eliminate you from the enquiry by examining those clothes. You can, of course, refuse.' He had been holding out the receipt all the time he had been talking.

'You're welcome to the clothes,' muttered Colin, taking the receipt. He even got Finch a bin-liner to put them in.

Natalie, he thought, I'm sorry. I'm so sorry.

'I thought my wife was in bed,' he said, answering one of the points the sergeant had made. 'I didn't think I needed to check where she was. She was going to watch a film – she often goes to bed and watches up there.'

'And you didn't look in on her, to say you were back?' Finch looked enquiringly at him.

'No.' Colin looked at the policeman, who seemed little older than the boys he taught. 'Are you trying to eliminate me from the enquiry, or do you think I killed Natalie for some reason?' he said.

'I don't know,' said Finch. 'But if you didn't, then there's no harm in answering my questions.'

'I have answered your questions,' said Colin.

'Yes, sir. Thank you for your co-operation.'

And he left.

Hannah tried to sleep, but all she could see whenever her eyes grew heavy was Mr Murray, standing there, looking at her so oddly, a pair of women's sandals in his hand. Kim musn't go telling the police that Colin had killed Natalie, not when Hannah knew that it wasn't true.

But Hannah hadn't told Kim about Mr Murray; she was scared to.

He'd had a pair of shoes in his hand, and he had seen her. He had seen her. She couldn't go to school – he'd find her, he'd recognize her. Should she go to the police? Say that she'd seen him there? No. No, she couldn't. She didn't dare.

She would just keep quiet, and hope that Kim did the same. She had promised, but Hannah didn't set much store by that. Kim wasn't the strongest of people – if anyone asked her questions, she might not keep her promise.

Oh, God. How could she think that Colin had killed anyone?

Lloyd felt guiltily pleased that he was going to be let out of school early, in order to head the murder enquiry. He'd be home tomorrow, see Judy tomorrow after all, and had something like real police work to do.

But a little girl had died, and that was nothing to feel pleased about. And recalling him was unnecessary; Judy was just as capable as he was of running a murder enquiry, but she didn't have the rank. Nor did he, strictly speaking. It would be the Detective Super from headquarters who had overall charge. But he had felt that his personal intervention wasn't necessary, providing Lloyd came back.

'Mrs Hill can get it under way,' he had said. 'She knows what she's about.'

He wasn't sure how Judy would feel about that. She had been acting DCI for the best part of two months, and the first serious crime that had come along, they were going to bring him back to take over once she had done the groundwork; it seemed hardly fair.

He wondered if they would have done that if he'd been in the middle of the course, rather than at the end; probably not. But the headquarters Super would have taken personal charge, and Judy couldn't stand the man.

He'd point that out to her, if things got sticky.

Erica lay facing away from the bedroom door; she didn't turn round when Colin came in.

'Are you asleep?' he asked quietly.

'No.'

'It's . . . it was Natalie,' he said. 'You know, from the drama group. The girl with the Russian name.'

Erica stiffened at that distancing of himself from the girl.

'That policeman seems to think I did it,' he said, with a nervous little laugh, as he got into bed, pushing Sherry down to the bottom with some difficulty. 'Bloody dog,' he muttered.

'Why does he think that?' Erica asked.

'I don't really know. I can't imagine why he thinks I should have had anything to do with it. I think it's because I was washing my tracksuit. He's taken it away.'

Erica frowned. 'Can he do that?' she asked.

'I don't know. I said he could – I could have refused. But it seemed sensible to let him have it, if he was that bothered. It's coming to it when you can't wash your clothes without being suspected of murder.'

'Why were you washing them?' she asked.

'I always wash them.'

'No, Colin.' She sat up and looked at him. 'I always wash them,' she said.

He gave a weak smile. 'You know what I mean,' he said. 'They always get washed straight away, and I thought you were in bed.'

'That doesn't usually turn you into a housewife,' she said.

His face grew alarmed. 'Good God, Erica, *you* don't think I had anything to do with it, do you?'

Erica looked at him coldly. 'I don't think you killed her, if that's what you mean,' she said steadily.

He looked baffled. 'Then what the hell do you think?' he asked.

55

'I think you were screwing her,' she said. 'That's what I think.'

Colin stared at her. 'What?'

'I said I think you were screwing her,' she repeated slowly and carefully.

'Natalie?'

'Are there others?'

Colin's eyes were wide. 'What? I don't believe we're having this conversation,' he said. 'What in God's name makes you think that?'

He knew why they were having this conversation, all right, thought Erica. And that sergeant knew. 'The car wouldn't start!' she shouted. 'I ask you – was I expected to believe that?'

Sherry raised his head and gave a little whine, because Erica had raised her voice, and he was trying to get over.

'Why would I lie about that, for God's sake?' demanded Colin.

'Because you don't need a car for a training run. So there had to be some reason for your not bringing it home.'

'There was! I couldn't make it go!'

'It's going all right now, though, I see.'

Colin sighed. 'Patrick fixed it.'

'Patrick fixed it? Good for Patrick.' Erica lay down again, her back to him. 'I don't want to hear any more,' she said.

He pulled her round to face him. 'Jesus Christ!' he shouted. 'You think I was having it off with a fifteen-year-old girl? What the hell is going on?'

'Leave me alone,' she said, pulling away from him.

'What is this? The only contact I had with that girl was the drama group! I don't even know her other name! What's got into you?'

The dog barked.

'Ssh, Sherlock,' said Erica, and he put his head back between his paws, looking doubtfully at her.

'This is ... This is ...' Colin shook his head. 'It's crazy,' he said. 'It's a nightmare. It's not happening.'

He must be an asset to the drama group, thought Erica, as she watched his performance. He just thought that if he kept denying everything, eventually she would dismiss the evidence of her own eyes. He had some sort of answer, something ... he wanted her to spell it out for him, so that his explanation wasn't too evidently prepared. She wasn't about to do that.

'I want to get some sleep now,' she said. 'I have to go in early and do letters about the uniform.'

Colin blinked. 'What?' he said.

'The head came round tonight – asked me to go in early and do letters to the parents saying that school uniform needn't be worn during the heatwave.'

56

He shook his head slightly. 'Erica – I don't think that's going to be the first thing on his mind tomorrow morning,' he said. 'Natalie has been murdered.'

'I'm well aware of that,' she said. 'But the school still has to be run.'

'No one's going to be worrying about getting letters out!'

'The pupils will still be there, still wearing winter uniform. It will still be a heatwave. I'm going in early to get the letters done for distribution by the form teachers, so I would like to get some sleep now.'

'I don't believe this.' Colin shook his head. 'You're accusing me of adultery with a teenage girl I barely know – that policeman thinks I *murdered* her, and all you can worry about is letters about the school uniform?'

Erica shook her head. 'That's not all I can worry about,' she said. 'But it's all I can do anything about.'

Colin stared at her without speaking for a long time, then got up. 'I don't know what's got into you,' he said. 'I . . . Maybe it's the shock. I don't know. I think I'll sleep in the other room,' he said.

'You do that,' said Erica.

He left, banging the door. After a moment, Sherry crept up the bed, to lie alongside her again, and Erica wept silently into his coat while he fell blissfully asleep.

Chapter Five

Colin woke, surprised to find that he had slept, but sheer exhaustion had seen to that. He felt far from refreshed; it took him a moment or two to get his bearings. The wallpaper was wrong. He was facing the wrong way. Of course. He was in the spare room. The dog-house.

He heaved himself out of bed and into the bathroom, where he took his first shower of the day, shaved, and looked at himself in the mirror. He looked the same. A bit tired, maybe, but substantially the same man looked back as had looked back yesterday.

But the police had taken his clothes away for forensic examination, because they suspected him of having murdered Natalie, and he still couldn't understand how that had happened. What had he done, what had he said, to make that sergeant so suspicious of him? Erica thought he'd been having an affair with her – he could hardly blame her for jumping to that conclusion, after the way Sergeant Finch had reacted.

He looked the same, but he wasn't. He was someone fighting for a life that he had taken for granted yesterday.

He went into the bedroom to get dressed, and found the bed made. She would have got up early, of course, because she was determined for some reason to go into work and do these letters to the parents. Her way of dealing with it, he supposed. Think about something else, something mundane, while your husband comes under suspicion of murder. But she wasn't downstairs either. She must have gone to work so early that she would be lucky if the school was open.

It took him a little while to work out what was really wrong about this morning, why the house seemed so very empty. The dog wasn't here. Colin frowned. She must have taken him for yet another walk, to see if he could find any more bodies for him to be accused of murdering.

If only she hadn't blurted out that she had gone to the Green to meet him, none of this would be happening. That was what had made the sergeant begin to wonder about Colin's involvement.

Erica hadn't come back by the time he was leaving for school; she must be taking the damn dog with her. He supposed the head would

58

make allowances, especially since she had gone in early for him.

He unlocked the garage and pushed up the door, his shoulders drooping a little at the thought of school, of seeing Erica, of the police being all over the place, which they surely would be. He was a suspect. A *suspect*. It seemed like a nightmare, but the sun into which he backed the car was real enough. His mail was still piled up on the back shelf, obscuring his view as he backed out on to the driveway.

He got out, and moved it on to the back seat, frowning a little. He thought he'd spread it out on the shelf, not piled it up like that. He shrugged, got back in, and drove the short distance up Larch Avenue, sweeping in to the school by the back entrance, round to the car park.

Walking through the grounds to the school building was an odd experience. There was a muted sound, not the huge crescendo of noise usually produced by adolescents bursting with energy and health, eager to let everyone know. People looked shocked, and hurt, and stood in little groups, discussing what had happened.

The younger ones were excited; they hadn't known Natalie, they didn't really appreciate the dreadfulness of what had happened. Police cars sat around, and they were intrigued by it all.

A handwritten notice on the door said that everyone had to assemble in the hall at eight forty-five; it was almost that now, as the head strode towards him.

'Ah . . .' The head waved his hand around. 'Colin. How is . . .' Another moment's panic. 'Erica? It must have been a terrible shock for her.'

Colin didn't answer. The head must know how she was, surely.

'Yes,' the head went on, clearly not expecting an answer. 'Terrible. Tell her to take her time – I'm not at all surprised she didn't feel like coming in. Tell her . . . well, you know what to tell her.'

'Yes,' muttered Colin. 'Thank you.'

She'd done it again. She'd done her disappearing act, like she had after she'd discovered that letter. He knew where she was, but he wouldn't try to contact her. She would come home when she was ready to, like before.

Lloyd stood outside the door of the cramped murder room, where he couldn't be seen by the occupants, who sat variously on or at desks.

Judy stood at the far side, a plan of Ash Road Green behind her. A board beside it bore the name of Natalia Ouspensky, and an enlarged photograph of a blonde girl with a friendly smile. The times she had been seen, a description of her clothing, not much else, not yet.

59

The general hubbub was quietened when Judy stood up, and faced her crew. 'Right,' she said. 'Listen.'

It took a moment or two, but eventually everyone was aware that the briefing was about to start.

Judy looked at them, mostly seasoned professionals, mostly male, many of them drafted in from other divisions for the enquiry. Lloyd felt a little apprehensive; you could feel the hostility, just because she was a woman. You could feel them want to see her fall flat on her face.

'Natalia Ouspensky,' she said. 'Known as Natalie, or Nat, to her friends. Aged fifteen years one month.'

Lloyd listened as she outlined the events of the night before as far as they were understood to have happened.

'Natalie had head injuries,' continued Judy, 'and she had been strangled. There may well have been a sexual motive, as you'll see from the photographs. At any rate, her knickers were found in her pocket, and her tights had been used to strangle her.'

'Bra?' asked someone.

'It seems she wasn't in the habit of wearing one,' said Judy. 'Her shoes were found...' She pointed to the map. 'Here, at the depot, in the doorway, about sixty yards from where she had been seen alive. Sherlock the bloodhound also led us to the shoes. Maybe we should recruit him.'

Some smiles.

She told them about the car, then. 'If a car was involved,' she said, 'that suggests an older man, rather than a boyfriend. Some of you may know that Mrs Cochrane's husband Colin teaches at Oakwood School. He was known to the dead girl, and was in the area at the time, so he could become involved in the enquiry.'

'How well did he know the girl?'

'He was involved in the same drama group at the school, which met last night, and he was running in the area at the time of Natalie's death. For this reason, we are treating the last alleged sighting before her death as unsafe, and we are not reporting it to the press.'

'What are we telling them?'

'As far as they're concerned, Natalie left home at seven-thirty in a neighbour's car. She was dropped at her grandmother's, where she stayed for an hour, then left there at eight-forty. We have had no other reported sighting since that time until Sherlock found her body.'

She read out the names of the detectives that she wanted to conduct enquiries at the school.

'I want you to talk to Natalie's friends,' she said. 'I want to know what sort of girl she was, and I want to know who her boyfriends were, if any. I have given the head an undertaking that these interviews are purely to get information about Natalie that we can't get elsewhere – boyfriends, and so on. So if you do have reason to suspect anyone you speak to of involvement in the crime, you must caution them immediately, and the interview must cease until the appropriate people can be present.'

'My God, the kiddiewinkies won't get too much hassle from you, will they? It was probably her boyfriend that did it.'

Judy nodded. 'Probably,' she said. 'Which is why I'm not going to have intimidation thrown at us in court. If we are dealing with an adolescent killer, then we're going to get him, and he won't wriggle out of it.'

'Why does that mean we have to give undertakings to headmasters?'

Judy addressed the room, not him. 'If we're going to find out what sort of girl Natalie really was, as opposed to the one her mother thinks she was, we need to be on good terms with the school,' she said. 'So don't throw your weight about. Natalie's mother thinks she wasn't into boys, but the contraceptive pills in her room suggest otherwise. Her friends will know about any boyfriend, and we have to find out who he is.'

Lloyd smiled. She was handling her hecklers so far, without pulling rank – an unwise thing to do when you needed team-work above all else. A suicidal thing to do if the rank was temporary. She wasn't falling into any traps so far.

'If we turn up a boyfriend or boyfriends, it could very well be that he or they will have to be asked to give a sample of blood for DNA analysis, if only for elimination purposes. In any event, the procedure will be explained in detail. He will be told exactly what DNA analysis is, and how it works, and what it means if we get a match.'

'Great. Why don't we give them a bag of sweets and a balloon as they leave?'

Judy ignored that, as she detailed another lot to do an extended door-to-door. Ash Road again, to catch those who were unable to be spoken to yesterday, and Kings Estate, on the route from Natalia's grandmother's house to the bus stop. 'We want anyone at all who saw her between eight-forty, when she left her grandmother's house in Henry Way, and ten-twenty, when Sherlock the bloodhound found her body. It was daylight until about nine, so we stand a good chance.'

'Sherlock was wasting his time, for all we're going to do about it, if we mustn't upset the kiddiewinks. You want a gang of nannies on this, not cops.'

Judy looked at the speaker. 'Whoever murdered that little girl is going to get caught,' she said quietly. 'Arrested, charged, prosecuted, put away. No one is going to walk away from this because he didn't have his rights explained to him, or wasn't told that he could have a solicitor and didn't understand what he was signing. No one is going to have any come-back at all on how this enquiry was conducted from day one.'

Her glance took in the entire room now. 'I imagine that it will shortly be DCI Lloyd who'll be in charge of this investigation, but today, in the absence of anyone more senior, it's me. And if you – if any of you – jeopardize our case against a potential suspect, it's me you'll answer to, not DCI Lloyd. And I've got more to prove than him – do I make myself clear?'

There was laughter, nods of appreciation. Judy's supporters were at last becoming vocal, as though they were at a football match they were beginning to think their team might just have a chance of winning.

Lloyd grinned. Attagirl, Judy.

'Natalia was an only child. Her father died three years ago in an accident at work,' Judy went on. 'Her mother has a boyfriend, who does live there, but he wasn't there when I saw her last night. He's a long-distance lorry driver, and was supposed to be on the road. DC Marshall – I want you to check him out. I want to know that he was where he was supposed to be, because I'm pretty sure that Natalie knew her killer, felt at home with him. Felt safe with him.'

'Is there any suggestion that he abused her?' asked Marshall in his slow, Glasgow drawl.

'No,' said Judy. 'I'm just covering all the angles. So be discreet – he probably has nothing to do with it.' She looked round. 'One other thing,' she said. 'How Natalie died is not to be discussed outside this room with anyone. God forbid that there's another murder, but serial killers have to start somewhere, and if we do get another one, I want to know for a fact that it is by the same hand, and not a copy-cat killing. Any questions?'

'Yeah. What are you doing other than playing at being the investigating officer?' asked the most persistent of her hecklers.

'Going to the post-mortem,' said Judy sweetly. 'Do you want to swap duties, Sergeant?'

He smiled, and lit a cigarette. 'No thanks,' he said.

'After that I'll be at the scene, and then at the school, if anyone wants me. All information has to be channelled through DS Sandwell. Evening briefing will be at six o'clock sharp. Let's get on with it.'

Lloyd allowed the exodus to sweep round him, and finally caught her eye, receiving a wide, genuine smile of welcome.

He went into the room, empty now save Judy and Sandwell, who diplomatically found something he had to do elsewhere.

'They sent for me, I'm afraid,' he said.

'I thought they might let you finish the course, since you were due back in a couple of days anyway,' said Judy.

'Does it bother you?' he asked.

She smiled. 'No, of course not. They couldn't let me take charge of it.'

'You sounded as though you were doing all right to me,' said Lloyd. 'The grammar wasn't all it might have been, but . . .'

'Were you listening to all that?'

He grinned as she went faintly pink.

'Well . . . I've got a date with Freddie,' she said, to cover her slight embarrassment. 'Tom'll let you see the witness statement, and what we've got so far.'

'What's this about Colin Cochrane's involvement?'

'It's very flimsy stuff, but it does involve Tom's nose, and it's quite interesting.'

'Oh, good,' said Lloyd. 'I've been a bit concerned about police-men's noses lately.'

He went into the CID room and let Finch bring him up to speed, as he insisted on calling it.

Finch's suspicion of Cochrane seemed a touch premature, in Lloyd's opinion, but he gave the sergeant his blessing to do some gentle digging about him at the school, on the pretext of being an interested fan. Finch could get away with that; with his fair curly hair and look of eager innocence, he had fooled a great many people into believing he was harmless. As harmless as a cut-throat razor.

And he knew, of course, that Finch would be right about the deodorant – his sense of smell had come in handy in the past. But it was a popular brand, and there was no real reason to suppose that that meant she had been with Cochrane.

Lloyd was less interested in jumping to conclusions than he was in finding out as much as he could about the victim. Judy had had a look in the girl's bedroom, and found nothing of any interest other than the contraceptive pills, but her mother had been too distressed to be interviewed.

She wouldn't be feeling any better today, Lloyd thought with a sigh, but it had to be done. And talking about her daughter might just help.

Patrick wasn't listening to the head as he spoke gravely about what had happened. He doubted if anyone was; everyone knew what had happened.

He was scanning the sea of faces in front of him for one particular face, and he couldn't see it. His legendary inability to remember

63

faces meant that he had had no idea who the girl was, or whether she was in his class, even.

He could see her face now, in his mind. She had long dark hair, with a sort of elfin look, and large, dark eyes. He would know her if he saw her again, but try as he might he couldn't see that face in the rows of people who sat in front of him. The staff were sitting awkwardly on the stage, as they were given to doing when there were gatherings of the whole school, apparently. That was fine at prize givings and the like, but it seemed absurdly theatrical this morning.

Everyone looked pale and drawn, especially Cochrane. Patrick hadn't even been able to talk to Erica; she hadn't come in at all. And he couldn't find this girl. He had to. It was desperately important. Because whatever he had made himself believe last night, the truth was still there to be reckoned with, and he had to find that girl. She had to be somewhere, for Christ's sake. He began again, from the back, where the older children were. Students.

He rubbed the back of his neck, and looked at every female face in turn, but she wasn't there. And he had to talk to Erica. He'd ring her at lunchtime. No, better than that. He would go and see her.

Judy stood stiffly and silently by the table, looking up at the lights. The stiffness and silence was occasioned entirely by her horror of post-mortem examinations, but Freddie, well into his grisly task, had obviously misinterpreted it. He looked up.

'I think I owe you an apology for last night,' he said.

Judy allowed her eyes to meet his. She didn't speak.

'I was unforgivably rude about Lloyd and to you, and I seem to have made a rather clumsy and very unromantic pass at you,' he said. 'I'd had a very hard day. It's no excuse, but it's the reason. Am I forgiven?'

'Nothing to forgive,' said Judy.

'I didn't mean what I said about Lloyd. Sheer envy prompted that bit of bitchiness,' Freddie said, then carried on as though he had said nothing personal at all. 'The vaginal swabs were positive,' he said. 'So DNA identification shouldn't be difficult, if you get a suspect. And there's good news on that front – they've got digital profiling now. The result should only take a few days to come through.'

'Good,' said Judy. It was an unbelievable improvement on the old system, which had taken up to six weeks, but she couldn't enthuse about anything right now.

'No external or internal bruising, no sign that she put up any resistance.' He carried on working as he spoke. 'No sign of any sexual violence of any sort,' he added.

She had never fainted. It had taken superhuman effort to stay conscious at her first post-mortem, and she wasn't going to start now that she was almost inured to it, just because she had seen the victim on a bus prior to her death.

She tried not to think of the body as a person, but it was difficult not to see her flashing a smile at the boy on the bus, running off home. She'd gone home, changed, gone to her gran's, left there to get a bus ... and then what? Met a boyfriend?

'So you don't think it was rape,' she said.

'I didn't say that. But if it was,' said Freddie, 'no force was used, and no resistance offered.' He bent over the body. 'So ...' The words came out in little groups as he did something unspeakable to the corpse. 'Either she consented to sex ... before any of this happened, or ... she was in no condition ...' He made a little grunt as he succeeded in removing whatever it was, ' ... *to* resist,' he finished, straightening up and favouring Judy with a brief smile before making some unintelligible notes into the microphone above his head.

'That just meant that the victim was healthy,' he explained, when he had finished. 'She has no toxic substances in her body. Heart, liver and lights all sound as a bell.'

Judy didn't want to think about Natalie as a healthy teenage girl. She much preferred her victims entirely unknown to her. 'Can you tell me any more about the head injury?' she asked.

'Not much.' He bent to his task again, and didn't speak for some minutes. 'I can see two distinct blows, and then any number. Can't give you any indication of the build or weight of her attacker, either, I'm afraid.' He rinsed his gloved hands, and signalled for the body to be taken away.

The cleaning-up operation wasn't much better than the post-mortem itself. Judy felt sick.

'I can tell you how it was done, though,' Freddie said, and stepped back. 'Someone put a hand over her face.' He demonstrated on his own face. 'Like this. There are marks of the thumb and little finger of a right hand on her cheekbones. Her assailant pushed—' He pushed his own head back. 'Her head hit the edge of the concrete pipe. No great strength required. Just one forceful, unexpected push.'

He took his hand away from his face. 'That first blow didn't do a terrific amount of damage, but she slid down the edge of the pipe, I think, from the slight grazing to her back. That could be how her skirt got pushed up.'

'Rather than by her assailant?'

Freddie shrugged. 'It's perfectly possible,' he said.

But Freddie still hadn't ruled out rape.

'And while she was in a sitting position,' he went on, 'her head was repeatedly struck against the concrete, which was when the real harm was done. When her attacker let go, she was either pushed inside the pipe or fell inward of her own accord. And after some minutes, she was strangled.'

Judy wanted out of here. 'Is that when you think she was sexually assaulted?' she asked.

'I don't think anything,' he said automatically. 'But if she had removed her own underclothing and put it in her pocket prior to the attack, I would have thought that she would just have removed the tights and pants together, wouldn't you? It's quicker.'

Judy was no expert in alfresco sex, but it seemed a reasonable supposition. She nodded.

'I would therefore have expected to find the pants still inside the tights, or lying about near the body, if he'd pulled them away from one another. I don't think he could have pulled the tights out of her pocket and left the pants in there unless they had been put in separately, which seems unlikely.'

Judy nodded again, not trusting herself to speak.

'Which is why I am not ruling out the possibility that the removal of her underwear was subsequent to the attack, and that a sexual assault took place then, either before or after she was asphyxiated.'

Judy closed her eyes. Poor little Natalie.

'If it's any consolation, I doubt that she knew much about it,' said Freddie.

Judy opened her eyes, startled to hear Freddie departing from his usual clinical attitude.

'Her mother said that she had a quick meal at home before she went out,' he said. 'The digestive processes have taken their natural course in the time you would expect them to have taken. That suggests that there was no prolonged period of fear.'

Judy was grateful to Freddie for saying it, but the whole thing had only taken fifteen minutes. Not, in her layman's opinion, enough time to have affected the digestive processes anyway.

Freddie smiled sympathetically, something Judy hadn't realized that he could do.

'Time of death,' he went on. 'Well, that tallies with the witness's statement. Even by the time I examined her, she was obviously very recently dead. With the temperatures that the police surgeon took, which were higher than normal because of the asphyxia, I'd say between nine-thirty and ten-thirty, and probably somewhere between the two is about right.'

Judy nodded.

'In other words,' Freddie went on, 'she could certainly have been killed while this lady was in the woods with her dog.'

'And the assailant's hand could have muffled any cry,' Judy said, at last finding her voice.

Freddie nodded. 'Yes,' he said. 'So there's no reason from my point of view to doubt your informant. She would have been unlikely to hear anything, and I doubt if there would have been time for the victim to cry out at all, come to that. The first head injury probably caused her to lose consciousness to a degree, as I said. The subsequent blows to the head would have rendered her at best semi-conscious.'

Judy escaped then, having to make herself walk through the labyrinthine corridors instead of run, which was what her whole being was telling her to do. She would never, never get used to mortuaries and bodies being opened up like sardine cans. Never.

Kim kept looking at the empty table where Natalie would have been sitting. They were in the form room; lessons were disrupted because of the police being at the school, and anyway no one could have concentrated.

Mr Murray had just left the room, and had told them to stay there.

'He's a bit weird, isn't he?' said one of the girls, leaning back in her chair to speak to Kim.

Kim frowned. 'Who?' she said.

'Mr Murray,' she said.

No, he wasn't. He was nice. Kim shrugged.

'Haven't you noticed?' said the girl.

'No,' said Kim.

'He looks at you funny,' she said.

'At me?' said Kim, astonished.

'No! At everyone.'

'Does he?' said Kim, disbelieving.

'Well,' she said, 'he was looking at me when he came in here. And Marian – she said he looked at her, too. And Debs says he stared at her in assembly this morning.'

Kim sighed. This was bound to happen, she supposed, after something like this. They'd think men were following them home next. 'Maybe he just fancies girls with long hair,' she said. 'I've not noticed him looking at me funny.'

Poor Mr Murray.

She hadn't told Colin where she was.

She had done this before; come here to think, when staying in the house had seemed impossible. The last time had been when she had found that letter.

Erica felt the tears coming again, the tears that she had cried all night, and had only controlled once she was up by a considerable effort of will.

She shouldn't be doing this to him, not really. The police suspected him of murder, and he hadn't killed the girl. Just had an affair with her. And now she had disappeared without telling him where she was. The police might think that he'd done away with her too.

No. No, that was nonsense. They didn't start accusing you of having done away with your wife just because she had gone out without telling you. But Colin would be worried. Half of her wanted him to be, but the other half knew it wasn't fair to add to his problems, even if they were of his own making. The police must have found out that he'd been seeing Natalie, she thought, otherwise why would Sergeant Finch have been asking all those questions? Why would he have taken his running things away? It wasn't anything she had said, even if Colin thought it was.

Anyway, she wasn't going to stay away, not like last time. She had just needed somewhere to go, somewhere quiet to think. She wouldn't leave Colin wondering where she was. It wasn't fair, leaving him alone like that this morning, really.

But she had been alone, she thought, blowing her nose. She had been alone all summer while he must have been seeing that girl, every time he went to athletics meetings. Taking her with him, as likely as not. She had known there must be someone.

She had known really, ever since the letter she had found at the end of last term, the one that said all those things about what they had done together ...

Had she been checking up on him when she had taken the dog to the Green? She didn't know. She didn't honestly know. But it didn't take a genius to work out what had happened. Colin had heard Sherry bark, looked up and seen her, then had just taken off as fast as he could. He wanted her to face him with it so that he could try to convince her that she was mistaken.

She wasn't. She wasn't, and she wasn't going to give him the chance to deny it. He couldn't deny it if he wasn't even supposed to know it had happened.

She stood up. She would go home now. Colin would have gone to work.

'Colin Cochrane works here, doesn't he?' asked Tom, settling himself down with a coffee in the staff room, which was occupied by a sole female, pretty and plump.

'Yes,' was the short, and, Tom felt, would-be dismissive reply.

He wondered a bit about that. There was nothing the police had done to indicate that Cochrane was a suspect, unless he'd told them himself that they had removed his tracksuit and trainers for examination, which seemed a little unlikely. Not the sort of thing Cocky Colin Cochrane wanted to get into the papers, Tom was sure, however innocent he may prove to be.

So why the hostility? It was there, quite definitely. Perhaps she just didn't care for total strangers joining her on a free period that she had thought she would be spending in peace.

'Tom Finch,' he said, extending his hand. 'I'm a DS with Stansfield CID. We're here about—'

'I know why you're here,' she said.

Tom nodded. 'The headmaster said I could get a cup of coffee in here,' he said. 'I hope you don't mind me being here. But it's thirsty work, interviewing.'

'I fail to see what Mr Cochrane has to do with your enquiry,' she said.

'Oh, it was just that I met him last night,' said Tom. 'It was his wife's dog that—' He broke off. 'I'm sorry,' he said. 'I'm being a bit insensitive. Did you know Natalie?'

'She was in my biology class,' she said, softening slightly. 'I didn't know her particularly well, but obviously it's been a terrible shock. I'm Mrs Kane, by the way,' she added.

'I'm sure you don't need me rabbiting on about Colin Cochrane,' said Tom, picking up his mug, making as if to leave. 'I just – you know. I've only seen him on the telly before.'

'Please. Stay, if you want. It's not your fault this terrible thing's happened. I thought you'd been listening to school gossip, which is absolute nonsense. What did you want with Colin?'

Gossip? Tom hadn't heard any gossip, but the staff did seem to like Cochrane. Mrs Kane obviously did, so he wouldn't get told any rumours about him by her. He'd try the kids. A much better bet.

'It must be funny, working with him,' he said, apparently quite uninterested in gossip.

'Funny?' said Mrs Kane.

'Well, with him being famous, and all that. If I was him, I'd have packed all this in by now.'

Mrs Kane's eyebrows rose. 'Some people are dedicated to what they do,' she said.

'Yes,' said Tom. 'I suppose they are. The thing is, I've got a son – he's six.' He delved into the wallet in which he really did keep a photograph of his children. 'That's him,' he said. 'He's really good at sport – better than you'd expect a kid that age to be. A lot better. I don't know how young you should start them and I thought Colin might . . . I didn't really get much chance to talk to him last night.'

She sighed. 'Any other day I would have said that you could catch him at lunch,' she said. 'He lunches with me as a rule. But I think he may go home to see how his wife is.'

Tom nodded. 'Of course,' he said. 'She was very shaken up.' He

69

thought for a moment. 'He doesn't have lunch with his wife, then?' he asked. 'She works here too, doesn't she?'

Mrs Kane smiled. 'No scandal, I'm afraid,' she said. 'Erica prefers to bring sandwiches. The teachers are expected to eat with the pupils if they stay in school for lunch.'

'Oh.' Tom smiled. 'That's what I call dedication,' he said. 'No wonder Mrs Cochrane prefers sandwiches.'

Mrs Kane smiled back. 'Lunch can be a bit trying,' she said. 'But Colin would be pleased to talk to you about your son, I know. It's just I think he probably won't be there today.'

'He was saying last night that he's moving up to long-distance running,' Tom said, with a hint of pride at his inside knowledge of the great man.

'Yes, so I believe.'

'Doesn't always work, does it? If you're used to middle-distance.'

Mrs Kane smiled. 'Oh, Colin will try to see to it that it works,' she said. 'I've never met anyone so determined. So disciplined.'

Tom looked earnestly at Mrs Kane. 'How often does he do that run that he was doing last night?' he asked, awe-struck.

'Three or four times a week at least.'

Tom's eyes widened. 'That same run?' he asked. He outlined Colin Cochrane's run, only to have Mrs Kane join in with the last few stages.

'He might not go as far out as that each time,' she said. 'It depends how long a run he's doing. He sets himself a time, you see, and the round trip must be completed in the time he's set. I told you – he won't give up once he's got hold of something. But I don't think he's being very sensible.'

'Do you think he's overdoing it?'

'He . . . he's a bit obsessive about it, I think,' she said. 'But then, he's like that about everything. He's one of these people who can't just have an interest in something. He becomes hooked on it.'

Tom finished his coffee. 'Well . . . let's hope he makes it,' he said, getting up and going to the door. 'It would be a shame to see him retire from running altogether.'

'I think he should,' said Mrs Kane. 'He's not getting any younger.' She looked up at Tom. 'He comes in here some mornings worn out,' she said. 'I don't honestly know why he's doing it at all, but he does it too much too often, if you ask me.'

Tom couldn't but agree that he'd done it once too often now.

Hannah strained to hear what the doctor was saying to her mother. She had been ill all night; her mother had found her being sick and had called the doctor first thing.

'I think it's just the shock, Mrs Lewis,' he was saying.

It wasn't shock. It was fear. It was not being able to close her eyes without seeing Murray standing there holding Natalie's shoes.

'This is a very mild tranquillizer, just to help her get some sleep,' he said. 'Just one now, and one this evening if you think she needs it.'

Hannah began to cry at the mention of the word school. Silent tears, cried into her pillow. She couldn't go to school; as long as she was here, she was safe. He didn't know who she was, she was sure of that.

'Once she's had a sleep, and feels more relaxed, try and get her out into the fresh air,' said the doctor. 'It can do her more good than I can. And try to make sure that she does go back to school soon. Tomorrow, maybe, or the next day. She'll feel better when she's talked about it to her friends.'

No. No. They'd make her go back. But she couldn't stay away for ever.

Oh, God, what was she going to do?

Chapter Six

Lloyd was at the council depot when Judy arrived. Plan in hand, he was pacing out the distance between where Natalie Ouspensky had been found by Sherlock, and where she had been seen by Mrs Cochrane. Where Sherlock had found the shoes, where her killer might have parked his car.

'Why would he leave her shoes here?' he asked, by way of greeting.

Judy still had no answer to that; she told him Freddie's findings on the body.

'Mm,' said Lloyd, when she'd finished. 'What are your thoughts?' he asked.

Judy shrugged. 'I haven't really formulated any,' she said, and looked round.

The Green looked different in the bright, warm sunlight. Last night the building had been black and sinister; today it was a council depot. The adventure playground had been traps for the unwary; today it was an arrangement of tyres and pipes and nets and ropes, perfectly obvious, perfectly innocent. The grass was quite long, and covered with clover and buttercups; the trees that ringed it were green and welcoming, not secret and shifting.

But her notion of how it had been last night was coloured by the fact that it was where a body had been discovered; she tried to imagine it before then, before it had any ominous connotations. Moonlit. Quiet. A balmy evening, solitude.

'She told Mrs Cochrane to mind her own business,' said Lloyd. 'And walked up there.' He strolled up towards the adventure playground, Judy following.

'Let's say she was here with someone,' he said. 'What happened next?'

Judy looked at him. 'Freddie seems to think that she was just standing here talking to someone who suddenly cracked her head against the pipe, then raped and strangled her, not necessarily in that order,' she said.

Lloyd's eyes grew wide. '*Freddie* thinks that?' he said. 'He must have been a great deal more forthcoming than usual.'

He wasn't half, thought Judy. Aloud, she said that he hadn't really been himself. 'He's been given an ultimatum by Mrs Freddie,' she said. 'It's murder victims or her.'

Lloyd smiled. 'And Freddie has, of course, chosen murder victims,' he said.

'He hasn't told her yet, but yes, he has. I don't think he's too cut up about it.' She looked sternly at Lloyd. 'That wasn't a pun,' she said.

'Has he made a pass at you yet?' he asked, with a smile.

Judy sighed. 'Why don't you just get out your crystal ball, tell us who killed that little girl and save us all a lot of time and money?' she asked.

Lloyd grinned. 'It doesn't work that way,' he said.

'It was a very oblique pass, and he apologized for it this morning,' she said. 'And I'm beginning to think I should take him up on it. At least he can't read minds.'

'It's the Welsh wizardry,' said Lloyd, melodramatically. 'You can have no secrets from me.'

That was probably true, and something she preferred not to think about. 'Well, anyway,' she said briskly, 'that's his theory, and if he's right, then what happened next was an unprovoked attack, probably by a psycho.'

'Well, since he's obviously not going to say it this time, I'd better,' said Lloyd. 'Theories always come to grief. And I'm going on the assumption, for the moment, that she knew her attacker.'

Judy nodded. 'I thought that last night,' she said. 'But I'm not so sure now.'

Lloyd shook his head. 'She didn't just stand there and talk to a total stranger,' he said. 'Not here. Not at night. It's too lonely. Too exposed. She was with someone she knew and trusted.'

'Being with someone she knew and trusted doesn't rule out his being a psycho,' Judy said.

'I know,' said Lloyd. 'But let's assume consent, just for argument's sake.'

If the girl had consented to sex, then they would have wanted privacy, thought Judy. Mrs Cochrane was around, and they would presumably have wanted to keep out of sight. There wasn't a lot of choice, really. She looked at the pipe; that was where she had been found, where she had died. But it was hardly somewhere one would go from choice.

'What do you think about in there?' she asked Lloyd, pointing over to it.

'What do I think about it?' he asked, puzzled.

'For somewhere to have sex,' said Judy.

'Sure, if you want,' he said. 'But I'd just as soon wait until we get home.'

She hit him.

'That's a sackable offence,' he said.

'Sorry, sir. But does it strike you as somewhere a girl like Natalie would agree to have sex?'

He shrugged. 'It would keep them dry if it started to rain, it's hidden from view, it wouldn't be any more uncomfortable than anywhere else. Why not? And what is a "girl like Natalie"? I think she might have been a bit hard to control, from what her mother said.'

Perhaps. But Judy just couldn't see Natalie agreeing to it; her background, her mother, her whole way of life seemed to argue against it. Natalie would like her creature comforts, Judy was certain. 'I take it you don't agree with Freddie,' she said.

Lloyd shook his head. 'Whoever it was beat her unconscious and strangled her. I don't think that any intermediate or subsequent sexual assault would be non-violent in those circumstances.'

Judy felt a little dubious about that. 'It depends what sort of psycho you've got,' she argued. 'Perhaps he just wanted her acquiescent.'

'Perhaps,' said Lloyd. 'But let's say they were together. Why would it become violent?'

He sat down near the middle of the see-saw, leaning on it and letting go, letting it rock up and down as he thought.

'The attack has to have taken several minutes,' he said. 'Which means that any preceding activity can't have taken very long. Perhaps she said something disparaging about his technique.'

Judy snorted. 'If everyone whose girlfriend was less than complimentary about—' she began.

'I know, I know,' he said, interrupting her. 'We'd be knee-deep in corpses. But she presumably did or said something to provoke him.'

'But did she?' said Judy. 'You'd expect there to have been shouting if he had got so angry with her that he did her that much damage. But no one heard anything at all.'

Freddie could be right. Judy was no keener than Lloyd on the idea, but he could be right. Whoever she was with just . . . did it. Wanted her unable to resist.

'How did you get on with Natalie's mother?' she asked, not wanting to entertain Freddie's theory right now. The physical evidence didn't really suggest rape to her, either. And if Natalie had consented, then provoked him to violence, Judy wanted to know a lot more about her.

Lloyd rocked up and down on the see-saw. 'She started off saying that Natalia didn't go with boys,' he said. 'I had to tell her about her being on the pill so that she would give that up. Then she said that she had had a few boyfriends, but nothing serious.'

Ah. Judy began to rethink Natalie. If her mother hadn't wanted to admit to boyfriends, then presumably she didn't think that Natalie had been settling for a goodnight kiss on the front porch. But that didn't immediately bring you to having it off with someone in a surplus storm drain.

'She had been wondering if Natalia had met someone special,' Lloyd went on. 'Because she had been out a lot over the past six months. She has no idea who, though.'

Judy frowned. 'Why keep him a secret,' she said, 'if she didn't do that with the others? Someone mother wouldn't approve of?'

'Black?' suggested Lloyd. 'Asian? Only I didn't get the impression that that sort of thing would bother Mrs O. unduly.' He thought for a moment. 'Someone a lot older than her?'

'Married?' said Judy.

'Married seems quite likely,' said Lloyd, pushing himself off the see-saw. 'And perhaps it gives us a motive, if she was threatening to tell his wife, or whatever. And there's the car ... Much more likely, if it was a married man.'

Judy had been having to accommodate the idea of a married man having an assignation with Natalie in that pipe, and that had seemed less likely than ever. But the car – yes. She was with him in the *car*, and they had a row.

But the time factor was against that. The car would have had to arrive, Natalie and her boyfriend would have had to have been together for some minutes, at least, however poor a performer Lloyd thought he was; then the row, then the murder. Then he had to get away – all before Mrs Cochrane came out of the woods.

'Mrs O. did say that she had found it quite difficult to bring up Natalia on her own,' Lloyd carried on. 'She has to work, and Natalia's been pretty well doing her own thing for the last three years. I got the impression that she wasn't all that easy to control, as I said.'

'Married brings us back to Colin Cochrane,' said Judy. 'I know he's just a wild guess, but they can be right. And Tom's not stupid.'

'No, he's not. But don't encourage him – he thinks he's got this all sewn up, and we're a long way from that.' He looked thoughtful. 'I suppose Mrs Cochrane really did see Natalia alive, did she?'

Judy shrugged. 'Well, I told the troops not to take it as gospel,' she said. 'But I think she did.'

Lloyd grunted. 'I think I'll get back to the station – see what's been coming in.'

Judy headed up the hill to Oakland School. She was going to talk to Baby Otter.

'What are you doing here?'

Patrick had had more effusive welcomes in his time, not least from Erica. 'I just came to see how you are,' he said.

75

'I thought maybe Colin had sent you,' she said.

'Colin? Why would he send me?'

'To tell me you had to mend his car yesterday,' she said.

Patrick nodded. 'I did,' he said.

Erica's eyebrows rose. 'You mean it really wouldn't start?' she said.

'It was something and nothing,' he said. 'Only took about an hour – but I told Victoria it took a couple of hours, so don't go landing me in it, will you?'

Erica stepped back, inviting him in.

The dog padded over to him immediately, and Patrick tickled its ears. 'It was this fella who found her, they tell me?' he said. He sat down, and patted the large head that was laid in his lap. 'It must have been a terrible shock for you,' he said.

'Yes.' Erica sat down too.

'It was just when you didn't come in to work, I was worried. I'm not here to provide an alibi for your husband, if that's what you thought I was doing.'

She sighed. 'I know you're not,' she said.

'What were you doing there, at all?' he asked. 'At that time of night?'

'I had the dog,' she said defensively.

Patrick smiled at Sherlock. 'What use would this great lump be if you'd met this nutter?' he asked.

Erica put out a hand and touched Sherlock's ear. 'Well, I didn't meet him,' she said.

Not quite, thought Patrick. Not quite. But you very nearly did.

'Kim, isn't it?'

Kim nodded, and stood just inside the door. She had already spoken to the police, because Mr Murray had told them that she was a friend of Natalie's, though what qualified him to judge she didn't know. Still, he was right. But now she had been called out of class to come and talk to a detective inspector. It was a woman; that had surprised her.

The woman smiled. 'I'm DI Hill,' she said. 'Have a seat, Kim.'

They were in Mrs Cochrane's office, DI Hill behind the desk. She looked all right. She looked cool, in light, smart summer clothes instead of the heavy dark uniform that Kim wore. She was in her thirties, Kim supposed. She had a nice smile.

She had managed the other interview all right. She had said that Natalie had been to discos and things with boys, but other than that she knew nothing. She hadn't let on how well she had known Natalie, because that way she could get away with keeping her information to herself. She wished, with all her heart, that Natalie had never told her, and it was getting easier to pretend that she never had.

'Please?' The inspector indicated the seat.

Kim edged forward and sat, as requested, ready to be interviewed again, though she didn't know why. But nothing had prepared her for the inspector's opening question.

'You're Baby Otter, is that right?'

Kim's mouth opened. How could she know about that? It was a private joke, nothing more. She looked at DI Hill in sheer awe.

'No magic powers, Kim. You shouldn't write things on the back of bus seats if you want to keep them private.'

Kim still didn't see how she knew. Was it really only yesterday that she'd done that? And Natalie had crossed out the I. She still couldn't really take it in; Natalie was dead. Dead. It seemed unreal, impossible. She would be back tomorrow. But she wouldn't. She wouldn't, because someone had killed her. And she knew something the police didn't know, and Hannah had said not to tell them.

Kim hadn't wanted to come to school today, but her mum had said she would probably feel better here with everyone else than brooding about it at home, because she had to go in to work, and she didn't want to leave Kim on her own. But nothing made you feel better about your best friend having been murdered.

'This must have been a terrible shock for you,' the inspector said. 'And I'm sorry that I have to come barging in asking questions. But I'm sure you understand how vital it is that we know as much as possible about Natalie.'

Kim nodded.

'She was Pink Champagne, I take it. Did the names mean anything?'

Kim shook her head. 'Just silly names we gave one another when we were kids,' she said.

'So you've known Natalie a long time?'

'Since the juniors.'

The inspector nodded slowly. 'I'm sorry,' she said. 'This must be very difficult for you. But I'm sure you want her killer found.'

Kim nodded again. She did. She wanted whoever had done that caught and dealt with. She ought to tell her, she ought to. Just tell her what Natalie had said. But she had promised Hannah, and Hannah was off sick today, so she couldn't be released from her promise.

Kim wasn't sure why she had promised. What the hell did it have to do with Hannah, anyway? But Hannah had always behaved as though Colin Cochrane was her own personal property, and she had promised.

It was true that it would cause an awful lot of trouble for him, and it was hard to believe that he would have done anything like that. She had rung Hannah for advice; there wasn't much point in ignoring the advice she'd been given.

'Tell me about this drama group,' said DI Hill. 'You're a member, aren't you?'

'Yes.'

'That was where you'd been when I saw you on the bus yesterday?'

She had been on the bus, of course. She had to have been, otherwise how could she have known about her writing on the seat? 'Yes,' she said again.

'Natalie was a member?'

'Yes.'

If her monosyllabic replies were irritating the inspector, she gave no hint of it. She had a big notebook open in front of her, and she would jot things down now and again.

'There was a boy on the bus,' Inspector Hill said. 'Right at the front. Natalie seemed to know him. Is he a member of the drama group?'

'Dave Britten. No.'

'Was he Natalie's boyfriend?'

'Used to be,' said Kim.

'Was she seeing someone else?'

Kim shrugged.

'I have to know,' said the inspector. 'Even if it's just to eliminate people from the enquiry. I have to check. And our enquiries here have led us to believe that Natalie had had one or two boyfriends over the last two years. Is that true?'

'One or two,' said Kim. Several, actually.

'But the feeling seems to be that she may have found a steady boyfriend during the holidays.'

'I don't know,' Kim muttered.

The inspector put down her pen and sat back. 'Kim,' she said, 'I know this might be hard to believe, but I was fifteen once. And I had a friend that I'd had since the juniors.' She smiled. 'I have never known anyone as well as I knew her, and no one has ever known me as well as she did. Did Natalie have a steady boyfriend?'

Kim could feel herself grow red, and the silence that followed the question grew unbearable.

'I don't know his name.'

'What do you know?'

Kim didn't speak.

'What do you know?' she asked again.

She didn't want to get him into trouble. She didn't want to get anyone into trouble.

'What do you know?' Just the same question, over and over. Not impatient, not demanding an answer. Just asking, over and over.

'She told me he was married,' she said, not looking at the inspector, trying not to let the tears come, but they were coming despite her efforts.

'Did she tell you anything else?'

'No,' she said, her voice agonized, tears streaming down her hot face.

The inspector produced tissues from somewhere, and handed them to her. 'I think she did, Kim,' she said, her voice quiet.

Kim shook her head. Her whole world seemed to be closing in, to have become this question. Hannah was right; she would ruin his career, his marriage. But what if he had killed her? What if?

'Kim,' said the inspector.

That was all; just her name, a slight warning in her voice. Kim didn't have to answer. The head had said that it was up to her whether she saw the police at all on school premises. But she ought to tell her. Whatever she had promised, whatever harm it would do. Natalie had been done terrible harm. Kim raised her head. 'She said he was a teacher,' she whispered.

'Did she say which teacher?' The inspector's voice hadn't changed now that she had won; there was no triumph, no increased urgency, no shock, no disapproval. Just the same quiet tone of voice.

'No,' said Kim, wiping the tears that wouldn't stop coming. 'No, honestly, she didn't, she didn't.'

'I'm sorry this is so distressing for you,' said the inspector. 'But I need to know what you're not telling me.'

'That's all Natalie told me!'

The sun was shining outside, lighting the office with an almost golden glow; Kim wished with all her heart that she was out there, away from this claustrophobic room.

'Whatever it is,' the inspector said, as though Kim hadn't spoken, 'it can't hurt Natalie now. Was she putting pressure on this man?'

'What?' said Kim.

'Threatening to tell his wife, or something?'

'I don't know,' said Kim.

'Was she the kind of girl who might do that?'

Kim shook her head.

'Tell me what she was like,' said the inspector.

Kim got herself under control. She could tell her about Natalie, she supposed. 'She . . . she wouldn't do anything like that,' she said. 'She really wouldn't.'

The inspector nodded. 'I know you're very shocked by what's happened,' she said. 'But – please don't think I'm criticizing, or being cruel – are you actually surprised?'

Kim stared at her. Of course she was – no. No, no, she wasn't. Not entirely.

'No,' she whispered, after she had been made to think about it. 'I worried about her.'

'Because she went with a lot of boys, or because of something more specific?'

'Because . . .' Kim tried to put it into words, but it was difficult. 'Because she never thought,' she said. 'She never thought, not really. She never thought before she did anything.'

'About the effect it would have on other people?'

Kim looked away. 'Or herself,' she said. 'She never knew when to stop.'

'Who was Natalie seeing, Kim?'

'She didn't tell me who it was!' Kim shouted.

'But you think you know.' Still the same, quiet voice.

'It's just gossip, I don't know.'

'What gossip?'

Kim shook her head.

'If it's gossip, I'm going to hear it anyway.'

DI Hill looked nice. She looked like Kim's mum, in a way; she didn't look as though she would let you wriggle on the end of a stick until you told her what she wanted to know. But that was what she was doing, and she wasn't going to stop.

Kim looked down at her hands. 'Someone . . . someone said that Mr Cochrane was having an affair with one of the girls at school.' She looked up, now that the words were out. 'That doesn't mean he killed her!' she said.

'No, it doesn't,' said the inspector. 'And it doesn't mean that it was Natalie he was having an affair with. Come to that, it doesn't mean he was having an affair at all. Gossip's like that.' She was writing as she spoke. 'I do take gossip with a pinch of salt, so don't worry about that.'

Kim blew her nose, and wiped away the tears.

'Thank you,' said the inspector. 'And I'm sorry. I really am.'

No, she wasn't. She'd got what she wanted.

But there was something else that Kim thought she ought to know. Possibly the only thing she had intended telling her, and she still hadn't said it. 'She . . . she seemed worried about something,' she said.

The inspector frowned a little. 'Did she?' she asked. 'She seemed quite cheerful when I saw her on the bus.'

Kim nodded. 'Maybe I don't mean worried,' she said. 'But she was . . . funny. In a funny mood. As if she was thinking about something else all the time.'

'Did you ask her if she had something on her mind?'

Kim shook her head. 'I didn't see her on her own,' she said. 'But there was something bothering her. Well, no, she didn't seem bothered, just—' She broke off.

'Preoccupied?' suggested the inspector.

Kim nodded. Preoccupied. That was the word.

She wanted to tell Patrick, but she mustn't, not even him. They had talked about what the police were doing at the school, and Patrick said that someone had chatted to him about Colin, but that he thought he was just a fan.

Erica doubted it. 'What did he look like?' she asked.

'Young. Well – he looked like one of the sixth-formers, but he's got two kids, so I suppose he must be older than he looks,' said Patrick. 'Curly fair hair.'

Oh, God. Detective Sergeant Finch. He hadn't seemed much like a fan of Colin's last night. Erica wasn't sure how much of this she could stand. She wanted to know what he had been 'chatting' to Patrick about, but he didn't attach any significance to it, and she mustn't be the one to make it clear that there was any.

She felt so alone, so helpless. She began, despite her best efforts not to, to cry again. Patrick was beside her, his arm round her shoulders.

'I saw her,' she told him. 'I saw her alive. About quarter of an hour before Sherry—'

Patrick patted her like a baby as she cried. 'There was nothing you could have done,' he said. 'Nothing. Don't cry, there's a good girl. Don't cry.'

He kissed her as he spoke, little comforting kisses, and she didn't try to stop him. They sprang apart as they heard the front door open, and by the time Colin came in Patrick was back on the other chair and the dog was looking inscrutable, his head on Patrick's knee as though it had been there for hours.

Colin frowned. 'What are you doing here?' he asked.

Poor Patrick. That was the second time someone had asked him that.

'I came to see how Erica was,' he said easily.

Colin sat down, tight-lipped. He looked at Erica, then at Patrick. 'I have to speak to Erica,' he said pointedly. 'Alone.'

'No sooner said,' said Patrick, amiably, getting up. He gave Erica and the dog a final pat each. 'Take care of yourself, love,' he said. 'See you later, Colin. I'll show myself out.'

Colin waited until the front door closed before he spoke. 'I thought I'd better find out if you had come home,' he said.

'I hadn't gone far,' said Erica tiredly. 'I just couldn't face school.'

'Or me, it would seem,' said Colin.

Erica sighed. 'Or you.'

'Mrs Ouspenky's boyfriend's in the clear, Sarge,' said DC Marshall, as Tom Finch walked into the murder room. 'He was in a Happy Eater between ten and eleven last night, half way to Doncaster. He has six fellow diners, a tankful of DERV, and a timed and dated receipt to prove it.'

'Good,' said Tom, though it didn't sound as though Marshall had been obeying the instruction to be discreet. Never mind. 'One less to worry about,' he said.

'Tom – just the man,' said Bob Sandwell. 'Those clothes you sent over to the lab?'

Tom looked at Sandwell, startled. 'They can't have checked them out already,' he said.

'No, but they found something in the pocket that'll interest you.' Sandwell pushed over a piece of paper encased in plastic. 'It's been laundered,' he said. 'But it's legible. It's not been for fingerprints yet, but there doesn't seem much hope.'

Tom took it. A typewritten letter, faded, but as Sandwell had said, legible.

It began 'Dear Colin,' and was dated the sixth of September. It said that the writer would wait for him on the Green, at the adventure playground, that evening. It went into graphic – not to say porno-graphic – detail about what the writer and Colin had done together the last time they had met, and what they would do this time. If it had ever been signed, the signature had been laundered away.

Tom smiled broadly. 'Bob Sandwell, I could kiss you,' he said.

'I shouldn't have let you read that – it's got you over-excited.' Sandwell took it back. 'I'll get copies made,' he said, 'and send this off for prints.'

'So, he didn't go anywhere near the Green, didn't he?' Tom said, jubilant. He and Sherlock should set up in business together. Together, their noses would conquer the world.

'Maybe he didn't,' warned Sandwell.

Tom pulled a disbelieving face. 'With all that on offer?' he said. 'Has the DCI seen it?'

'No, it's just come in.'

'Do us a copy. I can't wait to see his face when he reads this,' said Tom.

Colin hadn't really expected to find Erica there, never mind Patrick Murray. Still, at least he had confirmed to Erica that the car really had broken down.

'He said it only took an hour to fix it,' said Erica.

'Erica, you can't believe I had anything to do with what happened to Natalie,' he said wearily. 'You just can't.'

She looked at him steadily. 'I know you didn't kill her,' she said.

'I didn't do anything with her!'

'You left her there, Colin!'

Colin closed his eyes.

'You just . . . left her there,' Erica said again, her voice accusing.

He opened his eyes slowly. 'How . . . how do you know that?' he asked.

Erica frowned. 'How do you suppose I know?' she asked.

Natalie must have spoken to her. My God, no wonder she thought the worst. 'It . . . it isn't how it seems,' he said. 'It's not what you think. Whatever she said, whatever she told you, I wasn't having an affair with her, Erica. I swear to you. She's been writing these letters – she sent one yesterday, saying she'd meet me there. That's all. I swear. That's all.'

'Are you still trying to tell me it was all in her mind?' Erica asked. 'It was just a teenage fantasy? Nothing to worry about?'

Yes, he thought helplessly. Yes. 'It's the truth,' he said, his voice weak. 'What did she say to you?' he asked.

'She told me to mind my own business.'

'I've never had anything to do with her! Whatever she said, you must believe me.'

'She didn't have to say anything!'

'She must have – and it's lies. All lies.'

'I knew you'd do this,' she said. 'I knew it.' She looked away.

'Erica – it's all in her imagination.'

'Go away, Colin,' she said. 'Go back to school.'

'What?' he said. 'How can I go back to school when you're accusing me of God knows what?'

'If you won't leave, I will,' she said. 'I know what I saw.'

'You didn't see me,' said Colin.

'No,' she agreed. 'I didn't see you. You made damn sure of that.'

She was snapping on the dog's lead, she was leaving, and he couldn't stop her. It was a nightmare. A nightmare. Surely to God he would wake up soon?

There were names now; boys that Natalie had been known to consort with. A lot of names. Lloyd decided to wait until Judy got back from interviewing this girl who was reputed to be Natalie's best friend. She would know the latest boyfriend, presumably.

'You'd better put Cochrane on that list,' Tom Finch said, knocking on the open door as he spoke. He smiled. 'And at least I won't need kid gloves to deal with him because he left adolescence behind a long time ago,' he added.

'What have you got?' asked Lloyd.

'Cochrane. On toast.' Tom held out a sheet of paper. 'It's the best we can do,' he said, as Lloyd reached for his glasses. 'A photocopy of a letter that's been washed, spun and tumble-dried isn't going to be too good. The original's gone to see if we can get any prints from it. Not much chance of that, but since it was found in Cochrane's tracksuit . . .'

Lloyd read the letter with some difficulty, not just because the copy was very pale. He wasn't sure that someone who was anticipating a reunion after two celibate months should be reading it, really.

When he got to the end, he slid his glasses down his nose and looked at Tom. 'Natalia's mother will dispute that any of these lads had anything to do with Natalia,' he said, nodding to the details on his desk about her possible boyfriends. 'Never mind that she wrote this letter.'

'Who else could have written it?' asked Tom. 'And there are rumours about Cochrane and a schoolgirl going round like wildfire.'

'Since the murder?'

'Someone told me that they heard it yesterday afternoon,' said Tom.

Lloyd took off his specs and handed the letter back. 'Why would she type it?' he asked.

'They all do,' said Tom. 'Keep it. That's your copy.'

Lloyd frowned. 'All who do?' he asked.

'Kids. They've all got computers with word processors now, you know. It's how they do their homework – it's how they do everything. My sister's kids don't know what a pen's for.' He grinned at Lloyd. 'It even fixes their spelling for them,' he said.

'Time you got one, then, isn't it?' said Lloyd automatically, but he was thinking about Natalia's room. She did have a computer; he had seen it. He told Tom.

'There you are, then,' he said.

'But this sort of thing?' said Lloyd. He wasn't convinced. It seemed a very calculated way of dealing with what was a very passionate letter. And the lack of a signature bothered him.

'Probably got washed away,' said Tom.

'Maybe,' said Lloyd. He sighed. 'I hate to sound like Methuselah, but you used to be able to check typewritten letters,' he said. 'Match up the type with the typewriter.'

'Well,' said Tom. 'I don't suppose you know what sort of software she was using?'

Lloyd had put in a number of hours on the subject, and knew

84

enough to know that even Tom couldn't tell what software someone was using from seeing the computer in an off mode.

Tom grinned. 'I just thought you might have seen a manual or something,' he said. 'Some programs have a safety net affair.'

Lloyd heard the spelling of the word program. He had had to come to terms with program and disk before he could even begin to come to terms with the actual beast. But now, for the first time in his life, he found himself actually wanting to hear what a computer man had to say.

'You type your letter, print it out, and then delete it if you don't need to keep it,' said Tom.

So far, so good.

'Some programs let you rescue it later, even if you have deleted it. Providing you haven't deleted enough things after that to have wiped that one out, if you see what I mean. It's like a sort of waste paper basket that gets emptied when it's full, on a first-in first-out basis.'

'You mean it holds what you've done even if you've told it not to?' said Lloyd, wondering at the tyranny of this technology that the world was worshipping. But then, the world had always worshipped tyranny, so it was no real surprise.

'It might have. It might not, of course. Shall I send someone to check out what's what?'

'Please,' said Lloyd, absently. Cochrane could deny that Natalia had written it, as long as it remained anonymous.

'Shall I bring Cochrane in?' Tom asked.

Lloyd nodded. 'Discreetly, Tom,' he said. 'And voluntarily, if at all possible.'

'Sir.'

Chapter Seven

It was relatively easy to be discreet at the school, Tom discovered; neither Cochrane nor his wife had turned in for work.

'I think Mr Cochrane went home at lunchtime,' said the head. 'Mrs Cochrane didn't come in at all today. I wasn't surprised, after what she . . .' The sentence tailed off. 'But it is most unusual – No, to be quite accurate, it's unheard-of for Mr Cochrane not to be here when he's supposed to be.'

'Well, I'll pop down to his house, then,' said Tom.

'Oh, good,' said the head. 'I'm a little worried. It's so unlike him, not even getting in touch . . . I rang, because I thought something must have happened. But it was just their answering machine.'

'Perhaps his wife wasn't too good,' said Tom. 'She did take it very hard.'

Very. He had wondered about that. All right, no one wanted their dog to turn up a dead body, least of all that of a teenage girl. But there had been more to it than that, he had known that there was.

'He probably thought he ought to stay with her,' Tom said.

'But not even ringing in?' The other man shook his head. 'I'm worried, Sergeant . . . er . . .' He waved his hand about. 'I'm worried. Mr Cochrane is someone you could honestly set your clock by. I really am worried.'

So was Tom. Worried about Mrs Cochrane's insistence that she'd seen the girl alive. She hadn't told him that; that little gem hadn't come out until Judy got there. He'd sent a car for Judy straight away, but even so, Erica Cochrane had had twenty minutes to think about it. He had taken her at face value then. Just some woman who had stumbled on a body. He had given her some time to get over it. Idiot. She was covering for her husband; he had given her time to work out what must have happened, and amend her story accordingly.

Cochrane was once again fresh from the shower, bathrobed and deodorized, when Tom got to his house. Who was it who kept trying to wash her hands? Lady Macbeth? He smiled. Lloyd would be proud of him.

'Is your wife here, Mr Cochrane?' he asked, stepping into the hallway.

'No,' he said. 'She's gone out with the dog. What do you want with her?'

'Oh, nothing much,' said Tom. 'It'll keep. Your headmaster's very worried about you, you know.'

'I should have rung,' Cochrane said. He did not invite Tom further in.

'We thought your wife must be ill,' said Tom.

'Well . . . she's certainly not herself,' said Cochrane. 'I didn't feel that I could go back to work this afternoon.' He looked irritated at having found himself accounting for his behaviour to Tom, of all people, and said so. 'I don't know why I should be explaining all this to you,' he said. 'What are you doing here? Have you brought my clothes back?'

'Sorry. We don't work that quickly,' Tom said. 'But I take it you do have some other clothes, do you, Mr Cochrane? There has been a development which we would like to discuss with you at the station, if you wouldn't mind coming with me.'

'The station?' he said. 'Can't you just tell me whatever it is here? What development?'

'I think it would be better down at the station,' said Tom.

Cochrane disappeared back upstairs without a word, then came down again, tucking his shirt into his trousers, a tie draped round his neck, a jacket over his arm. He wanted to make a good impression, it seemed to Tom.

Cochrane looked at him in the mirror as he did up his tie. 'You made up your mind last night,' he said. 'No evidence – no reason. You just decided you were going after me. Why?'

Your deodorant, mate, thought Tom. 'If you'll just come with me, sir,' he said.

'Jealousy? Because I'm well-known, and I earn a lot of money?' Cochrane slicked his hair back with the comb on the hall table. 'Is that it?'

Tom was always supremely unmoved by insults; it was par for the course as far as he was concerned to be called a fascist pig and worse.

'I could sue you for wrongful arrest.'

'I'm not arresting you, sir. Just asking you to help with our enquiries.'

Cochrane turned to face him. 'And if I refuse, that makes me look as though I've got something to hide, is that it?'

'We think you can throw some light on some new evidence, sir,' said Tom stolidly.

'This is personal,' said Cochrane. 'You decided last night that you were going to involve me in this,' he said. 'Do you get brownie points if it's someone well-known?'

'Sir.' Tom indicated the door. 'If you wouldn't mind.'

Cochrane walked ahead of him to where the car sat with a uniformed constable at the wheel, and got in.

Tom sat beside him in the back, and listened politely to the running commentary about citizens' rights as the car drove along Ash Road. Cochrane hadn't thought it necessary to leave a note for his wife, Tom had noticed. Because she would be able to guess where he'd be?

And just what was her part in all this? She had gone to meet him, and had found a body, not a live person, Tom would be prepared to bet. The body of a girl who was in the school's drama group, as was Cochrane. A girl she reluctantly admitted knowing, but whose name she claimed not to know. She hadn't been going to tell them that her husband taught at the school – it had had to be dragged out of her.

And Natalie? A girl who liked having a good time, by all accounts. A girl who had been writing Cochrane steamy love letters that raised more than an eyebrow, and who had arranged to meet Cochrane last night at the adventure playground. Which was where Sherlock had found her body.

A body on which Tom had smelt Cochrane's deodorant, and on which the dog had smelt Cochrane's scent.

'Fasten your seat belt, Mr Cochrane,' he said, and smiled a little as Cochrane complied.

It's going to be a bumpy ride, he thought. Lloyd would have been even more proud of him for that. He couldn't remember which film it came from, though. That was going to annoy him.

The car made the short journey along Ash Road and turned right up to the police station, where Tom shepherded his charge into the building. He installed Cochrane in an interview room, and went along to the DCI's office.

Judy Hill was in there. 'I had a word with Britten,' she was saying to Lloyd. 'It seems that he and Natalie were seeing one another steadily from January until about April, then she began to lose interest. She finished it at the end of last term.'

'Did she give a reason?' asked Lloyd, beckoning Tom in.

'She dumped him, in his words. She said she had started seeing someone else.'

Lloyd nodded. 'I take it that the verb "to see" is being its usual elastic self in this context?'

'Oh, yes. And I gather he wasn't the first.'

'He definitely wasn't the first,' said Tom. 'I spoke to someone who reckoned his brother and Natalie got it together over a year ago.'

Lloyd looked up. 'Over a *year* ago?' he repeated. 'She's only just turned fifteen now.'

'They start young these days, guv. Natalie did, anyway, by all accounts.'

Lloyd looked pained, but it wasn't Natalie's morals that were bothering him. 'Tom,' he said. 'Call me Lloyd. Call me Chief Inspector. Call me sir, if you want. Call me Baldie. But please stop calling me guv.'

'Sorry, guv.'

'Isn't Inspector Hill your guv, anyway?'

'You're both my guvs, guv.'

'What rank do I have to achieve to escape being called guv?'

'The one you're after,' said Tom, with a smile. 'I'd have to call you sir until I got promotion too. Then I could call you guv again, guv.'

Lloyd laughed. 'I take it you've got Cochrane waiting to see us?'

'I certainly have. I reckon he's had a bust-up with the missus.'

'Oh?'

Tom explained the circumstances, and sighed. 'I screwed up,' he said to Judy. 'Sorry.'

She frowned. 'Did you?' she asked.

'She worked it out, didn't she?' said Tom. 'She realized what must have happened, and told you she saw the girl alive to cover for her husband.'

Judy looked less than convinced.

'Why did she take the dog on to the Green at all?' asked Tom. 'Not the sort of place many women would go alone after dark, is it? You have to go past the council depot and it's like midnight in the coal hole down there.'

'There's supposed to be a light,' said Judy. 'Vandals got it weeks ago and it hasn't been replaced.'

'Even so. The Green itself isn't lit, is it? There's open ground right opposite her. Why not go there?'

Judy shrugged. 'She thought she would be bound to meet up with her husband, because he always came back that way from his training run.'

'But he wasn't there when she got there, was he? Instead of finding him she found Natalie's body, and she's lying when she says she was alive.'

Lloyd, who had been reading Mrs Cochrane's statement, looked up, pushing his glasses down. 'Why should she leap to the conclusion that her husband had murdered her?' he asked.

'Because I reckon she knew he was having it off with her,' said Tom. 'Cochrane could have taken the dog out when he came back, but she left minutes before he was due home, didn't she? So, like I said. Why did she take the dog to the Green at all?'

'Go on, then,' said Judy. 'Why?'

'She went to check up on him, that's why. And finds Natalie's

89

body. So she tells you that she saw the kid alive, because she knows that fifteen minutes after she left the house, hubby would be home and out of the frame.'

'Why would she be so keen to cover up for him?' asked Judy.

'Because women are like that.'

'Are they?' Judy smiled, shaking her head. 'Has Freddie ever talked to you about theories?' she asked.

'Yeah, I know. They always come to grief. But I was with these two last night, and there was grief there already, believe me.'

Lloyd tipped back his chair. Tom could see Judy tense up, as he was doing himself.

'Well,' he said, rocking gently back and forth, 'is it much of an alibi? We don't know when he got home.'

'He had told her he would be home at ten,' said Tom. 'And he's got a thing about being bang on time.'

'I can try to find out if he was,' said Judy. 'That's a very flashy car they've got – the neighbours might notice its comings and goings.'

'An interesting situation,' said Lloyd, coming down again, much to Tom's relief. 'If someone did see him come home at ten, he's got an apparent alibi, which as far as Tom's concerned makes him guilty as sin.'

'It all depends when she died, doesn't it?' said Tom. 'We've only got his wife's word for it that she was alive at ten o'clock. She could have been dead half an hour by then, according to the doc.'

'She could,' said Lloyd, seriously. 'Judy, see if you can get any more from Mrs Cochrane. And talk to the neighbours.' He stood up. 'I think Mr Cochrane's had enough time to stew now, don't you, Tom?'

Tom couldn't wait. They'd see how cocky Mr Cochrane was after this.

Patrick tried to keep his mind on his work, but it wasn't easy, what with the police fetching kids out of class all afternoon, and his drawing a blank with Erica. He had hoped to make certain that she was on his side; he might have been able to do that if Colin hadn't come home unexpectedly.

Colin Cochrane never did anything unexpectedly, and he had had to choose today to step out of character. Patrick needed to be certain of Erica; he needed her to trust him, and then perhaps he could get out of this all in one piece.

That policewoman was a bit of all right, he thought, his mind settling into its familiar grooves as he sidelined his problems for a moment and reflected on the pleasanter aspects of life. A few years older than him, but then so was Erica. Older women were a great deal less trouble, he had found. And if the worst came to the worst, a detective inspector in his corner might be very useful indeed.

She had asked him about Natalie, but he had said that he had only taught at the school for one day, and couldn't be of much assistance. She had asked if he knew a girl called Kim; he had said that she had already been interviewed, but she had wanted to see her all the same.

Kim had been with her a long time, and had looked less than happy when she had been released. Poor kid. Natalie had been her best friend – Patrick had known all about Kim from the start. He felt he ought to do something.

He'd told Kim that she could come to him if she was worried about anything, or just needed someone to talk to. He was always at the school until at least seven, he'd said, so even if it was after hours, he'd be available.

He felt it was the least he could do, but he hoped that she didn't take him up on it. He really didn't want to think about anything but his own survival.

Erica watched anxiously at the window as the police inspector she'd met last night spoke to their neighbours. What about? Anxiety was gnawing at her, making her feel ill, as she waited to see if she would be next on the inspector's list.

Colin had called her, said that he was at the police station, helping them with their enquiries. He seemed to be blaming her, which was hardly fair. She had done everything she could to keep him out of it.

He had said that if they let him go he would be staying at the Derbyshire. She was glad that he wouldn't be coming home. She didn't want to go through any more conversations like the one they had had at lunchtime.

If they let him go? Was he just being bitter, trying to make her feel bad? It wasn't her fault he was there. If he had kept his hands off that little bitch, he wouldn't be in this trouble.

Oh, God, that woman was coming up the path. Erica opened the door. 'Why have you taken Colin to the police station?' she asked, as the inspector came in.

'Oh, something came up that we wanted to discuss with him,' she said.

'What?'

'I'm sorry, Mrs Cochrane, but I can't tell you that.'

'What were you talking to my neighbours about?'

Inspector Hill thought for a moment before she spoke. 'They tell me that your husband didn't come home until about twenty past ten last night,' she said.

Erica shook her head. 'That can't be right,' she said, without a moment's hesitation.

'Oh?'

Erica sat down. It couldn't be right. 'Colin said he would be back at ten,' she said. 'He's never late.'

'They seem quite certain,' said the inspector. 'They were saying goodnight to a guest. Did your husband tell you that he was home earlier than that?'

'No,' said Erica. 'We didn't discuss it.'

'So you've no reason to doubt what your neighbours have told me?'

Yes, she had. She had every reason to doubt it. But they had no reason to lie. Erica didn't understand; she shook her head. 'It's just that he's never late,' she said again. 'Never.' It was impossible to explain that to anyone who didn't know Colin.

And it didn't make any sense. Where had he gone?

'He didn't come home the usual way, did he?'

They knew he was lying about that. Erica looked at Inspector Hill, and decided against trying to reinforce any lies Colin may have told. She didn't think she would be very good at pulling the wool over these shrewd brown eyes.

'Colin didn't kill that girl,' she said. 'Why are you interviewing him?'

'We're talking to lots of people,' said the inspector easily. She opened her notebook. 'But I'd like to go over your statement,' she said.

Erica gave a short sigh. 'You'd better sit down,' she said.

'What made you decide to take the dog on to the Green?' she asked.

Jealousy. Curiosity. Hope that she was wrong, that she would see Colin running home. 'He had to go out,' she said, nodding to the dog, whom the inspector was absently patting.

'But why the Green?'

'Why not?' Erica didn't know how long she could keep this up.

The inspector smiled. 'I don't care much for women being advised not to do this and that because of men's behaviour,' she said. 'But the Green is unlit and lonely. It was an odd time of night to take the dog there, wasn't it?'

Oh. Was that all? Erica could explain that.

Colin had told them the route that his training run took, and now they were sitting just looking at him.

Eventually Lloyd spoke. At least he was conducting the interview; Finch was just sitting there. 'So between nine-thirty and ten o'clock you were ... where, exactly, Mr Cochrane?' he asked.

Colin thought. 'At half past nine I was just entering the Branwell industrial estate,' he said. 'I run through there to Byford Road ... that takes about twenty minutes, I suppose. So I'd be on Byford Road by about ten to ten.'

'And you usually go down Woodthorpe Close and cut across the Green, I understand?' said Lloyd.

'Normally.'

There was silence, then. Colin tried not to let it get on his nerves, but it did. 'I decided not to,' he said. 'I carried on along Byford Road until I got to Beech Street, and I ran down that way.'

Lloyd frowned slightly. 'But I've been told that you are a very precise man,' he said. 'That you time these runs to the minute. A detour must have put your timing out, surely? Why would you do that?'

Colin didn't answer. Why he had done that had nothing to do with them. It wasn't his fault that she had ... His mind flinched away from the consequences of Natalie's infatuation with him.

More consequences, and more. Because here he was in a police interview room, with his words being taped, under caution.

He looked at the two men who sat opposite him. They seemed convinced that he had killed Natalie. It didn't make sense; they had no evidence.

'Look – why am I here?' he demanded. He jerked his head towards Finch. 'He said that there had been a development. This is just the same stuff that he asked me yesterday.'

'Oh, we'll get to that, Mr Cochrane,' said Lloyd, like some sort of smooth salesman. 'Bear with us, if you will. For the moment, I'm just trying to establish for myself where you were.'

'Why? What am I supposed to have to do with any of this?'

Lloyd ignored that, and pushed his glasses back up his nose to read. 'So you went down Beech Street towards Ash Road. And – though you live in Ash Road – you didn't go home, is that right?' He pushed his glasses back down and looked at Colin over them.

'That's right, Chief Inspector. I went to the school, and picked up my car. It has valuables in it. I didn't want to leave it at the school all night.'

'Quite, quite, Mr Cochrane. Car theft's a problem that we are doing all in our power to curb, I do assure you.' He got up from the table and walked around, his hands in his pockets, to Colin's side, and sat on the edge of the table. 'So you picked up your car, and you got home – with your valuables – when?'

'Nineteen minutes past ten.' Colin didn't look at him. He felt like a criminal. They were making him feel like that, just by their body language. For the first time in his life he understood just for an instant why juvenile offenders seemed to get worse, not better, after their first brush with the police.

'You looked at your watch?' said Finch.

'Yes, I did.'

Finch smiled. 'Now why would you do that?' he asked.

'I had told my wife that I'd be home at ten. If I say ten, I mean it. I don't like being early, and I hate being late. I checked to see how late I was.' He addressed Lloyd, rather than Finch.

Lloyd nodded, almost as though he was thinking of something else. 'Would you be prepared to give us a sample of blood for DNA analysis, Mr Cochrane?' he asked, sliding off the table. 'DNA analysis produces what is sometimes called a genetic fingerprint,' he went on. 'No two human beings—'

'I know what it is! I don't see why I should. I had nothing to do with this girl.'

'It's your privilege, for the moment, to refuse,' said Lloyd, and glanced at Finch. 'Odd how we can make suspected drunk drivers give a sample of blood but we can't make suspected murderers do the same, isn't it?' he said.

'You have no reason to suspect me of murder!' Colin shouted.

Finch produced a sheet of paper in a plastic cover, and passed it over the table. 'Do you recognize this, Mr Cochrane?' he asked.

'Sergeant Finch shows Mr Cochrane a letter found in the pocket of his tracksuit top,' Colin heard Lloyd saying, and the words seemed to echo as he stared at the letter, feeling the blood rush to his face and pound in his ears. Dear God. He'd forgotten it was there.

'The sergeant asked if you recognized this letter, Mr Cochrane,' said Lloyd.

He nodded, speechless.

'Mr Cochrane nods,' said Lloyd.

He had forgotten all about it. Gradually, the pounding subsided, and he waited for the questions.

'Right, Mr Cochrane,' said Finch, and Colin could see that he had been waiting for this moment. 'Did Natalie Ouspensky write that letter to you?'

'She must have done,' Colin muttered.

Finch leant over, his ear cocked. 'Sorry?' he said.

Colin raised his voice. 'I said she must have done,' he said.

'Don't you know? If I'd been getting up to those tricks with someone, I think I'd remember who.'

Colin looked at the letter, and shook his head.

'Are you saying you don't know who wrote that letter to you?'

'I do now,' said Colin. 'But I didn't.'

'You didn't find out who she was until you met her last night, is that what you're saying?'

A shake of his head, a reminder, a spoken denial.

'I didn't meet her,' he said. 'I didn't go. I deliberately avoided the Green. I found out who had written it when you told me that was who had been murdered.'

'I think you'll have to explain that, Mr Cochrane,' Lloyd said.

'It's obvious! She was there hoping to meet me, but I avoided her, and she was there, alone, when some . . . some maniac killed her.' He didn't want to think about it, about his responsibility for her death. She had told him she would be there. She had told him. He had left her there, just like Erica said. In the dark. On her own.

Lloyd was looking puzzled. Theatrically puzzled. Almost strip-cartoon puzzled. You could practically see the question mark in a bubble over his head. 'The thing is,' he said, 'the pathologist doesn't see it like that at all.'

He sounded very Welsh now. Welsh, and terribly interested, as though he was discussing a particularly good play that they had all seen, not poor little Natalie's murder.

'No,' he went on. 'He doesn't think she met a maniac. At least, not one with I AM A MANIAC printed on his tee-shirt. He thinks she was quite at ease with whoever killed her. The opinion – the professional opinion – of the pathologist and several of the investigating officers is that she knew – and trusted – whoever killed her. She was wrong to, obviously, but she did, we think.'

Colin wasn't sure if that made him feel better or worse.

'She knew and trusted you, Mr Cochrane,' said Finch. 'She was waiting to see you. You knew she would be there. Do you suppose anyone else did? Not the sort of thing she'd advertise, I don't suppose.'

'Maybe . . . maybe someone followed her there,' Colin said, almost thinking aloud.

'Yes,' said Lloyd, enthusiastically. 'Yes, could be, could be. Except . . . you do different lengths of run, you said. I mean, it might be two, three – even four hours. She would have no way of knowing exactly when you were going to come across the Green, would she?'

'No,' said Colin dully. 'I'm usually there at about nine, though.'

'So she'd be there from about nine, wouldn't she?'

'Yes, I suppose so. If she knew my usual times.'

'Well, she knew you'd end up there, so I think we can assume she knew when that was likely to be. And she was there from nine, let's say.'

Colin sighed. 'Let's,' he said.

'Half past nine, it would be dusk, and nobody about. If I'd followed her there I think that's when I'd have killed her, if I'd been going to kill her. I don't think I'd have waited for a lady and a dog to come along before I did it. No. I'd have done it once it was dark, and quiet ... half past nine, quarter to ten, say. What would you say, Mr Cochrane?'

Colin stared at him. My God, he'd been worrying about Finch. 'I didn't kill her!' he shouted. 'I've just told you! I avoided her. I didn't go across the Green. As I got to Woodthorpe Close I remembered the letter, and I ...' He closed his eyes. 'I didn't want to deal with some teenager with a fantasy ... I just kept running along Byford Road.'

'You were aiming to get home by ten, you said?'

Colin nodded. No one bothered telling him to speak for the tape.

'But you didn't get there until twenty past.'

'No. Because I took the long way round.'

'It's not that long a way round, is it, Mr Cochrane? I doubt if it's even a mile.'

'It's only about half a mile, two-thirds at the most,' said Colin tiredly. He wasn't looking at either of them now.

'And yet you seem to be saying that it took you twenty minutes,' said Lloyd. 'I don't believe you, Mr Cochrane.'

'Tough,' said Colin.

'It wouldn't take me twenty minutes to walk half a mile, never mind run, and I'm not a world-class athlete,' Lloyd continued. 'As you may have noticed.'

Yes, Colin could see that he probably wasn't. He hadn't been asked a question; he saw no reason to respond, and Lloyd didn't pursue it.

'And you maintain that you didn't know who had written this letter to you?' asked Finch.

'Yes,' said Colin. 'I've never known. Not until now.'

'*Never* known?'

Again, Colin shook his head. This time he was asked to speak for the tape. 'No,' he said.

'What's that supposed to mean? Have there been other letters?'

Colin sighed. 'They began last term. I didn't know who was sending them.'

'Did they always arrange meetings?'

'No. This is the first one to do that.'

'Were they all like that?'

'Yes. It's not all that unusual,' said Colin.

'Not unusual?' Finch repeated.

Colin looked up slowly. 'If you're on television and under seventy, you get all sorts of letters,' he said. 'They're sometimes very ... explicit about what they'd like to do.'

'Trouble is, Mr Cochrane, she says you've actually done these things with her.'

96

Colin sighed. 'I know. That's what made these letters different. But it's a fantasy. Make-believe.'

'Is it? So when did you get this letter?'

'Yesterday morning. It was in my pigeon-hole at work, like all the others have been. That means, to save you time, that they were part of the internal system – they came through the office, not the post. That means that it was someone at the school who was sending them.'

'How many would you say you had received?'

'I don't know.' Colin shrugged. 'A dozen or so, altogether.'

'And you kept them.'

Colin frowned. 'No,' he said.

'You kept this one.'

'I meant to get rid of it. I just forgot about it.'

Finch looked totally disbelieving. 'You made this detour in order to avoid her, but you forgot you had her letter in your pocket?'

Colin rubbed his eyes. 'I remembered then, but I forgot when I got home.'

'Because you were so keen to get your running things into the machine?'

'I just wasn't thinking about it, that's all!'

'No,' said Finch. 'I'm sure you weren't.'

'I didn't go to meet her. I'm desperately sorry that she was murdered while she was waiting for me, but it wasn't my fault!'

'No? Before this one, you say you've had eleven other letters?'

'I wasn't counting. Something like that.'

Lloyd was merely listening to the conversation now, his chair tipped back. He took no part in it. He didn't seem terribly interested.

'And what did you do about it?'

Colin blinked. 'What was I supposed to do about it?' he asked.

'Did you show them to anyone? The headmaster? Another teacher? Your wife?'

'Would you show them to your wife?' Colin demanded.

Finch picked up the letter and looked at it for a moment. 'Yes,' he said. 'Yes, if there was no reason not to.'

'And what if she believed it?'

Finch grinned. 'That wouldn't be very likely,' he said. 'I'm not that much of an athlete either.'

'Oh, for—' Colin put his hands over his eyes. Erica had believed the one she had seen, whatever Finch's wife would or would not have done. But he wasn't about to tell them that.

He'd told them everything they needed to know. He'd told them about the letters, about the detour . . . He didn't have to discuss the ins and outs of his marriage with these people.

He let his hands slide down. 'If you start making enquiries into

97

this sort of thing, it becomes public knowledge,' he said. 'I didn't want that.'

Finch smiled.

'Look! Adolescents go through phases. Making a big fuss is no way to deal with it. I just ignored them.'

'By putting them in your pocket?'

'I didn't want to dispose of it at the school.'

'I think you met her, Mr Cochrane,' said Finch. 'I think you met her, like you've been doing for months. I don't think you were running through any industrial estate at nine-thirty. I think that's what you do all the other nights you go out training. But on Tuesdays, it's Natalie.'

'That's not true!' Colin shouted, jumping to his feet.

Lloyd's chair thumped down. 'Sit down,' he said quietly.

Colin had almost forgotten he was there. He took a deep breath, and sat down. 'I don't know how or why I'm here,' he said, his mouth dry. 'I knew Natalie from the drama group. I didn't even know her surname, not properly. I didn't know that she was the one who was writing those letters. I didn't go to meet her. I thought it was a harmless fantasy that whoever was writing those letters would grow out of.'

'Why did you keep this one?' asked Finch.

'I took it home to dispose of it,' Colin said. 'It was a fantasy. Nothing more. Do you think I'd forget I had it if it had been true?'

Finch picked up the letter again. 'She's got some imagination,' he said.

Colin looked at him with something approaching loathing. 'Some people do,' he said.

'Like you,' said Finch.

Colin had always thought that if you just lived your life without hurting other people, this sort of thing couldn't happen to you. But it could. He licked dry lips. 'I would like some tea,' he said, his voice quiet, a little hoarse from shouting. 'And I'd like to make a phone call.' He looked up at Lloyd. 'I can make a phone call even if I'm not under arrest, can I?' he asked.

'You can indeed,' said Lloyd. 'Sergeant Finch will show you where the telephone is.' He leant over to the machine. 'Interview suspended fifteen forty-five,' he said.

Kim heard the bell that signalled her release from school with mixed feelings.

She wanted to get out of here, to get home and away from everyone talking about Natalie, though it had helped, in a way. But her talk with the inspector had unsettled her. She felt as though she had betrayed someone, and she wasn't even sure who.

98

Hannah, she supposed, though that was silly. But she ought to call in on her way home, see if she was all right and tell her that she had had to break her promise. It wasn't as though Hannah had any reason to want Colin Cochrane's name kept out of it, except that she idolized him.

But Kim liked him too. He was good fun in the drama group, and she really couldn't imagine him having an affair with anyone, never mind a pupil. And she was quite certain that he could never have . . .

Her mind flinched away from the word. Poor Natalie. Yes, she had been right to tell the police everything she knew, even that Natalie might have very easily got in over her head with someone. And the inspector had said that rumours didn't mean anything, so she wasn't jumping to conclusions about who the someone was. Not officially, at any rate.

She had given her Dave Britten's name without a qualm, and he hadn't been seeing Natalie for months. But that was because she knew Dave, knew that he would never kill anyone. She had told the other policeman the other boys she knew had been with Natalie. So why did she feel so bad about Colin Cochrane? She hadn't said it was him, just that there were rumours. She had just said what Natalie had told her, and what she had heard.

But he was well known, and this sort of thing couldn't be kept quiet. If it got out, it would be in the papers, and if it wasn't him, if it wasn't true, then Hannah was right. It could ruin everything for him for no reason at all.

She wished she had talked to someone else first. Not Hannah – that was silly. Hannah was always going to take Colin Cochrane's side. She should have talked to someone who would have given her proper advice. Someone like Mr Murray.

She walked slowly in the afternoon sunshine to Hannah's house. She didn't want to tell her, but it would be easier just to get it over with. She would have to remember to phone her mum at the salon, so that she didn't worry if she got home first.

Judy hadn't been back in her office two minutes before Lloyd came in and sat, infuriatingly, on her desk.

'Cochrane's having tea and biscuits,' he said. 'Aren't we civilized? How did you get on?'

She told him what she had found out from the neighbours, but that was old news, apparently.

'His wife stuck to her story,' she said. 'She saw Natalie alive and well at nine fifty-five, and the dog found her dead fifteen or twenty minutes later.'

'Do you still believe her?' asked Lloyd.

Judy nodded. 'Yes,' she said. 'Though she was a bit thrown when

I told her that her husband didn't get back until twenty past ten.'

'He's got a thing about time-keeping,' said Lloyd. He got up and walked to the window. 'He doesn't want to give us a sample for DNA,' he said.

'Finch could be right,' said Judy doubtfully. 'She could be lying. She definitely thought Cochrane would be safe at home by ten, so it would have been an alibi, of sorts.' She swivelled round to look at him. 'I just don't think she *is* lying,' she said. 'If she was making it up, why would she say she saw her in such a specific spot, standing by the wall opposite the depot – why not just say she saw her on the Green itself?'

'I think you could both be right,' said Lloyd. 'You and Finch.'

Judy could feel a theory coming on.

'We said that something had to have happened between their being on intimate terms and her being murdered,' he said.

No, thought Judy. You said that. She still hadn't made her mind up about the order in which all the things that had happened to Natalie had occurred. But she was unobtrusively jotting down Lloyd's musings. They were almost always right.

'And that she was there with someone when Mrs Cochrane saw her,' Lloyd went on. 'Suppose that was Cochrane? He met her, as arranged. It was five to ten – time for him to be on his way home. But – as Finch said – Mrs C. turned up, checking up on him. He hears someone coming and makes himself scarce, but Natalia hangs around.'

Judy frowned. 'Why would she do that?' she asked.

Lloyd turned to face her. 'She can't run as fast as him,' he said.

'Isn't that ungrammatical?'

He smiled. 'It's . . . colloquial,' he said.

Got him, for once. Judy felt inordinately proud of that. 'All right,' she said. 'How does that make him angry?'

'That doesn't,' said Lloyd. 'But Natalia sees a way of forcing the issue. Mrs Cochrane follows the dog into the woods, and Natalia goes to where Cochrane's lying low, tells him who she's just seen, and starts making things difficult for him. He loses his temper . . .'

'Kim said that Natalie wouldn't do something like that,' said Judy.

'He goes off to the school to fetch his car, Mrs C. comes out of the wood, and Sherlock finds Natalia's body,' said Lloyd. 'He picks up the car, and gets back at twenty past. She has no idea that any of it had anything to do with her husband. She simply reports what she saw, and what she found.'

'Mm.'

Lloyd looked offended. 'Mm?' he repeated. 'Mm? Is that the best you can do? What's wrong with it?'

Judy thought about it. Most of it made sense. Perhaps it all did. What was wrong with it was something that she couldn't tick off neatly in her notebook, because it was what Tom Finch would call a gut feeling. She took refuge in facts.

'If he was leaving to go home at five to ten,' she said, 'and he's got a thing about being on time, then he obviously hadn't intended picking up his car. So why would he do that after he'd just murdered someone? Wouldn't he rather just get home?'

'Ah,' said Lloyd. 'No. Because he had blood on his tracksuit – why else was he washing it? He could run along a road without anyone seeing it, perhaps, but could he walk up his garden path in full view of the neighbours? No. So he needed the car, because that way he could get right into the house without being seen.'

That seemed like very quick thinking on the part of someone who had just done away with his lover, Judy thought.

'What about the tyre marks?' she asked.

'Coincidence,' he said. 'You said that yourself.'

She had. But why would someone be leaving there in a hurry? There had to be a reason. And murder was as good a reason as any.

Lloyd left to continue his interview with Cochrane, and Judy thought about what he had said. It did make sense, and if Cochrane was refusing to let them have a sample ...

But theories were dangerous. Everyone seemed to have one about this, and no two were alike. Judy flicked through her notebook, already full of statements and questions and comments. Very few facts.

Fact – Natalie had had sexual intercourse. Fact – Natalie had been murdered. Fact – presumably – Cochrane had been twenty minutes later than intended getting home. Fact – until proof to the contrary was found – Cochrane's missing twenty minutes were the ones in which Natalie had died.

But there, as far as she could see, the facts ended and the theories began. And both Lloyd's and Finch's depended on the one thing that had struck her as wrong. She didn't believe Natalie had written that letter.

The interview resumed at sixteen-thirty hours.

'Mr Cochrane,' Lloyd said. 'Before the refreshment break, you asked why you were here at all, so I'll tell you.'

Cochrane looked a little apprehensive.

'In a case like this, it's our job to suspect people who were known to the deceased – it's not often a complete stranger, you know. We have to talk to people who have a possible motive, people who had

101

the opportunity. And we have circumstantial evidence which points, for the moment, to you.'

'What circumstantial evidence?' challenged Cochrane. 'You've got a letter that could be from anyone. You've got a detective sergeant who doesn't believe any man washes his own clothes. You've got the fact that I chose not to run across the Green, which was a departure from the norm. You can't charge me with murder on those grounds. This whole thing is ridiculous. I had nothing to do with any of it.'

'We don't want to charge you with murder,' said Lloyd. 'But, like it or not, you have come under suspicion. Looked at another way, we have been told – and give considerable credence to the information – that Natalia was seeing a married man. A teacher. And we have a letter inviting you to meet a female person – who uses the school's internal mail system – on the Green on Tuesday evening, with the promise of sexual favours. The letter indicates an ongoing relationship with you.'

Cochrane sighed. 'I've told you. It's some sort of fantasy.'

'And Natalia was found murdered on Ash Road Green last night, at a time that you could very easily have been there. You were twenty minutes later than intended getting home, and you account for this by saying that you added half a mile to your run. You do see, do you, why we must regard you as a possible suspect?'

Lloyd looked out of the high window at the sunshine touching the trees that ringed the station car park. It was a shame to be cooped up in here on a glorious day like this, he thought. Even more of a shame for Cochrane if he was telling the truth, which, despite the scenario he had just outlined to Judy, Lloyd thought he was.

But there wasn't a policeman alive who hadn't learned the terrible lessons of others' mistakes, of other times when inconclusive circumstantial evidence was discounted because the interviewee seemed to be telling the truth.

It didn't go down very well with the families of victims if they found out that the murderer had been interviewed at the outset, and his less than perfect explanations accepted. Especially not if he went on to kill again, and that was clearly Judy's fear. But less than perfect explanations were often all that the innocent could provide; all the police could do was keep up the pressure.

He left the next bit to Finch. His aggressive style was odd, compared to Judy's, with which Lloyd was much more familiar. But it was time to let him have another go.

'Weren't you surprised to find that your wife wasn't at home when you got back last night?' Finch asked.

'You know that I thought she was,' said Cochrane. 'I thought she'd gone to bed.'

102

'Didn't you think it odd that your wife didn't call hello to you?'

'No.'

'But you were late, and that was very unusual, wasn't it?'

'I didn't think about it.'

'Do you always wash your own clothes?'

'No.'

'How often do you wash your own clothes?'

'Not often.'

'How often? How many times have you done it before?'

'A few. When Erica's been away, or sick, or something.'

'If she's in bed watching a film?'

'Not necessarily.'

'Which film?' Lloyd asked, interrupting the rapid questioning which Finch favoured in the hope that the interviewee would trip himself up. Lloyd preferred to let them talk, but that wasn't why he was interrupting, because Finch's method often worked.

It was the mention of a film that he was interested in. He had checked the TV listings yesterday; that was why he had gone out to that Godforsaken pub in the middle of nowhere. He'd already seen the only film that was on – he'd even checked the regions, to see if he was missing anything by not being at home.

'I don't know!' Cochrane said.

'A video?' asked Lloyd. 'Or a satellite channel?'

'No, we don't have satellite. Just some film on the television.'

'I think there was only one on,' said Lloyd. 'And it finished at ten.'

'That's right. That's why I said I'd be back at ten.'

'But your wife left the house at quarter to ten, according to her statement,' Lloyd went on. 'The film wouldn't have been finished by then. Why would she leave just before the end?'

'Perhaps she didn't watch it after all.'

'Perhaps not,' said Lloyd. 'But if she didn't watch it at all, why wouldn't she have taken the dog out earlier, when it was still light?'

'You'd have to ask her that!'

Lloyd went back to his contemplation of the sky. He very possibly would ask Mrs Cochrane about that. It was another little puzzle. And little puzzles always interested him. Finch was convinced that Mrs Cochrane wasn't being straight with them, and if she hadn't been watching a film at all, that might explain why.

'Do you deny that what is described in that letter ever took place between you and the writer?' demanded Finch.

'Of course I do!'

'Do you deny meeting Natalie Ouspensky on the Green at any time last night?'

'Last night or any other night! I was nowhere near the Green!'

103

Lloyd took a hand again. 'In that case, tell us where you were during the extra twenty minutes.' He turned to face him. 'Now.'

Cochrane sat for a moment without speaking, then took a breath. 'I was running,' he said. 'I never had anything to do with Natalie in my life. I don't know how I've got involved in any of this.'

'Then try to remember if anyone saw you on your run,' said Lloyd.

Cochrane shook his head. 'I run that way because it's quiet,' he said. 'There's very little traffic, and no pedestrians.'

'How convenient,' said Finch.

'There was a lorry in the industrial estate,' Cochrane said. 'The people with it saw me, but I don't know who they are, so what good does that do? They're probably not even local.'

Probably not. Lloyd sat down and looked across at Cochrane. 'In that case,' he said, 'your only hope is DNA, Mr Cochrane. And you have refused to let us do a test.'

'If it will get you off my back,' Cochrane said, 'you can do whatever you like.'

Theories. Lloyd felt that his always seemed to come to grief as soon as he uttered them; perhaps that was why he did utter them. 'Good,' he said, and he meant it. He just hoped that Cochrane really did understand what DNA was all about. 'We'll arrange for that to be done.'

Now, they would have to hope that the rest of the team had come up with something, because unless Cochrane was stupid – and he seemed to be far from that – he had not been with Natalie last night.

'Does this mean the interview's over?' asked Cochrane.

Lloyd nodded. 'Interview terminated seventeen twenty-five,' he said. 'Thank you for coming in, Mr Cochrane. We'll be in touch about the test.'

'And, just so that we're not in any doubt,' said Cochrane, as he rose, 'it will prove, beyond any doubt, that I was not with Natalie?'

'It'll prove you didn't have sex with her last night,' said Finch. 'Unless you did. It's as simple as that, really. It doesn't prove that these letters aren't true.'

Cochrane nodded. 'Last night will do,' he said.

Finch stood. 'I'll show you out,' he said.

Lloyd rubbed his eyes. It had been a long day; he'd had an early drive back to Stansfield, and had come straight to work. He needed some rest and recreation, but he had a briefing to attend, and lots more work to do before he could knock off for the day.

Judy was already in the murder room; Lloyd asked her to do the honours, and confessed that his theory had just been knocked on the head by Cochrane's changing his mind about the test.

The room filled up as he brought her up to date; she made notes, as ever, then called the murder team to order, waiting until the murmur of conversation finally ceased.

'The house-to-house has turned up two people who saw Natalie waiting at the bus stop at about quarter to nine,' she said. 'One of these people came back to get something she had forgotten, and Natalie was no longer at the bus stop. That was at ten to nine, but the bus was late and didn't get there until five to nine, according to the driver. He doesn't remember picking anyone up at that stop.'

'So she went off with someone?'

'Perhaps,' said Judy. 'Or started walking. We need to find anyone who saw her after that, but there's been no joy so far. She may have been offered a lift, and the tyre marks near the scene make that likely, so we need to find anyone who saw a car arriving at or leaving the service road at Ash Road Green. We've had no response to the radio appeal so far.'

'What about the ex-boyfriends? Are any of them possibilities?'

'The most recent is one David Britten, and you have his description. He isn't a strong suspect, and there is a possibility that the killer had access to a car, which makes any of the boys unlikely.'

'What about Cochrane?'

'Colin Cochrane has been interviewed – the chances are that he will be eliminated from the enquiry by DNA analysis. It looks as though Natalie may have been seeing a married man, but probably not Cochrane.'

'Does that mean we're back to square one?'

'Not quite. There's a strong probability that Natalie went to the Green from the bus stop. I'm hoping we might come up with something from the bingo club regulars tonight. We want to know if anyone saw her hanging around the Green from about nine. And ask them about cars. You have details of Colin Cochrane's car in front of you, but, once again, we are not regarding him as a prime suspect.'

Lloyd skipped the rest of the briefing, and went along the corridor to his office to try to shift some of the work that persisted in coming in whether there was a murder to be investigated or not.

The theory was that murder room personnel dropped everything but the murder; he was supposed to have someone who took over the day-to-day running of the department. In practice that wasn't possible, and it was after seven before he felt that he had made enough of a dent in it to be going on with, and turned his thoughts back to the matter in hand.

He had believed Cochrane, even before his decision to cooperate, if only because the man had no pat explanation for the things that had happened to him. He was bright; if he had murdered Natalia, he would have thought of something better than anonymous love letters, a last-minute decision to take a detour from his normal route, and refusing to say why the last half-mile apparently took him twenty minutes. Everything he had said had rung true; Cochrane struck him as someone who simply didn't know why this was happening, and resented it.

Time to pack it in, he told himself. Time to winkle Judy out of her office and have her to himself at last. He walked through the deserted CID room and knocked on her door, but she wasn't there; in the quiet building, he could hear her making calls from the murder room, and he resigned himself to a wait.

He picked up Judy's copy of the letter to Cochrane, and read it again for some sort of clue to the personality of the writer, but it was difficult, with the purple prose, to get hold of anything, except that it began and ended like a letter from a youngster, and the bit in between wasn't quite the same.

It was good to be back, he thought, sitting on the edge of Judy's desk. He had missed Judy, missed her professionally as well as personally. He had been sorely in need of her sheer common sense when he had been faced with his theoretical problems; he always allowed himself to be distracted by non-essentials.

Judy could cut away the wood and find the trees; she was the sort of person who should be in command, because she always was.

'What's wrong with the chairs?' she predictably asked, as she came in.

'Any thoughts on this?' he asked, waving the letter at her.

Judy nodded and took it from him, sitting behind her desk. 'You know what it reminds me of?' she said.

Lloyd twisted round to face her, and grinned. 'Modesty forbids,' he said.

She gave him one of her looks. 'It reminds me of those big fat books that women write,' she said. 'You know, sex and shopping sagas.'

Lloyd's eyebrows rose. 'I've never read one,' he said. 'Are they like that?'

'Very. I've tried to read a couple, but I tend to give up at about page sixty when I get to saturation point with descriptions of sexual gymnastics and interior decor.'

Lloyd took the letter from her and read it again. Like Tom, he had been rather too taken with the advanced sexual techniques it described to notice that it was a little too advanced, grammatically, for the average fifteen-year-old, given that he thought they were all entirely uneducated in the first place.

That was what had seemed different about the bits in between the sexy bits; the syntax, of all things.

106

'You think she copied it from a book?' he said.

Judy shrugged a little. 'I think she could have,' she said. 'But she could have written it from experience, I suppose, if she's good at that sort of thing.' She smiled a little sadly. 'I mean at writing about it,' she said. 'She seems to have got the knack of the practical side.' She took a breath, almost as though she had something to confess. 'I think she might have been quite good at spelling, if that's any indication,' she said, her voice light, trying and failing to sound cheerful. 'I wouldn't know about her literary ability.'

Lloyd heard then, for the first time, of Judy's original encounter with Natalia, when she had seen her on the bus home. It didn't have any bearing on the case, but it was unlike her not to have told him before now. It still upset her to think of it, obviously, so he didn't dwell on it.

'The punctuation and grammar are good,' he said. 'Even the bits in between the lurid passages. But they are more basic – the whole style is more basic. You're right. It does read as though it's copied from a book, but I think it's by someone who knew what she was doing.'

Judy looked a bit puzzled.

'You know – like when you paraphrase what it says in history books for an exam. So that you've not too obviously memorized it – alter the vocabulary slightly – bring it down to your perceived level.'

Judy smiled. 'I was more your maths and science type,' she said. 'You don't get many marks for making artful alterations to the text books.'

'But I didn't notice any books in the house,' Lloyd went on. 'In her room or anywhere else. The two usually go together – writing ability and reading.'

Judy thought about that. 'And we're saying that, either way, she has to have been a reader in order to have written that letter, aren't we?' she said.

'Are we?' They doubtless were. He didn't have her clarity of thought.

'Either these things happened, and she has a natural ability for kiss-and-tell memoirs – which you think means that she will almost certainly be a reader – or she copied it, or paraphrased it, in which case she had to know that she could. So she has to have read that sort of book, at least to the same extent as me.'

'Which is, you tell me, page sixty,' said Lloyd, and smiled. 'You should try reading real books – you'd enjoy them much more.' He slid off her desk. 'Well, we can find out about her reading habits from her mother,' he said. 'As to her writing ability . . . her English teacher can presumably tell us about that.'

107

Tom knocked, and put his head round the door. 'I'm off now, if I'm not needed any more tonight,' he said.

'Right, Tom,' said Judy. 'See you tomorrow.'

'Goodnight, guvs,' Tom said.

Lloyd returned his goodnight, smiling at the little joke, and turned back to Judy, plucking the pen from her hand as she sat making notes.

'What – ?' She looked up, exasperated with him, as she so often was. 'What are you doing?' she demanded.

'Closing you down. It's time to go home. Way past time.'

She took her pen back. 'But I want to try to track down her old English teacher,' she said. 'This Mr Murray's new – he won't know what Natalie was like at English. And I want to get some notes down before I forget them.'

'I said, it's time to go home,' Lloyd repeated. 'You will have written down anything important at the time.'

Judy sat back with a little gasp. 'You can still actually take me by surprise when you do that,' she said.

'Do what?' he asked, in injured innocence.

'Pull rank,' she said. 'If you wanted to talk to someone, you'd be dragging me round half the county until midnight. And we have to be able to prove that Natalie wrote this letter if we think Cochrane murdered her.'

'Agreed. But it doesn't have to be tonight. You can't get in touch with anyone until tomorrow morning anyway. And we are checking out Natalia's computer. If there's a copy of this letter on it, we won't need to bother any English teachers, will we?'

'Well, why didn't you tell me that?'

'I just did.'

Judy put away the few things she had on her desk. Lloyd's desk always looked as though a small dumper truck had tipped its load on it; he wished he could be more like her.

'Your place or mine?' he said.

'Yours,' she said immediately.

Lloyd pulled a face. 'Yours will have less dust,' he said.

'Well . . .' she said. 'Mine has probably got more dust, in fact.' She looked at him. 'If you tell anyone this, I'll kill you,' she said. 'But I've been keeping your flat hoovered and dusted.'

He smiled broadly. 'Why?' he asked.

'I didn't like to think of it being neglected for weeks,' she said.

Judy was very fond of his flat. He rather suspected she was fonder of it than she was of him. 'My place it is, then,' he said.

Hannah had known, really, that Kim would never be able to keep her mouth shut about Natalie, so it hadn't really come as a surprise.

Her mother had invited her to stay for tea, but neither of them had really been able to eat. Or talk, not properly.

'Did I hear you telling Hannah that the police had talked to you, Kim?' asked Hannah's mother, talking through the programme they were pretending to watch.

Kim nodded.

'Well, I hope you told them what they wanted to know,' she said.

Kim went pink.

'You knew her better than any of the other girls,' Mrs Lewis went on. 'Who she hung about with, that sort of thing. I know she had a bit of a reputation – I hope you told them that.'

'You're making it sound as if it was her own fault she got killed,' Hannah's father said, from the depths of the sofa.

'It very likely was,' said Mrs Lewis. 'Girls like that often come to sticky ends.'

It was her own fault, Hannah thought miserably, wishing with all her heart that they would change the subject.

'And the police need to know where to look. No one will be safe until whoever did that is behind bars.'

Hannah looked at Kim.

'I just answered their questions,' she said, half in reply to Mrs Lewis, half in defence of her treachery.

'Do they have any idea who did it?'

'I don't know,' said Kim.

'Mum! They've been asking Kim questions all day. She doesn't need you doing it as well.'

Her mother looked apologetic. 'Sorry. But I'm worried,' she said to Hannah. 'And I don't want you going out after dark until this man's caught, do you hear?' She looked at Kim. 'I'm sure your mum feels the same,' she said.

Kim nodded.

'Hannah's dad will run you home tonight anyway, whether it's dark or not.'

'Oh – it's all right. My mum said she'd come for me. She finishes at eight.' She looked at Hannah. 'Do you think you'll be coming to school tomorrow?' she asked.

The very idea made Hannah feel sick. 'I don't know,' she said.

'The doctor said you should,' said her mother. 'But I think you've got some sort of tummy bug. Maybe you should stay off another day.'

One more day. That wasn't going to be enough. He'd see her. He'd recognize her. But . . . if it had been two days, and she hadn't been to the police, surely he would realize that she wasn't going to tell on him?

But she would much rather not put it to the test.

109

Chapter Eight

Tom drove home, windows open in the soft summer evening, his head still buzzing with questions and answers.

His theory had bitten the dust good and proper now that Cochrane was taking the DNA test in the absolute belief – knowledge, even – that it would clear him. But, he thought, there was that letter, and Cochrane's reluctance to say what he was doing during the twenty minutes in which Natalie died. He hadn't had sex with her, but *someone* had . . . supposing that was *why* she died?

Judy was getting a blood sample from the boy that Natalie had been going out with immediately prior to Cochrane; she said that she had seen Natalie with him on the bus, and that the relationship was still friendly.

Perhaps it had never stopped being friendly, Tom thought. Natalie had never been slow in coming across, by all accounts, and if Natalie had been expecting Cochrane at nine, she might have given up on him. If she ran across this Dave Britten, she might well have had a quick jump with him instead, going on her reputation.

But Cochrane *had* turned up. He had seen what she was up to, the boy had taken off, and Cochrane had bashed Natalie's head against the concrete in a rage. Then he had strangled her, and gone up to the school to get his car.

And if Colin Cochrane had killed Natalie, he might wish he hadn't been so cooperative about the DNA test, because Natalie's killer would have had only to graze a hand on that concrete, just left enough blood or tissue for a sample – and they could work with minute samples – for them to have a DNA fingerprint. Saliva, hair. Anything.

He doubted that Cochrane knew that. Of course, they hadn't heard yet if there had been anything found at the scene that didn't belong to Natalie, but it was always a possibility on a close contact killing.

And what if Erica Cochrane *had* watched that film? What if she hadn't left home at quarter to ten? What if she was there when her husband got in at twenty past?

His tracksuit would be covered in whatever it was he was so keen to wash off; he has no option, and confesses all to his missus, who bungs his stuff in the machine and works out how to give him an alibi.

She phones the police from the house, says she's found a body, and *then* she takes the dog to the Green, thinking – as people quite often did – that if she reported the murder then she wouldn't come under suspicion, and neither would hubby.

But then she had tried to be too clever. Given time to think, time to calm down, she had thought of saying she had seen the girl alive at five to ten, believing that Cochrane could say that he was home at ten, having picked the car up from the school. Except that she didn't know that the next door neighbours had seen him come home; that had given her a jolt, by all accounts, when Judy had told her.

Of course, Cochrane was doing a very good impression of an innocent man. But then, thought Tom, he was in the drama group.

Kim was being driven home, her mother chattering as she always did, as she had to the Lewises when she had called for her on her way home from work. It was one of the evenings that she worked for the hair salon in the supermarket, and she had heard from a customer that Colin Cochrane had been taken away by the police that afternoon.

Hannah's mum had been horrified. He was such a nice-looking man, who would believe that he would do something like that, it just went to show that you never knew.

'Well,' Kim's mum had said, 'it seems there's been talk about him and one of the pupils – I hadn't heard that, but that's what they were saying.'

They didn't *know* it was Natalie, Kim thought miserably. They didn't even know it was anyone. It was just gossip, that was all. The inspector had said so. And Mrs Lewis had assumed straight away that he must have done it, just because the police were questioning him.

But they *were* questioning him, and Kim knew why.

'Are you all right, love?' her mum asked. 'You're very quiet.'

'Yes,' she said.

'Soon be home. Hannah's not looking at all well, is she? I think her mum must be right. She must have some sort of bug.'

Her mother drew up outside the house, where Kim's Auntie Janice was keeping an eye on her little brother. Kim braced herself for more questions as soon as she got in. People thought it would be good for her to talk about it.

'Listen, love,' said her mother. 'I know nothing can make this any easier, but – well, if you want, we could go away for a few days. Janice says she'll stay with Mark. It might help to take your mind off it.'

111

Her mum couldn't afford to go away for a few days. Kim smiled. 'I'm all right,' she said.

'Well, if you want to, you just tell me and we'll go. I'll explain to the school.'

'I'll be fine,' said Kim. 'Honestly.'

'Good God, you've stocked the fridge!' came the startled voice from the kitchen.

Judy smiled. 'Well, I haven't eaten for seven weeks,' she called back.

He came into the living room. 'Does this mean I've got to make you dinner?' he said.

'Oh, I don't know.' She walked over to him. 'I'd be quite prepared to skip it.' She made to kiss him, but he pulled away from her. 'What's the matter?' she asked.

'Did you skip lunch?' he demanded.

'Well – yes. I was busy at the school. And I could talk to the teachers at lunchtime without causing too much disruption.'

'Did you have breakfast?'

'Er . . . no,' she said guiltily. 'Not really. I had some toast. I'd arranged for the garage to look at my car first thing, you see, so I had to get the bus into Stansfield early, and—'

'When did you last eat?'

'I had a packet of crisps at the school – oh, and some biscuits.'

'It's half past seven,' he said, and looked at her, shaking his head. 'I'll make something to eat.'

She followed him out into the hallway and into the tiny kitchen.

'How do you think you got on at Bramshill?' she asked, sitting at the kitchen table.

'I don't think I actually did myself any harm,' he said, as he pulled things out of the fridge. 'As to how much good . . .' He shrugged.

She must have got the right sort of food; not as simple a job as it might seem where Lloyd was concerned. That was a relief, anyway.

'It'll have helped,' said Judy, firmly. 'It's bound to. But even if they do away with the rank, that doesn't mean that they do away with the holder,' she pointed out.

'They do if the holder has you coming up behind him,' he said, then ducked away from any retribution.

'That had better be a joke,' she said.

'Not really.' He turned. 'When euphemisms like "early severance exercise" start being bandied about, they don't intend having over-paid inspectors on the books when they've got ones already there who can do the job just as effectively.'

'But there would still be the same amount of work,' Judy argued. 'We're stretched as it is. As soon as something major like this happens, we're seriously undermanned. They can't get rid of people wholesale.'

'Perhaps not,' said Lloyd. 'But if they do have to choose between us, they'll choose you. So would I. You're younger, for a start. So I wasn't exactly joking. And Sheehy's no joke anyway,' he said.

Judy knew that. 'At least they threw out the fixed-term contract idea,' she said.

'Do you remember the Lord Chamberlain?' Lloyd asked.

She didn't, not really. She knew he was some sort of Court official, but she wasn't deeply into royalty and its servants.

'Stage entertainments used to be censored,' Lloyd said.

'Oh, yes, I know what you mean. They had to be approved by the Lord Chamberlain, isn't that it?' It seemed like a very rapid change of subject.

'Correct,' said Lloyd.

He had somehow managed to get two saucepans and a frying pan on the go already. She would still have been looking in the fridge, and deciding to go out for a pizza. Judy realized that she was very hungry, as a wonderfully appetizing smell began to fill the little kitchen.

'And if you wanted to get something a bit near the knuckle past him,' Lloyd went on, 'you put something really outrageous before it in the script. He was so eager to blue-pencil the shocker that he missed the one that came after it.'

'You think the Sheehy Report worked it that way?'

'I think everyone works everything that way these days. Say you're going to destroy all the dogs on the dangerous breeds list, then commute it to muzzle-wearing. Instant acquiescence. No one protests, no one petitions – at least they're not putting them all down, they say. We won that one, they say. Did we hell – we just got conned.'

She caught his hand. 'You'll be all right,' she said. 'I'd back you against the system any day. And Bartonshire's got room for both of us, I'm sure.'

He sat down at the table with her. 'Malworth's Superintendent is due to retire this year some time,' he said. 'I thought I'd go for it. Strike while the iron's hot, and all that.'

Judy tensed up. She knew what was coming next, and she didn't want to discuss that of all things on his first night back.

'If I got it,' he said, 'I'd want a base in Malworth, and your flat's the obvious choice.'

She shook her head. 'It wouldn't work,' she said.

'I'm not talking about marriage!' He leant back and attended to the meal as he spoke. 'We might as well,' he said. 'It's time we put it on an official footing, anyway.'

'No, Lloyd,' she said.

'Are you saying you would make me keep on this flat even if we were sharing yours?' He turned back to face her.

'I'm saying I would make you keep on *living* in this flat,' she said steadily.

'Why, Judy?' he asked. 'Why won't you even consider our living together on a normal, everyday basis like other people?'

She looked at him. 'Because,' she said, 'if this turns into a row, I can just get up and leave.'

He sighed. 'It's not going to turn into a row,' he said. 'I haven't even applied for the job, never mind got it.' He got up, and took warm plates from the oven.

She always forgot to put plates in to heat when she did the cooking. It drove Lloyd into a frenzy. She addressed his backview as he dished up the meal. 'You'll get it,' she said. 'If you really want it. But I don't believe you do.'

He paused for a second in what he was doing, then turned and grinned at her. 'I'd run a mile from Malworth,' he said. 'Besides, I don't think the uniform would suit me.'

Judy relaxed at last. She had been ninety-nine per cent sure that it was a bluff, but the one per cent uncertainty had made for very thin ice to skate on. Still, she must be getting better at detecting Lloyd's play-acting. That was something.

'I just thought I'd see if a seven-week absence had made your heart grow any fonder,' he said, putting down the food, getting knives and forks.

She looked at him. 'It couldn't,' she said. 'And you know it.'

He just raised an eyebrow, and sat down. 'Eat,' he said.

She did. Lloyd opened a bottle of wine from the fridge, and there they were, eating a meal it would have taken her a day to think about, and hours to prepare for, and too long to cook, so nothing would have been quite the way it should have been. It had taken him twenty minutes, and everything was lovely.

After the meal, they retired with their tiny cups of high-octane coffee to the sitting room and the sofa, where Judy kicked off her shoes and curled up beside Lloyd. 'I missed you very much,' she said, and kissed him, to absolutely no response.

'I understood from our telephone conversation that you had managed perfectly well without me,' he said, in a mock huff, picking up his coffee, taking a sip.

'I managed perfectly well without you, and I missed you very much.' She kissed him again. His only response was to hold his cup out of the way.

'When?' he asked, taking another drink.

She laughed. 'What do you mean, when?'

114

'When did you miss me?' He finished his coffee in one final gulp, putting down the still steaming cup. 'In the morning, at night, at home, at work? When?'

'All the time,' she said, and kissed him again.

This time he didn't ignore her. And she hadn't just missed him; she had been lonely. Lloyd was her best friend, her boss, her lover, even her cook now and again, as tonight. She had felt as if everyone she knew had deserted her. She had chided herself for feeling like that; he was only going to be away for a few weeks, she had known he was coming back, and she had even seen him, albeit fleetingly, on the weekends he could get away.

It was ridiculous, she had told herself, to feel somehow bereft. What about women whose men went to sea for months at a time? They didn't go into a decline, did they?

But then, neither had she. She had enjoyed taking charge at work, and she hadn't been sitting twiddling her thumbs at home, either. She had her own life, her own interests, which rarely included Lloyd. It wasn't as if they ever went out much together – come to that, they quite often didn't even see one another after work.

But always, wherever she was, whatever she was doing, she had been aware of there being something missing, and she had felt very alone. She was making up for all that now, as she welcomed him home.

He sneaked a look at his watch behind her back.

She pulled away from him. 'Am I boring you?' she asked.

He grinned.

'Is there a film on or something?'

He looked hurt. 'Would I be bothering with some old film on my welcome home night?' he said.

'Sorry,' she said.

'I'm recording it,' he said, and grinned as she aimed a smack at him. He disentangled himself from her and stood up.

She put out a hand for assistance, but he shook his head. 'No,' he said. 'You wait there.'

'I rather hoped I might be coming with you,' she said.

'Just popping into the kitchen. Shan't be a tick.'

He was up to something. She drank her cool coffee, and thought that it perhaps tasted less like tar when it was hot.

'Here we are,' he said, coming back in with a bottle of champagne and two glasses.

She smiled. 'I should send you away more often,' she said.

'Ah, this isn't a homecoming celebration,' he said, and handed her the glasses to hold while he opened the bottle with a satisfying pop, and didn't spill a single drop. He poured some into the glasses, stopping at exactly the right moment for the froth to rise to the top without going over, then touched her glass with his.

'Happy anniversary,' he said, just as she took her first sip.

She almost choked. Oh, my God. What had she forgotten now? 'What?' she said. 'Anniversary? Which anniversary?' They had met in February, more years ago than she was now prepared to count, but it had been February. She knew that.

'The seventh,' he said solemnly.

Her eyes widened. 'Have we celebrated the other six?' she asked.

'No,' he said.

'Thank God for that. I thought my memory had finally gone altogether.' She drank some champagne while she thought about it, and he topped up her glass.

'Why haven't we celebrated the other six?' she asked, deeply suspicious of this so-called anniversary.

'The first two seemed inappropriate, as you were still living with your husband at the time,' he said.

A little dig at her reluctance to end her already dead marriage, of course.

'And the next two didn't seem like landmarks, really. The fifth would have been, but you were away that time.'

She had been on the Junior Command course two years ago, but she had been kept busy, so there hadn't been too much time to brood. She had missed him; just not as acutely as this time.

'Six seemed a silly number to celebrate,' said Lloyd. 'I thought I was going to miss it this year too, but here we are.'

What was this anniversary? She had come to Stansfield seven years ago, but that had been in April. 'Anniversary of what?' she asked, giving up.

'Of the time you finally let me have my wicked way with you,' he said, and glanced at his watch again. 'Your actual words were that it might not solve anything, but what the hell – or some tender, romantic tosh like that – and they were uttered on Monday the seventh of September, seven years ago.' He counted down. 'To the minute,' he said. 'Twenty-one fifteen hours.'

She nodded, dumbstruck. She definitely hadn't forgotten the occasion. And it had indeed been early September, she had remembered that. But not the date, and certainly not the time. Only Lloyd would have made a mental note; only Lloyd would remember to remember.

'So why is the seventh anniversary a landmark?' she asked.

'The seven-year itch,' he said. 'I haven't got it.'

She smiled. 'Neither have I,' she said.

116

'So let's celebrate,' he said. 'We can take the champagne with us.'

Colin pushed his empty glass over the bar. 'Another one in there, please,' he said.

The young barman picked up the glass, his face doubtful. 'You're not driving, are you, sir?' he asked.

'Resident,' said Colin.

'Sorry,' said the barman, cheerfully getting another. 'But we've been told to check.'

He stood at the bar, drinking whisky and soda, wondering what had become of his life.

'Colin.'

He looked up to see Patrick Murray, and raised his glass to him in a sardonic toast. 'Top of the evening to you, Patrick,' he said. 'How did you know I was here?'

'I didn't. This is my local.'

Oh yes. Patrick lived in the town centre, in one of those maisonettes that he and Erica had looked at.

'How is everything?' asked Patrick.

'Fine,' said Colin. 'Everything's fine. The police are accusing me of murder, my wife's accusing me of infidelity with a minor . . . Everything's fine.'

Patrick glanced at the interested barman, and took his arm. 'Let's sit over there,' he said, steering him to a more private corner of the sparsely peopled lounge bar of the Derbyshire.

Colin sat down heavily in an easy chair, and looked at Patrick, who bent his head close, speaking in a low voice.

'The police don't really think you had anything to do with this, do they?' he asked. 'Everyone's saying that they took you in for questioning this afternoon.'

'Yes,' said Colin, nodding. 'Yes. They . . . they think I was with her. Last night.'

'What makes them think that?' asked Patrick.

Colin shook his head and took another gulp of his drink before he launched into explanations. 'Natalie had a fantasy,' he said. 'About me. Unfortunately . . .' He smiled, pleased to have got the word out; it hadn't been very easy, which was odd, because he'd only had two drinks, not counting this one. 'Unfortunately,' he said again, with bravura, 'she wrote it down.' He tossed back what was left of his whisky.

Patrick picked up his empty glass. 'Same again?' he asked, and went to the bar without waiting for a reply, returning with a whisky for Colin and a half pint of beer.

Colin took his drink from Patrick with a morose nod of thanks.

117

'They've taken my clothes, my shoes, my blood, even . . . They think I killed her,' he said.

'Ah, you're used to all that,' said Patrick.

Colin frowned. 'What?'

'They do random testing after races, don't they? For drugs? That's not because they think you're taking drugs, it's because they have to prove you're not.'

'I'd want my money back if I had been,' muttered Colin.

'That's more like it,' laughed Patrick. 'It's the same thing with the police. If they've found this . . . whatever it was that Natalie wrote, they've got to prove that you had nothing to—' He broke off. 'What the hell *did* she write?' he asked. 'A diary?'

Colin shook his head. 'Letters.'

'Letters?' repeated Patrick, baffled. 'Saying what?' he asked.

'Describing what we'd done together.'

Patrick whistled. 'No wonder you're in the shit,' he said.

'But we hadn't,' said Colin. 'It's not true.'

Patrick sat back and grinned. 'That's your story and you're sticking to it?' he said.

'No,' said Colin, wearily. 'I never touched the girl. And by next week I'll be able to prove to Erica that she's wrong. Because whoever was with Natalie last night, it wasn't me, and this test will prove that.'

'Then you've nothing to worry about, have you? It's all a mistake, and they'll realize that.'

'I've got Erica to worry about.' Colin stared into his drink, then lifted his eyes to Patrick. 'She thinks I was having an affair with Natalie. That's why I'm staying here. I can't go home to all that suspicion – you don't know what it's like.'

Patrick smiled. 'I've a fair idea,' he said, and sipped his cold beer. 'What makes her think that?' he asked.

'I don't know. She won't tell me.' He took a gulp of his drink as a full stop. 'The police made her think it. I think.'

Patrick smiled. 'Sure, it's not every man can produce evidence that he wasn't with another woman,' he said. 'You'll be in the clear, then, won't you?'

'I don't know,' said Colin.

'What's that supposed to mean?'

'It'll only prove I wasn't with her last night,' said Colin. 'It won't prove that those letters weren't true. Sergeant Finch was quick to point that out. They know that Natalie was seeing a married man. A teacher.' It was quite difficult getting the consonants not to stick to one another, he found. 'They think that was me, whether I was with her last night or not.'

'Ah,' said Patrick. 'I see.'

118

Colin frowned. 'What do you see?' he asked.

'You had been going with her, is that it?' asked Patrick. 'But it was over, and you were with someone else last night?'

Oh, God. 'No,' said Colin. 'I've not been seeing her or anyone else.'

'Then what the hell have you been doing?'

'When?' asked Colin, a little confused now.

'When you go out. Erica doesn't believe you've been running. She says you've lost interest in her. And you weren't where you should have been last night, were you?'

'No,' Colin sighed.

'That adds up to another woman,' said Patrick. 'And if that's what you were doing last night, tell the police, for Christ's sake – you can't afford to be a gentleman. You're mixed up in a murder enquiry.'

Colin looked at him. It was getting hard to focus, for some reason. Tiredness, he supposed. 'There isn't another woman,' he said. 'I *have* been running. There's nothing . . . nothing sinister about it. I've just been running.'

'Pull the other one,' said Patrick.

'Why does no one believe me?'

'Because,' said Patrick, 'you've been running all your life. But it's only this year that that's meant leaving Erica alone for hours on end, and not wanting to have anything to do with her when you did condescend to go home.'

Colin frowned. 'Why has Erica been telling you all this?' he asked. 'Are you—?'

'No!' said Patrick, offended. 'What do you take me for, for Christ's sake? She just needed someone to talk to, that's all.' He leant closer. 'Look,' he said, 'I'd be the last person to preach to you. But you have to box a bit clever. Erica's found out. All right, she's got the wrong end of the stick about last night, because you weren't with Natalie, but you can't blame her for that, can you? You have to . . .' He moved his shoulders a little. 'Duck and weave a bit,' he said. 'Finish it with this one, for one thing.'

Colin groaned. There was no getting through to him, and he might as well talk in language that Patrick understood. 'It is finished,' he said tiredly.

'Tell her that,' Patrick said. 'Tell Erica that.' He got up. 'But not until you've got your proof that you weren't with Natalie last night.' He smiled. 'Until then, I should just lie low, if I were you. Take it from one who's played away more than a few times. A couple of days to let everything cool down is just what you need – and proving that she was wrong about Natalie gives you a head start in the moral indignation stakes. But if you'll take my advice, you'll be straight with her about this one. Believe me – it works.'

It was genuine advice. This was Patrick trying to help. Colin looked up at him and smiled. 'Thanks, Patrick,' he said. 'Thanks for coming.'

'See you, Col,' said Patrick, patting his shoulder as he went.

Colin finished his whisky and called to the barman for another. Drinking was a rare pursuit; he was no fitness freak, but you couldn't run at his level and knock back too much of the hard stuff. Tonight, he could, because it was over.

Trust Patrick only to be able to think in terms of another woman. The effect on his marriage had been the same, though, as Patrick had pointed out.

He had been deluding himself, making himself ill, trying to prove everyone wrong. He was over the hill, but there were much worse hills. A very lucrative career awaited him in show business. Someone had even asked him if he would play himself in an episode of some sitcom. And he'd been offered a part in a pantomime, of all things.

All right, his fame might last the fabled fifteen minutes, but the advertising people paid very silly money to so-called celebrities during those fifteen minutes, and he was one. He could make certain of a secure financial future if it only lasted a couple of years.

Or he could carry on teaching. Or he could go back to teaching, once the public had tired of him and moved on to someone else. His career problems would be other people's dreams.

So if everything was so rosy, why was he sitting here getting drunk? He knew why. Because a man's wife ought to take his side.

Because he wasn't jumping on her every night in life, because she had seen one letter from a besotted teenager, because she had listened to one over-zealous cop, Erica had leapt to the conclusion that he had been with Natalie. That wasn't right. It was all wrong.

So he would just have another drink instead of thinking about it. He drained his glass and went to the bar.

'Another,' he said. 'Make this one a double.'

'They're all doubles,' said the barman.

'Have that on me,' said a voice. 'And I'll have the same, whatever it is.'

Colin looked up to see a bearded man whom he had never seen before in his life.

'You will have a drink with me, won't you, Mr Cochrane?' he said. 'Will Marlow, *Stansfield Courier*.'

'Yes, all right,' said Colin. He had had twice as much to drink as he had thought he'd had, but it hadn't really affected him. He could handle a local reporter, and he wanted company. 'Why not?'

Marlow was a very big tipper, he noticed, as the barman pocketed a note of substantial denomination. But it was none of his business what Mr Marlow did with his money.

'You again.'

Patrick shrugged. 'I wanted to see how you were,' he said.

'You saw how I was at lunchtime,' said Erica.

'Your husband hadn't been taken in for questioning at lunchtime. I was worried about you.'

Erica stiffened. 'You know about that?'

Patrick smiled a little. 'Everyone knows about that,' he said. 'It was Victoria who told me. It's all over the town. Colin's famous, remember.'

Didn't she know it? If he wasn't on television, silly little girls wouldn't throw themselves at him, and they wouldn't be in this mess.

'Do I get to come in?'

She sighed. 'Not if you're going to make a pass at me,' she said. 'I don't need that on top of everything else.' It was a lie; she felt she probably needed that more than she ever had. The warmth and protection of someone's arms would be very welcome indeed.

But not Patrick's, however attractive he could be. Colin was a friend of Patrick's; that was what had stopped her in the past, and to let it happen now would be extreme folly, whatever Colin had done.

'No passes,' he said. 'You will remain a nut I failed to crack.' He smiled.

'Very romantic. Come in, then. Give the neighbours something else to talk about.'

'I'm here on Victoria's orders,' he said. 'She wanted to let you know that we're here if you need us.' He walked in, and Sherry, as ever, trotted over to him, tail wagging.

'Hello, boy,' he said. 'Are you looking after your mistress?'

Erica closed the door. 'Are you looking after yours?' she asked.

Patrick looked up quickly. 'What does that mean?' he asked.

'You told me not to land you in it with Victoria,' she said. 'I presume you were somewhere you shouldn't have been last night.'

He smiled and sat down, complete with adoring dog, who leant against his legs. 'Ah, well,' he said. 'You know me. Nothing heavy, though – not a mistress. Just a friend.'

Erica shook her head. 'Do you want a drink?' she asked.

'No, thanks. And I honestly did come to see how you are,' he said. 'And Colin. What did the police want with him?'

Erica poured herself a gin and tonic. 'I really don't know,' she said.

'He's not still at the police station, is he?' asked Patrick, horrified.

'I don't know that either.' She looked at Patrick's worried face, and relented. He did seem to have come to offer moral support.

121

'Colin won't be coming back tonight, whether they let him go or not,' she said. 'I don't know if he's ever coming back.'

Patrick obviously didn't know which piece of information to deal with first. 'What do you mean, whether they let him go or not?' he said. 'And why isn't he coming back? Have you two had some sort of row? Surely they don't think he had anything to do with it?'

The poor man didn't know where to start with the questions. But she could give him some answers. She wanted to; she needed someone to talk to. Patrick, incorrigible womanizer that he was, was easy to talk to; she had spent all summer unburdening herself to him.

'He's gone to a hotel,' she said. 'I think they will have let him go. They have to, surely? He didn't kill Natalie.'

Patrick frowned. 'Do they think he did?' he asked.

She sat down and took a sip of her drink before she spoke. 'I think,' she said slowly, 'that Colin was having an affair with Natalie. I don't know what the police wanted with him, but I expect they've found out. It was nothing I said,' she added quickly, in case Patrick thought that.

'No, of course not,' he said, absently playing with Sherry's ear. 'I know you thought he'd been seeing someone, but . . .' He shook his head. 'Is that what the row was about?' he asked gently.

She shrugged. 'I don't even know if you'd call it a row,' she said. 'I know what he's been doing, and he won't admit it. He insists he's been training. His coach knows nothing about it.'

Patrick smiled suddenly. 'Thank God you're not *my* wife,' he said.

'And if he really was running the way he says he is, it would be wrong. It isn't what you're supposed to do,' said Erica. 'I told you there was someone else. You kept saying I was wrong.'

'Sure, you only got married in March,' said Patrick, and tickled the dog, who rolled over. 'Even I took a bit longer than that to start looking round. And I wasn't married to you.'

'Patrick,' she warned.

He smiled. 'Ah, you can't blame a man for trying,' he said. 'Especially when you've just told him your old man's away for the night.'

She had, hadn't she? She looked at him. 'You promised,' she said.

'All right, let's talk about you. How did you find out it was Natalie?' he asked.

Erica shook her head. 'It doesn't matter,' she said. 'I just know it was. But Colin didn't kill her, Patrick,' she said.

'No, of course not,' said Patrick. 'Colin couldn't hurt a fly, I know that.' He stopped tickling the dog, who whimpered. 'You don't think the police really believe he did, do you?' he asked.

Erica shrugged. 'They might,' she said. 'They took his running things away.' She took another drink. 'But even if they do, I don't see how they can prove it, because he didn't.'

Patrick sat back. 'I'll do anything I can to help,' he said. 'I don't know if there is anything, but if you think of something, just say the word.'

He meant it. He would probably say that Colin was with him, and get his lady friend to agree, if she asked him to. But she couldn't ask him to do anything like that. She smiled. 'Thank you,' she said.

'I could give you a cuddle, which you look as though you need,' he said. He got up with some difficulty, as Sherry was extremely reluctant to get off his feet, and almost fell, landing beside her on the sofa. 'That was supposed to be smooth,' he said, laughing. 'Come here and have a hug.'

She allowed herself to be cradled in his arms.

'You know,' he said, 'if that husband of yours doesn't want you, then he's a fool.'

He kissed her then, like he had at lunchtime, and she didn't try to stop him this time either. Little kisses, on her eyes, on her cheekbones, on the corner of her mouth. But this time no one came to interrupt them, and affection turned to arousal, the kisses from friendly to frantic.

She couldn't, she mustn't, let it happen. She broke away. 'You said you wouldn't do this,' she said.

He moved away from her immediately, holding up his hands in surrender. 'Sorry,' he said.

It had been a long time since anyone had wanted her so much; it hadn't been easy to call a halt. Erica stood up and got her clothes back into a semblance of order, then looked at him. 'I think you should go,' she said.

'Ah, you're not offended, are you?' he asked, looking up at her.

She shook her head. She wasn't offended.

'I could stay if you like,' he said. 'Just for the crack. No funny business, hanky-panky, jiggery-pokery, not if you don't want it.' He grinned. 'Mind, I'm a chronic liar,' he added.

She laughed, and the tension was broken. She was glad. She hadn't meant to hurt his feelings.

'Go home to Victoria,' she said.

As soon as he had gone, she wished she had let him stay.

Patrick went home to Victoria, as advised, to find her already in bed.

'Where have you been?' she asked, when he went up. 'And don't lie to me, Patrick.'

'With Colin,' he said. 'He's in a bad way. The police think he had something to do with that little girl, and so, it seems, does Erica.'

'Was she there?'

'No,' said Patrick, getting undressed. 'Colin's staying at the Derbyshire.'

She raised her eyebrows. 'So Erica was on her own, was she? And you didn't pop round to see how she was?'

'No,' he said. 'I was with Colin. I left him getting drunk.'

He told her enough of what Colin had said to remove some of the doubt about where he had been, but distrust still hung in the air. He reached for her as soon as she put out the bedside lamp; he needed the release after his aborted seduction of Erica, and, besides, it helped to allay suspicion still further. But his mind was on other things.

He had about four days, according to Colin. Four days in which it was essential to get Erica on his side. She hadn't told Colin what she had seen, that much was obvious. Colin had no idea why she thought he'd been with Natalie last night – he was blaming the police for putting the idea into her head.

Thank God for the Cochranes' crumbling relationship, their chronic lack of communication; that was all he could say. It had bought him time, and he desperately needed that. Erica wouldn't be a problem – it was just a question of how best to achieve his ends, how to make certain of her.

Not like this, he thought, even if she was panting for it. She would feel guilty afterwards, and she would blame him. That was the last thing he needed; she had to *want* to help him, and that meant making a clean breast of everything before Colin came waving his proof at her.

So, friendship had to be the key; she needed a friend right now, even a flawed friend. She was on her own, with rumours and accusations flying round about her husband. And they were friends; hadn't he respected her wishes and behaved like a perfect gentleman once she had said a final no?

He could have pushed it; this could just as easily be Erica. But that would have been a mistake. Her rejection of him had been a good thing, in a way.

Natalie's letters. Were they a good or a bad thing? She hadn't written to him, he was glad to say, but maybe the compromising letters started once you'd finished with her. He could imagine her doing something like that to get her own back. They had to be a good thing as far as he was concerned, really, because the police would think that they had crossed this married teacher that they knew about off their list.

That girl who saw him on the Green obviously hadn't said anything yet. It looked as though she intended keeping quiet, or she would have told the police, surely. She must just be keeping well out of it, sensible girl.

It was the luck of the Irish, it had to be, because not one potential witness had come forward, despite all the appeals on the local radio.

His body worked vigorously, his mind on all the pitfalls he'd avoided, all the close shaves. It was stimulating, living this close to the edge. Because he was going to be all right. He was. His enjoyable life wasn't going to be ruined by any promiscuous ... little ... slut like Natalie.

He rolled away from Victoria, breathing hard. He was going to be all right.

'In answer to your earlier question,' Lloyd said, breaking the long, golden silence. 'No. You're not boring me.'

Judy sat up, and smiled. 'I needed you,' she said simply, and kissed him.

It was patently true, but he chose to affect disbelief. 'Oh, sure,' he said. 'That's why you're so desperate to move in with me. Because you need me so much.'

'You know I do,' she said, lying back beside him.

'That's what you said before. But I don't know you do, do I?' He sat up then, and looked down at her. 'If I said that either we live together or we call it a day, what would you do?' he asked.

'I'd move in with you,' she said promptly. 'But you wouldn't issue an ultimatum like that,' she added.

'Wouldn't I? What makes you so sure about that?'

She clasped her hands behind his neck. 'Because you're too unselfish.'

He took her hands away, held them. 'And you're too selfish,' he said.

'I know.' She looked penitent.

'One day,' he said, 'I might have had enough of being unselfish, and then where will you be?' He pulled her up to him, and held her close to him, triumphantly glad that she wasn't some WCI from Northumbria.

But he wanted it to be like this all the time, and he never lost an opportunity to remind her of his ultimate objective. Her answer was that it wouldn't *be* like this all the time, as if he didn't know that. But he wanted that; he wanted to go to bed with her simply in order to sleep, he wanted them to grow used to one another.

'What would you do then?' he whispered mischievously in her ear. 'If one day you discovered that I had had enough, and had just upped and gone?'

She didn't answer.

'You take me for granted,' he said. 'And you'll miss me when I've gone – you see if you don't.'

'Don't even say it,' she said, her voice indistinct.

Startled, he pulled back to look at her. 'Judy?' he said. 'I wasn't being—' He broke off. There were tears in her eyes. *Tears.*

'Please,' she said, as they fell. 'Please, don't even say it.'

He had never even seen Judy cry, and now he had *made* her cry, when that was the very last thing he had meant to do.

'I couldn't bear it if you left me,' she said.

He stared at her, at cool, capable, together Judy, truly distressed by a throwaway remark that had meant nothing, and he didn't know what to do, except put his arms round her, and hug her to him.

'We'll do anything you like,' she said, through the tears. 'Get married, live together, whatever you want.'

He had waited years to hear her say that. But not like this. Not because of a threat he hadn't meant, and would never dream of carrying out. Not under some sort of duress.

'No,' he said. 'No. I don't want you to do that. I want you to feel right about it. I'm not going to leave you, you daft bat.'

She drew back. 'Is that the truth?' she asked, still tearful.

'I'd *never* leave you,' he said. 'Never.'

At last she relaxed a little, and he wiped her tears with his hand. 'I've no intention of leaving you,' he said. 'I wasn't being serious, Judy – I wasn't even *pretending* to be serious.'

'Sorry,' she whispered.

'I should think you are,' said Lloyd. 'Have some flat champagne.'

How like Judy to offer him what he most wanted in circumstances which made it impossible to accept. But he had really shaken her, and he had never meant to do that. He didn't partake of the flat champagne, but he made Judy drink hers for its medicinal value, which she did, slowly, not speaking, lost in thought.

He watched her until she put the glass down. 'Tell me what you're thinking,' he said, not expecting to be told.

She looked at him as if she was only now becoming aware of his presence again. 'I was just wondering how I ever got this lucky,' she said, the tears still not far away.

'Luck had nothing to do with it,' he said, lying back and drawing her down to him. 'It was your cleverly worded ad that did it.'

She smiled at last. 'Go on,' she said. 'I'll buy it.'

'How could it miss? "*Beautiful, independent woman with brown eyes, smashing legs, logical mind and a dislike of unreasoning arguments, seeks volatile bald male chauvinist with thickening waist and inflated ego for flaming rows and occasional patronizing lectures.*" '

She nodded. 'But luck did play a part,' she said. 'It was pure luck that it was right next to "*Lover of language, poetry, books and films seeks unromantic woman with little or no knowledge of the arts, shaky grasp of grammar and morbid fear of commitment, with a view to*

126

possible marriage." ' She smiled again, then looked worried. 'Have we really got nothing in common?' she asked.

'We've got this,' he said, rolling over, kissing her.

'Sex?'

'No! Though I'm not complaining,' he added hurriedly, lest she went off the idea. 'No, I meant us – you and me, together. Whatever we happen to be doing. For a great deal of the time we're not having sex.'

'We can't have ourselves in common,' she objected.

'Yes, we can. We go together. We . . . complement one another. Interlock.'

She looked a little dubious. 'Like pieces of a jigsaw?' she said.

He shrugged. 'If you're into tired old clichés, yes,' he said.

She poked him in the ribs. 'You just made sure I said it and not you,' she said.

'Naturally,' he said, smiling. 'But we are like pieces of a jigsaw. We're just different shapes, that's all. We still fit together.'

She pulled a face. 'Do you have to do that?' she said.

He grinned.

'Anyway, I'm a piece of earth and you're a piece of sky,' she said.

He liked that. He smiled. 'Maybe,' he said. 'But they do meet, remember. They meet on the horizon.'

'The horizon,' Judy reminded him, 'is an optical illusion.'

Lloyd shook his head. 'I'll bet even your fantasies are grittily realistic,' he said.

'What fantasies?' she said, putting her arms round him. 'I don't need fantasies.'

And she kissed him then, a kiss not calculated to ensure a good night's sleep, until she stopped kissing him, rather as though she had forgotten what she was doing.

Lloyd drew back to see her looking thoughtful.

'Speaking of fantasies,' she said.

He groaned. 'I know of no other woman who could be making love, utter these words, and be talking about work,' he said. 'But you are. I know you are.'

'Sorry,' she said.

He couldn't remember ever having had so many apologies from Judy in one night. 'All right,' he sighed. 'What?'

'I didn't just *see* Natalie on the bus,' she said slowly. 'I sort of fantasized about being her mother.'

Lloyd was beginning to feel he really had never known Judy at all. 'Do you regret not having had children?' he asked.

'No,' she said firmly.

'Right,' he said, relieved that he had not been wrong, and that this was going to be about work, not about starting a family. 'Carry on, Inspector.'

'But I was just ... wondering, when I saw her. What it would be like to be her mother. So I was watching her. Listening to her. Seeing how she behaved with her friends – and without them, when she was on her own.'

'And you don't think she wrote that letter,' he said.

'No,' said Judy. 'The girl I saw on the bus seemed too ... I don't know. Too adult. That's a very adolescent letter, in between the sexy bits.'

Lloyd nodded.

'And that means that it's very important to find out who did write it,' she said. 'Because if she *was* there, whoever she is, waiting for Cochrane, while all that was going on ...'

'Then she almost certainly saw something,' said Lloyd. 'But why wouldn't she have come forward?'

'From that letter, I'd say she's very immature,' said Judy. 'And if she did see anything, then I think she's probably very frightened. Too frightened to tell anyone.' She looked serious. 'And that's dangerous,' she said.

Hannah hadn't even tried to sleep. Colin had been taken away by the police, that's what Kim's mother had said.

They couldn't possibly think that Colin had done it – he hadn't even been there. She had waited and waited, but he hadn't come.

It was Kim's fault. She'd told them about Natalie going with a teacher, and Julie wouldn't have been able to wait to tell them those stupid rumours about Colin that seemed to have got round like wildfire. But they couldn't arrest him because of that. There had to be something else.

She knew what that was. She had known all along; that was why she had tried to stop Kim telling the police anything that would make them suspect Colin. She lay awake, her heart heavy with the knowledge that her letter saying she would meet him had probably caused all of this. They must have found it and thought it was from Natalie, because she was there.

It was her fault. Colin was suspected of murder, and it was her fault. She would have to tell them it wasn't Colin. She would have to do something. Tell them about the letters.

She could tell them what she'd seen. But the fear that gripped her as soon as she even thought about that made her almost faint. She couldn't. She couldn't.

She had to do something. Colin hadn't been there – she had to make them understand that. Natalie hadn't written that letter. Her

128

eyes widened as she thought of a way. She could do it. She could. But she would have to go to school, and that filled her with just as much dread as going to the police. Murray would see her.

She could go to Colin's house. Yes. Yes, she could go to his house. Early. Before he left for school. Oh, but he might see her, and she didn't want that. Really early, then, before he was even up. But what if he was still with the police? What if he never got it? He would. He would get it – they couldn't keep him there for ever – he hadn't done anything wrong.

She slipped out of bed and switched on the computer. If they believed the other letter they would believe this one, and it would prove that Colin hadn't even been there.

Chapter Nine

Nothing new had come in overnight; after the morning briefing, the squad dispersed on various duties, leaving Judy, Tom and Lloyd in the murder room.

Poor Lloyd, thought Judy. She must have petrified him last night, but she had had to deal with an overwrought pathologist, a distraught mother, a garage mechanic, hostile colleagues and a post-mortem all before just being alone with him, which had in itself brought her emotions dangerously close to the surface. The sudden, frightening thought that she might have taken him for granted for too long had just been one emotional jolt too many. Now that she was herself again, she couldn't really recapture that dreadful feeling; just the effect it had had on her. She felt more than a little silly, if truth be told, and grateful to Lloyd for behaving as though it had never happened.

'I think Natalie got tired of waiting for Cochrane and let someone else have a legover,' Tom said. 'Cochrane caught her at it and lost his rag – finished her off when he saw the damage he'd done.'

Lloyd looked at him over his specs as he read the night duty's reports. 'You have such a poetic touch,' he said.

'He did it, guv,' said Tom. 'If he washes his own clothes, I'm Groucho Marx. And I smelt that deodorant.'

Lloyd took off his glasses. 'It makes sense,' he said. 'But I don't want us concentrating on Cochrane to the exclusion of all else, because all this is purely circumstantial.'

Oh, get him, thought Judy. He had built up more fool-proof circumstantial cases than anyone she knew. Except, of course, that he didn't actually believe in them. He wanted them to be picked over and the bones extracted, because the flesh was pure invention, and he knew it.

Tom simply believed that he was right, and Lloyd was determined not to encourage that.

'Until we get forensic or eye-witness evidence to the contrary, I think we have to assume that what we have been told by Mrs Cochrane is true,' Lloyd went on.

'But, sir—'

'Don't make the facts fit your theory, Tom. Keep an open mind. We should get the reports on the physical evidence at the scene today – let's not speculate.'

But oh, *God*, he could be so irritating, thought Judy, watching Tom's reaction with a smile.

Tom was due at the forensic lab; he had turned to go, but he turned back again, deciding to put up a fight. 'He was having an affair with her, sir. The letters say so. She arranges to meet him on the Green. He can't account for twenty minutes of that so-called run, and his wife just happens to see her alive before Sherlock the bloodhound conveniently finds her dead? Come on, guv – even if I hadn't smelt his deodorant, it's got to be worth looking into.'

'I didn't say it wasn't worth looking into. Of course it is. But I'm sure the inspector will tell you what's wrong with your theory.' He smiled at Judy. 'You have the floor,' he said.

Judy looked at Tom, and smiled sympathetically. Lloyd in his wise and wonderful mood was perhaps the *most* irritating thing that could happen to a person first thing in the morning. It happened to her a lot more than it happened to Tom.

'The twenty minutes unaccounted for is your best bet from that lot, Tom,' she said.

'What's wrong with the rest of it?' he asked.

'Well, I don't believe that the letters are from Natalie, so I'd give you an argument there – and you haven't proved that they are, yet. And while Cochrane can't prove he was running, he's not obliged to. You have to prove that he wasn't, and you haven't done that yet either.' She smiled. 'Where were you on Tuesday evening?' she asked.

'Here, doing that stuff for the CPS,' he said gloomily.

'Did anybody see you?'

'No,' said Tom. 'I was here alone – but my wife didn't happen to see the victim alive, and my dog didn't find her dead.'

'No,' Judy agreed. 'But if they had, would that automatically make you a suspect?'

'I wasn't getting passionate love letters from the victim,' said Tom.

'Perhaps neither was Cochrane,' she said. 'And wasn't Mrs Cochrane's call logged at ten twenty-five?'

'Yes,' said Tom.

'So all in five minutes, despite the fact that he's just come in covered in blood and told her he's an adulterer and a murderer, they work out this elaborate alibi between them? And then she ad libs?'

'She didn't know the neighbours had seen him.'

'He did – I think he might have mentioned it. And what sort of alibi would it have been, anyway?'

'Well – like you said, they didn't have much time to organize it.'

'That they didn't. Even if she called us from their own phone, she would still have had to get to the Green – which is a ten-minute walk away – by the time the patrol car got there in answer to her call, and it was a fast response, as I remember.'

'Well, it could just—' Tom began.

'And the neighbours saw his car coming from the other direction,' she added. 'Down Larch Avenue, from the school. Their statement is available to investigating officers, if they care to look at the case-files now and then.'

Lloyd grinned. 'That's my girl,' he said. 'Theory demolisher to the gentry, Tom – you didn't stand a chance. And the fact is that there is no evidence that Cochrane was having an affair with Natalia, and there is no evidence that he killed her, therefore I don't want you concentrating on him until there is, all right?'

'Guv,' sighed Tom, and left.

'Was that discouraging enough?' Judy asked.

'It should have done the trick,' said Lloyd.

'No new thoughts from you?'

'No,' he said. 'Inspired guesses come from information received, and we have so far received very little real information at all.'

But it should start coming in today, thought Judy, now that all the appeals and enquiries would be sinking in, getting round. Now that the lab would have completed its work on Natalie's clothes and all the rest of it.

It didn't seem possible that no one had seen anything, particularly if Tom was right and a third party had been involved. The boy, or whatever, must have run away. Didn't anyone see that?

'I don't suppose you've come up with an answer to the little puzzle, have you?' Lloyd asked.

'The shoes?' She shook her head. 'I can't imagine why they were left down there, unless . . .' She hesitated before she said what she could imagine, because she didn't want to. 'Unless he was going to keep them, and changed his mind,' she said quietly.

Lloyd sighed. 'That means you still think there's a possibility of other victims,' he said. 'That we've got a potential serial killer who was thinking of starting a collection.'

She nodded. 'If Freddie's right about how it might have happened, then it sounds psychopathic to me,' she said.

'*If* Freddie's right,' said Lloyd. 'But theories, as you've just demonstrated, always come to grief.'

Judy hoped so. 'But I think Freddie's right about the underwear,' she said. 'If she had consented, we would be talking about a quickie, out in the open, remember, with someone else about – someone known to Natalie, someone who could get her into trouble if she caught her. She wasn't likely to be peeling things off one by one.'

132

'But that's an assumption,' Lloyd said. 'You're always telling me that you can't base logical thought on assumptions. Granted, it seems unlikely in the circumstances, but we don't know that she didn't. Let's just regard that as another little puzzle for the moment, along with the shoes.' He paused. 'And Cochrane's missing twenty minutes,' he said. 'And Mrs Cochrane's lack of interest in how her film ended.'

'I can do that one,' said Judy. 'She didn't watch it.'

Lloyd's face fell. 'Oh,' he said.

'Her headmaster came and asked her to go in to work early next morning,' said Judy. 'When he left, she remembered that the dog hadn't been out.' She smiled. 'Have I just jumped on a theory that hadn't even been voiced?' she asked.

Lloyd smiled too. 'Not really,' he said. 'It was just Finch's insistence that she isn't being entirely open with us. I thought perhaps she had something to hide. Of course, we only have her word for it that that was how she spent the evening.'

'And the headmaster's,' said Judy. 'I spoke to him on the telephone yesterday evening. He confirmed that he called on Mrs Cochrane at about ten past eight, and stayed for about an hour and a half, discussing the wording of a letter he was sending out to the parents.'

'Why?' said Lloyd.

Judy frowned. 'I think it had something to do with the uniforms,' she said. 'He's a bit long-winded.'

'No. I mean why did you seek confirmation?'

'Because I know what Tom means. She *was* evasive about her husband teaching at Natalie's school. It *did* take her too long to tell us that she'd seen Natalie alive. And she was really startled to discover that he hadn't got home at ten,' she said. 'Not just because he's never late – it was more as though she knew that he *must* have been home by then.'

Lloyd tipped his chair back. 'You wondered if Tom's first and second theories could be combined?' he said. 'If Cochrane had killed Natalia earlier – say nine-thirty – gone home, told his wife . . . *Then* they would have had time to concoct an alibi.'

'Well, I . . .'

'But instead of staying in the house, Cochrane went to fetch his car from the school, in case its presence raised any awkward questions about his movements. The neighbours saw him bringing it back, and pop goes the alibi?' He nodded. 'Not bad,' he said approvingly, letting the chair down.

Sometimes she knew why living with him would be a mistake.

'Cochrane would hardly be so eager to have a blood test, if that were the case,' he said. 'Would he?' He smiled magnanimously at her. 'But I can see why you were pursuing it.'

'I never said I thought any such—' Judy began indignantly.

133

'Pity the headmaster had to spoil it, really,' Lloyd went on, blithely ignoring her. 'But I don't think Natalia wrote those letters,' he said.

'*You* don't think—' Judy gave up, mid sentence. Lloyd was winding her up, and she wasn't going to let him do it to her. 'No,' she said. 'Neither do I.'

'Which brings us back to someone jumping out at her while Mrs Cochrane was in the woods with Sherlock,' said Lloyd. 'And I don't care for that theory at all.'

'But you did say there was a possibility of his doing it again, didn't you?' Judy asked quickly. 'When you spoke to the *Courier*?'

'I said we had to bear it in mind, yes. And made all the right noises about women not putting themselves at risk.' He stood up as Sandwell arrived back from his refreshment break. 'But I have every intention of getting him before he claps eyes on another solitary female,' he said grimly. 'So let's go to work and do that.'

Hannah didn't seem to have come back to school today, thought Kim, looking at the small group of people who always met up before going into school. Julie, Claire, a couple of others. No Hannah.

And no Natalie. She wondered when the pain would go, when she would stop expecting to see her round the next corner, when it would stop hurting just to think of her. She had never been close to anyone else who had died suddenly, never mind like that, never mind so young.

She and Natalie had had fallings out, and arguments, but they had always been together. Always in the same class, the same form. It was, she thought, a little bit like being widowed must be. Two-thirds of her life had had Natalie in it, and now she was gone.

Only people didn't think of it like that. Her mum knew, but other people didn't, not really. They would ask her questions, because she was Natalie's best friend, and they wanted to know what she had been like. They weren't being deliberately insensitive; they just didn't think.

What *had* she been like? Much too daring for Kim, really, though Kim had tried hard to keep up. Natalie had always been the first to do anything. Trying to smoke, which neither of them had taken to, for instance. Drinking alcohol, which they did do sometimes, but not much. Natalie had even taken one of some capsules that the boys had got hold of when they were in the first year at secondary school, but Kim hadn't done that. It turned out that they were cold capsules, so she hadn't come to any harm. Kim had never told anyone that.

She didn't think Natalie had tried anything else, but if she had, she hadn't told Kim. She doubted that she had, because Natalie had been the first to grow up, too, in every way. Except in the boob department, Kim thought, with a sad smile. She had outstripped Natalie there by the time she was thirteen.

She began to cry, then. She hadn't cried, not until now. And she couldn't, not here, with all these people. She blinked away the tears, pretended that the sun was in her eyes.

Natalie had had boyfriends first, of course, and had lost her virginity before her fourteenth birthday. She had sworn Kim to secrecy then, and said that she hadn't liked it. Another little smile, as Kim thought about that. It had grown on her, presumably, because there had been several boys since, and Kim doubted if too many of them had been refused. When Natalie had told her about this married man, Kim had despaired of her.

Her eyes grew wide, the tears gone with the jolt of the memory. Oh, my God. What had she done? She had forgotten, completely forgotten. She had been too upset, too shocked to think straight. They had arrested Colin Cochrane, and it was all her fault, and now . . .

And now, Colin Cochrane was walking in the gate. He looked pale, and it was odd to see him walking in rather than driving up in his flash car. He didn't have a tracksuit on, which was even more unusual, and he didn't have any kit with him, but he was there.

He wasn't under arrest. Kim almost fainted with relief.

The DI had been looking rather pleased with herself this morning, Tom had fancied.

Possibly because she had done a demolition job on his nice new theory, but in all probability her rosy glow was for a much earthier reason than that. Lloyd was looking quite chipper too.

The lab had continued the theory-busting, with a negative report on Cochrane's clothes. But they had added that the killer's clothes would be unlikely to have had blood on them, anyway. Any blood was likely to have been confined to the hands of her assailant, it had added. Lady Macbeth, thought Tom, darkly.

Natalie's own clothes had a tale to tell, though. Foreign fibres: two different sorts, and a small piece of black cotton, probably from a button. A dark brown human hair that didn't belong to Natalie. A dog hair that almost certainly belonged to Sherlock. It pointed out, smugly, Tom felt, that tracksuits didn't have buttons, and that none of these traces came from Cochrane's clothing. One set of fibres was grey polyester/wool, one white cotton.

But Freddie's report suggested that the killer needn't have come into close bodily contact with Natalie, so his theory still survived. Just.

It was, however, becoming much more likely that Mrs Cochrane was telling the truth, and that some nutter had chanced on Natalie while Mrs Cochrane was in the wood; she really had seen Natalie alive and found her dead.

'I've checked out Natalie's computer, Sarge,' said the computer whizz-kid he had sent. 'She doesn't have a word-processing program on it, and anyway she's got a dot matrix printer. That letter was done on an inkjet.'

It was a conspiracy. His perfectly good theory was being blitzed out of existence. 'What about the school?' Tom said sharply. 'Don't they have computers?'

'All schools do, I think.'

'Then get over there! See if she could have had access to a word processor with an inkjet printer, and check its files out if you find one.'

'Right, Sarge,' he said, turning away. 'I get all the exciting jobs,' he muttered.

Tom followed him out into the corridor, and called him back. 'We are investigating the murder of a fifteen-year-old girl,' he said, his voice low, as he quietly manoeuvred the constable into a corner. 'If you find that boring, you're in the wrong job, mate. All right?'

'Sorry, Sarge,' he said, offended.

'If those letters are in the files of any word processing program in this town, we need to find them,' Tom said. 'So shift yourself, because you're the only bugger we've got round here that can look for them fast enough.'

'Sarge.' He moved with a great deal more enthusiasm this time.

'Trouble?' said Judy, as she came out of her office.

'No, ma'am,' said Tom. 'Just motivating the staff.'

She smiled. 'What did the staff have to say?' she asked.

'Natalie didn't use her own computer if she did do those letters,' said Tom. 'We're checking out the school computers. How are you getting on with English teachers?'

'I'm not,' said Judy. 'The previous one has emigrated to Canada, would you believe? The school thinks it must have samples of Natalie's English Language work somewhere, but so far all they can offer us is the general assessment of her work that says damn all about her grammar and punctuation.'

Tom grinned. 'Well, I expect the DCI could have told you that,' he said.

'They're operating under a new system, is one excuse. They've only been back two days is another, and I've even been told that they've had a murder to contend with.'

'No! Really?' said Tom, then thought about the problem. 'What about her geography teacher?' he said. 'Or history? Some subject that she had to write about?'

'Brilliant,' Judy said. 'I'll try that.'

'Except that you think it's a waste of time,' said Tom.

'Yes,' she said, with a sigh. 'I really don't think Natalie wrote those letters, and your staff seems to agree with me.'

'I think I'm being worn down by the weight of evidence,' said Tom. 'Do you think Cochrane knows who did write them?' he asked. 'And isn't saying? He's mixed up with someone else, and thinks that he's damned if he says so and damned if he doesn't?'

'He could be,' Judy said. 'If the letters are true, then he'd be in big trouble.'

'But not as big as murder,' said Tom, with a sigh. 'And he does get pretty weird mail.' He was reluctant to let go of his theory, but the facts really didn't seem to fit it. 'They might just be fan letters, of sorts, I suppose,' he said, and grinned. 'Do *you* fancy him, ma'am?' he asked.

'I wouldn't know,' she said. 'I haven't even seen the man.'

'You must have seen him on the telly,' said Tom.

'No. Everyone keeps telling me he's famous, but I don't know him from Adam.'

'But he's in everything. You can't turn the telly on without him popping up. What sort of things do you watch?'

She smiled. 'I see a lot of old films,' she said.

'He's not in them.'

She went back into her office, and Tom walked back to the murder room, where Lloyd was just putting down the phone.

'We're going to nail this one, Tom,' he said. 'We've got prints from Natalia's shoes. The thumb and two fingers of someone's right hand – not Natalia's.'

'Yes!' said Tom, punching the air.

Lloyd looked pained. 'That, DNA, the trace evidence on Natalia's clothes . . . We can't miss.'

Tom had one last go. 'Are we going to ask Cochrane for a hair sample?' he asked. 'And prints? She could have been in close contact with two people, remember. The fibres could belong to whoever she was with before she was killed.'

'Yes,' said Lloyd. 'They could. But the fibres suggest a suit and shirt, and that doesn't sound like an old boyfriend to me. But we will leave no stone unturned, Tom.' He grinned. 'Meanwhile, could you tell Inspector Hill to draft out a possible description of the assailant's clothing from what we've got? I'm going to have a word with the Super.'

'Will do, guv,' said Tom.

Lloyd opened his mouth, and shut it again. 'Oh, what the hell,' he said. 'There are more important things to worry about than being called guv.'

He and Judy should have a reunion more often, thought Tom, picking up the phone as Lloyd left the murder room. He might even forgive a misused comma in this mood.

Colin had never tried to work with a hangover before. It was going now, thank God, but it had been torture first thing. And he hadn't had any proper kit. All his designer tracksuits were at home or with the police.

That chap Marlow had kept him up late talking, as well. He wasn't all that sure what he'd told him, but most of it had been off the record. He had wanted to know why the police had been talking to him, so he could put his side of the story, he'd said.

Now that his head was no longer aching, Colin wondered about that. He didn't suppose Marlow had actually heard anyone else's side. Oh, well – the whole town knew he had been questioned, so what difference did it make?

He had just seen off his final class of the morning. He showered and changed back into his suit. He hadn't made his usual pilgrimage to the office for his mail – he hadn't known how to cope with Erica. Patrick was right – he should just stay out of her way until he could prove to her that he was telling the truth.

But that was easier said than done if you both worked at the same place, and he had better go and pick up his mail, or she might come here with it, and he didn't want that.

He walked through the maze of buildings that covered what had used to be the cricket pitch, trying to make sense of what had happened to him, but he couldn't. And now he wasn't even living at home. The whole thing was more than a nightmare. It was as though he had been sucked into Natalie's fantasy world, and couldn't escape.

Erica was printing out; she looked up, but then she behaved as though the printer required her total absorption in order to work.

'Is this it?' he asked, picking up a bundle of letters.

'Yes,' she said, without looking at him. 'Your mail from home is beside it. One of them doesn't have a stamp.'

'Right,' he said, scooping up the fan-mail, a normal-sized bundle today, and putting his real mail in his jacket pocket. He would normally put it in the car, but he didn't even know if Erica had brought the car, and he wasn't going to ask.

He didn't go to lunch with Trudy Kane; he wasn't hungry, and women were proving too much like trouble at the moment. Instead, he trudged back to his lair, to the gym, where he could be alone. He felt less lonely that way.

Patrick ate lunch alone at a table in the oddly quiet dining hall.

138

Yesterday had been fraught, with the police there mob-handed, interviewing everyone who stood still long enough, but it had been easier to cope with, somehow, than today.

This morning had been both trying and tiring; he had had to think of so many things at once. Still no sign of that girl as he had sat on the stage during yet another assembly of the school, this time to listen to a talk from the police to the students, the female students in particular, about the importance of staying in pairs when going out in the evening, and even during daylight hours in lonely or secluded areas.

The head had said that students who had lessons at the Byford Road annexe could, if they wished, go the long way round rather than cross the Green, in view of what had happened. If they did use the Green, they had to ensure that no one was left straggling, and had to respect the police lines cordoning off parts of it.

Patrick had then gone to his form room to take the register, and there he had told one of his most magnificent lies ever.

He had never known Natalie, was how he had begun, for a start. Always best to get the real lie out of the way as soon as possible, he'd found.

He hadn't known Natalie, but it was clear from the grief that pervaded the school that she had been a valued friend to many of her fellow students.

He could, he thought as he finished his salad and reached for his pudding, hazard a guess as to how many, but he had not, of course, thought that when talking to the class. At the time of the magnificent lie, he had been a new teacher, trying to help his form come to terms with the death of a pupil of whom he had known nothing more than her difficult Russian name.

Thank God it hadn't been Smith, because he would have stumbled over it just the same when he had found himself looking at it. His heart had stopped beating when he had seen Natalie's name. A schoolgirl? In his school? In his form? And the little bitch hadn't said a word. Not one word. She had let him find out like that.

He wished, he had told them solemnly, that he had known her, but, sadly, having to ask how to pronounce her name when taking the register had been his only conversation with her.

All he could say to them in their bereavement was that life did kick you in the teeth from time to time, and that all you could do was show it that you wouldn't give up, that life went on. From what he had heard of Natalie, that was a sentiment with which she would have heartily agreed. She had had spirit, and that spirit would live on.

That last bit was true, he thought. Natalie had had spirit, all right.

He had drawn a neat line through her name in the register, and had got on with his job. That had been easier. The afternoon might not be too bad.

More than six hundred letters to get out, and a printer that only did fifty sheets at a time, Erica thought, savagely pushing the paper in, pressing the key.

She had been interrupted all day, but the last time it had been a policeman, who had insisted that he had to check the files in the word processor. The headmaster, he had assured her, had said it would be all right.

It was all right for him; he wasn't trying to get these letters out. It would *be* winter before she got them out at this rate.

She was trying not to think about Colin and Natalie, but it wasn't working, and now here was Colin again, even more haggard than he had seemed before lunch. 'What's wrong?' she asked. Silly question, but that was what she said.

'That letter? The one with no stamp?'

'Yes,' she said. 'What about it?'

He held it out, in its envelope. 'I think you should read it,' he said, closing the office door.

Erica took it. His hand was shaking. 'Colin, I think we—' she began.

'Just read it,' he said.

She pulled it out, recognizing its style before she had even unfolded it properly. She read as much of it as she needed to and looked up at her husband. 'What does this mean?' she asked.

'It means,' he said, 'that whoever has been writing those letters is still doing it. It means that it wasn't Natalie. It means,' he added, his voice rising until he shouted the last few words, 'that you might actually believe me at last that I had nothing to do with her!'

She stared at him, baffled. She had seen Natalie with her own eyes. 'How can I believe you?' she shouted back.

'Because you've got that letter in your hands! You got it at the house this morning. And it didn't come through the post. Natalie didn't write it. Look at the bloody date, woman!'

She looked at the letter, dated the day after Natalie had died. 'So she didn't write that letter,' she said. 'All that this proves is that there's more than one. I know you were with her, Colin – I know you were there! Stop lying to me!'

'Erica!' he roared. 'I *wasn't* there. I wasn't with her. I have never had anything to do with her *in my life*! Colin banged his fist down on the desk with each of the final three words. 'And I'm taking a blood test that will prove to you once and for *all* that I wasn't with her on Tuesday night!'

The door opened, the head came in, and Erica knew beyond a shadow of a doubt that Colin was telling the truth.

'Er . . . Mr Cochrane, Mrs Cochrane. I must ask you to . . . moderate your voices,' the head was saying.

Erica could hear him, but she wasn't taking it in. If Colin was telling the truth, then . . .

'I know,' the head went on. 'I do understand that you are coping with . . . with . . . a considerable crisis, but I'm afraid we do have the . . . school to consider.'

'Sorry,' said Colin. 'It was my fault.'

No, it wasn't, thought Erica, still shell-shocked by her realization. But surely even Patrick wouldn't . . .

'Oh, no one's to blame. I'll – I'll just . . . let you sort things out. If you could just . . . you know.'

The head escaped.

'I'm going to the police,' Colin said. 'If you won't believe me, maybe they will.'

Colin was gone; she looked at the closed door, her thoughts racing. She had to tell Colin, tell the police . . . she had to—

She made herself slow down, think things out. She had to talk to Patrick. But he would be in class now, she thought, looking at the clock.

Which was perhaps a good thing, because of course she should talk to Colin first. She would see him when he came back from the police. She didn't know if he would ever forgive her, but that was a bridge that she would cross when she got there, and not before.

Hannah woke up with the sun shining into her room; she frowned, and blinked. Didn't that make it late? She looked at the clock. It was almost two. She had slept all morning.

She hadn't slept at night; she had done her letter and crept out of the house as soon as it got light, cycling to Ash Road and delivering it. She had only just got her nightclothes back on when her mother looked into her room; she had assumed that she had been up because she was still being sick, and Hannah hadn't told her any different, so her mother had made a doctor's appointment, of course, without even telling her.

But it meant that there was no question of going to school; if she could stay away long enough, Mr Murray would realize that he had nothing to worry about.

And she might be free of this dreadful fear.

Cochrane had brought them a letter which he had thrust into Lloyd's hands with the air of one who thought that it exonerated him.

It didn't; now he was in an interview room with Judy sitting opposite him at the table. Lloyd had wanted her to interview Cochrane, and had been quite prepared to put Tom's nose out of joint in order that she should do so, but, as it happened, he hadn't had to.

Tom had got a phone call from the person he insisted on calling his snout, and had begged to be allowed to go and see him, because there was a chance that he could save face over the stake-out fiasco, as it had become known.

Lloyd had made a great play of being reluctant to take him off the murder enquiry, even for that short time, and by granting him permission he now had one sergeant who believed that he owed him a favour, instead of one who hated his guts for bringing Judy in over his head. A nice bit of work all round, really.

Now. Cochrane. A nasty bit of work? That wasn't how he struck Lloyd, and the evidence certainly didn't suggest it, but this letter had made its appearance, and Tom could be right. But he was going to let Judy do the talking, and he would be watching her as well as Cochrane. Judy's opinion of people was something Lloyd valued. He could tell from her body language whether she believed or disbelieved what she was hearing, regardless of what she was actually saying.

'I'm sure you'll understand that though you are here voluntarily, I do have to caution you,' Judy said. 'In view of the contents of this letter.'

Cochrane frowned a little at that, and Judy went through all the stuff that she was required to tell him about his rights; she never forgot any of it, unlike everyone else, because she used a little checklist in her notebook. Her notebook – not her official pocketbook, but a great thick shorthand pad – had once been more than necessary to her, because the trained memory that police officers liked to think they possessed had not been issued to Judy, despite her tidy and logical mind, or perhaps even because of it.

Lloyd's mind was as untidy and illogical as his desk, his memory an attic in which things got thrown in any old how. But unlike Judy, he never threw anything away. He, as he was wont to point out to her, remembered things without writing them down.

Now, the tape took care of the actual words spoken at interviews, but Judy still took notes, because out of that mass of demi-shorthand and question marks came the answers to questions that often no one had thought of actually asking. She noted everything: appearance, manner of response, lack of response; if the answer was there to be found once she had completed her enquiries into anything, she would find it.

Since cautioning Cochrane, she had said nothing at all; God knew how Cochrane must be feeling, because the silence, broken only by the hiss of the tape going round, was unnerving even Lloyd.

'Aren't you supposed to be asking me questions?' Cochrane demanded, eventually.

'Am I?' said Judy, looking up from her notebook. 'I thought you were going to tell me all about this letter.'

'Tell you what? I've told you everything I know.'

'You do realize it's an alibi?' Judy asked sweetly.

'What?' Cochrane stared at her.

'That's what this is,' she said, pointing with her pen at the letter. 'It makes it very clear where you were and what you were doing at the time of Natalia Ouspensky's murder – it even specifies the times that you were with the writer. A touch unusual, for a love letter, I'd say. But unfortunately it isn't signed, so I can hardly check it out until you tell me, can I?'

Cochrane stared at her. 'Christ,' he said.

'I take it that that name hasn't been given in reply to my question,' Judy said.

Judy didn't joke with people she thought might have murdered fifteen-year-old girls. Not even barbed jokes.

'Jesus Christ,' Cochrane said, putting his head in his hands. 'I didn't want a bloody alibi,' he said, his muffled voice tortured. 'What's happening? What's happening to me?'

'Well,' said Judy. 'What might have happened is that you have been having a relationship with the writer of these letters, that you were with her on Tuesday evening, and that you didn't want to tell us that because you are a married man, and she is quite obviously a pupil at your school.'

Cochrane didn't look up, didn't react.

'Or perhaps you didn't want to tell us because your meeting on the Green with the writer did indeed take place, and Natalie saw you. Perhaps threatened to tell someone.'

He looked up slowly, fearfully.

'Perhaps you killed her to keep her quiet, Mr Cochrane,' said Judy. 'And this is your girlfriend's attempt to keep you out of prison.'

He shook his head, his eyes wide with fatigue and worry.

'There are any number of theories that I could trot out, Mr Cochrane,' she said. 'But I won't. Because I think it's time you told us exactly what you were doing in the twenty minutes so far unaccounted for in your run.'

Judy believed he was innocent of Natalia's murder, Lloyd knew she did. But she had to keep going until they had no reasons left to disbelieve him, purely because of the letter that lay between them on the table.

An obviously trumped-up alibi was, as Cochrane had realized when it had been pointed out to him, the very last thing he wanted.

'You still think I killed Natalie,' he said, his voice weak.

'I don't,' said Judy.

It took Cochrane's tortured mind a moment or two to understand the words. 'What?' he said.

'I think this alibi is false,' she said. 'But not because you killed Natalie. I think whoever wrote this letter knows you didn't kill Natalie, because she was on the Green, waiting for you. And she knows that you were never there.'

For the first time Lloyd saw hope dawn in Cochrane's eyes. In his opinion, it was a little premature; he knew Judy.

'But if you have been having an affair with the writer of these letters, you must tell us, Mr Cochrane,' she said. 'Whether you were with her or not. You must tell us.'

'I haven't,' said Cochrane, helplessly. 'I swear to you. It's fantasy! . . . it's all fantasy. She's imagining it all.'

'Who is? Who wrote this letter?'

'I don't *know* who wrote it. It's not signed. I'm not meant to know.' He sighed. 'But if Erica doesn't believe me, why should you?'

'Mr Cochrane,' Lloyd said immediately. 'In your previous interview you said that you had never shown your wife the letters.'

He sighed heavily. 'No,' he said. 'But she used to open my mail for me, and she found the first one. It was just like that,' he said, pushing away the latest and most damning of all. 'Describing things . . . She never really believed me that I knew nothing about it.'

'But according to Sergeant Finch, you get all manner of letters from female fans,' Judy said. 'So why did your wife think that this one was for real?'

'She just did,' Cochrane sighed again. 'It came in the internal mail – that was the main reason, I suppose, because that meant it was from someone who actually knew me, and she was making it sound as though we'd been together.'

'But you do get letters of this nature?' she persisted.

'All sorts,' Cochrane said. 'Some of them are a lot . . . well, even more explicit than that.'

'And the first letter was in March, didn't you say?'

He nodded again.

'But you had only just got married,' Judy said. 'It seems a very harsh conclusion for your wife to come to unless she had a lot more to go on than that.'

He looked at Judy, and relaxed a little. 'Erica and I hadn't long been married, but we had had a relationship for a long time before that,' he said. 'We didn't live together, but . . . well, you know what I mean.'

144

Lloyd rather fancied that she did.

'So though we were, on paper, newly-weds, we had been together a long time, and . . . well, the way things were, it wasn't too difficult for Erica to imagine that something really was going on.'

'And she was imagining it, was she?' Judy asked, sounding a little like a nanny with a slightly wayward charge.

'Yes,' he said firmly. 'She was. But . . . well, things hadn't been going very well between us, and she thought that there might be someone else before she ever saw the letter.' He gave a sour little laugh. 'Before we even got married,' he said.

'Why would she marry you, if she thought that?' asked Lloyd.

Cochrane shrugged a little. 'When I sold my flat and bought the house, we decided she should move in with me,' he said, trying to explain. 'Keeping up the house and her flat seemed even more wasteful than before. It was more for convenience than anything else. It wasn't an earth-shattering decision.' He looked at Judy. 'But the head made it clear that he would rather we were married, especially with my being in the public eye. So . . .' He shrugged again. 'We got married.'

Lloyd couldn't resist sneaking a look at Judy, to find that she was glancing at him. The result of the Cochranes' change of domestic set-up had probably set his campaign back two years, he thought.

'I spent last summer at various athletics meetings,' Cochrane said. 'Big meetings. But I was in the studio, not running. I wasn't running, because I wasn't good enough.' He sighed. 'I was never top-flight. Britain's number two at my peak, which didn't last. But I had always been good enough to compete before.'

Judy frowned a little.

'There is a point to this,' he assured her, before he went on. 'Because of how it affected me. I knew I couldn't be a miler any more, but I thought I could move up to the longer distances. I didn't want to retire – I like athletics. I like the atmosphere, I like the life.' He shook his head. 'No,' he said. 'I don't like it. I live it. It means . . . meant . . . everything to me.'

Judy didn't speak now. She had got him talking, and that was what she wanted.

'But I failed in the trials. I broke down on the track.'

Lloyd sat down, interested.

'That was the first time I had ever failed to make the England squad for an international meeting since the Juniors, do you know that?' Cochrane asked him.

'No,' admitted Lloyd, with surprise.

'Not a lot of people do,' said Cochrane. 'Because I never had world records or Olympic medals. I got knocked out in the first heat more often than not. But I was always there, because even at that I was

145

better than most. When I was dropped, my world fell in. And Erica didn't know what was wrong. I couldn't very well explain to her that athletics meant more to me than she did, could I?'

'Perhaps not,' said Lloyd.

'I bought the house at the end of the season, because I was going to retire, and I needed to put down roots and all that,' he said. 'But I couldn't let it go, not just like that. We got married this March, and Erica moved in, but we ... well, things weren't working out, because I was hell to live with. She suspected that it was another woman, and when she came across that letter she thought that it was proof. The atmosphere got unbearable – I went to every meeting I could during this summer, just to get away, whether I was commentating or not.'

'But you must have known you couldn't run for ever,' said Lloyd. 'You must have known it would happen one day.'

'I must have,' said Cochrane. 'But it's like knowing you're going to die. You don't really believe it.'

'And at least you had another career,' said Lloyd. 'Two careers,' he added.

'That's what they said,' Cochrane agreed. 'And some people are natural teachers, but I'm not one of them. Patrick Murray is – he gets a buzz out of teaching. I don't. And being a so-called celebrity is no job for a grown man. I just felt lost.'

Lloyd nodded. His gloomy thoughts on his own career hadn't been all that different.

'And the running?' asked Judy, getting back to the point, which, as usual, Lloyd had allowed to get lost.

'I started this suicidal running programme last winter, to prove them wrong. But I failed in the trials again. I tried to give it up, but I couldn't. I ... I knew it was getting me nowhere, but—'

'What happened on Tuesday night?' Judy asked.

'On Tuesday night I was simply too scared to go across the Green,' he said. 'I feel awful about that now, but I didn't know how to handle a rabid teenage fan who had sex fantasies about me, and I just wanted to avoid her.'

'I can understand that,' said Judy. 'But what about the twenty minutes?'

'I hadn't allowed for not running across the Green,' he said.

'But that part of the run didn't take you very far out of your way,' she said. 'Certainly not twenty minutes out of your way.'

Cochrane flushed. 'No,' he said. 'But I'd said that I would be home by ten. I'm ... er ... I'm a bit obsessive about time,' he muttered, then blushed. 'I'm obsessive about everything,' he said in a low voice. 'To make it from Byford Road to the school in time to get home for ten, I would have had to run a four-minute mile.' He was blushing deeply, painfully now. 'And that's what I actually attempted, at the end of a three-hour run. I don't know how long it took me, because I collapsed in Beech Street. I was vomiting, I was shaking. I was a complete mess. In all meanings of the word.'

'You were sick on your tracksuit?'

He nodded. 'I had to sit on a wall outside some office until I could even walk again, and it was quarter past ten before I got to the car.'

'Did anyone see you?' asked Judy, coolly behaving as though Cochrane was not acutely embarrassed by his irrational behaviour.

'Someone might have seen me cross Ash Road,' he said. 'But I doubt it. And no one saw me in Beech Street. There's no one there at that time of the evening.'

The high colour had left his face; he had admitted how far his obsession with time had got, and Judy's total non-reaction was putting him at ease. Lloyd congratulated himself on not letting Finch loose on the man – they would never have got this far.

'I was relieved, at the time,' Cochrane said. 'Now, I wish I'd had an audience. I didn't know I would need one. Because none of this clears me, does it?'

'And when you got home?' said Lloyd, not answering his question.

'I did think Erica was in bed. I didn't want her to see me in that state, so I just stuffed the things in the machine and took a shower. Then all this happened.' He looked at Judy again. 'I didn't even want my wife to know what a fool I had made of myself,' he said. 'Never mind your Sergeant Finch. I hadn't had anything to do with Natalie – I didn't see what business it was of his, that's all. I never thought I'd get myself into this hole.'

Judy closed her notebook and regarded him for a moment. 'Maybe you should try explaining to your wife how you feel about having to retire,' she said. 'She might be a lot more understanding than you think.'

'That's what Patrick said, in a way.' Cochrane sighed, and looked from her to the Chief Inspector. 'This is a long way from police work,' he said. 'Isn't it?'

Lloyd shook his head. 'We had to be sure that these letters are what you say they are,' he said. 'That you really were telling the truth when you said you didn't know who'd been sending them. Because we have to find whoever it is – and if you have even a vague idea who it might be, it would make our job a great deal simpler.'

Cochrane shook his head. 'I honestly believed it was best to ignore them,' he said. 'I never tried to find out.' He smiled at Judy. 'I'm sorry if I've wasted a lot of your time,' he said.

She didn't react to his apology. 'We will need to take your fingerprints, Mr Cochrane,' she said briskly, standing up. 'And we need a sample of scalp hair.'

Cochrane sighed. 'A sample of blood. Now my fingerprints, my hair. Spending half my time in the police station, being cautioned, being taped. I had nothing to do with this! Any of it! When's it going to stop?'

'If they aren't your prints,' said Judy, 'and it isn't your hair, then you'll be one step further out of this hole, won't you?'

Cochrane got up slowly, wearily. 'Is this nightmare nearly over?' he asked.

Neither Lloyd nor Judy answered him, because the plain fact was that they didn't know.

Chapter Ten

Colin wasn't surprised by the silence that had followed his question. They couldn't make promises, he knew that.

The inspector terminated the interview, then looked thoughtful. 'Mr Cochrane,' she asked. 'When did you join the drama group?'

'Two years ago,' he said.

He had joined the drama group because it gave him a little bit of confidence before his first television appearance, and had continued to go along to it for the same reason. A couple of other teachers were in it – why weren't they being questioned over and over again?

Because they hadn't had a letter arranging a meeting on the Green that night, he told himself as they left the interview room. They hadn't behaved suspiciously with regard to personal cleanliness. It hadn't apparently taken them twenty minutes to run about half a mile. It was his own fault.

He was taken to have his fingerprints done, and to let them take samples of his hair, in what he hoped would be his final appearance in this drama. He was told that his fingerprints would be destroyed within five days if they had no bearing on the investigation, and he left, still absently wiping ink from his fingers as he walked away.

At last someone seemed to believe him that he hadn't killed Natalie, and once they had analysed his blood surely then even Erica would believe him that he hadn't been on the Green with her either, and he would be free of all this?

There was no point in going back to school now; he walked back to the hotel, wondering if he should try to speak to Erica. But Patrick had advised him to wait until he had the proof that he hadn't been with Natalie, and he thought that that was perhaps good advice, even if it had been offered as adulterer to adulterer. Patrick knew a lot more about women than he did.

He would do his best to avoid Erica for the next few days, like Patrick had said. She hadn't exactly been supportive, hadn't even asked if he wanted her to go to the police station with him. But all she had seen was what the police had seen; a letter giving him an alibi.

He walked through the town centre to the Derbyshire, and that

149

was when he saw the placard outside the newsagent:

LOCAL HERO QUIZZED IN SCHOOLGIRL MURDER

Dear God.

The DCI had lost his argument with the Superintendent that a description of the possible clothing worn by Natalie's attacker should be put out. There was, the Super had said, too much guess-work involved. It had seemed to Tom that the suggestion of a grey jacket or suit and white shirt was perfectly reasonable, given the materials involved, but the Super had said that it might stop someone coming forward who had seen someone in grey flannels and a tee-shirt. Tom supposed that it might, but he hadn't said that to Lloyd, whose good humour had evaporated, as it had a tendency to do, without warning.

Which was a pity, because Tom had had some news concerning the warehouse job, and he had rather hoped to beg another favour.

He looked up to see Judy coming into the murder room, waving the evening paper at him. 'Have you seen this?' she asked.

Under the headline 'COCKY' COCHRANE IN MURDER QUIZ was an interview with Cochrane himself; Tom glanced at Judy, then read.

Colin Cochrane, once one of Britain's best athletes, and now a frequent contributor to several childrens' television programmes, revealed in an exclusive interview that he has been questioned by police in connection with the murder of fifteen-year-old Natalia Ouspensky on Tuesday night.

Natalia was a pupil at Oakland School, where Cochrane teaches on a part time basis, and was last seen alive waiting at a bus stop in Henry Way on Tuesday night. Her body was found on Ash Road Green.

'I want to put the record straight,' said Cochrane, speaking in his hotel room last night.

Cochrane is temporarily separated from his wife Erica, a secretary at the school.

'I am in no way connected with this dreadful business,' he said. 'My only dealings with Natalia were through normal school activities.'

Natalia's body was found by Sherlock, the bloodhound belonging to Mr and Mrs Cochrane, whose house on Ash Road is less than quarter of a mile away from the Green.

Cochrane went on to make specific allegations concerning the

150

police's conduct of the case, which this paper is, for obvious reasons, unable to quote here.

Detective Chief Inspector Lloyd, leading the murder enquiry, was unavailable for comment this morning. A police spokesman said that many people were being questioned, and that it was against policy to name or discuss individuals.

Having made a highly successful commercial for Olympic deodorant, a contract worth several thousand pounds has been offered to Cochrane in connection with the launch of a range of Olympic products for men. He is also considering an offer to host a series of sports programmes and is hoping to publish a book to compliment the series. He fears that these projects may now be in jeopardy as a result of his involvement in the murder enquiry.'

'That's not going to make his temper any better,' Tom said. And the thing is . . . I've just been to see my sn – my informant.'

Judy smiled. 'It's all right,' she said. 'You don't need to translate it into standard English for me. Or for the DCI for that matter – he just likes making you do it.'

'I know. Anyway – ' Tom took a deep breath. 'He says the delivery's on for tonight,' he said, and closed his eyes, waiting for her reaction.

'Well,' she said. 'Hand your information over to someone else – you're on the murder enquiry.'

'It would only be a couple of hours,' he said. 'And it wouldn't really interfere with the enquiry. And if I did hand it over, I don't think anyone else would act on it, in view of last time.'

'Neither would I. Your sninformant is unreliable.'

'But he's not, ma'am! He says it was a mix-up between the buyers and sellers – it was the sellers that got it wrong, not him.'

'Talk to the DCI, then,' she said.

'Well, I hoped that you might . . .' He tried to look winning, but it wasn't going to work.

'Oh, no. If this goes – as I'm sure you would say – pear-shaped again, I'm not going to be the one who talked him into it,' she said. 'If the information seems sound, he'll get someone on to it. If not . . .' She shrugged. 'And I don't think he'll let you be in on it,' she warned, 'even if it does happen. You're murder room personnel.'

Tom nodded. He had known that would be the answer, really, but it had been worth a try. He tapped the newspaper. 'What's happening about Cochrane?' he asked.

'He's gone,' she said.

Tom stared at her. 'What?' he said.

151

'He's gone,' she repeated firmly, and took the paper back. 'I'd better take this along to the DCI,' she said.

'Do you mind if I come with you?' said Tom. 'I'd like a word with him.'

'Sure,' said Judy. 'But I've warned you – you're on your own about this warehouse thing.'

It wasn't about this warehouse thing.

In his office, with Tom and Judy uncomfortably awaiting his reaction, Lloyd put on his glasses, read the article, then threw down the paper in disgust. 'There was a time,' he said to Judy, 'when you could rely on newspapers to take some pride in their job, to act responsibly, to make some effort to ensure that what they printed was accurate before they went to press.'

Judy picked up the newspaper. 'They're certainly skating on thin ice,' she said. 'But their lawyers obviously wouldn't let them quote him on the harassment business, and they haven't really said anything about that, have they? They've got the press office statement more or less right. I suppose it's up to Cochrane if he wants to go public.'

Lloyd looked puzzled for a moment, then his brow cleared. 'I'm not bothered about the story!' he said. 'If he wants to hang himself that's his business. I'm talking about the appalling English – the grammar, the punctuation, the spelling! How are children supposed to learn if they don't get taught in school and that's the sort of stuff that gets printed in the paper? Call themselves professional writers?'

Tom laughed, as did Judy.

'It's not funny!' said Lloyd.

'It is,' Judy said.

Lloyd smiled. 'What made him do it, do you think?' he asked.

Judy looked wary. 'Who?' she said. 'The reporter or Cochrane?'

'Oh, I know what made the reporter do it – he's never been taught how to write English,' said Lloyd. 'But why would Cochrane do a stupid thing like that?'

She shook her head. 'He won't have done himself any good,' she said, then flashed a smile at Tom. 'I think Sergeant Finch wants a word,' she threw over her shoulder as she left.

Tom waited until the door had closed behind her, before he spoke. 'Have you really let Cochrane go?' he demanded.

Lloyd raised his eyebrows. 'Yes, Sergeant,' he said. 'I have.'

'But why, sir?' said Tom, remembering the difference in their ranks a touch too late. It was easy to forget with Lloyd, but not advisable when questioning his actions.

Lloyd sighed. 'Because we have absolutely nothing with which to hold him,' he said. 'Nothing that we've got places him anywhere near Ash Road Green on Tuesday night. Not his clothes, or his trainers – '

'He washed them, sir,' Tom reminded him.

' – not a single witness who saw him anywhere near the place. Those are not his prints on Natalia's shoes, and the hair that was found does not match Cochrane's in anything but colour. It is now obvious that Natalia was not writing him these letters.'

'Because of that letter he showed us today?' asked Tom. 'Anyone could have done that.'

'But not Natalia, Sergeant Finch.'

'It didn't have to be Natalia! All it had to do was give him an alibi. And guess where the only ink jet printer that we've found is situated?'

'Where?' asked Lloyd sharply.

'Erica Cochrane's office,' said Tom.

Lloyd nodded. 'And does she have the sort of word processing program which has this waste-paper basket system?' he asked.

'Yes,' said Tom. 'It was checked out.'

'And you didn't find this latest letter lurking in there, did you?'

'No, sir, but you can override it. And Natalie could have had access to that word processor every time she went to her drama group. The kids aren't supposed to go in the office – but you know kids.'

Lloyd sat back and looked at him. 'You have to have evidence before you start accusing people of murder,' he said. 'We have precisely none. No evidence at all against Cochrane on his supposed relationship with Natalia or the murder. No evidence at all that his wife is lying, covering up for him or manufacturing alibis for him.'

'If she did lie about seeing Natalie alive, then she wouldn't think twice about producing that letter,' said Tom.

Lloyd ran his hand over what was left of the hair on the top of his head. Probably why he went bald in the first place, thought Tom.

'Cochrane has been interviewed twice,' Lloyd said, his voice very Welsh and low. 'He has let us have his clothes for examination, had his fingerprints taken and given us a sample of his blood and hair. What more do you want from him, Tom? What is it about him that gets to you?'

Tom sighed. 'Nothing about him personally,' he said. 'Unless you count his deodorant. But his wife knows more than she's telling. I know she does – I've known it all along.'

'Well, if she does you're going to have to be content with finding it out the hard way,' said Lloyd angrily. 'By following leads and checking the door-to-door statements. By finding witnesses, and/or physical evidence. By playing with these expensive computers we've got to cross-reference similar attacks in other areas. By ploughing through interviews with known sex-offenders and child molesters like everyone else is having to do!'

153

'I know all that, sir!' said Tom. 'But Erica Cochrane's not being straight with us, and that's not to protect a convicted rapist, is it?'

Lloyd looked thunderous for a moment, then visibly calmed himself down. 'How did your meeting with your informant go?' he asked, changing the subject altogether.

'He says the delivery's on again,' said Tom. 'At seven forty-five tonight. The DI said you might be able to get someone to arrange something.'

'Is his information any better than it was before?' asked Lloyd.

'He's reliable, sir,' Tom said. 'It wasn't his mistake.'

'No?' Lloyd was looking through papers; Tom wasn't convinced that he was even listening.

'No, sir. The blokes taking delivery wanted the stuff delivered at nine forty-five a.m. on Tuesday, because no one would take any notice when the place was busy. Humphry Davy Court gets dozens of deliveries all day. But the blokes *making* the delivery thought that they must mean nine forty-five p.m., and that's when they tried to deliver it.'

Lloyd looked up.

'And it seems the drivers won't agree to a morning delivery, so it's tonight,' said Tom, now less than enthusiastic.

'I think you should arrange it,' Lloyd said, after a moment's thought.

Tom frowned. 'The DI thought you wouldn't even let me go on it,' he said.

'Well, she was wrong.'

Tom was far from happy about having his request granted. 'Are you taking me off the murder enquiry, sir?' he asked.

'No,' said Lloyd. 'But from now, you're on the warehouse job. You don't have too much time – you'd better get on with it.'

'Is it because I still think Mrs Cochrane's lying to us?' Tom demanded. 'Do you think I'd let that affect my efficiency? I can think one thing and work on another, you know!'

'Then go back to work and do that, Sergeant,' said Lloyd. 'Get this warehouse thing set up.'

Tom stood there, reluctant to leave matters like that.

'That *is* an order,' Lloyd added, mildly.

Tom stared at him. 'Sir,' he managed, through his teeth, and left.

'How's it going?' Judy asked DS Sandwell.

'Well,' he said. 'We've had dozens of reported sightings since the evening paper came out. Most of the lads are out checking them now, but I don't hold out much hope for any of them, really. One says she saw a girl getting into Colin Cochrane's car, but . . .' He shrugged. 'We'll see,' he said.

154

'I doubt very much that she was with Cochrane in the first place,' said Judy. 'I don't think he would have been so keen to let us have a blood sample if he'd been with her. In fact,' she said, 'I don't think he had anything to do with it. That nonsense in the paper isn't going to help, though.'

Sandwell looked unconvinced. 'You don't think Tom could be right? He went down there to meet her and saw her with someone else?'

'He could be,' said Judy. 'But there's nothing whatever to prove it. And whose prints are on Natalie's sandals, if that's the case?'

'The one she was with?' suggested Sandwell.

Judy shrugged. Possibly. Though what reason he could have had for neatly placing them in the doorway was beyond her. 'Any more hopeful sightings than that one? Anyone say they saw her with a boy?'

'No.' Sandwell smiled tiredly. 'Someone reckons they saw her getting into a spaceship,' he said. 'If that's any help.'

Tom came into the murder room looking like a thunderous cherub, and Judy almost laughed.

'I'm off back to the CID room,' he said. 'I'm not on murder room duties any more.' He took his jacket from the back of his chair and marched out.

Judy went after him. 'Tom?' she said. 'I thought you wanted to do the warehouse job. You have to get it set up.'

'I did want to do it. But I only got put on it because I'm convinced that that bastard killed Natalie,' he said. 'And he thinks I'm not being objective enough.'

'I take it you're talking about the DCI,' said Judy.

Tom lowered the heat to simmering point. 'Yes,' he said.

'Then I think a little more respect would be in order.'

'Sorry, ma'am.'

'Did the DCI say that was why he wanted you on the warehouse detail?' she asked. 'Did he say you were off the murder enquiry?'

'No, ma'am.'

'Then don't jump to conclusions,' she said. 'About Cochrane or the DCI.'

'No, ma'am,' he said.

Judy watched him trudge off down the corridor back to the CID room, and went along to Lloyd's office, where he was about to address a plate of sandwiches.

'Hi,' he said. 'Did you have a run-in with your sergeant, by any chance?'

'Yes,' said Judy. 'Why are you winding him up?'

'Because he needs winding up.' He pushed the plate over to her. 'Have a sandwich,' he said. 'It might be a long evening.'

155

'No, thanks,' she said. 'He's just a bit over-eager,' she pointed out. 'You haven't really taken him off the enquiry, have you?'

'No,' said Lloyd, biting into a sandwich. 'They're good,' he said, with his mouth full.

'Maybe later. He thinks you have,' she said.

'Well, that'll do him no harm,' said Lloyd. 'The canteen will be shut later, and I won't be leaving any,' he warned. 'Did you have lunch?'

'I told him not to jump to conclusions,' admitted Judy. 'Should I have left well alone?'

'No. Very good advice.' He fanned his coffee. Even Lloyd couldn't drink police station coffee straight from the machine. It came at boiling point. 'You should eat,' he said, sounding like a joke Jewish mother.

'Stop worrying about my diet,' she said. 'Why do you want him on the warehouse thing?'

'He's the best man for the job,' said Lloyd. 'I want the two delivery men caught, and I don't know anyone better at chasing villains.'

'But they're not significant,' said Judy. 'It's the other two who distribute the stuff – the lorry drivers won't know anything about the operation. We'll be lucky if they get community service. And Tom is murder room personnel,' she said.

Lloyd smiled. 'I think you'll find that it could have a bearing on the murder enquiry,' he said. 'Tom's actually getting the best of both worlds. He just doesn't know that yet.'

'Right,' said Judy. She hated it when Lloyd was mysterious; her pride wouldn't allow her to ask what he meant. 'Cochrane's pen-friend,' she said, changing the subject. 'I've got someone at the school checking up on the drama group, because if I was a love-struck teenager and the object of my affections joined a drama group – so would I. So I'm finding out which girls already at the school joined after he did.'

'Good thinking,' said Lloyd approvingly, maddeningly.

And what when they found her, if they found her? thought Judy. She would say that she had seen nothing and heard nothing like everyone else. And what about this car, or whatever it was that had skidded out of there? Had no one seen that either? Was this man invisible, or what? She was beginning to feel quite affectionately disposed towards Sandwell's alien theory.

Lloyd smiled when she said that. 'It's not so strange,' he said. 'The Green's partially screened off from the road – hardly anyone would be using it at that time. We know she probably didn't get the chance to call out, and the car . . .' He shrugged. 'Well . . . I think it's a bit like the rest of Tom's detection work. He's thought of an explanation, and wants to find evidence to back it up. But I doubt if the car had anything to do with it.'

Tom Finch knocked and opened the door. 'Guvs?' he said. 'Have you got a minute?'

Something had improved his demeanour since Judy had last seen him.

'Sure, Tom,' Lloyd said. 'What can we do you for?'

'I've got someone in the interview room that I think you'll want to talk to,' said Tom. 'Both of you.'

'Right.' Lloyd got to his feet. 'Who?' he asked, standing aside to let Judy walk ahead of him through the door.

She didn't actually pull him up for every act of male chauvinism. Asking Lloyd not to let ladies go first regardless of rank would be like asking a cat not to chase mice, so she didn't try.

'His name's Kennedy,' said Tom, leading the way down the narrow corridor to the informal interview room. 'He's spent the last couple of days in Yorkshire with his family. Grandson's christening.'

'Nice for him,' said Judy. She knew Tom Finch quite well; there was an air of suppressed excitement about him.

'Yes. He says he knew he'd get legless, so he let the train take the strain. Didn't want to be tempted to drive home after the do.'

'Highly commendable,' said Lloyd, exchanging glances with Judy.

Tom had something up his sleeve, obviously; Judy just hoped that it got them further forward on this enquiry, because the folk wisdom of murder hunts said that the breakthrough had to come within the first three days, or chances were it would never come. And with any luck this really could be the breakthrough; Tom clearly thought it was.

Lloyd hadn't asked why Tom was dealing with what had to be the murder, though he was supposed to be setting up the warehouse job, but he would, whether it wrapped up the enquiry or not.

'Mr Kennedy,' said Tom as they arrived at the interview room, indicating a small man who got up awkwardly, not sure whether one shook hands in these circumstances.

'This is DCI Lloyd and DI Hill,' he said. 'Would you mind telling them what you just told me, Mr Kennedy?'

Mr Kennedy eyed Judy, then turned to Lloyd. 'Well – like I told the sergeant,' he said. 'I got the train to Leeds, and left the car at the station. I know what I'm like – I'd have been all for driving back last night if I'd taken the car. It's just me, you see, now that the wife's gone.'

Lloyd smiled and nodded, and Judy took out her note-book. Tom Finch was enjoying this. It would probably take all afternoon at this rate.

'I was working late Tuesday, but the christening was at ten yesterday morning, so I didn't want to leave it till the morning to leave.

157

So I got the last train up on Tuesday night. It was a fair old rush. I didn't finish while nine, and the train was at twelve minutes past ten. But it was late anyway, so I needn't have—'

'Tell the Chief Inspector about Ash Road, Mr Kennedy,' said Tom, taking pity on them.

'Yes, well – I was driving along Ash Road, keeping my eye on the clock. It was five to ten, and I thought I could make it to the station by five past. Give me time to park the car and get it paid for, and all that.'

His until now fairly restive audience had become very interested in Mr Kennedy's story; Judy sat down, the better to note down what he was saying.

'Anyway, I was just passing the Green, when a car comes reversing out of there like a bat out of hell. *Reversing*, if you don't mind, right on to the main road at I don't know what speed. I had to swerve to avoid it.'

'Did you see what kind of car it was, Mr Kennedy?' asked Judy.

'I did, lass. But better than that, I've given this young lad its number. I didn't exactly mean to memorize it, but it's not the sort you forget. CCC 800 M.'

Judy had never seen Cochrane's car, but it didn't take too much working out.

'I am checking out the registered keeper, sir,' said Finch, smiling broadly.

Finch himself had a very crude expression that exactly described the way he was looking right now. Judy would tell Lloyd later what it was – she liked shocking him, because it was so easy.

'I knew nothing about this murder until I got the evening paper,' said Mr Kennedy. 'Living alone, you see. If the wife was alive she'd have been telling me all about it, but—'

'Thank you, Mr Kennedy,' said Tom. 'We may need a formal statement from you, but in the meantime, thank you for coming in. You've been very helpful.'

Tom showed his star guest to the door, and Lloyd looked at Judy.

'So much for my mind-reading abilities,' he said. 'It seems that the drama group will be sorry to lose Mr Cochrane.'

'What about Mrs Cochrane?' said Judy. 'Do you think Tom's right about that too?'

'Well . . . you both think that there's something she's not telling us,' he said. 'But let's find out what condition Cochrane admits to leaving Natalia in, shall we?'

A WPC appeared at the door. 'Sergeant Finch wanted the registered keeper of CCC 800 M,' she said. 'It's Colin Cochrane, of 12 Ash R—'

'Yes,' said Lloyd, interrupting her.

Tom came back as she left.

Lloyd looked at him. 'It's Cochrane's licence number,' he said. 'Surprise, surprise.'

'Yes, sir,' said Tom.

'Sergeant Finch,' said Lloyd. 'Your facial expression borders on insubordination. Only senior officers are permitted to look unspeakably smug. Sergeants and other ranks must content themselves with looking modestly pleased.'

'Sorry, sir.' Tom grinned. 'I'll get off to the school and pick Cochrane up, shall I?'

'No,' said Lloyd. 'DI Hill and I will go – and I think we'll try the Derbyshire first, in view of his general demeanour when he left here.'

Tom's smile vanished. 'But sir—' he began.

'You've got a date with a warehouse, I believe, Sergeant Finch,' said Lloyd. 'And I don't imagine you've done much about setting it up, since you were inadvertently asked to deal with Mr Kennedy.' He paused. 'Didn't Sergeant Sandwell get the message that you were on other duties?'

'But I can get someone to cover for me at Humphry Davy—'

'You will do it yourself, Sergeant. The inspector and I will call on Mr Cochrane.'

Finch looked irresistibly like a child who had had a lollipop snatched away. He turned and walked out of the room.

Judy looked at Lloyd. Vindictiveness wasn't in his make-up; he could get toweringly angry, but he never held grudges. 'What are you up to?' she asked. 'You wouldn't do him out of his arrest.'

Lloyd smiled. 'I have no intention of arresting Mr Cochrane,' he said. 'I may have to, if he's uncooperative, but I do hope not – it's such a hassle when you get here.'

Judy frowned. 'But if his car drove out of there at five to ten,' she said, 'that's when Mrs Cochrane got there. She must have seen it – Finch has probably been right all along.'

'Mm,' said Lloyd. 'Probably.'

'We have to assume that she did see it,' said Judy. 'And for all we know, Cochrane had just murdered Natalie and she found the body.'

'Mm,' he said again. 'Well – we'd better go and talk to him again, hadn't we?'

Kim had a decision to make, and she didn't want to make the same mistake twice. She should have taken Hannah's advice in the first place and not said anything at all, but she had and now she knew she had been wrong. She wanted to talk to someone, get advice about what she should do.

She had a free period, and now she was in the fifth year she was allowed to go home to do private study; she was walking home in the sunshine, walking past the Green. She stood for a moment and looked at the cordoned-off adventure playground, blue sheeting masking where it had happened. People had left bunches of flowers there; Kim hadn't been one of them. She didn't want to mark where something so awful had happened; Natalie knew that she was thinking of her, and trying to do her best by her.

Who she really wanted to talk to was Natalie. She would have been laughing at her. 'You don't need me to tell you what to do,' she would have said. 'Just do it, or don't do it – don't keep asking me if you should.'

But she wanted someone to listen to what she had to say before she did anything she couldn't undo. She would speak to Hannah – she would ring her when she got home. Hannah was the nearest thing to a best friend that she had now.

The evening paper was lodged in the letter-box; no one had taken it in yet. Kim pulled it out as she went in and glanced at it. Then she sat down on the stair and read it properly. This was worse than rumours. And why? Why would he talk to the papers? It made it look as though he had had something to do with Natalie, and he hadn't.

Up in her bedroom, she rang Hannah's number.

'Oh – hello, Mrs Lewis. Is Hannah there?' she asked.

'No, she isn't – is that Kim? I had to send her back to the doctor. She was up all night with this tummy bug she's got.'

'Oh, dear,' said Kim. 'Is she worse, then?'

'Well, I didn't feel I had to get the doctor out to her this time, but she's definitely not right. Can I give her a message?'

'No . . . I just wanted to ask her advice, really,' said Kim, the truth coming out automatically.

'Can I help?' asked Mrs Lewis.

'Oh – no. No, thank you. That is – it's about my English homework,' she said, as the plausible lie at last presented itself. 'Could you tell her that I was wrong about what I said before? I know it wasn't what I thought. She'll know what you mean. Maybe she could ring me back. I'm at home.'

'All right,' said Mrs Lewis, sounding slightly puzzled. 'But I might be able to help, you know.'

'Oh – wait – I'll speak to Mr Murray,' said Kim, almost to herself. Yes, of course. Why hadn't she thought of that before? 'I'll go back and talk to him,' she said, relieved to have made the decision. 'Thank you, Mrs Lewis.'

'All right, Kim,' she said. 'I'll tell Hannah you rang.'

Kim hung up and left a note for her mother, who was picking up her little brother from school. Mr Murray would tell her what to do.

The daily papers were in on the act now. Lloyd had indeed picked up Cochrane at the hotel and had steered him to the waiting car, wishing he had had the foresight to expect the invasion of reporters. For one thing, he would have made sure that he didn't look as though he'd been sleeping in his suit, which he rather thought he did. It was very hot, and difficult for him not to get creased at the best of times.

He had told them that Cochrane was helping them with their enquiries, but this had turned out not to be strictly true.

Cochrane sat with his elbows on the table, looking like someone who had given up. But he had not, Lloyd was convinced, given up protesting his innocence; Cochrane, it seemed to him, had given up imagining that he would be believed. Or even caring if he wasn't. He barely seemed to have taken in the question, never mind answered it. It was a simple enough question. Had he been driving his car out of Ash Road Green at nine fifty-five on Tuesday night?

Judy repeated the question.

Cochrane shook his head slightly. It was the first reaction they had got; Judy tried to build on it.

'For the tape, please, Mr Cochrane,' she said.

Cochrane looked at her from under his eyebrows, then half stood, and put his mouth close to the microphone on the wall. 'For the tape,' he said, and shook his head again. He sat back down. 'All right?' he asked.

Lloyd frowned. 'Have you been drinking?' he asked.

'Yes. Do you want to breathalyze me too? You haven't done that yet. What else? An intimate personal search for illegal substances? Can I choose which of you does it?'

This was a new Cochrane. He'd been drinking, but he was far from drunk, in Lloyd's estimation. This was a Cochrane very near the edge. It was mutiny, of a sort. He'd behaved exactly as he was expected to behave for as long as he could. Now he was past caring. But he couldn't afford to be.

'This is a very serious matter, Mr Cochrane,' Lloyd reminded him.

Cochrane smiled. 'Of course it's serious,' he said. 'I've found myself in a Kafka novel – how serious can you get?'

Lloyd raised his eyebrows a little. 'From your television appearances, I understood that you weren't much of a man for literature,' he said.

'I'm not,' said Cochrane. 'But I do know what *The Trial*'s about. I'm just prepared to admit that I haven't read it, unlike other people.'

Neither had Lloyd. But he could quote it, with a slight amendment.

'*Someone must have slandered Colin C, because one morning, without his having done anything wrong, he was arrested,*' he said, quietly.

'Quite,' said Cochrane.

'*No!*' shouted Lloyd, bringing the flat of his hand down on the table, making Cochrane jump.

Judy didn't even react; she knew his tactics. She just sat with her pen poised over her notebook.

'Not quite, Mr Cochrane,' Lloyd went on, his tone normal again. 'Because I have *not* arrested you, though every rule in the book says that I should have.'

Cochrane frowned.

'Natalia's body was found on the Green, and your car was seen speeding away from the scene. The body smelt of your deodorant – you have twenty minutes which you can only account for with an uncorroborated story, you washed the clothes you had been wearing when you were out, and then to cap it all you came in here with an obviously trumped-up alibi.'

'She smelt of—?' Cochrane began, but Lloyd carried on.

'But I didn't arrest you, because I don't believe you killed her. I think you've been having an affair with her, though.'

Judy reacted this time. Lloyd hadn't tested this theory on her.

Tom had said that afternoon that Mrs Cochrane would hardly be protecting a convicted rapist, but Lloyd thought that might be in essence just what she was doing. 'You know all about DNA, don't you, Mr Cochrane?' he said. 'You know that it can determine the identity of someone who has had sex with a woman, and you know how. But you had used a condom when you were with Natalia – so whatever we'd found to analyse, it had nothing to do with you, and you knew that. And you agreed to a blood test.'

'This is ...' The young man's head was shaking all the time.

Judy was writing everything down, not taking part in this.

'But you didn't drive home when you left there, did you? You drove up to the school to work out your cover story for your wife, now that she had proof of what you were doing. Because she's what *made* you drive out of there as though the hounds of hell were after you.'

'No – no, this isn't true.'

'And Natalia ran away from your wife, right into the arms of a homicidal maniac,' Lloyd said. 'Your dog found her body. Your wife was frightened – she didn't tell us what she'd seen. She was keeping you out of it, but in reality she was protecting a psychopath. And you were too fond of your own skin to tell us the truth, and let us get on with finding him.'

There was a silence, then Cochrane exploded, this time making Judy jump.

'I was never anywhere near the Green! I never touched Natalie! I have told you what I was doing – it wasn't very glamorous, and it wasn't very clever, and I'm sorry I can't produce three independent witnesses who saw me throwing up all over myself, but that's what I was doing! I wasn't with Natalie, I wasn't driving my car, I wasn't running away from my wife! Is that clear enough for you?'

Lloyd stared at him. He couldn't still deny it, for God's sake.

'Mr Cochrane,' Judy said, her voice calm. 'We *do* have a witness. An independent witness – one who saw your car reverse at speed on to Ash Road from the service road on the Green at five minutes to ten on Tuesday night.'

'None of this is real,' said Cochrane. 'It's a fiction. Someone's making this whole thing up.' He smiled. 'Someone's inventing it,' he said.

'Why would this man lie about seeing your car?' Lloyd asked.

Cochrane looked back at him with eyes that held no spark, no light. Just an acceptance of defeat. 'I don't think he's lying,' he said, still smiling. 'He's just saying what he believes. But he imagined it.'

Lloyd sat back. 'Like the writer of these letters imagined what you and she had done?' he asked. 'Like your wife imagined that you were having an affair? Does everyone involved with you imagine things?'

'Yes,' said Cochrane, his expression not changing. 'Yes. But all this is the work of someone *else*'s imagination – it must be, because none of these things happened. This is Natalie's fantasy,' he said. 'It must be. Natalie's making the whole thing up.'

Judy glanced at Lloyd, who shrugged a little. Perhaps Cochrane was Freddie's psychopath, after all. Natalia was dead when Mrs Cochrane found her, as Finch kept insisting, and she was covering up for her deranged husband, for reasons best known to herself. 'Natalia's dead, Mr Cochrane,' he said. 'She isn't making anything up now, if she ever was.'

Cochrane sat forward. 'And I wasn't driving my car at nine fifty-five on Tuesday night,' he said. 'It was at the school. I'd left it there because it wouldn't start.'

'Why did you go back for it, in that case? What made you think it would start then?'

'Patrick said he'd mend it for me.'

'Patrick?'

'Patrick Murray. He's good with cars. He said he'd see what he could do and—' Cochrane broke off.

'Yes?' said Lloyd.

'Patrick,' he said, his eyes alive again. 'He must have been driving my car – it must have been him. He had the keys.'

'Is this the new English teacher?' asked Judy.

'Yes – don't you see? *He* must have been driving it!'

163

'How did you get the keys back?' asked Lloyd, refusing to react to Cochrane's sudden animation but excited all the same, even if his latest theory had been wildly wrong. 'You drove it home, remember.'

'He left them under an ornamental tree thing at the back gate,' said Cochrane. 'Don't you see? Don't you see? Patrick has to have been driving it!' His eyes widened. 'That's why the mail was piled up like that!' he said. 'It must be – I didn't leave it like that, covering up the rear window. I don't do that.'

'Perhaps,' said Lloyd. He didn't know what Cochrane was talking about, but it hardly mattered. They were just one step away now.

Cochrane looked at him open-mouthed. 'Perhaps?' he repeated. *'Perhaps?'*

'I'll check it out.'

Patrick Murray had only just started at the school – a perfect hunting ground for a sex killer. Would Natalia have felt safe with him? Yes, probably. A teacher. Offered her a lift home, perhaps.

Cochrane had slumped back down, elbows on the table, head in hands, because of Lloyd's lack of enthusiasm, but Lloyd couldn't afford any of that right now. They still had to prove it.

'If Patrick Murray wasn't driving my car,' Cochrane said, 'then you're all – every last one of you – all just part of Natalie's fantasy.'

Murray would have to be going some to beat Cochrane in the weirdo stakes, thought Lloyd.

Cochrane looked up at him and gave him a half smile. 'But I'm still just about sane enough,' he added, 'to think that that isn't very likely.'

'I'm sorry,' said the girl at the other end of the line. 'Mr Cochrane isn't in his room.'

'It's his wife,' said Erica, a little desperately.

'Sorry,' she said. 'He isn't in the hotel at the moment.'

'You mean he isn't taking my calls,' said Erica.

'He just isn't —'

Erica put the receiver back on the rest. Surely he wasn't still with the police? He had gone there of his own accord – they couldn't keep him all afternoon, surely? She would just have to go to the hotel, find out for herself. But . . . she sighed. She did have to talk to Patrick.

She picked up the receiver again.

Patrick shook his head as he read the paper over the shoulder of the teacher whose evening paper had caused the staff room to come to a standstill. No one was even answering the phone.

The earwigging barman must have tipped off the reporter last night. And Colin had been getting drunk; this Will Marlow must have thought it was his birthday, with Colin slagging off the police to him. It would be in the nationals tomorrow, Patrick had no doubt.

And he didn't fancy Colin's chances with the head once he saw the paper; he might be a bit vague and like everything to be frightfully friendly and informal, but he wasn't going to take kindly to this.

Good. Erica would suffer too, and he, Patrick, would be on hand to comfort her, to be a tower of strength, to be a friend in need. Things were working out just fine.

Someone finally answered the phone, and called out Patrick's name. He made his way through the crowded staff room, still buzzing as the evening paper was passed from hand to hand, no one going home in the middle of this juicy bit of scandal. No one could remember seeing Colin this afternoon; they were rather hoping to see what would almost certainly be a show-down between him and the head, but it looked as though they might be cheated of that.

'Hello, yes?' he said, his finger in his ear.

'Patrick, it's Erica. I need to talk to you.'

He smiled. This was perfect. Perfect. She was rattled by the news-paper report. She needed a friend, and he was it. 'I'll be down directly,' he said.

He ran down the stairs through the reluctantly departing teachers, knocked on the office door and went in.

She had been crying. 'Close the door,' she said. 'Lock it.'

He nodded, and shut and locked the door. 'Erica,' he said, as he turned to face her. 'It wasn't really his fault. He was drunk – I think the barman at the hotel set him up.'

She frowned. 'What?' she said.

'This stuff in the evening paper. Don't worry about it. It'll be a storm in a teacup. He was very down – this bloke Marlow just took advantage.'

'I don't want to talk about the evening paper,' she said, looking faintly puzzled.

Patrick frowned. 'Haven't you seen it?' he asked. 'Colin's sounding off about the police questioning him.'

'Yes, I've seen it,' she said. 'I'm not surprised – are you?'

He closed his eyes briefly. This was not a moment of his choosing, but from her tone of voice it was the only one he was going to get.

'It was you,' she said. 'In Colin's car. Wasn't it?'

What to do? Claim ignorance? Futile. She knew it was him. The question was clearly rhetorical. 'Yes,' he said, and sat down opposite her. The Cochranes had clearly ignored his advice and had started communicating. It had always been a gamble. Where was Colin? Why weren't they presenting a united front?

165

'How could you do that?' she asked.

'Which?' he asked in return. 'I've lost count of the terrible things I've done this last two days.'

'How could you let Colin take the blame?'

'Ah, no,' said Patrick. 'No, I didn't do that – I wouldn't. When Victoria said the police had taken him in, I thought they must know about the car, and I'd have to tell them it was me driving it, not him.'

Erica looked more than a little sceptical. 'I didn't see you rushing off to confess,' she said.

'But they *didn't* know about the car,' Patrick said. 'You hadn't even told him what you'd seen, not then.'

She gave a short sigh. 'I still haven't,' she said.

Hope. Hope was creeping through his soul again. If the police didn't know yet, there might still be a chance.

'They are going to be told,' she warned him, seeing his relief. 'I just wanted to talk to you first.'

Patrick nodded. 'It's more than I deserve,' he said.

'I know,' she said. 'But I couldn't just – tell them. Not without warning you.'

'Thank you,' he said.

She looked at him, her head shaking. 'I can't believe you took Colin's car to have sex with a fifteen-year-old girl,' she said.

'No, no – no. It wasn't like that.'

'Are you saying you didn't have sex with her?' she asked sharply. 'Because I heard what was going on, Patrick.'

'No. I did have . . . I did.'

'And you used Colin's car! Because you didn't want to risk picking up an under-age girl in your own car? It would be better if Colin got the blame for it?'

'No. It's not the way you think it was.' Patrick had to try to explain to her. To both of them. Why was Colin letting Erica do this on her own? 'Where is Colin?' he asked.

'For all I know, he's still with the police!'

Patrick's hopes nose-dived. 'He's where?' he said.

'Oh, don't worry, Patrick,' she said, her voice heavy with sarcastic concern. 'Colin doesn't know either.'

Patrick blew out his cheeks. There really was hope, if he just played it right. That was all he had to do, and he could be home free. He leant on the table. 'Erica,' he said. 'I don't suppose you could possibly think again about telling the police?'

Her mouth fell open. 'This has been a nightmare for Colin,' she said. 'And it's still going on!'

Patrick licked his lips. 'I know, I know,' he said. 'But *he* knows they've got the wrong man. They're doing a DNA test – you know? Genetic fingerprinting?'

She nodded. 'I know,' she said.

'By next week they'll know they've got the wrong man too,' said Patrick, desperately.

Erica blinked at him in disbelief. 'Another week of this? That'll seem like a lifetime to Colin! They suspect him, Patrick – don't you understand what you've done?'

'Yes,' said Patrick desperately. 'But hear me out, Erica, please. Everything they've done – taking away his clothes, taking a blood sample – don't you see? That will all go to prove he wasn't there. Because he wasn't.'

'So what?' she cried. 'The only reason he doesn't know the truth now is that he keeps avoiding me! Do you seriously think I'm going to let this situation go on? I'm telling the police, Patrick, make no mistake about that. I just haven't told them yet because you—' She broke off and looked at him, some of the anger going as she saw his stricken face. 'You've been very kind to me,' she said. 'And I'm . . . very fond of you. I felt I had to tell you first.'

Kind to her. Fond of him. That was good, that was good. 'No,' he said. 'I've caused you nothing but trouble. You didn't have to do anything for me.'

'You've caused plenty of trouble now,' she said. 'But that doesn't alter the fact that you were around when I needed you, and you didn't put any pressure on me when . . . well, when it would have worked.' She shook her head. 'But you knew what I must have thought when I saw the car!' she said. 'You knew, and you said nothing, Patrick! You let me go on thinking that Colin was there with her!'

'Yes,' he said, sitting forward. 'It was wrong of me. But I *was* there, Erica. Anything that they've found there will point to me. A DNA test would *prove* that I was with her. They'll charge me if they find out.'

'They will find out,' she said.

'But it doesn't have to happen,' said Patrick.

'It does, Patrick.'

Patrick sat back and ran his hands down his face, parting them to look at Erica. 'You know I didn't kill her,' he said. 'Because you saw me leave, and you saw her alive and well.'

'I know you didn't kill her,' she said, her voice flat.

'Please – think about it, Erica. Colin is going to be cleared. You know he had nothing to do with Natalie, and in a few days the police will know he had nothing to do with Natalie, then everyone will know. His life will go on as normal.'

Erica was shaking her head in disbelief. 'Normal?' she said. 'I accused him of having sex with a minor,' she said. 'The police thought he'd murdered her, for God's sake! Look at the paper! Look what you did to him! Normal? He's not even living with me now! Do you think his life is going to be normal once the dailies get hold of this?'

Patrick shook his head. That was a tough one. 'No,' he said. 'Right. But . . . he's going to be cleared – that's probably money in the bank to him. He can sell his story.'

'Don't you dare be flippant about this!' she said.

'No. I wasn't . . . I just meant that it won't harm him professionally – not once people know the facts.'

'What I did can't be undone,' she said.

Patrick was losing; he fought desperately to regain ground. 'It's not like you accused him of . . .' he said, deliberately shying away from the word. 'Natalie wasn't a child, you know.'

'Oh,' she said, sitting back a little. 'I wondered when Natalie would get the blame.'

Miscalling Natalie wasn't going to work. He had to retrieve the situation somehow.

'And whatever she was like, it's still a crime,' she said. 'And I accused him of it.'

'Yes. Right. But . . .' Patrick sat forward again, and kept his voice low. 'If you tell the police about me, then I lose my job, my wife, and my liberty as likely as not.'

'You went cruising in Colin's car, picked up one of your own pupils from a bus stop, and seduced her! You deserve whatever you get!'

Patrick shook his head. 'It wasn't like that,' he said. It wasn't. He had to make her understand.

'I don't care what it was like!'

'Just—' Patrick held up a hand. 'Just listen, please. I didn't pick her up from a bus stop. Well – yes, I did, but not the way you mean. I already knew her.' He paused before the make-or-break statement that would seal his fate. 'I'd been seeing her since the beginning of June,' he said.

Erica stared at him. 'What?' she said. 'She only turned fifteen last month!'

'I didn't know how young she was. I didn't know she was still at school.' The truth. The truth. He, Patrick Murray, was having to rely on the truth to get him out of trouble. 'And I didn't find out until Tuesday morning when I took the register. I swear, Erica, I didn't know.'

She had gone silent. He plunged on.

'On Tuesday evening I saw her by chance, and I only picked her up to tell her that it was impossible for us to go on seeing one another.'

'Oh, that's what you were doing, was it?' said Erica. 'At the council depot? Explaining to her how impossible it all was?'

'No,' sighed Patrick. 'That was what I meant to do, and I tried to, but . . .'

'But? You knew how old she was then!'

Patrick hung his head. 'I know,' he said. 'I know it was wrong.'

'And then you left her there – you just drove off and left her there!'

He looked up. 'Yes, I did,' he said. 'And now she's dead. I have to live with that, Erica. But if you tell the police they'll charge me, and I'll go to prison for sure because of what happened afterwards. And that had nothing to do with me. You know it had nothing to do with me.'

Erica closed her eyes.

Patrick got up and walked slowly round the desk, crouching down beside her, moving in for the final assault. 'Erica,' he said. 'What's happened to Colin has happened. And it didn't happen because of what I did, however wrong that was, because you're the only person who saw the car, and you haven't told anyone. It would have happened anyway, and it won't change what's happened if you tell them about me. It'll just finish me. Is that what you want?'

'She wouldn't be dead if you hadn't left her there,' said Erica, her eyes still tight shut. 'Why shouldn't you be finished?'

Now. Now was his chance, his only chance. 'Because I didn't hurt her, Erica,' he said. 'I just made love to her, that's all. It was wrong, I know. But I'd been seeing her all summer, and it . . . it just happened. I just made love to her, that's all, like I'd done a dozen times before.'

'Love!' she said, her voice full of contempt.

'Yes,' said Patrick, seizing his chance. 'Love. I loved her, Erica.'

'You were trying to pull me all the time you were seeing her,' she said, opening her eyes but looking out of the window, away from him. 'You tried to get me into bed last *night*! Love? Don't make me laugh.'

'I was flirting with you before, that's all,' he said, his voice low. 'It's my nature to flirt. And it was only because I knew you wouldn't have any of it. I loved her, Erica, and that's the God's honest truth.'

She still wouldn't look at him, but he was getting through to her now that he was lying in his teeth. He was.

'And last night was different,' he said. 'We were both hurting . . . I just thought we'd be good for one another, that we both needed a bit of comfort, that was all. Not because I didn't love Natalie.'

'I don't think you're capable of love, Patrick,' she said.

'I can understand that,' he said. 'But I did truly love her. I was . . . devastated when they told me what had happened. A moment's panic – and God knows what I left her to face. I don't know who killed her,' he went on, desperately. 'But throwing me into the ring is just going to make it take even longer to find him.'

169

He had never worked so hard in his life. Sweat trickled down from his hairline and settled uncomfortably in his collar. 'I was a coward,' he said. 'And a fool. But don't tell them,' he pleaded. 'Please.'

'I'll have to tell Colin,' she said.

'But he'll tell the police,' said Patrick. 'You know he will.' He caught her chair and swivelled it round so that she was looking at him. 'Erica,' he said, suitably on his knees. 'Ask yourself what good it would do to destroy me. It won't bring Natalie back. It won't change anything that's happened. Colin's going to be in the clear any day now. And it's not all my fault, Erica – not all of it.'

She looked down at him. 'Oh, Patrick,' she said.

'I made a stupid mistake,' he said. 'One stupid mistake. I've already paid for it by losing Natalie – don't make me pay for it again with everything I've got left.'

She closed her eyes again and sighed. There was an eternity before she spoke.

'I won't tell anyone,' she said, quietly, tiredly, reluctantly.

But she had said it, she had said it. Patrick resisted the impulse to kiss her. He didn't imagine that would go down too well. But he was safe, he thought, as he left her and went back up to the now deserted staff room.

He settled down to do what he always did after school; preparing lessons that he hoped his students would find diverting and amusing, and not just educational. He possibly liked this bit better than anything else about teaching.

He thought he heard someone at the staff room door, and lifted his head to listen. He could feel rather than hear someone on the other side. 'Yes?' he said. 'Is someone there?'

The door opened slowly, hesitantly, and Kim, the girl who had been Natalie's best friend, put her head round.

'Hello, Kim,' he said. 'Do you want me?' He smiled. 'How long have you been out there?' he asked.

She didn't answer, didn't come any further in.

'I know,' he said. 'You collect door numbers. Fascinating hobby.'

She smiled, which was a start. 'Could I talk to you?' she asked, in a voice so quiet that he had a job hearing it though she was only ten feet away.

'You can,' he said. 'But if you want me to hear what you're saying you'd better come further in.' He got up and pulled a chair round to face his.

She sat down, he sat down, but she was looking at her feet, slightly pink, tongue-tied.

'Right,' he said, realizing that he was going to have to open the conversation, or they would be here all night. 'I won't ask what's

170

wrong, because I know what's wrong. This whole dreadful business.'

She nodded. 'The police have been questioning Mr Cochrane,' she said.

Patrick shook his head, smiling. 'Don't jump to conclusions, Kim,' he said. 'Everyone wants whoever did that to Natalie found – the police have got to ask questions. They spoke to you too, remember. Don't take any notice of what it says in the paper.'

'They think he killed her,' said Kim.

Oh, God. Half the girls in the school were in love with Colin. He wanted to reassure her; he took a deep breath. 'No,' he said. 'I don't think so. It's just that they think . . . well, I'll tell you something,' he said. 'I probably shouldn't, but it might set your mind at rest. They're questioning him because they think Natalie had a . . . sort of crush on him.'

'Natalie?' said Kim, incredulously.

'You don't think that's likely?' asked Patrick.

'No,' she said.

No. She obviously had known Natalie quite well, then. He smiled. 'They're probably wrong,' he said. 'But anyway, I think that's all it is. They're hoping he can—'

'It isn't all there is,' said Kim, the words coming out in a rush. 'They suspect him because of something I told them. That's what I want your advice about.' She looked down at her feet, and took another moment before speaking. 'At the beginning of the holidays, she told me she was going with a married man,' she said. 'A teacher.'

So that was how they had got hold of that. Patrick stood up and went to the window, opening the blinds a little to the evening sun.

'That's what I told the police,' she said. 'And there was that rumour about Mr Cochrane. That's why they keep questioning him, because they think it was him she was seeing, but it wasn't – I know it wasn't. Because now I've remembered something else Natalie said.'

Had she, now.

'She said that he didn't know she was still at school,' said Kim. 'He didn't know how young she was. So it can't have been Mr Cochrane, can it?' she said.

He turned and looked at her. The afternoon light streamed in through the half-closed venetian blinds, casting dusty strips of sunshine over her, neat and demure in her school uniform. He should have guessed that Kim would know all about him – he had heard all about Kim, hadn't he?

She didn't look like a blackmailer, but she was, and a very accomplished one at that, telling the police just enough to take the heat off him, then letting him know, oh-so-shyly and hesitantly, that she could just as easily switch it on again.

My God, butter wouldn't melt, he thought, as she looked earnestly back at him, her eyebrows drawn together as she considered this weighty problem. 'I think I ought to tell the police,' she said.

He turned back to the window. He liked schools. He liked them when they were full of teachers and pupils and comings and goings; he liked them when they were quiet, and he was alone in their chalky, echoing rooms. Oakland didn't use chalk any more, but somehow its dust still seemed to be suspended in the air.

Oakland School suited him admirably; the ancillary staff had been reduced to Erica and the caretaker now that all that came out of the budget. The contract cleaners came in the morning, and the building was always quiet at night.

Tonight it was quieter than ever; all the extra-curricular activities had been suspended, so that the children – my God, no, not children, not if his experience of them was anything to go by – so that the students didn't have to go home at dusk.

'It could be stopping them finding out what really happened,' she said.

'What is it you want?' he asked, still not looking at her.

'Advice,' she said, still shy, still hesitant.

He smiled. 'On whether or not you should go to the police?' he asked.

'Yes.'

He liked schools, he liked Oakland, and he loved teaching. He wanted to have his life the way it was right now, and he had fought hard to keep it. But all that hard work with Erica could go slipping down the drain, with just one word from modest, unassuming Kim.

'No,' he said. 'I don't think you should go to the police.'

He had never been blackmailed before; he knew you were supposed never to give in to it, that it was regarded as the worst crime next to murder, but ... well, that rather depended on where you were standing.

Hannah was riding as fast as she knew how towards the school, and Kim, and Mr Murray, hoping against hope that she could catch Kim before she saw him, but knowing that too much time had elapsed if she really had just been on her way.

Kim had rung while Hannah had been at the doctor's. She had been wrong, she had said, and that had to be about Colin – it was the only thing they had discussed. Without giving her mother time to object, Hannah had jumped on her bike and headed for the school.

She pedalled furiously; she had to stop Kim telling Murray that she knew it wasn't Colin who had been with Natalie. Why did she have to go to him, of all people? Because Kim never did anything

172

without checking with someone else first, that was why. And she didn't know that she was checking with the man who really had been with Natalie.

Breathlessly, desperately, she propelled her bike up Larch Avenue to the rear entrance of the school, cycling illegally round to the front door, the only one open after four-thirty, where she threw down the bike and ran along the corridor to the office.

'Is Kim Walters here?' she asked, skidding to a halt at the open office door.

Erica Cochrane was over by the printer; she jumped at the sound of Hannah's voice. She had been crying; it was obvious. Good, thought Hannah, her loathing for Mrs Cochrane transcending even this crisis.

'Has she got short brown hair?' Mrs Cochrane asked, blinking away tears, trying to sound normal.

'Yes,' said Hannah, still trying to catch her breath, wondering what had happened now that Mrs Cochrane was in such a state.

'She's up in the staff room, seeing Mr Murray.' The last word was lost in a sob.

Hannah wasn't going up there. She had no wish to meet Mr Murray. And she needed to know what the matter was with Mrs Cochrane. 'Is there something wrong?' she asked urgently. 'Is it Colin?' She felt a little uncomfortable as Mrs Cochrane looked at her strangely.

'You're one of those girls that used to hang round the house,' she said, walking towards Hannah as she spoke. 'And it's thanks to people like you that he's been arrested! Get out. Get out of here.'

Arrested? Hannah stared at her, horrified. But her letter was supposed to stop them thinking that Colin . . . The paper had said that Colin was in a hotel, of course. The bitch hadn't given him the letter.

'Just get out!' shouted Mrs Cochrane. 'Just leave me alone! Leave Colin alone! Get out!'

Hannah got out.

173

Chapter Eleven

Mr Murray didn't seem to think it was a good idea to tell the police, but Kim didn't honestly feel that she could keep what she knew to herself. He had said that perhaps her information wasn't as valuable as she thought it was, that the police could prove whether or not Mr Cochrane had been with Natalie on Tuesday night.

She had pointed out that it wasn't just Tuesday night, or just the police. His wife ought to know that it really couldn't have been Colin. He had said that Mrs Cochrane was still in the building – why didn't she go down with him and tell her what she had just told him?

But she couldn't. Not straight to her face. He had smiled and said he had thought not. Her information was only valuable when it came to the police.

He had really been very strange; half the time she had no idea what he was talking about. He had asked her what she wanted; she had said that she had just wanted to know if she would be doing the right thing by going to the police with what she knew, because she didn't want to get anyone else into trouble, not after all the trouble she'd caused Mr Cochrane.

Natalie would have laughed at her, but she would have helped. Mr Murray wasn't laughing, but he wasn't helping either, not really.

He'd gone back to looking out of the window. Perhaps he thought she might get into trouble for not telling the police in the first place. That hadn't really occurred to her.

'Do you think I'll get into trouble?' she asked.

He didn't turn round, just kept looking out of the window. 'Now why would you get into trouble?' he asked.

'Because they've spent all this time thinking it was Mr Cochrane she was seeing, and that's all my fault. They could have been looking for who it really was.'

'Oh, but you've only just remembered, haven't you?' he said. 'So that's not your fault, is it?' He sighed. 'Let's stop this nonsense. How much do you—?' He broke off. 'Kim,' he said urgently, beckoning her over to the window.

She got up and walked over a little nervously.

174

'Do you know that girl?' he asked.

Hannah stood with her bike by one of the trees lining the driveway round to the rear of the school.

'Oh, yes,' Kim said. 'That's Hannah.'

He opened the window, and called Hannah's name. She looked up. 'Wait there!' he shouted. 'Wait there!' He turned to Kim. 'Will you do me a favour?' he asked. 'Will you wait here? I've just got to—' He broke off. 'Will you? I won't mess you around any more. Just trust me. I'll be back.'

'All right,' she said, bemused, and he was off.

She frowned and looked out of the window to where Hannah had been, but she was gone, cycling as fast as she could up the incline to the rear exit, past the virtually empty car park. She obviously had no intention of waiting for Mr Murray, whose feet Kim could hear rattling down the stairs.

She saw the car back out just as Hannah passed; she shouted uselessly, saw Hannah swerve and tumble off the bike just as the car hit it. Mrs Cochrane got out and rushed to where Hannah was getting up. She was all right; she was standing, Mrs Cochrane's arm round her shoulders as she helped her into the car. After a moment it moved off up the drive, and Kim saw Mr Murray rounding the corner of the building just as the car disappeared. She had no desire to continue her strange conversation with him; Hannah was obviously frightened of him for some reason, and it was very odd, him not wanting her to go to the police. Kim followed Hannah's example, running down as fast as she could to beat him to the front door, then carrying on towards home.

'Why didn't you take your latest theory out for a test drive first?' Judy asked Lloyd, when they were alone in his office.

Lloyd smiled. 'I must have got out of the habit,' he said. 'But it was possible. There's always been some doubt about the sex and the violence being perpetrated by the same man.'

Judy frowned. 'Do you "perpetrate" sex?' she asked.

'Not very often,' said Lloyd.

He was too far away to be hit. And his theory still presupposed that Natalie had written those letters. Today's letter rather bore out Judy's contention that Natalie had not, Judy would have thought, since poor little Natalie was dead by the time *it* was perpetrated.

'Mrs Cochrane could have produced that letter herself, as Finch pointed out,' said Lloyd.

Judy sighed. 'Let me ask the question before you answer it,' she said.

'The fact is,' said Lloyd, 'that Erica Cochrane must at the very

175

least have seen her husband's car leaving, which she didn't tell us, so she's obviously protecting him – what we have to find out is to what extent.'

True. 'But the letter just got him into worse trouble,' Judy said.

'But she didn't know that it would,' argued Lloyd. 'It distanced Cochrane from Natalia, and gave him an alibi – that's all she was thinking about, if she did do it.'

'But he clearly didn't want an alibi,' said Judy.

'No. And I think that that's because he really wasn't there,' said Lloyd. 'That Murray was driving his car, and that Murray killed her, just like Freddie said.'

Judy had found Murray rather attractive; she had difficulty casting him in the role of murderer. 'I liked him,' she said. 'He doesn't behave like a psychopath.'

'Neither did Christie.'

No.

'This woman who says she saw Natalie get into Colin Cochrane's car,' Judy said. 'I'll tell Bob we want a description of the driver, if it's a genuine sighting.'

'With any luck she'll know whether or not it was Colin Cochrane, at least,' said Lloyd.

'So she will,' said Judy. 'I keep forgetting he's famous.'

'I don't,' said Lloyd, with an enigmatic smile.

Lloyd was being mysterious again and, when Murray was brought in, declined Judy's invitation to come and talk to him on the grounds that he had to wait for Tom coming back.

Judy walked along to the interview room, unsure of the line she intended taking with Murray; it was this indecision that had prompted the invitation. 'Mr Murray,' she said. 'Thank you for coming in – and for letting us take your fingerprints.'

Murray smiled. 'I wasn't too sure if I had a choice,' he said.

'We all have choices,' said Judy, sitting down, trying to remember that she might be talking to Natalie's killer.

'Oh, we do,' agreed Murray. 'And invariably make the wrong ones.'

'Interview with Patrick Joseph Murray,' she said, glancing at the clock. 'Commencing nineteen hours fifteen. Present are DI Hill, DC Marshall. Could you say your name for the tape, please?' she asked.

'Patrick Murray,' he said, and listened gravely to his rights.

'Now,' said Judy. 'Mr Cochrane has told us that he couldn't start his car on Tuesday evening, and that you agreed to look at it for him.'

'That's correct – as I told this gentleman here.'

'Yes. Did you return the keys to Mr Cochrane?'

'In a manner of speaking. I left them under a sort of plant pot thing at the back gate. Because the caretaker would have gone by the time Colin came back, you see – in fact, he'd gone by the time

I'd finished.' He smiled as DI Hill wrote that down. 'I thought you had the tape for all that now?' he said, pointing to her notebook.

'Bad memory,' she said. 'I got into the habit.' Then she glanced down at it. 'Mr Cochrane's car was seen at a time when he claims not to have been driving it,' she said. 'Did you drive it that evening, Mr Murray?'

Murray shook his head. 'I got in and started the engine,' he said. 'Made sure I'd fixed it. That's all. I drove it along the drive at the school, and reversed back into his parking space.'

'You didn't drive it on the road?'

'No,' said Murray.

'Perhaps you wouldn't mind telling us where you were at five minutes to ten on Tuesday evening?' Judy asked.

Murray appeared to be trying to dredge up the details of Tuesday evening; Judy was much too used to Lloyd to be taken in by that.

'Five to ten?' he repeated. 'I'd be at home, I expect.'

Judy looked at Marshall.

'The thing is,' Marshall said slowly, like he said everything, 'when I went to ask you to come here, I went to your house first. Your wife said you'd still be at the school – that's how we knew where to find you.'

Patrick Murray smiled. 'Yes,' he said, encouragingly.

'And I asked your wife what time you got home on Tuesday evening,' he said. 'I said you might be a witness to something I was investigating. She thought it was nearer half past ten when you got in.'

'Ah, then, she'll be right,' said Murray, not a bit put out.

'So – perhaps you wouldn't mind telling us where you were?' repeated Judy.

Murray looked like a small boy who had been caught trying to steal sweets. 'That's just it,' he said. 'I would,' he said. 'I really would mind. You see . . . I was with a friend.'

'Does she have a name, this friend?' asked Marshall.

'Oh, she does indeed. But I don't want to tell you her name.' He lifted his hands helplessly. 'So where does that leave us?' he asked.

Judy wasn't entirely sure where it left them. Hang on to him, she had been told by Lloyd. Don't let him go. She had pointed out that she could hardly arrest him on what they had, but Lloyd had put touching faith in her ability to persuade the man to stay.

Victoria Murray had indeed told Marshall that her husband had come home at ten-thirty; she had added that he had almost certainly been with another woman. She had confirmed that he had told her that he had been mending Cochrane's car. 'The idiot's got himself involved in something because he can't stop lying,' she had said. 'Not because he was murdering anyone.'

'Well,' Judy said. 'It leaves us with the fact that someone was driving Mr Cochrane's car at five minutes to ten. He says it wasn't him, and you say it wasn't you. Maybe you have some other suggestion? Did anyone see you leave the keys under this plant pot thing at the back gate?'

Murray shook his head. 'Doubt it,' he said. 'Even the caretaker had gone, as I said.'

'Larch Avenue is quite a long street,' she said.

Murray looked slightly puzzled. 'Yes,' he agreed. 'And steep. I pity the kids puffing their way up there on their bikes. Mind, they shouldn't smoke so much.'

'It could take us quite a while to organize a door-to-door, to see if anyone saw the car being driven out of the school, and by whom.'

He nodded. 'And you'd probably not find anyone who did,' he said. 'They'd all be watching the telly between eight and ten. There was a good film on.'

'So I believe,' said Judy, and looked him in the eye. 'Who were you with, Mr Murray?'

'I don't know if you have ever indulged in an extra-marital relationship,' Murray said. 'But secrecy is ... well, paramount. And since I know that telling you the lady's name will not advance your investigation one iota – if you can advance an iota – I would really much rather not say.'

'Who were you with?' asked Judy.

Murray nodded over to the tape. 'At the beginning of this interview, you said I didn't have to answer any questions,' he said. 'I'm choosing not to answer that one – all right?'

'Then perhaps you won't mind answering some questions about Mr Cochrane's car,' she said. 'We'd like to know exactly what was wrong with it, and exactly what you did with it.'

It was, she discovered, an inspired choice of question, even if it had been asked out of sheer desperation. The answer was, to her, incomprehensible, but Marshall was interested, and it was going on for ever.

Lloyd waited impatiently for Tom. Judy couldn't hang on to Murray for much longer, not unless he'd confessed to the whole thing, and that seemed less than likely.

The job had gone swimmingly this time. All four had been arrested, all the stolen goods recovered while still in the lorry, making transporting them to the station a great deal easier than it might have been – and now Lloyd wanted to talk to the lorry driver and his mate.

The door opened and Tom knocked on it. 'They've been charged,' he said. 'We got a cough from the two who hired the warehouse, and the other two have put their hands up to handling.'

Lloyd beamed at him. 'Good,' he said.

'And the custody sergeant says you can only talk to them in his presence, and not about the stolen goods.'

'Fine,' said Lloyd. 'Now you can go and ask Mrs Cochrane to come in and help us with our enquiries. I think she has a little explaining to do.'

Finch brightened at last. 'Yes, sir,' he said, and left before Lloyd changed his mind.

The custody sergeant was highly suspicious of Lloyd's motives. 'You can't put any questions to them about tonight,' he said. 'They've been charged.'

'I know,' said Lloyd.

'And they've been bailed,' he said. 'I think they're only staying out of curiosity.'

'Yes,' said Lloyd, as he was ushered into the interview room. 'Good evening, gentlemen,' he said.

The two men, one young and spotty, one middle-aged and surly, looked back at him.

'We're not grassing anyone up,' said the youth.

'Wouldn't dream of asking you to do any such thing,' said Lloyd, sitting down opposite them. 'Nothing like that at all.'

'What, then? asked the older one. 'Only if we help you, you've got to say. In court.'

'I will make certain that the court knows of your public spirited-ness,' said Lloyd. 'This sort of thing goes down well.'

Two pairs of highly suspicious eyes looked back at him, but only for a moment. Then they looked away, like they always did.

'Now,' said Lloyd. 'Correct me if I am wrong, but I believe that you actually tried on Tuesday evening to deliver the goods in connection with which you have been charged.' He raised his eyebrows in a query.

Stony silence. Then the middle-aged one looked at the sergeant. 'He can't ask us about that,' he said.

'No questions can be put to you about the matter on which you have been charged,' the sergeant said. 'But this question seems to be about your previous visit.'

'Exactly,' said Lloyd. 'It doesn't matter to us how many times you tried to deliver there. But you did try on Tuesday night, didn't you?'

'Yes,' said the older one, grudgingly.

'Now, what I want to know is . . . did you see anyone while you were there?'

'Of course we didn't! Or we'd have got rid of the bloody load then, and we wouldn't be sitting here, would we?'

'No – I don't mean that. I mean, did you see anyone in the vicinity? Anyone at all?'

179

'No,' he said.

Lloyd sighed. He had been on a roller coaster ride with this. Sure that he was right, then with the sighting of the car sure that he was wrong. But this time he had been so sure, once he knew about Murray having Cochrane's keys.

'Yes, we did,' said the youth to the older man. 'We saw him off the telly – remember?'

'He doesn't want to know about that!' said the other. 'He means real people.'

'He does want to know about it,' said Lloyd. 'Who did you see?'

'Him,' said the boy. 'You know. That bloke that used to be a runner. Whatsisname – you know – Colin Cochrane!' he remembered triumphantly, and turned to the other. 'We couldn't believe it, could we? Seeing him like that.'

Lloyd smiled at them. 'And . . . what time was that?' he asked.

'Hang on,' said the older one. 'Are we getting him into bother?'

Lloyd shook his head. 'You're getting him out of it,' he said. 'What time?'

The man looked at him for a long time, gauging him. Lloyd put on his open, honest, blue-eyed look. 'He is in deep trouble,' he said. 'You're his only alibi.'

'We got there at nine forty-five sharp,' he said. 'We waited for over five minutes, then got out of the lorry and banged on the door. That's when we saw him.'

'And where exactly was he when you saw him?'

'Passing the end of the cul-de-sac.'

'Humphry Davy Close?'

'Yeah. Running on to Byford Road.'

'At ten minutes to ten?'

'Yeah.'

'Thank you, gentlemen,' said Lloyd, and got up, leaving the interview room, closing the door quietly, checking that there was no one around. 'Yes!' he said in a fierce whisper, punching the air.

Colin Cochrane looked up wearily when Lloyd went into the interview room. 'What now?' he said.

'You're free to go, Mr Cochrane,' said Lloyd.

Cochrane stared at him. 'Was it Patrick who was driving the car?' he asked. Then, disbelievingly, 'Did Patrick *kill*—?'

'I don't know, Mr Cochrane. I just know that *you* weren't driving your car at five to ten on Tuesday night, and that was the only reason that you were here. So you're free to go.'

'How do you know it wasn't me?'

Lloyd smiled. 'Your lorry,' he said. 'You were right. The men had seen you. And they identified you.'

'But . . . how did you find them?'

'Well,' said Lloyd. 'We don't just harass people, you know. We do act on what they tell us.'

'Is the nightmare over now?'

Lloyd indicated with a movement of his head that that was still a little way off. 'But we're getting there, Mr Cochrane,' he said. 'We're getting there.'

Patrick had told the inspector and the sergeant in minute detail what had been wrong with Colin's car. DC Marshall had been quite interested – he had even suggested to the inspector that might be what had gone wrong with her car; Patrick had offered to have a look at it for her, but she had politely turned him down.

He was going to bluff his way out of this, with any luck. God knew he had that aplenty. The only place they could possibly have found his fingerprints was in the car, which was fine. The only person Natalie had confided in had turned out to be an amateur blackmailer, so she hadn't told the police. And as long as they didn't know which of them had been driving the car, he didn't see that they could keep him here. Not on Colin's say-so.

Colin was in it up to his neck, and, as far as they were concerned, Colin was her married boyfriend. Patrick was an innocent bystander, whom Colin had tried to implicate. He was anxious to be seen to be cooperating fully with the enquiry.

There was a knock at the door, and DI Hill suspended the interview.

'If you wouldn't mind staying where you are, Mr Murray,' she said, and he was left with DC Marshall, until another man came in. He wasn't a big man, but his presence in the room somehow made Patrick feel much smaller, and a good deal less lucky. He was introduced as Detective Chief Inspector Lloyd.

'Are those the clothes you were wearing on Tuesday night?' he asked.

Patrick automatically looked down at what he was wearing. 'It's the same suit,' he said. 'It might be the same shirt – if it is, it's been washed, I hasten to add.'

'Could you remove them, please?'

DCI Lloyd was Welsh; dealing with a fellow Celt was sometimes good, sometimes not. They gave him paper overalls to wear, and DC Marshall bore off his clothes. Inspector Hill came back, decency having been observed, and the interview was recommenced, with the change in personnel noted. He was reminded that he was under caution.

'Mr Murray,' said DCI Lloyd. 'I have just been given information

181

by two independent witnesses which confirms that Mr Cochrane wasn't driving his or any other car at five minutes to ten on Tuesday evening. He was running along Byford Road.'

Patrick smiled, despite his worsening situation. 'Ah, I'm glad,' he said, suddenly as Irish as the chief inspector was Welsh. 'I'm glad. Poor Colin's taken a bit of a hammering over this.'

Lloyd nodded agreement. 'So who was driving it?' he asked.

Patrick had one more, rather desperate, attempt at bluffing. 'Joyriders?' he suggested.

Lloyd studied him. He didn't look at him – he studied him. 'Joyriders?' he repeated.

'Found the keys, made off with the car. Inspector Hill said that someone might have seen me leave them.'

'So joyriders stole the car, then parked it neatly where it had come from, and put the keys back where they had found them? Have you heard of many joyriders who have done that, Mr Murray?'

Patrick smiled. 'It's unlikely,' he said. 'But not impossible. Maybe Natalie was one of them, for all I know. Maybe she got left down there with one of the others.'

'Who then killed her?'

'Could be.'

'You weren't driving Mr Cochrane's car?'

'Not on the road,' said Patrick.

'You weren't with Natalia?'

'Me? No.'

'Perhaps you would be prepared to let us have a sample of blood,' said Lloyd. 'Just to be certain?'

Patrick looked at him. 'For this . . . er . . . DNA test, would that be?' he asked. 'Like Colin?'

'Yes.'

'Do I have a choice?'

'We all have choices,' the inspector said again.

'And make the wrong ones,' Patrick added, again. 'I'm probably making the wrong one now. But no.'

Lloyd nodded. 'You are making the wrong one,' he said. 'Because your refusal can – and will – be indicated at any subsequent trial. Your prints were found on Natalia's shoes, Mr Murray. Do you still say you weren't with her?'

Her shoes. He'd left his fingerprints on her shoes. You had to know when to fold your cards. 'Yes, all right,' he said. 'I was with her.'

'Patrick Murray, I am arresting you on suspicion of the murder of Natalia Ouspensky on . . .'

Don't panic, Patrick, don't panic, he told himself, as he found himself being led away to what they called the custody suite, being

182

told that he had the right to inform someone of his arrest. Thanks, but no thanks.

He had known, from the moment that the inspector had said the car had been seen, that he couldn't really bluff his way out. 'It was the bugger I nearly rammed, wasn't it?' he said, when they were back in the interview room. 'He told you after all. I thought I'd got away with it.'

'Are you confessing, Mr Murray?' asked the inspector.

Patrick looked over at her. 'I'm admitting that I was in Cochrane's car,' he said. 'And that I was with Natalie. But I didn't kill her,' he said. 'And I can prove it.'

Lloyd sat back, a little as though he was at a concert, preparing himself to listen to the music. 'Then do so, Mr Murray,' he said.

'Right,' said Patrick. 'Well . . . I came to Stansfield just after Easter, for an interview at Oakland. I got the job, obviously, but they didn't need me until September.'

She was writing it down. Patrick admired her doggedness. Lloyd was less patient.

'Is this relevant?' he asked.

'Oh, I think so,' said Patrick. 'You see, my wife didn't join me here. We were going through a sticky patch. I made friends with the Cochranes, but I was lonely.'

Lloyd didn't seem terribly moved by that, but Patrick ploughed on.

'By June my wife still hadn't come, and I honestly thought my marriage was over,' he said. 'I started going out. And I met Natalie at a disco.'

Two stony faces looked back at him.

'I took her out a few times, and . . . and we made love. Like you do.'

'Did you know how old she was?' asked Lloyd.

'I knew she was young, but she told me she was seventeen. Said she hadn't been able to get a job yet. I had no reason to disbelieve her.'

Lloyd nodded. 'Go on,' he said.

'I started at the school on Tuesday, and I was taking the register when I saw her name. She was right at the back of the class, practically hidden. I hadn't seen her. That was the first time I knew that she was still at school. Still a minor.'

'Were you angry?' asked the inspector.

Patrick turned to her. 'Angry?' he said. 'No. No – I was shocked, but . . . well, I thought there was no harm done.'

Lloyd sat forward a little. 'I have a sergeant,' he said, 'who would by now be telling you to cut to the chase. Would you do that, Mr Murray?'

'Yes,' he said. 'Right. Well – I always work until about seven or so. Colin was having trouble with his car, and I said I'd look at it.'

He smiled. 'Your tape has details of that,' he said. 'But it was a temporary repair – I wanted to be certain it would hold.' He shrugged. 'I took it out for a test run,' he said. The truth. It seemed to have been a long time since he had told the unvarnished truth – even his confession to Erica had had the odd improvement made to it. 'Just a run through the streets. And I saw Natalie waiting at a bus stop.'

'You hadn't arranged to meet her?' Lloyd got up as he asked the question.

'No. I didn't even know she knew anyone round there. I was just testing the car.' He was always so much more convincing when he was lying. This sounded pathetic.

'Go on,' said Lloyd, who had begun to tour the room.

It was a bit off-putting. Patrick was giving a performance, even if it was the God's honest truth – the audience wasn't supposed to mill around.

'I picked her up. I thought we had to get things sorted out – I had to tell her that we couldn't see one another again.'

No one said anything; Lloyd was stopping now and then to glance at the posters on the wall, Inspector Hill was writing in her notebook, and neither of them seemed to care whether he ever said another word.

'What happened . . .' Patrick began, and pulled a handkerchief from his pocket to mop up the perspiration. It was so damned hot. 'What happened was that she said we ought to go somewhere we wouldn't be seen together. She suggested the place – not me.'

'Really?' said the inspector.

Yes. Really. DI Hill had been more inclined to believe him when he had told her a pack of lies, he knew she had.

'When we got there, she . . . came on to me,' he said. 'I didn't go there for that, but she . . .' He shrugged.

Lloyd was leafing through the booklet on the Police and Criminal Evidence Act that Patrick had been told he could refer to at any time.

'She . . . she . . . wanted us to . . .' Patrick mopped the sweat from the back of his neck. 'So we did,' he concluded.

'You had sex, in a borrowed car, with an under-age pupil,' said Lloyd, not even looking at him, still browsing through the booklet. 'Is that what you're too shy to say, Mr Murray?'

'I didn't want to,' said Patrick.

Lloyd's eyes went heavenward.

'I didn't . . . I . . .' Patrick closed his eyes. 'All right, I wanted to – but I didn't mean to. I've never had much willpower,' he said. 'And we'd been seeing one another all summer – I couldn't really see the difference. I pointed out to her that we were in Colin Cochrane's

184

car, of all things, but she – she persuaded me. She asked what harm we were doing Colin.' He looked at Lloyd. 'More than I could ever have imagined,' he said. 'That's what harm we were doing him.'

Lloyd let the booklet drop and swing on its piece of string. 'So far,' he said, 'we have had a defence of your morals – which sound pretty well indefensible, I may say. But I understood you to say that you were going to explain why I shouldn't now charge you with murder, Mr Murray.'

If only he knew where Hannah had gone. Or even knew her other name. But she had vanished by the time he got down there, and when he had got back up to the staff room, Kim had gone too. She had said she would wait. Fifteen-year-old girls were much more trouble than they were worth. Perhaps he could get away without mentioning that bit.

'I was trying to leave,' he said. 'But Natalie ... well, she didn't want to go ...'

He had told her to hurry up; she had retrieved her pants from the floor of the car, and tried to pull them on in the confined space, lifting herself off the seat. Her shoulders had caught a pile of letters and sent them spilling down over both of them on to the floor.

She had laughed and had begun to pick them up; he had told her to leave them, to get out of the car and make herself presentable. They had both got out, and he had got into the driver's seat.

He couldn't be late getting the car back, he had said, starting the engine, but Natalie had been in no mood to hurry; there was plenty of time, she had said, leaning in the open driver's window to kiss him, to tease him. She found Cochrane's deodorant and started spraying it about until he got it off her.

He had told her to do up her shirt; she had said he'd unbuttoned it so he could button it up again. He had told her he didn't have time for all that. He had told her to do what she was told. But none of it had worked.

'Make me,' she had said.

He had got out of the car, and she had giggled as he caught hold of her. He had pushed her against the wall, and ... and he had no willpower, and ... well, he hadn't buttoned up her shirt.

But in the middle of it all he had heard Sherlock's unmistakable bark, looked up, and seen Erica Cochrane.

'So I just got in the car and got the hell out of there,' he said.

Lloyd's face was grim. 'Could Mrs Cochrane see you?' he asked, his voice low.

Patrick shook his head. 'Not to identify me,' he said. 'It was too dark. I only saw her for a second, in the headlights.'

Inspector Hill looked up from her notebook. 'Let me get this straight,' she said. 'You are saying that when you saw Mrs Cochrane you immediately stopped what you were doing, got into the car, and drove off – leaving Natalie there?'

'It was survival of the fittest, as far as I was concerned.'

'Survival being the operative word,' said Lloyd. 'Not, I think, of the fittest.'

'Maybe not,' said Patrick. 'But I didn't kill her. She was alive when I left, and Erica Cochrane's told you that. It's lucky for me Erica saw her – I told her to get out of sight.'

'A tall order,' the inspector said. 'Given where she was. Standing in front of a sheer wall.'

Her delivery was always the same; always calm, always quiet, unlike the chief inspector, whose emotions, real or manufactured, were on display.

'What construction do you imagine Mrs Cochrane put on what she had just witnessed?' she asked.

Patrick shrugged. 'That it was Colin who was with her,' he said.

'That didn't bother you?'

'Not really. She already thought Colin had a bit on the side. For all I know, he has.'

Lloyd shook his head a little. 'And Mrs Cochrane would then believe that she knew who this "bit on the side" was, wouldn't she?' he asked.

'She might as well think it was Natalie,' said Patrick. 'Again – for all I know, it was.'

Lloyd waited for him to say more, but Patrick didn't see the need to expand on what he'd already told them.

'That's it, is it?' Lloyd asked. 'This proof?'

'What more proof do you need?'

'More than that,' he said. 'Mrs Cochrane saw her husband's car – naturally she would have thought it was her husband who was using it, and she didn't tell us that. We therefore have no reason to believe the rest of her story – she could have found a body, couldn't she? She could be lying to protect her husband.'

'Not now, she couldn't,' said Patrick. 'She's known since this afternoon that I was in the car, not Colin. Do you think she would still be keeping quiet about it if she thought I'd killed her? She found her alive, just like she told you.'

Lloyd nodded, accepting that, and Patrick relaxed a little.

'But there is still a little puzzle, Mr Murray,' Lloyd went on. 'You see, we can't work out – and your account doesn't explain – why Natalia's shoes were sitting in the depot doorway.'

And they had his fingerprints on them. The full story, then, the bit he had hoped not to have to recount, but that had always been a forlorn hope.

186

'I parked Colin's car at the school, and I was picking up the envelopes to put them back on the shelf, when I found Natalie's shoes.' He looked at the disapproving Inspector Hill. 'Even I couldn't let the kid go home in bare feet,' he said.

Lloyd was looking puzzled now, the animated eyebrows low over his eyes. 'But if you went back, in what way does Mrs Cochrane's statement that she was alive when she saw her benefit you?' he asked. 'For all we know, you went back, discovered that Natalia had failed to keep out of sight, and lost your temper with her.'

Patrick smiled. 'My temper is always exactly where I left it, Mr Lloyd,' he said. 'I don't lose it. I went back and left her shoes – I didn't even see Natalie, and I've got a witness to that fact.'

'Couldn't you have mentioned that earlier?' demanded Lloyd.

'Well, to be honest, it's not really going to be much use now,' said Patrick. 'But she can clear me, once you find her, because Erica Cochrane saw Natalie alive after I left, and this girl in an Oakland School uniform saw me arrive back, with Natalie's shoes in my hand. She watched me put them down, and she watched me leave. She knows I never even saw Natalie.'

Lloyd sighed loudly, and scraped his chair back, getting up. 'A girl in an Oakland School uniform?' he said.

'I tried to find her, but all the kid knew was that she saw me with a pair of women's sandals in my hand, and then Natalie was found murdered. She's not been back to school since. All I can tell you is that her name's Hannah.'

'How do you know her name at all?'

'Because I saw her tonight, and one of the other girls told me her name. But she ran away, because she's petrified of me. I was in the staff room when I saw her, but by the time I got downstairs she had gone. Just . . . vanished. Her bike was lying on the ground, but she was nowhere to be seen.'

Lloyd looked less sceptical than he had, but even more sombre. 'What time was this?' he asked.

Patrick did a calculation. 'Sixish,' he said. 'This Kim girl was with me, but she had gone when I went back. She probably knows where Hannah lives, but I can't remember Kim's other name.' He looked at the industrious inspector. 'I've a terrible memory for names,' he said. 'And faces. But you can't write them down.'

Lloyd made an exasperated noise. 'Does this mean we have to get hold of the register in order to find Kim in order to find Hannah?' he demanded.

'I know Kim,' said the inspector, almost absentmindedly as she went leafing backwards through her notebook. 'Her name is Walters. But if I remember . . .'

'Go and ask her,' said Patrick. 'She'll tell you where to find

Hannah. It's crazy – this girl thinks I'm the murderer, and she's the only person in the world who can vouch for the fact that I'm not.'

The inspector looked up from her notebook. 'You do realize what you're saying, don't you, Mr Murray?' she asked, and went back to her task.

Patrick's mouth opened. No, he hadn't realized what he was saying. That hadn't crossed his mind. No wonder Erica had been prepared to cooperate. How was he to know, for God's sake?

'It's not my fault!' he said. 'I *told* Natalie to get out of sight.'

'Hannah,' the inspector said, not even acknowledging that Patrick had spoken. 'There's a Hannah Lewis on the list of girls we got from the drama group,' she told Lloyd. 'She's our best bet.'

The chief inspector agreed. 'Interview suspended, twenty hundred hours,' he said. 'In the meantime, Mr Murray, I'm sure you'll understand that we must put you in one of our cells.'

He sounded really upset about that, thought Patrick. But the worst had happened; the bleak future that he had outlined for Erica's benefit was a virtual certainty. It had always been, really, from the moment he had discovered what had happened to Natalie. There had been moments when he had thought that he had got away with it, that's all. They hadn't lasted long.

But now, unless Hannah had really vanished into thin air, she would be found, and he would at least be able to prove that whatever else he was, he was no murderer.

'Oh, I understand all right,' he said. 'And believe me, I want you to find her.'

Tom looked up as Judy and Lloyd came in. 'No joy on Mrs Cochrane, sir,' he said. 'No one's at home. The caretaker says she left the school at about six, he thinks. She was working late.'

'Was she, indeed?' said Lloyd. 'And she's disappeared too,' he added grimly.

'Who else has disappeared?' asked Tom.

Things began to fall into place as Judy told him Murray's story. He had been wrong about Mrs Cochrane as well, it seemed, but not that wrong. She had been stringing them along, but she hadn't found Natalie dead. She had found her very much alive, and at it with someone she not unnaturally assumed was her husband.

'I've put out a general alert for Mrs Cochrane,' said Judy, as they drove to where Hannah Lewis lived. 'Meanwhile, we may have found our witness, with any luck.'

Tom had a feeling that whatever luck they had had, and that was precious little, might well have run out. The lorry driver and his mate being able to corroborate Cochrane's story was luck, he supposed, but he wouldn't have taken advantage of that. He took a breath. 'The DCI stopped me making a fool of myself over Cochrane,' he said. 'Didn't he?'

She smiled. 'He does have a rather unique way of doing people favours,' she said.

'Then I'll do him one,' said Tom, with a grin. 'Something can't be rather unique.'

'Don't you dare start that!' she said.

Tom laughed. 'Don't worry,' he said. 'I'm not equipped to. I had a teacher who had a thing about that.'

As he had gloomily predicted, they did not find their witness. What they actually found was Mrs Lewis, who almost passed out when Tom identified himself and Judy.

'What's happened?' she cried. 'Where's Hannah? What's happened to her?'

'Nothing that we know of, Mrs Lewis,' said Judy, her voice as reassuring as she could make it, given that they had no idea what had happened to Hannah or Mrs Cochrane. 'May we come in?'

'Where is she?' said Mrs Lewis again, as they walked into a pleasantly furnished, tidy sitting room. 'She went to the school to meet Kim, but she's not at Kim's – I just rang. There's no answer from the school. Something's happened to her, I know it has.'

'We don't know that,' said Mr Lewis.

Tom hadn't even noticed that he was there, but he was. Sitting on the sofa, silent until that utterance. For all Tom knew, invisible until then.

'Try not to worry,' said Judy. 'We think she may just be with a friend – she may have been mistakenly frightened of someone. We'll find her, don't worry. In the meantime, can you tell me what Kim said when you rang her?'

'Kim wasn't there – it was her mother I spoke to, and that's what worried me.' Mrs Lewis was on the verge of tears.

Tom caught Judy's eye, and looked up towards the ceiling.

'Mrs Lewis,' said Judy. 'Has Hannah got a computer? A word processor?'

Mrs Lewis was startled out of the tears. 'Yes,' she said.

'Would you mind if Sergeant Finch had a look at it?' asked Judy. 'It's important.'

Mr Lewis gave consent, challenged by Mrs Lewis, but Tom was already on his way to find Hannah's bedroom. He left Judy trying to find out exactly why Kim's mother had so alarmed Mrs Lewis, and went up to her room.

It didn't take long. She hadn't even taken the precaution of deleting the file. Presumably her parents were not into computers. Today's letter, Tuesday's letter, and a number of other letters. They were looking for the right girl, then, he thought. But if it was Murray she was afraid of, perhaps she hadn't witnessed the murder after all.

'And Kim is with her aunt at the police station?' Judy was saying.

'That's what Mrs Walters said. I was just going to ring the police about Hannah when you came. Kim's been phoning her at all hours of the day and night – she's got Hannah into trouble, I know she has.'

No, thought Tom. If Hannah was in trouble, she had got herself there by not coming to the police in the first place. But Judy was probably right. She would be lying low with a friend, knowing that all this was about to break about her head. He said as much in an edited version, but Mrs Lewis dismissed the idea.

'She would have come *home*,' she said.

'I'm not so sure,' said Mr Lewis.

'Oh, do be quiet, George!'

Kim Walters, it transpired when they contacted the station and DC Marshall, had been very anxious to let them know that the man who had been seeing Natalia was not Colin Cochrane.

Judy smiled. 'Better late than never,' she said, as Tom headed for the Walters' residence.

The reason for this knowledge did prove Patrick Murray's contention that he had not known until Tuesday that Natalie was only fifteen. But he had known then, and he would be charged with the offence. Tom felt a little sorry for him; Natalie had hardly been corrupted by Murray's attentions, and in truth he would be charged with being a cad, basically. And it wasn't every day that ungentlemanly conduct ruined your entire life.

Kim, when they saw her, assured them that Hannah was quite safe – she was with Mrs Cochrane.

Erica had reversed out of Colin's parking space, and had almost driven straight into the girl she had already frightened out of her wits when she had screamed at her to get out of her office. The headmaster had heard her. Again. And come in and told her to take a few days off if things were as bad as they seemed. And had gone on at her about the evening paper.

She had had enough. She had finished the damn letters, left them on his desk, and gone to the car. She hadn't been looking where she was going. She had scrambled out of the car, praying that she had done no damage.

'Oh – please,' the girl had said. 'Please – he's coming after me.'

Erica had tried asking who was coming after her, but had got no coherent response.

'Please help me!' the girl had shouted, almost hysterical with fear. 'Please, Mrs Cochrane, please! Don't leave me!'

She had been terrified. Erica had helped her to the car.

'Drive off,' the girl had pleaded. 'Please, please, get me away!'

Erica had driven off, looking round just in time to see Patrick Murray run round the corner of the building. Patrick? Was this girl afraid of Patrick? She had tried to take her home, but the girl was afraid even to do that, because 'he' would find her.

Erica had taken her to her own house, allowing the girl to calm down a bit before she asked her any questions. She had driven right into the garage and had let the distraught girl through into the kitchen, where Sherlock had come loping up to be fussed and fed. Erica had been in the middle of giving him his dogfood when the girl had got nervy again.

'Mr Murray knows where you live,' she had said. 'He might have seen us – he'll come here. I can't stay here.'

The girl had wanted somewhere to hide, and Erica had thought then of her own bolt-hole.

'What's your name?' she had asked, as she had driven away from Ash Road.

'Hannah Lewis.'

'Do you want to tell me what all this is about?'

No reply.

There the conversation had ended, and now Erica was making tea while Hannah looked at her books. The books had been left in the flat when she had moved in with Colin; there were too many for the house to accommodate. She would have to think what to do with them when the flat got sold, if it ever did.

'Why are you so afraid of Mr Murray?' she asked, in the hope that a direct question might elicit some sort of answer. Her own feelings about Mr Murray were in as much turmoil as the girl's, but it was difficult to imagine him forcing his attentions on her.

She could see Hannah in the other room, leafing through a book, but she deliberately didn't look at her when she spoke, busying herself with her tea-making activities.

'I saw him,' Hannah said. 'On the Green. On Tuesday night.'

'You were there?' asked Erica, sharply.

'Yes,' Hannah said. 'And I saw Mr Murray. He had Natalie's shoes in his hand.'

'Her *shoes*?' Erica echoed. Patrick hadn't told her that bit. 'What on earth was he doing with them?'

'Holding them,' the girl said. 'Then he just put them down – and he knows I saw him.'

Erica had made a terrible mistake on Tuesday night, but it hadn't been her fault, it hadn't . . .

Sherry, keen to be allowed off the lead, had pulled a little as they had neared the blackness of the unlit council depot which heralded his freedom from constraint. Erica had let him lead the way, let him pull her excitedly down the path.

She had pulled his lead tight when they reached the bottom, and she had seen the dark shape of a car parked in the depot courtyard, its engine running, the driver's door open, lighting the empty interior. It had been facing her, its headlights dazzling her. It might have been burglars, or anything; Erica had hung on to Sherry as he strained to be allowed to go.

Beyond the car, she had seen something moving at the embankment wall opposite the depot, which had resolved itself into two dark shapes, so intimately involved with one another that at first she had taken it to be just one. Embarrassed, she had turned to go, but Sherry had barked, wanting to go on, and he was a big dog to argue with. Erica had been pulled back into the headlights against her will, as the car door had slammed, and the engine had been raced.

She had watched, almost mesmerized, as its tyres squealed and spun on the concrete, the driver trying to accelerate away before he'd even taken the handbrake off.

Her puzzlement had turned to disbelief as the car shot backwards up the service road, and she had checked its number, in case she wanted to report the incident to someone. It had been Colin's car; but it couldn't have been, she had told herself, as the area had been plunged in darkness once more. He'd said it wasn't going, for one thing. But she had known that she hadn't been mistaken; Colin's number plate had cost him a lot of money, and it wasn't the kind you could mistake.

Then, as her eyes had become once more accustomed to the half-light from the road above, she had seen the girl. Half naked, hopping about on one foot, still trying to get her knickers back on, for God's sake. She had stuffed them in her pocket as Erica had approached.

'What the hell do you think you're doing?' Erica had demanded, grabbing hold of her arm.

'Mind your own business,' she had said, shaking her off, and had walked away, towards the adventure playground.

Erica had thought it was Colin who had been with her. What else could she have thought? Sherry had smelt someone he knew – that was why he had been so excited. But he had smelt Patrick, of course, whom he knew just as well.

She poured boiling water on the teabags. 'And you think he killed Natalie,' she said. 'That's why you're afraid of him.'

'Yes,' said Hannah.

'You've got it all wrong,' Erica said brightly. 'But it's nothing we can't sort out over a cup of tea.'

Hannah had been on the Green that night. And she was one of

those girls that had hung about the house. Not just one of them, either – she was the one who had kept coming after Colin had asked them not to.

She loaded a tray with sugar, powdered milk, cups and saucers and the pot of tea. 'No biscuits, I'm afraid,' she said, her voice still determinedly cheerful. 'I don't keep things like that here. Just books, a few sticks of furniture, and non-perishables.' She set the tray down on the coffee table.

Hannah had called him Colin, in the office. Not Mr Cochrane, which was the natural thing to call a teacher. Colin.

Erica carried on making polite noises, finding out how Hannah took her tea, handing it to her.

Hannah was the letter writer. *She* was the one who had arranged to meet Colin on the Green, not Natalie.

'When you were on the Green on Tuesday evening,' she said. 'You were waiting for Colin, weren't you? Like you said you would, in that letter.'

Hannah looked back at her, then nodded briefly.

'And the other letters?' Erica went on. 'You wrote them, too, didn't you?'

'Yes.'

'Were they true?'

'No.' Hannah looked into her teacup.

'Why, Hannah?' asked Erica. 'Why did you do that?'

Hannah drank some tea. 'You opened his mail,' she said. 'I'd seen you do it. I knew you'd see one of them, sooner or later.'

Erica frowned. 'Why did you want me to see them?' she asked.

'Because he married you,' Hannah said. 'He didn't even say he was getting married. He just did it, when we were on the Easter break.' She looked up then. 'I wanted to split you up,' she said. 'I wanted you to believe them.'

She had got her wish, thought Erica. She had split them up, even if it had taken Natalie's murder to do it. She shook her head. 'You shouldn't have done that,' she said.

Hannah looked away. 'I know,' she said. 'But I hated you. I really did. I . . .' She looked back at Erica. 'I'm sorry,' she said. 'And I'm really grateful to you for getting me away from Mr Murray . . . bringing me here. I . . . I am sorry about the letters – especially the one arranging to meet Colin. It was stupid. He didn't turn up, or anything,' she added. 'Don't think that.'

'But why did you write the last one? The one he got this morning?' asked Erica, pouring her own tea, carefully, slowly, trying to keep her hand steady.

Hannah had caused it all. Everything. Everything that had

happened since March, everything that had happened on Tuesday night, everything that had happened since. She had blamed Natalie. But it was Hannah's fault. And she had been there, on the Green. All the time.

'I had to do something,' Hannah said. 'I knew Colin hadn't killed Natalie, because he wasn't there.'

Erica nodded slightly. 'Why didn't you just go to the police?' she asked, her voice light.

'I couldn't,' said Hannah. 'I was afraid of what Mr Murray would do.'

Erica sprinkled milk on her tea, watching it swirl into the dark liquid as she stirred. 'You should have gone to the police, Hannah,' she said. 'You really should.' Her spoon slowly moved round and round in the teacup as she spoke. 'And there was no need for you to be afraid of Mr Murray.' she added. 'Because *he* didn't kill Natalie.'

Colin had walked miles. Not running, not this time. Not any more. Just walking, enjoying the freedom from suspicion at last, trying to sort out his thoughts. His life. His feelings for Erica, his obsession with athletics. That was all it was, all it had ever been. But he had never been unfaithful to Erica, not since the day they had met. Not with a woman. But athletics had amounted to much the same thing. He was obsessed by something that meant more to him than anything – much more than she did, or ever would.

And that was why he hadn't been able to retire gracefully, to move into the comfortable world of TV celebrity, fleeting though it probably was, insubstantial though it doubtless was. It was pleasant, clean work with a pay-packet that so outweighed its responsibilities as to be laughable. But he hadn't been able to let athletics go.

Love wasn't like that; if a loved partner died, the survivor mourned, then moved into the next phase of his life. Obsession was like that. Never letting go. And they had thought that he could have murdered a fifteen-year-old girl, because of this obsession. He had almost begun to believe that he had.

He had gone home, then, not sure if Erica would want him back, not sure if he wanted to go back. He wasn't going to turn into another person; he wasn't going to stop being obsessive overnight. But now that he knew that he was, perhaps they could live with it. Or perhaps he could do something about it. Just facing it, on Tuesday night, when he had made himself ill, had helped.

But Erica wasn't there, even if he could have explained all that to her. The dog was; he was pleased to see Colin, and Colin had to admit that he was pleased to see him, because his presence meant that Erica was coming home. He wasn't sure that what he and Erica had was love, but it deserved another chance, whatever it was.

He foolishly imagined that it would be Erica when he heard the doorbell, but she would have her key, of course. He opened the door to Inspector Hill and Sergeant Finch, and thought for one ghastly moment that he was being sucked back into the fantasy.

Not Natalie's fantasy; he knew that now. Someone else's. Natalie had just got sucked in too, and she had died for it. And he still didn't know whose fantasy it was.

'Mr Cochrane, is your wife here?' the inspector asked.

'Erica? No,' he said. 'What do you want with Erica?'

'Do you know where she is? It's very important.'

He frowned. 'Not for certain,' he said.

'If you know where she might be, then tell us,' said Finch.

Colin shook his head. 'I want to know why you're looking for her,' he said.

'We just want to speak to her,' said Inspector Hill.

Colin's mouth fell open, and he stared at them. They didn't just want to speak to her. They were looking for her. Urgently. 'Erica?' he said. 'You think Erica had something to do with ...?'

'Just tell us where she is, Mr Cochrane – please,' said Inspector Hill. 'Before the situation gets any worse than it is.'

Worse? There couldn't be a worse. But ... she had been so certain that he had been with Natalie. So totally unprepared to believe his protestations. Oh, dear God. What had she done?

'I think she might be at her flat,' he said. 'It's been on the market for months, but ... she goes there sometimes.'

He gave them the address in a daze, listened as Finch relayed the information on his radio, watched them walk down the path, get into their car and go.

He would never have believed that the nightmare could reach such depths.

Hannah could hear the frantic banging on the door echoing through the almost-empty flat, hear her own name being called, Mrs Cochrane's name being called, as the nylon knot was pulled tighter and tighter round her neck. Her oxygen-starved brain could barely take in what was happening, but they were *there*, outside the door. The police were *there*, and she summoned all her strength for one last desperate effort before consciousness finally ebbed.

Then faraway voices. Just voices. She couldn't see.

'She's alive. What about the other one?'

'Just. Ambulance required at ...'

In and out of consciousness then, as more people arrived, more voices.

195

'She's coming to. You'll be all right, love, don't try to move.'

Dim shapes. Someone comforting her, someone examining her head.

'I don't think the head injury's too bad.'

A stretcher.

'She . . . she tried to . . .' It hurt to talk. Her throat hurt. Her voice sounded odd. But she had to tell them.

'Don't talk, love. You'll be all right, don't worry.'

The ambulance. Now she was fully conscious, fully aware. She tried to tell them, but they told her not to talk. It didn't hurt so much now; she wanted to talk.

She had a lot to say.

Chapter Twelve

Colin sat in the waiting area, alone now that the doctor had left.

They were operating, but the doctor's prognosis had been less than optimistic. Erica had lost a great deal of blood; in her weakened condition the operation itself might kill her, if that girl hadn't already done the job.

The doctor could, and had tried to, explain the medical problem, but no one could begin to make him understand, or believe, the circumstances. The police had said that the girl had also been admitted; Colin didn't even know her name to ask about her, but he gathered that it was whoever had been writing those letters, and that they thought Erica had tried to harm her in some way.

The police had been at the hospital, leaving only when it had become clear that Erica was on the critical list, and they were in no danger of her giving them the slip.

She might, one of them had said guardedly, have to face charges, and Colin was only too well aware of what charges he had meant. It was obvious; they thought she had killed Natalie, and then tried to kill this girl.

He had brought a nightie and dressing-gown, but they had said she wouldn't be needing them yet. The 'yet' had come a heartbeat too late.

He saw the doctor walking towards him, his face serious. And Erica wouldn't after all be facing charges.

Morning. Patrick opened his eyes to the new day, and reviewed his situation.

They were preparing a case against him for the Crown Prosecution Service, he had been told last night. He had been charged, and eventually he would know whether or not he would go to court to answer that charge.

It had been late before they had finally let him go; Victoria had been in bed by the time he had got home. He glanced over at her as she slept. Soon she would be awake, and wanting an explanation of where he had been.

197

He would have to tell her. Whatever happened, what he had been doing on Tuesday night was going to come out. He had known from the moment he had seen Hannah standing there that damage limitation was the best he could hope for, but he had never dreamed of anything like this.

He had thought that she must have seen Natalie, minus her shoes, complaining about being abandoned like she had. And that even if Natalie hadn't shopped him, Hannah had seen him, large as life, holding the shoes, and would surely have put two and two together.

He had thought she might tell someone – the head, Victoria – someone. He had hoped she wouldn't, of course, but he had known in his water that his unwitting dalliance with a schoolgirl wasn't going to have a happy ending.

But this? Natalie murdered? When the shock of hearing that had worn off, he had just been waiting for the knock on the door. But Hannah hadn't gone running to the police with her story, and . . . well, it had seemed just possible that he had got away with it.

He would have to tell the head. He would have to give evidence in the murder trial, even if he wasn't charged with his own offence.

Doomsday scenario? He would lose his job, his wife, and he would go to prison.

Damage limitation? Stay out of prison, because Kim could prove that Natalie hadn't been straight with him in the first place, and he really hadn't known that he was committing an offence, not until that last time. He had told them about her attempted blackmail. They had laughed; said that a guilty conscience did some funny things. It seemed that she had merely been seeking his advice after all.

But that made it more likely that she would tell the truth about what Natalie had said to her, and while his conduct on Tuesday night could by no stretch of the imagination be considered gentlemanly, he could hardly have foreseen that it would result in Natalie's death. It really was quite likely that he would not be charged with the sex offence.

But he would have to give evidence at Erica Cochrane's trial, obviously, and it would all come out then anyway. It was just possible that he could hang on to Victoria, somehow, like he had before. There was no way he could salvage his job.

And right now, he had to tell Victoria everything, before she found out some other way. He owed her the truth, anyway.

'Where were you this time?' she asked, as soon as she opened her eyes.

'Oh, you wouldn't credit it,' he said.

She sat up sleepily. 'I don't suppose I will,' she said. 'But try me, anyway.'

'The head only called a staff meeting about the uniforms,' he said.

198

'What did we think about the students not having to wear them during the heatwave? It went on for hours.'

She gave him a heavy-lidded look of disbelief.

'Then we all went to the pub. Mind you,' he added, 'do you blame us?'

'I suppose not,' she said, her voice resigned.

Lies were so much easier. People almost always believed him when he was telling lies. He smiled at her as she closed her eyes again.

Well ... perhaps he wasn't exactly being believed. But what he had said had been accepted. And he could hardly hit her with all this when she was still half asleep, could he?

He showered and shaved, skipped breakfast and went to school, where a second and more profound shock awaited him.

Erica was dead. At first, the words meant nothing; he couldn't take them in. *Erica*? The head asked him to keep it quiet – he was telling the staff, but not the students.

Erica was dead – killed, the rumour had it, in self-defence. First Natalie, and now Erica. The two people he had got close to – in very different ways – since his arrival in Stansfield, were dead. Sudden, violent deaths that made no sense at all. He sat in the head's office and stared into space, trying to come to terms with it.

'Are you all right?' asked the head.

Patrick nodded. Yes, he thought. Yes. And if a thought crept into his mind through the numbing blow of that news about the luck of the Irish, about the fact that dead women didn't come to trial ... well, it was only human, wasn't it?

Judy sat in the Walters' living room, with Kim, Mrs Walters, and Kim's aunt. Mrs Walters had packed her son off to school, untouched as he was by the events of the last two days, but she had kept Kim at home.

Kim sat on the big, comfortable sofa, between her mother and her aunt, her face unhappy, but surrounded by support and love and prepared to answer still more questions if she had to.

Judy's night had been spent largely at Barton General, where she had waited until the medical staff had allowed her three minutes with Hannah; she had gone home then and fallen into bed to be awakened by the call that had informed her of Erica Cochrane's death. She hadn't gone back to sleep.

'It's dreadful,' Mrs Walters said, taking her arm from Kim's shoulders, only to allow her sister to take over. 'It's just dreadful. When I think ...' She looked up at Judy. 'Something like this – you think it's bound to be a man, don't you? You think you're safe with a woman. Kim thought Hannah was safe.'

'I know, Mrs Walters,' Judy said, and leant over, putting her own

199

hand over Mrs Walters', as they were clasped and unclasped in helpless agitation. 'Please don't distress yourself,' she said. 'Hannah really is going to be all right.'

'But she had to . . .' Mrs Walters looked at Kim, then back at Judy. 'Hannah's mother said that Hannah had to defend herself with a knife,' she said, dropping her voice to a whisper. 'And that woman's dead – what's that going to do to poor little Hannah?'

The enormity of what she had done might well hit Hannah at some point, but she had seemed entirely under control when Judy had seen her. In much better shape than either Kim or her mother. 'Well, we don't know exactly what happened yet, Mrs Walters,' she said. 'We haven't spoken to Hannah in any detail – that's why I just want to go over a few things again with Kim.'

Kim put her arm round her mother, her aunt's arm still round her. Holding on to one another, now acutely aware of how suddenly people could be taken away.

Judy took out her notebook. 'Kim,' she said gently, trying not to make the child feel any worse than she already did. 'When you looked out of the window, after Mr Murray had gone down to talk to Hannah, you said that she was cycling away, looking over her shoulder.'

Kim nodded.

'And that she seemed very frightened? Is that what you told my colleagues?'

'Yes,' she said, in a small voice. 'I thought she was trying to get away from Mr Murray, but it must have been . . .'

Judy could see the tears coming as she spoke, and waited until she had got herself under control again before she carried on.

'You've been very helpful to us, Kim,' she said. 'I know how difficult all this has been for you – please don't worry about these questions. I just want to get things clear.'

Kim nodded again, manfully holding herself together, and Judy moved on to the difficult part. 'Now – there isn't a right answer to this next question,' she said. 'I just want your impression of what happened next – after you saw Hannah cycle away.'

'Mrs Cochrane's car hit Hannah's bike,' Kim said. 'But Hannah sort of threw herself off before it did.'

Judy nodded, writing that down. 'Do you think Hannah cycled into Mrs Cochrane's car because she wasn't looking where she was going, or that Mrs Cochrane's car reversed into Hannah's bicycle?' she asked.

Kim closed her eyes. 'Mrs Cochrane's car reversed into Hannah's path,' she said, after a moment. 'I think.' She opened her eyes and looked a little uncomfortable. 'But I could see the accident was going to happen,' she said. 'I probably closed my eyes. I always do that, like when you drop a plate or something, and you know it's going to break.'

Judy smiled. 'I think everyone does,' she said.

'But I did see what was going to happen, so I suppose Hannah would have seen Mrs Cochrane's car, if she had been looking where she was going,' Kim went on. 'And Mrs Cochrane should have seen Hannah. It was a bit of both,' she said.

Judy smiled again at the desperately honest assessment of the situation. 'That's fine,' she said. 'Then what happened?'

'Mrs Cochrane got out, and helped Hannah up.'

'Did Hannah still seem frightened?'

Kim nodded.

'Then she got into Mrs Cochrane's car,' Judy said. 'Did she get in by herself? Or did Mrs Cochrane help her in?'

'I . . . I don't – ' Kim swallowed hard to try to stop the tears. 'She . . . Mrs Cochrane . . . she had her arm round her, but . . . I don't know!' she almost shouted, in the end.

'Who opened the passenger door?' asked Judy, changing tack slightly.

'Mrs Cochrane,' said Kim, miserably.

'Did she shut the door? Before she went back round to the driver's side? Or did Hannah close it herself?'

'I think Mrs Cochrane closed it,' Kim said.

'Think?' Judy asked, her voice gentle.

'Mrs Cochrane closed it,' said Kim.

'Good,' said Judy. 'You're doing fine, Kim.'

But Kim wasn't, of course, doing fine, and the slender hold that she had had on herself gave as tears dripped down her cheeks again. 'I didn't know she was in danger,' she sobbed.

'Kim, you mustn't blame yourself,' said Mrs Walters, cradling her in her arms, rocking her backwards and forwards like a baby. 'Hannah's going to be all right – you heard the inspector.'

Judy watched as the girl cried miserably on her mother's shoulder. What a great job this was, she thought.

'I think we could all do with a break,' she said.

'Good idea,' said Kim's aunt. 'I'll get some tea for everyone.'

Tea. That would make everything all right.

The murder room had been packed up, the team had been stood down and had gone back to normal duties – within the textbook three days, no less. This was usually a moment to celebrate, an excuse to go across to the pub and tell one another how clever they had been. Not this time, thought Lloyd. This time the prime suspect was

201

dead, and they had another investigation on their hands. But not one that needed a murder room.

He had been proved right; he had known in his bones that Cochrane had been telling the truth, and he had indeed. But he had still allowed himself to be taken in by appearances, something that he warned junior officers about over and over again. Mostly, he would say, things are just the way they seem, but not always – beware of that. Despite his own good advice, he had still been looking for a man for Natalia's murder, and had thought that he had found him when Murray's involvement was made plain.

He had discovered Cochrane's unknown alibi witnesses, and had believed that he had cracked the case. But Murray's interview had sidelined everything, and he had felt like a player who had been taken off just after he had scored a goal.

But then he was, and always had been, a little detached from this enquiry. He hadn't been there when the body was found; he hadn't been at Erica Cochrane's flat where Hannah had been discovered lying unconscious, and Erica Cochrane dying.

Someone had to go and talk to Cochrane, who was owed some sort of explanation of these terrible events. And since his staff were involved in the real business of the day, Lloyd thought that he had better go himself.

He wasn't looking forward to it.

Kim's mother's arm was so tight round her shoulders that Kim seriously doubted if she would ever let her out of her sight again, but she wished she could speak to the inspector alone, just for a moment. It would hurt her mother's feelings if she said that, though, so she didn't.

Not that she had anything to say that her mother couldn't hear; she would just feel better without an audience, really. She looked at the inspector, who in turn looked at Kim's mum, not speaking, until her mum realized that it might be better if she wasn't there.

Kim didn't know how she had done that, but she had known that she would.

'I think I ought to go and give Janice a hand,' her mother said, taking her arm away, and patting Kim on the shoulder. 'Is that all right, love?'

Kim smiled, her mother left, and now she was alone with the inspector, and she didn't *know* what to say. But she had seen Mrs Cochrane just after Mr Murray had left the office. She had looked so sad. So hurt. And later, Kim had thought Hannah was running away from Mr Murray; she had told the police about *him*, because she had thought that nothing short of being afraid for her life would have made Hannah accept a lift from Mrs Cochrane.

But perhaps she hadn't accepted a lift. Perhaps Mrs Cochrane really had bundled her into the car when Hannah was still dazed from the accident. It just hadn't looked like that. If anything, Mrs Cochrane had seemed reluctant ...

She couldn't say that. She couldn't. But as it turned out, she didn't have to.

'Kim,' said the inspector quietly. 'When you said you didn't think she was in any danger ... It wasn't Hannah you meant, was it?'

Kim shook her head, tears coming into her eyes to be angrily blinked away. 'Hannah hated Mrs Cochrane,' she said, her voice no more than a whisper that the inspector had to lean over to hear. 'She had ... you know, a thing ... about Mr Cochrane. And she hated Mrs Cochrane.' She looked at Inspector Hill, expecting disbelief, but all she found was someone who was listening. Not dismissive, not shocked, just listening. 'I think ... I *thought*,' she amended, 'that Hannah wanted to go with her. And I thought that that was because she was so afraid of Mr Murray that even Mrs Cochrane would do.' She shook her head. 'But I've no right to say that,' she said. 'I was so far away, and ... and ...'

Kim knew what Hannah had told her mother, what she had presumably told the police. It hadn't seemed like that to her, but she *was* very far away, and Hannah ought to know what happened, after all. But all the same.

She took a deep breath. 'But it's Mrs Cochrane who's dead,' she said defiantly, before she changed her mind about saying it.

Inspector Hill nodded.

'And ... and, well ... people were saying that Colin was going with Natalie, and if Hannah thought that, she would be much more likely than Mrs Cochrane to—' She broke off. That wasn't fair. That really wasn't fair. She didn't know Mrs Cochrane. For all she knew, she might be perfectly capable of jealous murder. She had no right to say that Hannah was. 'That was a terrible thing to say,' she said.

'No,' said the inspector. 'It might be wrong, but it isn't terrible.' She sat beside her, put her arm round her like her mother had. 'When the police investigate a murder,' she said, 'we find ourselves thinking – and discussing – all sorts of possibilities. That a child's own mother killed him, perhaps. If we're wrong, we're glad. But we don't feel bad for having thought it. The unthinkable does happen.'

She was nice. Not like she'd been the other day, when Kim had felt like a fish on a hook, being drawn to the surface against her will.

'And don't worry,' she said. 'I understand your concern – and I'm not taking anything at face value.' She smiled. 'I've been taught not to, by someone who checks for himself if someone tells him it's raining.'

Kim smiled too, and sniffed back the tears.

'Thank you,' said Inspector Hill, closing her notebook, standing up just as Kim's mum came back in. 'I'm sorry to have had to put you through so much,' she said, and then smiled at Kim's mother. 'I'll see myself out, Mrs Walters. Kim may be required to give evidence at some future date, but we'll let you know.'

Her mother looked up at the inspector. 'What happens to Hannah now?' she asked. 'Will she have to go through a trial or anything like that?'

'That depends on a lot of things way outside my control,' said Inspector Hill. 'And, as I said, we don't actually know the full story yet.'

'Hello, Hannah,' the woman said, as she came into the interview room.

'About time too!' said Hannah's mother. 'I don't know who you people think you are.'

'This is DI Hill,' said Tom Finch, with a nicely wicked comic timing, Hannah thought.

He'd told Hannah to call him Tom, when he had picked her and her mother up from the hospital, doggedly polite in the face of her mother's rudeness.

'She wants to ask you a few questions, Hannah,' he went on. 'We just need to get everything clear, you know?'

'Just call me Judy,' said the inspector, as Tom set up the cassette recorder. 'How do you feel now, Hannah?'

Hannah smiled a little. 'Not too bad,' she said.

'Now, Hannah,' the inspector said. 'You are here because Mrs Cochrane died from stab wounds inflicted by you, and we have to talk to you about that.'

'But she was trying to kill me,' Hannah said.

She couldn't think of the inspector as Judy, the way she thought of Sergeant Finch as Tom. She sounded too like a headmistress. A headmistress trying to sort out a playground fight.

'Yes, I know. But I'm afraid it isn't as simple as that, Hannah. The inquest may well produce a verdict of lawful killing, but in order to do that they have to know what exactly happened, to the best of your recollection. We need to know now, so that we can tie it in with our forensic evidence.'

'It's perfectly obvious!' said Mrs Lewis, who Hannah would swear had not shut up from the moment Tom Finch had appeared, apologetically, at the hospital. 'And it's ridiculous to make Hannah do this so soon after something like this has happened to her!'

The inspector smiled sympathetically, but it was manufactured sympathy. Hannah's mother was rubbing this woman up the wrong way, as she so often had with others. Teachers, youth club workers, swimming instructors. Anyone Hannah had ever had anything to do with.

'I know it must seem very callous, Mrs Lewis. But we have to talk to Hannah while the events are very fresh in her memory. The inquest will be opened and adjourned – it could be several weeks before it's actually heard.' She turned to Hannah. 'I'm sure it's nothing to worry about,' she said. 'Neither this, nor the inquest. We just want to know what happened – as far as you are able to tell us.'

'It's all right,' said Hannah. 'I don't mind, honestly. Mum just fusses.' She ached all over, and her throat hurt. She just wanted to get all of this over with.

'Right,' Inspector Hill said. 'We will be taping this interview, Hannah, but you are not obliged to answer any questions. Anything you do say, however, may be given in evidence.'

'You're treating her like a criminal!'

'Hannah has, even if it was in self-defence, taken someone's life, Mrs Lewis,' the inspector said.

'So had that woman! And she would have taken Hannah's if she hadn't managed to stop her!'

'All violent death has to be investigated, Mrs Lewis. This is a formal interview in which the caution, the tape, and everything else is to safeguard Hannah's rights.'

'It's outrageous.'

'And I must ask you, Mrs Lewis, to let Hannah answer any questions put to her herself.' She turned again to Hannah. 'You are here voluntarily, Hannah, and are free to leave at any time. You are also entitled to free, independent legal advice.'

'She doesn't need legal advice! And if we can leave, that's what we're doing.' Mrs Lewis stood up. 'Come on, Hannah,' she said.

Hannah didn't move. She was the one being interviewed – it was up to her whether she stayed or not. And she was staying.

'I strongly advise you against leaving, Mrs Lewis,' said Judy. 'I would be quite within my rights to arrest Hannah.'

Her mother stared at the inspector. '*Arrest* her?' she said, her voice barely audible, for once.

'Yes,' said Inspector Hill coolly. 'Please don't make me do it, Mrs Lewis.'

Tom watched, lost in admiration for Judy's style, as the formidable Mrs Lewis, who had dismissed her husband at the hospital with a wave of the hand, telling him to go to work and keep out of the way, sank back down into the chair.

He always wondered whether Judy would really carry out the odd threat that she was given to making, but she sounded about as comforting as a dentist's drill when she issued them, so he had never had occasion to find out.

'Good,' said Judy. 'The sooner it's all sorted out, the better.'

So everyone kept saying. Tom felt badly about interviewing the girl so soon after such a dreadful thing had happened to her, but her injuries were superficial, and the attempted strangulation had been halted before any real damage had been done. Hannah seemed to have suffered no psychological ill-effects, and the doctor had said they could talk to her. 'A very pragmatic young lady,' he had called her.

Tom was never entirely sure what pragmatic meant, but the DCI had said it meant that a proper, recorded interview could be done, and that was what they had to do, because the attempted strangulation had been halted by a knife plunged twice, the second time fatally, into Erica Cochrane, and even alleged murderers were entitled to have their own deaths investigated as fully and as speedily as possible.

'I think we have to start with Tuesday evening, don't you?' Judy said.

Hannah expressed the desire not to have her mother present, but Judy explained that she was being interviewed with regard to the death of Erica Cochrane, and an adult had to be present.

Hannah gave a sidelong glance in her mother's direction. 'It'll upset her,' she said to Judy. 'You've seen what she's like.'

Judy smiled a little. 'Well,' she said. 'I can't say I blame your mum for being upset. You seem remarkably calm about it all.'

'Not much point in getting into a flap,' said Hannah. 'It's happened.'

'True.' Judy sat down and took out her notebook. 'So, let's get down to it,' she said.

'All right,' said Hannah.

'You wrote a letter to Mr Cochrane telling him you would meet him at the adventure playground on Tuesday evening – is that right?'

Hannah, so apparently calm a moment before, went a painful pink. Poor kid. That was why she hadn't wanted her mother present, of course.

Mrs Lewis was, predictably, staring at her daughter now. 'What letter?' she demanded.

'Just a letter,' mumbled Hannah.

'I want to know!' said Mrs Lewis.

'Mrs Lewis!' said Judy. 'I must ask you not to interrupt this interview!'

Judy had an enormous store of patience; Tom had seen it last her through hundreds of no-comment interviews, through dozens and dozens of voluble parent-overseen interviews, watched it finally produce answers from seasoned pros who simply couldn't match her in that department, and who eventually told her what she wanted to know. But she must have forgotten to top up this morning.

'You'd written him a lot of letters, hadn't you?' she asked, her voice calm again now.

Hannah nodded again.

'Is that why you didn't want me here?' her mother asked. 'Because you've been writing love letters to him, is that it?'

'Mrs Lewis,' Tom said, hoping that his intervention would stop Judy from actually hitting the woman. 'If you don't mind . . .'

'I do mind! I mind finding out from you people that my daughter's been writing love letters to some teacher!'

'I knew you wouldn't understand,' muttered Hannah.

'Of course I *understand*,' said Mrs Lewis. 'What bothers me is that you thought I wouldn't!' She looked at Judy. 'She's always had a crush on him,' she said. 'Of course I understand,' she said again, with a little laugh.

Hannah didn't seem comforted by that. But then, Mrs Lewis didn't know the nature of the letters. Judy would, Tom was sure, keep the content of the letters out of it if she could, but it seemed unlikely that she would be able to.

'I'm not sure I understand,' said Judy. 'Why *did* you write those letters, Hannah?'

Hannah thought for a moment before answering. 'I love him,' she said quietly.

'It's just a teenage crush,' Mrs Lewis assured Judy. 'You must have had a crush on a teacher too – everyone does.'

Tom had had a crush on a teacher. Just when he was beginning to understand what people saw in the opposite sex, an exchange teacher from France had come to the school, and Tom had followed round like a puppy this exotic, curvaceous creature, ten years younger and ten times sexier than any of his home-grown teachers. He understood.

But he hadn't written her letters, and, even if he had, they wouldn't have been the kind that Hannah had written. Even if they had actually been doing such things, he wouldn't have written letters about it. The sudden thought of that goddess from his youth performing such acts quite perturbed him. He quickly summoned up an image of his old maths master instead, but that very nearly made him laugh. He thought of his bank balance, and that did the trick.

'Those letters implied that you and Mr Cochrane were having a relationship,' Judy said. 'Were you?'

'What are you suggesting?' demanded Mrs Lewis, horrified. 'How *dare* you sit there and—'

'Mrs Lewis,' said Judy. 'I have asked you several times—'

'I'll be having a word with your superior officer, my lady! Suggesting such a thing – Hannah is fifteen years old!'

Judy didn't reply; her cool gaze remained on the outraged Mrs Lewis for a moment before she looked back at Hannah. 'Were you having a relationship with Mr Cochrane?' she asked again, her tone of voice not one whit altered from the previous time.

'No,' said Hannah, brick red now, and physically squirming. 'I just sort of . . . made things up. It was just a game, really.'

'The letters weren't true?'

'No!'

'What did they say?' demanded Mrs Lewis. 'What was in them?'

'But you did go to the Green to wait for him, didn't you, Hannah?' asked Tom, jumping in with a question to get off the subject of the letters. 'That is why you were there, isn't it?'

'I always waited for him on the Green – he didn't know I did,' said Hannah. 'It was just so I could see him. He always came back across that way when he was out running.'

'But you told him you'd be there this time, didn't you?' asked Tom.

'Yes,' she said. 'I thought – I thought this time I could talk to him – that was all – I wasn't going to do any of those things.'

'What?' said Mrs Lewis. 'What things?'

'And what happened when you got there?' asked Tom, still anxious to leave the topic that embarrassed Hannah so much that she hadn't even told the police that she had been there.

This was, after all, what they needed to know. No one seriously thought that Cochrane had been having it off with Hannah for months. But that was indeed something else they had to be sure about, so all he could really hope for was a deferment of Hannah's discomfort.

'I waited for hours – until almost ten o'clock. But he still hadn't come, so I was just going to leave, when I saw Colin's car parked there, and . . . two people by the wall.'

Tom hoped that Judy wasn't going to insist on knowing what the two people were doing, and this time she did let it pass.

'But it wasn't Colin,' she said. 'It was someone else, with Natalie.'

Tom drew a breath, about to prompt her with another question, but a quick look from Judy silenced him before he had formed the first word.

'And he suddenly got into the car and reversed up the service road really fast.'

'What happened then?' Tom asked after a long silence; it did seem to reduce the violent outbursts from Mrs Lewis when he asked the questions, and he really felt that one of them ought to be asking them.

'I saw Natalie running up towards me. Her blouse was undone, flapping about. And she didn't have any shoes on.'

'Did you speak to her?'

'No. I didn't want her to see me,' said Hannah.

'Why not?'

'Well – you know. Not after what I'd seen her doing. I was embarrassed. So I hid.'

'Where?' asked Judy.

'Behind a tree.'

'Did you see anyone else?'

'Mrs Cochrane,' Hannah said. 'Well – I saw the dog first, and then her.'

The silence that fell after she had said that was clearly unnerving her.

'Go on,' Tom said, encouragingly, and this time the look that he got suggested that if he uttered another word Judy would garotte him.

'The dog was running about, but he still had his lead on, and . . .' She tailed off, looked at Tom.

He didn't let his expression change.

'Mrs Cochrane was running up from the depot,' she said.

Judy sat silently, writing in her notebook, not even looking at the girl.

'I thought she was chasing the dog, but she wasn't, she was—' Hannah broke off.

There was a long moment before she spoke again.

'She was chasing Natalie,' she said, her voice small.

Judy still didn't speak; Tom felt sorry for the girl, having to tell her halting story without the comforting reassurance of questions. It seemed very hard on her.

'She caught up with her at the big pipe,' Hannah went on, eventually.

Stony silence, until Hannah's hoarse, damaged voice began again.

'She pushed her head against the pipe. Natalie sort of slid down, and . . .' She looked down. 'I ran away,' she whispered. 'She must have seen Colin's car.'

Still nothing from Judy, not even now that the girl had told her what she had witnessed. No feedback, no encouragement, no reaction at all. She just sat there, calm and poised, the very opposite of the little girl across the table from her.

'I never thought she would kill her,' Hannah said defensively.

A reaction then, at last; a fleeting reaction, as a mixture of anger

209

and sorrow of almost personal intensity crossed Judy's composed face just for an instant, then was gone. She still didn't speak.

It hadn't occurred to Tom until that moment that Judy might be finding this difficult too – she had seen the girl so soon before she was murdered, after all. Now she was talking to someone who could have stopped it, could have got help, and who had been too afraid of the consequences, too embarrassed by what would come out about her fantasy life, to do anything at all.

Judy wrote in her notebook for a moment or two, then finally spoke again. 'Did you see anyone else at that point?' she asked.

Hannah nodded. 'Mr Murray,' she said. 'As I was running towards the footpath to Ash Road. He had a pair of shoes in his hand, and I realized that he was the one who'd been with Natalie.'

'Hannah,' said Tom gently, now that the silence had been broken, and he felt free to join in. 'Why didn't you tell Mr Murray what was happening? You knew that Mrs Cochrane had got hold of the wrong end of the stick – you knew he could sort things out.'

'I didn't want to get involved,' said Hannah. 'I just wanted to get away.'

Murray had said that Hannah had looked frightened. He had thought that she was frightened of him, had thought that that was why she had stayed away from school. But it had been the furious Erica Cochrane that Hannah had been afraid of on the Green, it had been Erica Cochrane that she had wanted to avoid.

'He went over to the depot and I think he must have left the shoes there.'

As ever, Judy wrote that down too, then looked up, her face stern. 'I can understand your being frightened and confused at the time,' she said. 'But once you found out that Natalie was dead, why didn't you tell anyone what you had seen?'

'I was too scared to tell anyone. I . . . I'd lied to my mum about the drama group last term.'

'Oh?' said Judy and Mrs Lewis in unison.

Hannah looked shame-facedly at her mother. 'I told you it went on until nine, because that's when Colin usually finished his run.' She looked down at her hands.

'But, Hannah,' said her mother. 'You had seen that woman attack Natalie! What did that matter?'

'I was scared to say what I'd seen,' Hannah said, and looked up at Judy. 'Because you were interviewing Colin, and that was all my fault.'

It was all perfectly possible, thought Tom. Panic, shock, did strange things to people. No reason to suppose that it was anything but the truth, and yet he too looked at his inspector and he knew that she didn't believe a word of it.

'How was it your fault?' demanded her mother.

Hannah's eyes hadn't left Judy's. 'I knew you must have found the letter saying I would meet him, and think it was from Natalie. That's why I wrote that one on Wednesday night, because I knew Colin had never been there.'

'What do you mean, you wrote one on Wednesday night?' asked her mother.

'Mrs Lewis,' said Judy, dangerously near the end of her tether. 'You must allow us to ask the questions.'

Mrs Lewis sighed loudly.

'Tell me about yesterday evening,' Judy said crisply.

'My mum told me that Kim was coming back to the main school to see Mr Murray. I went over to meet her.'

'Why?'

She shrugged. 'I'm not really sure,' she said. 'I wanted to see her. I think I might have been going to tell her what I'd seen.'

Tom frowned. 'You think?' he queried.

'I don't know,' she said. 'I was getting desperate to tell someone – I knew I should have told the police, and I was scared of what might happen because I hadn't. I think I wanted to talk to her, that's all.'

Yes, Tom could see that she might want to confide in a friend.

'But you didn't,' said Judy. 'You didn't talk to her – you left before she came out of her meeting with Mr Murray.'

'Because Mr Murray saw me and recognized me,' explained Hannah. 'I wasn't sure what he wanted. He'd been with Natalie, and I thought he'd want to talk about what had happened. I didn't want to talk to him – I just got on my bike and ...' She looked at Tom again, having sensed a more sympathetic response than she was getting from Judy. 'The next thing I knew there was a car heading straight for me,' she said.

Tom said nothing, and Hannah continued.

'I was a bit dazed after I came off the bike. The first thing I really remember is being in her car, and then we were in the Cochranes' garage.'

She was looking at Judy again now, as she spoke.

'We went into the kitchen, and she fed the dog. That's when I took the knife.'

They had wondered where the knife had come from.

'Why?' asked Judy.

'Just ... for protection.'

'It's just as well she did!' said Mrs Lewis. 'Are you going to charge her with that, too?'

Judy ignored her. 'Did you have any reason to think that she would attack you?'

211

'She had shouted at me,' Hannah said. 'Earlier on. At the school.'

Judy's eyebrows rose, and she wrote that down. 'What about?' she asked.

'A crowd of us used to hang about their house,' Hannah said. 'To see Colin. She didn't like it, and Colin asked us not to go. When the others stopped, I still went. She recognized me from then. She said it was my fault Colin had been arrested.'

'So, after what you'd seen her do to Natalie, you thought you might need protection?' asked Tom.

'Yes,' said Hannah. 'The cutlery drawer was open, and I could see this knife, so I just . . . took it. While her back was turned.'

'Go on,' said Judy, her voice hard.

'Then she took me to that flat,' Hannah said. 'She said she knew somewhere I'd be safe. I had let her think that I thought Mr Murray had killed Natalie, so she was pretending she was trying to protect me. She made tea – she said we had things to discuss.'

'What things?' murmured Judy, as she wrote.

'She asked if I had written the letters. I told her I had.'

'And what happened then?'

Judy was still being cool and efficient and detached. Possibly even not detached. Maybe hostile would be a better word, which was really very odd. She didn't seem to give a toss about Hannah's feelings.

'I was looking at her books – she was standing beside me, talking about the letters, and then she . . . she . . .' The girl tailed off.

Oh, God, here we go again, thought Tom, as Judy waited.

'She just suddenly pushed me, said that she had killed Natalie because she thought she'd been with Colin, but she had got the wrong one. I got the knife then, but she caught my wrist and made me drop it, and pushed my head hard against the corner of a shelf. It made me sick, and she pushed me down on the floor and sat on me.'

The doctor's examination had told them most of that. The cuts and bruises were ones that they saw quite often in casualty on a Saturday night after the pubs closed. Hannah had vomited, another aspect of hand-to-hand combat not unknown to the medical profession.

'She was pulling her tights off. I could feel the knife underneath me – I got it and stuck it into her, but it made no difference. I tried to push her away, but she put the tights round my neck and pulled them tight. I couldn't breathe – but I could hear people at the door, calling out. I managed to stick the knife into her again. That's all I remember until I was in the ambulance, really.'

Now, the DI closed her notebook. 'Your recollection's very clear,' she said. 'Thank you, Hannah. I'll get someone to type up your statement, and then you can sign it.' She stood up, neatly putting her chair under the table. 'You might want to think about what you've said – you may want to add to it, or alter it,' she said.

Hannah shook her head.

'Well, think about it anyway,' advised Judy. 'I hope not to keep you too long. In the meantime, perhaps you'd like to get something from the canteen?'

WPC Alexander bore Hannah and Mrs Lewis off to the canteen, but Judy wasn't exactly breaking her neck to get this statement typed by anyone.

'Let's talk to the DCI,' she said, her face grim.

Chapter Thirteen

Lloyd sat at his desk, Finch and Judy facing him, and sighed.

Tom Finch was of the very strong opinion that this case was closed. But. But, there was always a but. But Judy was immovably convinced that Erica Cochrane had done nothing at all to either Natalia or Hannah.

Listening to Hannah had been like listening to a short story on the radio, she had said. You could hear the fiction being woven. Her drama lessons hadn't been wasted on her; all the improvisation techniques had been put to good use. But not, Judy had said, good enough use. Hannah had been too busy mooning over Colin Cochrane in the drama group to learn how to act all that convincingly.

Natalia's friend Kim, it appeared, had cast some doubt on Hannah's story. Not much – her eye-witness account could have been of an abduction. But she certainly hadn't seen it like that at the time, and even the events of last night hadn't swayed her, which did merit serious consideration.

Lloyd would like nothing better than to tell Cochrane that at least his wife had not been a murderer, but that was beginning to look very unlikely, because whatever Judy and Natalia's best friend Kim thought, Hannah's story was hard to fault in any detail.

'Come on, guv,' Finch said. 'We've got a result – you know we have.'

That was just what they didn't have. They had, as far as he could see, a draw. If Lloyd had felt like a substituted player before, he now felt like nothing more than a referee. Finch had all the evidence on his side, and Judy only had her instinct. But Judy's instinct was something that Lloyd would, if he had to, bet his life on.

She was saying that Hannah Lewis was their psychopath, and if her instinct was right, then the appalling truth was that unless she could prove it they would, in the end, have to let her go. They could bring charges with regard to Erica Cochrane, but no court would let them hold her in custody on that, and her self-defence plea would be accepted by the CPS as unshakeable.

Judy believed with all her heart and soul that Hannah could and would murder anyone else who crossed her – like her mother, for instance. Or Kim. Or Patrick Murray. They had all irritated her in the very recent past. And it was Mrs Cochrane who was dead, like Natalia's best friend Kim had pointed out. It was Hannah who had taken the knife.

So the referee was playing extra time, much to his sergeant's bafflement, but Finch kicked off with as much vigour and enthusiasm as he had shown at the beginning of the match.

'Erica Cochrane thought she saw her husband at it with Natalie,' he said. 'She lied to us about what had happened that night. Hannah's not making that up, is she?'

'No.' Judy looked up from her notebook, which she had been studying without success.

Her note-taking had let her down this time, thought Lloyd. Or her instinct, with any luck. But he had a dreadful suspicion that it was her note-taking.

'But even if Mrs Cochrane didn't tell us about the car,' Judy went on, 'she told us that Natalie was alive when she saw her first. Why would she do that if she had killed her? Wouldn't it have been safer just to say she'd found the body?'

'That *was* what she said,' Finch reminded her. 'To start with.' He warmed to his argument. 'Think about it, guv,' he said. 'She only told us that she had seen Natalie alive once I had asked her about the car. But I didn't tell her why I was asking about a car, did I?'

Judy frowned a little, and checked back through her notebook. 'No,' she said. 'You didn't.'

'She assumed someone had seen it – she thought she'd landed her husband right in it. *That*'s when she said Natalie was alive when she saw her first – not before. Because she thought he would have been home by ten, and out of the frame.'

One nil, back to the middle of the park. Judy's turn to kick off now.

Right on cue, she did. 'But you thought then that she was simply trying to protect her husband – not that she had actually done it. I still think that is what she was doing. She thought Cochrane was the last person to have been with Natalie before the murderer, and she was just keeping him out of it.'

'She had just topped the kid,' said Finch.

'If she had just murdered Natalie, why didn't she go home the way she had come, along the pathway?' asked Judy. 'That way she could have kept her head down, and not got involved. Why was she climbing the banking at all, if it wasn't in order to get to the phone?'

'She was running away from the scene of a crime – she thought her husband was at home, and she could hardly go home in that state, could she? And she *was* in a state – remember?'

Judy nodded.

'And last night,' Finch said. 'You're not saying Hannah did all that to herself, are you? She's covered in cuts and bruises that the doc says are consistent with what she says happened. You can't fake that sort of thing!'

'No. But she would be covered in bruises, if Mrs Cochrane was fighting for her life,' said Judy. 'Hannah Lewis went voluntarily to that flat, and took a knife with her.'

'She'd seen the woman attacking Natalie! She came to in her car, in her company, whether she liked it or not. She just made sure she could defend herself if the worst came to the worst, and it did. And,' Finch added, 'she could have said that Erica Cochrane took the knife, couldn't she? But she didn't.'

'Only because I'd have wanted to know how come she tried to strangle her, in that case,' said Judy.

'She'd already had one run-in with her in the office – the head's confirmed that. He heard Erica Cochrane yelling at her to get out. He had told her not to come back to work until she got herself sorted out.'

It was, as they said, good end-to-end stuff.

'Why would she take her intended victim to her own flat in order to murder her?' Judy asked. 'It doesn't make sense. None of it makes sense, if you really look at it.'

'She wasn't going to leave her there, was she?' said Finch. 'She'd have dumped her somewhere.'

'How was she proposing to remove her? Bump her down two flights of stairs? Prop her up in the lift?'

One all.

Finch gathered himself for his next attack. 'Hannah knew that Murray had borrowed Cochrane's car,' he said. 'Only Murray himself knew that – and he has never spoken to Hannah. Hannah saw him with Natalie, like she said.'

'That hardly proves that Hannah didn't kill her,' countered Judy.

'It takes away her motive – she knew that it hadn't been Cochrane. Unlike Mrs Cochrane, who thought it *was* him until Murray told her different.'

Two one.

'Do you seriously believe that someone of Hannah Lewis's intelligence saw what she says she saw, and didn't *tell* anyone? Didn't tell Murray when she saw him – while it was going on, according to her – didn't tell her parents, and even once she knew that Natalie had been murdered, didn't tell the police – because she would be found out in a lie?'

It did seem unlikely, and even Finch had to shrug a little.

'It wasn't the lie that worried her,' he said, after a moment. 'It was those letters. She was scared of her mum finding out about them. When you're fifteen you get things out of perspective, and I'd be scared if my mum found letters like these now!'

'Quite. So who was more likely to get Natalie out of perspective? A mixed-up, sex-obsessed, fantasizing teenager or a mature woman?'

Foul. 'We're not in the business of more likely,' said Lloyd. 'You're the one who insists that logic can get you anywhere, and logic says that she knew Natalia hadn't been with her idol after all, so there was nothing to get out of perspective.'

'Did she know that?' said Judy. 'We only have her word for it that she saw Murray. Mrs Cochrane could have told her it was him.'

She could. Perhaps that last goal was offside. But Judy obviously hadn't marked that bit of information down as a probable lie, or her response wouldn't have been delayed. If she had believed Hannah at the time, then it was probably because she was being told the truth.

'And what about Natalie's blouse?' said Judy.

'What about it?'

'Why hadn't she even begun to button it again?'

'Because she was being chased by someone who wanted to kill her!' said Finch.

'So we're being asked to believe. But Natalie had no reason to expect Mrs Cochrane to run after her, did she? What she was doing had nothing to do with Mrs Cochrane. The natural thing to do is to walk away from an embarrassing situation – and you would button yourself up as soon as you could.'

Lloyd sighed. Once, they had believed that all they needed was a suspect. They had enough physical evidence to bury anyone, they had thought. But all that physical evidence was on Murray. The fibres were from his suit and shirt, the hair was his, the fingerprints were his, the unnecessary DNA test that was being done would prove that he had been with her. And while Lloyd regarded the man as beneath contempt, it was clear that he hadn't murdered Natalia. His heart was heavy as he prepared to blow the whistle for time-up.

'I think we're going to have to let Hannah go,' he said to Judy.

'Hannah Lewis murdered Natalie,' said Judy. 'And she murdered Mrs Cochrane. She did, Lloyd, as sure as I'm sitting here. I know she did.'

Lloyd nodded slightly. 'Could be,' he said. 'But knowing isn't enough. Unfortunately, we don't have a shred of evidence.'

Finch was trying hard to score again before the final whistle.

'We've got plenty of evidence on Erica Cochrane, though,' he said. 'She saw what she thought was her husband giving Natalie one right in front of her eyes. Then she was face to face with the girl. We have an eye-witness to her attacking Natalie.'

217

'An eye-witness who just happens to be besotted with Erica Cochrane's husband, and who failed to mention seeing anything at all until now,' said Judy, almost absently, as she leafed gloomily back through her notebook. 'An eye-witness who just happens to have killed Erica Cochrane before we could hear her side of it.'

Finch shrugged off the tackle. 'When we arrived on the Green, Mrs Cochrane was in a right state – she looked like she'd gone three rounds with *someone*, that's for sure. You saw her yourself.'

'But Natalie didn't look like that,' said Judy. 'She looked as though someone had just suddenly hit her head against the piping without any warning. Why would Mrs Cochrane get all messed up if Natalie didn't fight back?'

'She got like that trying to get away. And she lied to us about what she had actually seen. And last night, Hannah was quite definitely unconscious when the area lads broke in, with a pair of tights still round her neck!'

'And a superficial injury to the back of her head,' said Judy. 'Natalie's head injuries weren't superficial.'

'Mrs Cochrane didn't have a handy piece of concrete piping in her living room,' said Finch.

Lloyd rubbed his eyes. 'I always thought that if you cleared up the little puzzles,' he said, 'the big one wasn't as puzzling as you thought it was. But we've cleared up the little puzzles, and it's got us nowhere.'

Judy frowned a little. 'All of them?' she asked.

'I think so,' said Lloyd. 'We know why her shoes were where they were, we know why Cochrane was twenty minutes late, we know why Natalia's sexual encounter was non-violent, despite the murder. And none of it helps.'

Finch sighed extravagantly. 'Erica Cochrane had the means, the motive, and the opportunity, as any Perry Mason would tell you,' he said.

'We don't have to prove motive,' murmured Judy, checking her notebook once more. She looked up. 'And the means was a pair of tights,' she said, just a hint of triumph in her voice.

The moment Lloyd had seriously doubted would ever come was here; his gun-dog was pointing at last.

'You forgot Freddie's little puzzle,' she said. 'The tights.'

Lloyd frowned. Surely she wasn't going to let him down? 'We've solved that one,' he said. 'That only puzzled Freddie because he thought it was a quickie out in the open,' he said. 'Natalia was in the car with Murray for about an hour. She could have done a long, slow strip tease for him for all we know.'

'She could have,' said Judy. 'But if she did, she didn't take off her tights.' She smiled. 'And we do have a shred of evidence,' she said.

A shred of evidence, Lloyd discovered as she explained, wasn't a figure of speech; it was precisely what they had got and nothing more. Judy's last-minute goal hadn't won the match; it had merely saved it. This game was going to end in a penalty shoot-out.

And they would find out how good a goal-keeper Hannah Lewis was.

Hannah had done what the inspector had suggested; she had thought about her statement.

She didn't think she had gone wrong anywhere, but now they were in the interview room again, waiting for more questions. Detective Inspector Hill was going to try to catch her out. She had known that she wouldn't leave it there; she had felt the waves of disbelief, which at first had unnerved her, then had presented a challenge that she had taken on, eye to eye.

The only bit that had really bothered her was when DI Hill had gone on about the letters. She had thought she might tell her mum what was in them, but she hadn't. Now, she wanted to get this bit over with; she had had three sleepless nights, and had no desire to toss and turn through a fourth.

'This is Detective Chief Inspector Lloyd,' said Inspector Hill, and looked at Hannah's mother. 'He is my senior officer, Mrs Lewis,' she said. 'If you have any complaints about me.'

Her mother didn't make a complaint. She just looked huffy.

This was the last lap. Not one she had envisaged during the first wakeful night. Then, fear of discovery had been almost overwhelming.

Colin's plight had claimed the next night, when she had devised her new letter to try to get him off the hook. By the next day, discovery had seemed inevitable because Kim was actually going to tell Murray that she *knew* it wasn't Cochrane who had been seeing Natalie, that she could prove it. Murray would have had no option but to go to the police before they came to him, and he would have told them that Hannah had been there. And she hadn't got there in time to stop Kim talking to him.

Everything had seemed hopeless, and even more desperate when Murray had called her name from the staff room. Sheer panic had claimed her once more, and all she could do was run. She had never in her life been so glad to see anyone as she had been to see Erica Cochrane, of all people. And then, in the Cochranes' kitchen, a whole new solution had dawned, one that would leave Hannah free of suspicion, clear poor Colin, and get rid of his wife, all in one go.

Inspector Hill was going through the rigmarole with the tape, reminding her that she was still under caution, telling her her rights all over again.

'I'm not entirely happy with this statement, Hannah,' she said, when she had finally got the preliminaries out of the way.

Hannah was. Oh, she could have cried, she could have been upset and afraid – she had thought about doing it that way. But her drama teacher had always said that you should use as much of yourself as you could in a part, especially if you were improvising. Being as much herself as possible was what she had finally decided. It was less easy for anyone to catch you unawares.

She was glad of that decision now, as she looked back at the cool inspector, whose watchful eyes missed very little, Hannah was certain.

And she had felt calm, once she had known what she was going to do, once she had realized that she could get Erica Cochrane out of the way for good. Not at all like she had felt after she had killed Natalie. That had been quite unprepared for, and sheer panic had claimed her. But this, though it had been devised in Erica Cochrane's kitchen in a split second, and carried out with only seconds to spare, had been thought out very carefully all through her third sleepless night, at the hospital, and no one was going to catch her out.

Not even you, she thought, looking back at the inspector without even trying to disguise the fact that it was a game that she was going to win. It was going to work, it really was, because Erica Cochrane couldn't refute one word of it. She was dead. She was dead, and Colin was free of her at last.

The brown eyes that looked directly into hers were just as uncompromising as before, but Hannah was confident now, despite that. It didn't matter whether or not she believed her, because it *could* be true. It *could* all be true, and there was nothing the inspector could do to disprove it.

She still hadn't asked her anything. Hannah could play at that game too, but her mother couldn't.

'Well?' she said. 'What aren't you happy about? Don't just sit there.'

The brown eyes widened very slightly, and her mother was put in her place once again.

Hannah smiled a little.

'I had hoped you might tell me the truth this time,' said the inspector.

'I've told you the truth,' Hannah said.

'Have you?' she asked. 'Let's go back to yesterday when you went over to the school,' she said. 'You told us that Erica Cochrane shouted at you.'

'She did.'

'Yes, we've had that confirmed. What . . .' The inspector paused. 'What puzzles me is why you were in the office.'

'I wanted to know if Kim was there.'

220

'But you had stayed away from school, hadn't you? Because you were afraid of Erica Cochrane?'

Hannah had to think for a moment. 'No,' she said. 'Not because I was afraid of her. She hadn't seen me – I was just upset about it all.'

The inspector nodded. 'So it didn't worry you – going to see her?'

'I . . . I knew other people would be around. The headmaster's always there. And Mr Murray works late – Kim said.'

The inspector's boss didn't seem very interested in any of this. He had tipped his chair back while they had been speaking; he sat poised on the chair's two back legs now, not looking at her, apparently lost in contemplation of something on the ceiling.

'Then, later, she took you to her flat.'

'Yes.'

The inspector frowned a little. 'Did she force you to go to her flat with her?' she asked.

Hannah shook her head.

'So you went with her to her flat, despite the fact that you had witnessed her murdering Natalie?'

'I didn't see her murder her!'

That had been carefully thought out too. If she said she had actually seen the murder, no one would believe that she hadn't told Mr Murray when she ran into him, or her parents, when she got home. But a quarrel, a fight . . . that was different.

'Neither you did. You saw her assaulting Natalie, though – that didn't worry you?'

Hannah had foreseen this trap, had been surprised that it hadn't been sprung during the previous interview. She had anticipated the question, and she had the answer. She had been quite disappointed before, but now she had the chance to show how clever she had been.

'Of course it worried me,' she said. 'But when I found myself in her car, I let her think that I thought Mr Murray had done it, like I told you. So I thought it would be safest if I did what she suggested, in case I made her suspect that I knew what had really happened. I took the knife, though. Just in case.'

'Yes, so you did. With considerable foresight, as it turned out.'

'Now, look here,' said her mother, tired of behaving herself. 'Hannah's answered all your questions – she's told you exactly what happened. You just let her sign that statement and go.'

Chief Inspector Lloyd's eyes dropped to her mother, and he stopped rocking gently to and fro, but he remained precariously balanced on the chair's back legs. 'Just a few more questions, Mrs Lewis,' he said, his voice Welsh and reassuring. 'Bear with us.'

'I don't see what other questions you can possibly have!'

'Just a couple,' he said, going back to his previous rocking. Hannah hoped he would fall. It seemed almost inevitable that he would.

'You see,' said Inspector Hill, 'we spoke to Mr Murray yesterday. As you suspected, Hannah, when you saw him he was bringing back Natalie's shoes.'

Hannah frowned, dragging her eyes, and her attention, back from the chief inspector. 'So?' she said.

'He said he had to bring them back – he couldn't let Natalie go home with bare feet,' she said. 'I've checked with him. He is quite sure – and I think you'll agree that he was in a good position to know – that Natalie wasn't *wearing* any tights.'

God, had it taken them until today to find that out? She had been proud of that touch, using Erica Cochrane's own tights. 'I wasn't wearing any either,' she said.

The inspector frowned. 'What's that got to do with it?' she asked.

'She used her *own* tights to strangle Natalie, like she did with me.'

'I don't think we said anything about Natalie having been strangled,' the inspector said, not to Hannah, but to Chief Inspector Lloyd, who didn't seem to be taking much notice of her. 'We can check the tape, but I know I didn't mention it. After all, it was my idea not to release the manner of Natalie's death, and you didn't see the murder, did you?' she said, turning back to Hannah.

This was pathetic. That trick was as old as the hills, and even if she had slightly fallen for it, it wasn't going to catch her out. No wonder Chief Inspector Lloyd was having nothing to do with it.

'She told me,' she said. 'Mrs Cochrane told me. She told me exactly what she did to Natalie, because she was going to do it to me as well. It should have been me in the first place, that's what she said, so she was going to kill me in exactly the same way. She was insane with jealousy. She was enjoying telling me.'

'When did she tell you?' asked the inspector.

'While she was taking her tights off.' Gotcha, she thought, triumphantly. Gotcha.

Inspector Hill's demeanour hadn't altered, but Chief Inspector Lloyd looked very crestfallen at the failed manoeuvre. He let the chair fall forward, and looked at the inspector, his shoulders drooping slightly in disappointment. Then he looked at Hannah, his blue eyes hard.

'If Mrs Cochrane used her own tights to strangle Natalia,' he said, 'how come she was still wearing them just minutes after the murder?'

What? This time panic was making her head spin, just like after Natalie. Think, Hannah. Think. It's a bluff. They can't know for sure whether she was or not.

'We might not have noticed,' he was saying, becoming Welsher by the syllable. 'But she had tried to climb up the bank to get to the phone – her tights were all laddered and torn. In shreds, they were.'

Hannah stared back at the blue eyes that hadn't left hers.

'The inspector here noticed it straight away,' he went on. 'Well – women notice things like that, don't they? But she's a policewoman, you see, so she made a note of it at the time. 'Informant dishevelled,' it says. 'Tights torn. Slight injury to leg.' We're trained to suspect everyone at the scene, you see, and it did seem suspicious – Mrs Cochrane being all messed up like that.' He smiled. 'But it wasn't suspicious after all. Because it proves she didn't do it – doesn't it?'

Hannah tried hard to get her thoughts under control. It didn't prove that she had. 'Then someone else must have done it,' she said.

Chief Inspector Lloyd frowned deeply as he gave that full consideration. 'So – as you see it, Mrs Cochrane beats Natalia senseless, then someone else altogether comes along and strangles her?'

'Yes.' Prove they didn't, Mr Smartass. Prove they didn't.

'The trouble with that,' said Inspector Hill, 'is that they would have had to tell you all about it, wouldn't they? Or – like the chief inspector says – how could you have known? Even Mrs Cochrane didn't know that she had been strangled, and she found her. I didn't know, until someone gave me a torch. It was too dark to see inside that pipe without one.'

Hannah stared at her, the panic rising.

'No one knew how she had died, Hannah,' she said. 'No one but the investigation team – and the murderer. And since we've just established that Erica Cochrane *wasn't* the murderer, that means she couldn't have said those things to you – and she couldn't have tried to commit a carbon copy of Natalie's murder.'

Her voice seemed to be fading away.

'But someone in that flat tried to produce a carbon copy – and that rather leaves you, doesn't it?' she was saying.

Hannah closed her eyes, and the room seemed to be spinning.

'You used your own tights on Natalia Ouspensky,' the chief inspector's voice said. 'And you used Erica Cochrane's tights on yourself.'

Her head felt like it had when she had pulled the nylon tights across her throat, tighter and tighter, until she had passed out. No such luck now.

She opened her eyes and slowly lifted her head to look at the inspector, and Chief Inspector Lloyd, then at her mother, shocked into total, blank, horrified silence.

She hadn't thought up an answer to that, and she wasn't going to. The game that she had seemed to be winning so easily had slipped from her grasp; it was over. The inspector had won, after all.

Inspector Hill sat impassively, pen poised over her notebook. 'The truth this time, Hannah,' she warned.

The truth . . .

She had been watching Natalie and Murray, when suddenly Murray got into Colin's car and sped out backwards. She had seen Natalie walking towards her, doing up her blouse. She hadn't seen Mrs Cochrane – Natalie had told her about that. Natalie had told her that Mrs Cochrane must have thought it was Colin she had been with. She had laughed about that.

'The sod's gone off with my shoes – look!' She had laughed about that, too.

And Hannah had been so relieved that Natalie hadn't been with Colin that she had laughed with her. They had reached the adventure playground by that time, and Natalie had asked her why she was there.

She had told her that she was waiting for Colin.

'What for?' she'd asked.

'What do you think for? The same as you and Mr Murray,' Hannah had said.

Natalie hadn't believed her, so Hannah had told her the things that she and Colin did together, all those things she had put in the letters, all the things she had imagined doing with Colin.

But Natalie hadn't been impressed at all; she had just laughed again. And this time, she had laughed at *her*. So Hannah had stopped Natalie laughing. Then she had made a proper job of it. After that, she had unbuttoned her blouse again, so everyone would know what sort of girl she was.

And then last night, she had sat in the almost-empty flat and listened as Erica Cochrane had told her what she had done to Colin, what she had done to her, shaking with anger as she spoke, and stirring her tea all the time.

Her voice had echoed; the room had a coffee table and a couple of chairs in it, and nothing else. It wasn't somewhere Hannah would have chosen to get away from it all.

'Do you understand what you've done?' she had finished.

'I split you up,' Hannah had said. 'You're here, and he's in a hotel.'

'The police,' she had said, suddenly, and had stopped stirring her tea at last, leaving the spoon in the cup as she had stood up. 'We have to go to the police.'

Hannah had felt in her pocket, felt the handle of the knife. 'The police?' she had said.

'Yes. You were there. You might have seen something that can help them.'

'So were you,' Hannah had said. She had taken out the knife, and held it against Erica Cochrane. 'I'll go to the police by myself,' she had said. 'Afterwards.'

Mrs Cochrane had frozen like a statue, her eyes on the blade of the knife. 'Afterwards?' she had said, still not moving. 'After what?'

'After I've killed you. Then I'll tell them what I saw. I'll tell them you killed her, that you brought me up here and tried to kill me, because you found out that I had written those letters.'

Mrs Cochrane's eyes had never left the knife-blade; she hadn't moved a muscle. 'They . . . they won't believe you,' she had said.

Hannah had pushed the point of the knife against her. 'They will,' she had said. 'When I've finished.' Then she'd pulled her hand back and thrust the knife in.

But it hadn't killed her. Mrs Cochrane's hands had clamped round her wrist, and they had fought for the knife. Hannah hadn't minded at first, because there would be cuts and bruises as well, and signs of a struggle, which would all help. Sooner or later, the knife would find its target, she had thought.

The fight had been silent and fierce; over and over again Hannah had got the blade within a millimetre of Mrs Cochrane's throat, her eye, her face, but she would push her away again, despite her injury, fighting for her life.

Natalie had been much easier, because she had been half unconscious when Hannah had actually killed her. This might really be quite difficult, she had realized, just as her arm had been pushed hard against the wall, jarring her elbow, and she had dropped the knife.

She had bent down to retrieve it, and Erica Cochrane had pushed her over, sat on her, tried to pin her arms to the floor. But Hannah had reached the knife before she could do that, and with the second thrust Mrs Cochrane had slumped over.

Then she had removed Mrs Cochrane's tights, and knelt underneath the corner of the shelving, standing up quickly, delivering herself a literally sickening blow to the head. Its effects had delayed her; the police had been breaking down the door before she had been quite ready for them.

Hannah had hardly been aware of the urgent knocking at the door at first; then, it had filled her head as she had prayed for oblivion, when her own grip would of necessity relax, and she would be able to breathe once more, her fiction complete.

It had very nearly worked, better than she could ever have hoped. The fight had given her details that she would never have been able to invent, and injuries that she could never have inflicted upon herself.

There was silence when she had finished, broken eventually by the inspector.

'But why, Hannah?' she asked. 'Why did you kill Mrs Cochrane? She hadn't guessed that it was you. Why?'

'I had to,' said Hannah. 'You had arrested Colin. I couldn't let

Colin take the blame for what happened to Natalie. It was much better if she got blamed. She wasn't good enough for him anyway.'

She felt better, in an odd sort of way. And she had wanted to tell *someone*. After all, it had really been very clever.

Patrick prepared Monday's lessons. It always calmed him, sitting quietly in an empty staff room, doing what he liked best.

Second best? No, he thought, after some thought. Best. He'd sooner give up women than teaching. And he still might have to give up both for a while.

Hannah Lewis had been charged with the murders; the police had come to tell him, just after four. Someone alive and kicking, someone who would have to stand trial. And he would be called as a witness, he had been told. He'd rung to tell Victoria the first part, but not the second.

He would have to tell her, though. The luck of the Irish had finally run out, he thought, as he packed up and headed for home, where he had a wife who put up with him, tolerated his shenanigans. Loved him, he supposed. But perhaps not for much longer.

He opened the front door and mentally squared his shoulders. It had to be faced.

'Are you all right?' Victoria asked him as he went in.

He smiled. 'Yes, sure,' he said. 'I hope Colin's OK, though.'

'Haven't you been to see him?' she asked.

'No,' said Patrick. 'I didn't think I should intrude, really.'

She nodded. 'I know,' she said. 'It's difficult to know what to do for the best.'

It was. But sometimes you had no choice, whatever the inspector said. 'Victoria,' he said. 'There's something you should know.'

'Yes?' she said, her voice dubious.

He smiled. 'I love you,' he said.

These things took a while coming to court, after all. He might not be charged – and you never knew – Hannah might not be charged, come to that. Anything could happen between here and Armageddon. Look what had happened to Erica. He might not have to give evidence at all, and baring his soul might be premature.

Sufficient unto the day, he thought, as he kissed his long-suffering, accommodating, forgiving wife, was the evil thereof.

And that was in the Bible, so it must be right.

Colin sat in the armchair where he had been sitting since Chief Inspector Lloyd's second visit of the day.

Sherlock had been sleeping; he was hungry now. He woke up and came stumping over to where Colin sat, and placed a large, trusting head in his lap.

Colin mustered a smile, and spread the dog's ears out over his knees, stroking them. The silly creature liked that. 'It's you and me now, Sherlock,' he said.

Sherlock lifted his eyes at the sound of his name, and his tail wagged.

Colin was glad that Sherlock was just as happy to be with him as he had been with Erica. He couldn't have borne it if the dog had been looking for her. But Sherlock's love was given to anyone and everyone, even someone who had never previously had much rapport with him, and somehow that was helping Colin.

Hannah Lewis had been charged with both Natalie's and Erica's murder, Lloyd had said. Erica had been an innocent victim. Lloyd had been relieved to be able to bring that news, but it wasn't news to Colin. He had never thought anything else, not from the moment the police had told him she had been taken to hospital. It didn't make Erica any less dead.

But life went on. 'Dinner,' he said, and Sherlock jumped up.

Colin was feeding him when someone came to the door. Another test. Try and pay the milkman, or whoever it was that came on Fridays, without breaking down. You can do it. You can.

It was Trudy Kane.

'Hello,' he said.

'I didn't think you should be on your own,' she said, almost argumentatively, as though he had already told her to leave. 'If you don't think it's seemly, I'll go. But I think you should have company, so you should be with someone, and people are funny after something like this. It doesn't have to be me. Just don't stay here on your own, that's all.'

He smiled, and stood aside to let her in. 'I'm not alone,' he said, as the dog came through to fall in love with whoever had arrived. 'This is Sherlock,' he said. 'He's been a great help. But his conversation is limited.'

His voice broke on the last word, and he did break down. He was aware that he was being – with the very best of motives – earmarked before he'd even buried Erica, but he did need company. And at least it wasn't the milkman.

Kim's mum had made her pack a case, ready for tomorrow.

'No arguments,' she had said. 'We're going.'

A seaside hotel, for a week. She couldn't really afford it, Kim knew that.

But she did want to get away from all of this horror. From

questions. The police said it would be all right. They said that some-one was being charged with both the murders. They hadn't said who, but Kim knew, just as she had known when her mother had told her what Hannah was saying about Mrs Cochrane.

Then she had realized how insistent Hannah had been about her not telling the police anything. How ill she had looked. How certain that it hadn't been Colin Cochrane who had killed Natalie. Why she had felt that by talking to the police it wasn't Natalie or Mr Cochrane that she was betraying, but Hannah.

Everyone had been behaving as though it was Hannah who had died in that flat, but it hadn't been. It had been Mrs Cochrane. And that, for Kim, had been the final straw. The terrible suspicion that had lurked at the back of her mind had forced its way into her conscious thoughts.

But if that policewoman hadn't come to see her ... would she have said anything?

Probably not.

Tom watched Hannah being taken away to a youth detention centre, feeling as shell-shocked as Judy looked now that he had heard the whole story.

They walked in silence back to the empty CID room, and Tom sat down at his desk, looking with something approaching fondness at his paperwork.

'You were right, guv,' he said, as Judy went towards her office.

'So were you,' she said. 'About a lot of things.'

Tom didn't exactly feel flushed with success. He had had the wrong people down for it all along. 'Name one,' he said.

'Cochrane's deodorant,' she said. 'And that Mrs Cochrane hadn't told us the whole story. That Sherlock had smelt someone he knew. That Hannah knew exactly who Natalie had been with,' said Judy. 'Jealousy wasn't her motive at all – I was wrong about that.'

Tom shook his head. 'Who could have guessed what it really was?' he asked, as Lloyd came in, and Judy slipped into her office and closed the door.

'Guessed what what really was?' asked Lloyd.

'Hannah's motive,' said Tom. 'That she killed Natalie because she *laughed* at her.'

Lloyd smiled. 'I've heard of flimsier motives,' he said. 'And I can see that you were never laughed at when you were at school.'

'No, I wasn't,' said Tom. 'But even if I had been, you don't *kill* people for it.'

'Not unless you're psychotic,' agreed Lloyd. 'But you want to. Believe me, you want to.'

Tom frowned. 'You weren't laughed at as a kid, were you, sir?' he asked.

'I was. And if I'd been unbalanced, I could have killed.'

'But why were you laughed at?'

'Because,' said Lloyd slowly, 'I wasn't called Tom.'

Ah. The ultra-secret name. Lloyd had to be the worst keeper of a secret in the world. There couldn't be a single person at Stansfield nick that didn't know about him and Judy, and it wasn't from her. But no one at all knew his first name; he kept it strictly to himself, and Tom had failed, despite several attempts, to get the tiniest of clues from Judy.

'I still could kill,' warned Lloyd. 'Remember that. I might not always be the well-adjusted chap you see before you now.' He knocked on Judy's door.

Tom smiled.

Judy was sitting at her desk, smoking, her hand shaking slightly. She looked up as Lloyd came in, closing the door behind him. She wasn't sure she had forgiven him for his 'women notice things like that' when she was in no position to thump him.

'Well done,' he said quietly.

Maybe. It had been Lloyd's idea, of course, the build-up with slightly awkward questions for which Hannah would have ready answers, to lull her into a false sense of security.

'An uncorroborated confession,' she said, releasing smoke. 'That's all it is.'

He smiled, and sat on the edge of her desk. 'And a shred of evidence,' he said.

'They might not even prosecute,' she said. 'If they do, she could retract the confession. The courts are paranoid about that now. She could get off.'

Lloyd looked at her seriously. 'It's out of our hands, Judy,' he said. 'We've done our bit. And Freddie might find something in the post-mortem on Mrs Cochrane that backs up the confession, now that he knows what he's looking for. How much blood she'd lost, for instance – he's not convinced it's consistent with Hannah's original story. And they're going to try to get prints from Natalia's skin – the thumb and little finger, remember?'

Judy nodded. It wasn't something that worked very often.

'Forensic are going over that flat with a fine-tooth comb right now. They could turn up some more evidence. And they think the button thread found on Natalia's body could be from a school blazer.'

'Natalie had a school blazer – that could have been picked up in her own wardrobe.'

229

Lloyd smiled. 'It all helps,' he said. 'Anyway, I don't think she will retract the confession. She's proud of it.'

Judy shivered. But he was probably right. He usually was. Even about Mrs Cochrane unwittingly protecting the psychopath. Like he said, they had done their job, and Freddie would do his, conscientiously as ever. She felt a little more confident of success.

Someone knocked, and waited to be told to come in. Judy was surprised to see Tom, who never stood on ceremony. Presumably he had thought he might catch them in a passionate embrace if he didn't announce his presence.

'I ought to be going, guv, if that's all right,' he said. 'I've got a dinner date tonight. It's our wedding anniversary.'

'How many years?' asked Judy.

'Seven,' said Tom.

She glanced at Lloyd. 'Congratulations,' she said to Tom. 'Give Liz my love.'

'I will. Thanks.'

'Where are you taking her, Tom?' asked Lloyd.

'That new place in Barton – everyone says it's worth the money. What's it called? It's in Grainger Street.'

'Pennyman's,' said Judy. She and Lloyd had been there a couple of times since it had opened. The manager was a friend of Lloyd's, but that didn't get him a discount. It was worth the money, but no wonder Tom had been so anxious about his expenses. He was going to need them.

'That's it,' said Tom. 'Pennyman's. I think Liz deserves the best for putting up with me for seven years.'

'What time are you supposed to be there?' asked Lloyd.

'Eight o'clock, so I'd better get a move on.' Tom went to the door. 'She'll be amazed that we're actually going to get where we're going for once,' he said, then stopped and turned, and snapped his fingers. '*All About Eve*,' he said, triumphantly.

Lloyd immediately looked interested, as if Tom could possibly be going to say anything about it that he didn't already know. Judy practically knew the dialogue backwards.

'What about it?' he said. 'Is it on somewhere? Are you going to see it?'

'No,' said Tom. 'It just suddenly popped into my head. I've been trying to remember for days which film that quote came from – you know. "*Fasten your seat-belts, it's going to be a bumpy ride.*" '

Lloyd shook his head. ' "Night", Tom,' he corrected.

'Night, guvs,' said Tom cheerily, and left, carefully closing the door again.

'Oh, well,' said Lloyd. 'Never mind.'

Judy frowned as he reached across her for her phone, and got out his address book.

She squinted at it as he dialled the number. It was open at P. She sighed. Tom had put ideas into his head, obviously.

Candlelit dinners for two were all very nice, but she did like to be asked first, and the last thing she wanted to do was get dressed up to go out. Anyway, they probably wouldn't have a table available, and even if they did, it would hardly be fair on Tom and Liz to have them sitting there all evening, so, all in all, she didn't think that this was one of Lloyd's better ideas.

But maybe he wasn't booking a table for tonight, she thought. He might just be arranging for them to have a night out next weekend, or something.

'Oh, hello,' he said, perching on her desk again. 'My name is Lloyd – could I speak to the manager, please?'

Oh, God, he was even going to pull strings to get them in, so it must be for tonight. She didn't want to go out. She wanted to go home. She wanted to have a bath and an early night.

'Bill? Lloyd here. Listen, some friends of mine are dining with you tonight at eight – Mr and Mrs Tom Finch? Would you trust me for a bottle of champagne to be sent to their table with my compliments?' He beamed. 'Thanks, Bill,' he said, and hung up.

Judy laughed at herself. She should have known that Lloyd would be the last person to horn in on Tom's evening out. She should have known that it would be a generous impulse, something she wasn't convinced she had ever had.

'You are an incurable romantic,' she said.

'I know,' he said. 'Will you marry me, Jude?'

She sighed, and looked at him for a long time before she answered. 'Very probably,' she said, crushing out her cigarette and standing up. 'Let's go home.'

She had never seen him look quite so startled. Or, she realized, with a rare pang of guilt, quite so *happy*.

But she hadn't said when.